CELTIC Cross

SARA SHERIDAN

CONSTABLE

CONSTABLE

First published in Great Britain in 2021 by Constable

A CIP catalogue record for this book
is available from the British Library.

ISBN: 978-1-47213-484-4

Typeset in Dante by SX Composing DTP, Rayleigh, Essex
Printed and bound in Great Britain by Clays Ltd, Elcograf S.p.A.

Papers used by Constable are from well-managed forests
and other responsible sources

Constable
An imprint of
Little, Brown Book Group
Carmelite House
50 Victoria Embankment
London EC4Y 0DZ

An Hachette UK Company
www.hachette.co.uk

www.littlebrown.co.uk

This one is for the tearaways and the misfits.
You know who you are.

Chapter One

Truth lies beyond

Edinburgh, June 1959

Mirabelle didn't see why it was necessary to be blindfolded but McGregor pulled the car over and insisted.

'You're enjoying this far too much,' she said, as he removed the floral silk scarf that was loosely knotted around her shoulders and tied it round her eyes, before turning the car off the main road. She had been daydreaming as they passed the wheat fields in the sunshine. Now she found herself focusing on the sound of the engine, the sensation of the cool air through the rolled-down window and the fact that, when he turned left, the road wound in an arc and then twisted sharply. The technique felt familiar – an old habit of hers to map a blind route through the movement of a vehicle.

'I'll help you get out,' he said, when he stopped the engine.

It was odd how time elongated when your senses were deprived, she thought. It felt like it had been half an hour since he'd fixed the scarf over her eyes, but it couldn't have been more than ten minutes, perhaps less.

He took her hand and helped her onto what felt like beaten track. As she took her first step onto the uneven surface she realised she shouldn't have worn such heels.

'Are you ready?' he asked, after only a few steps, putting a hand on each arm to steady her.

'This had better be good,' she said, with a smile.

'Well, tell me what you think.' He fumbled with the knot. Mirabelle closed her eyes, waiting for him to unmask her completely before she opened them.

They were standing in front of a small stone house set in a copse of sycamore and pine trees. She blinked. Between the tree trunks water sparkled in the sunshine.

'Are we visiting someone?' she asked. 'Are we staying here?'

He hadn't told her to pack a bag. McGregor's expression was quizzical.

'Not today,' he said. 'Do you like it?'

'It's very pretty. Is that the Firth of Forth?'

'It is. Down the track there's a jetty and a small boathouse. They go with the house.'

'It's absolutely charming.'

'Good. I've put in an offer on it. A successful offer, I might add.'

McGregor drew a key from his pocket and unlocked the front door. 'I should carry you over the threshold.'

'We're not married yet,' Mirabelle parried, curious, as she walked past him into a bright hallway with a flagstone floor. A crystal vase of blowsy garden roses on the oak table scented the air. Over them a mirror in a carved oak surround that had split with age reflected her image in a fitted, satin, orange and white dress, her hair swept into a chignon. She tied the patterned scarf back into place as McGregor appeared in the frame behind her.

'Now I've sold my cousin's estate, I thought it would be nice to have a weekend place and this is only twenty-five minutes from town. I know I should have asked, but I wanted to surprise you. It's my gift. Your wedding present.'

Mirabelle was glad the old place was gone. She liked the Highlands but the estate was a lot of work to run and this was far less remote. Anyway, after the family tragedy it had felt impossible to settle there. Nonetheless, McGregor was jumping the gun. 'But we haven't decided where we want to live,' she said.

'Whether we're here or there,' he gestured, meaning Edinburgh or Brighton, 'we'll need somewhere for holidays or weekends. This is on the right side of town for Turnhouse.'

'It sounds very glamorous, flying up to Scotland for a weekend.'

McGregor had made little secret of the fact he wanted to settle in Edinburgh now he had retired from the force. Mirabelle was, as yet, not opposed but also not completely convinced. She had spent a couple of months in the city during the winter, the memory of which, today in sunny June, seemed like an impossible dream of clouded breath, pink fingers and glowing windows too early in the afternoon. Could it ever have been so dark and so cold?

'That's what I love about you most. You're always glamorous.' He kissed her and her stomach fluttered, though she pushed him aside to explore. The house was Georgian by her reckoning, the proportions measured. In the sitting room there was an ornate pine fireplace, and the smell of woodsmoke lingered around the comfortable pale green three-piece suite.

'Who lives here?' she asked.

'Nobody,' McGregor said. 'The last occupant was an old lady who'd lived here for decades. The place is being looked after by a housekeeper who walks over from South

Queensferry. We're lucky it's come up – it hasn't been on the market since it was built. Everything round here was developed at the same time – the 1750s, I think.'

Upstairs, Mirabelle peered out of the window. To the rear, running down to the water, the garden was well-tended. A small vegetable patch was planted down one side next to a lawn with two wicker chairs placed in the sunniest spot.

'The furniture is lovely,' she said.

'We can buy that, too, if we want it.'

'My, what a pretty bedroom.'

McGregor's grin was wide as the Forth. 'Climbing roses outside the window. I thought you'd like that. And that view is tantalising, isn't it? The water looks inviting.'

'It helps that it's a sunny day.'

He nodded. 'I'd say a storm here would be fun, though. We could stoke the fire. And when it snows, we'll walk along the foreshore and watch it coming down. The light is quite extraordinary. Am I forgiven for not consulting you?'

'It's lovely.'

McGregor checked his watch. 'Good,' he said. 'I'm glad you like it because it comes with an entail.'

'A what?'

'An entail.'

'Like a curse?'

He laughed. 'Well, sort of. We have to be approved.'

'Approved? By whom?'

He took her hand, pulled her through the hallway and back down the stairs. 'I'll explain on the way.'

There was no blindfold this time as McGregor started the car and they wound further down the track. Mirabelle found herself fascinated by the movement of the water and a sailing boat making its way elegantly up the firth and under the huge girders of the rust-red rail bridge, which she could just glimpse, far off, in the rear-view mirror. 'What is that?' she asked, catching a flash of something else through the trees.

McGregor sighed. 'It's why I put the blindfold on. They're building a new toll bridge just past the harbour. On this side of the village. For cars. The site is a mess, but it'll be cleaned up when it's finished in a couple of years. It's quite impressive. The bridge will be over eight thousand feet long, though it's all mud and scaffolding now. I didn't want to put you off.'

Mirabelle turned in her seat and strained to make out the skeletal outline of the first sections of the bridge through the trees, the works starting on opposite banks. 'It'll be huge,' she said, realising the scale of it.

'They say there'll be a hundred houses built at the access points on both sides of the water. When the bridge is finished the traffic will bypass the village. I can't see that it will affect us in the longer term. The harbour is naval, these days – HMS *Lochinvar*. It's a training facility – mine-sweepers or something. Anyway, none of it is too close to the house.'

'Too close for what?'

'To intrude, darling. Shore Cottage sits on the edge of the estate up the road. We'll be closer to them than to the village and the family that lives there would block permission for anything that crowded their land. It'll become an enclave here – close enough to the shops and the pub in South Queensferry but still isolated. I know you like to be near the shore. We'll need to drive under a bridge to get here is all – eventually. And it's not even ten miles from Edinburgh – twenty-five minutes in the car.'

'So you said,' she replied quizzically, noting that McGregor had still not explained this entail business.

* * *

He turned the car inland, down another track marked 'Private Road' and pulled up at a high, rough-hewn sandstone wall into which was set a huge wooden double door, studded with spikes. To one side a ten-foot-tall carved Celtic cross was mounted on a wide, granite plinth. This didn't look like an estate. Mirabelle had visited a few now round Scotland and she'd never seen one that was walled in this way and without a gatehouse. 'It doesn't look as if they welcome visitors,' she said.

McGregor got out of the car and opened the door for her. 'Best behaviour,' he said, with a wink, and tugged the iron bell-pull.

It took a while for anyone to answer. They were out of sight of the water and the air smelt strangely of old books and fresh herbs. She was curious but enjoying the mystery and, for once, she decided she didn't want to ask too many questions. Eventually a smaller door, inset into the larger gate, opened with a creak and, to Mirabelle's surprise, a nun stood in the void. Her face was lined, her cheeks pink as summer roses and her eyes a watery blue. Mirabelle thought she looked as if she had been painted onto delicate china. 'Can I help you?'

'We're here to see Mother Superior,' McGregor replied. 'Alan McGregor and Mirabelle Bevan.'

The nun stepped back to let them onto a wide, cobbled pathway with lavender and roses on either side. Ahead an archway opened onto a complex of buildings. 'This way,' she said, striding ahead so that the hem of her robe lifted to reveal a pair of sturdy black boots with dried mud caked round the soles.

Under the arch the sound of women's voices singing reached them from the other side of a quadrangle where the door lay open to a pretty chapel covered with Boston ivy. The nun led them past it, into the building and up a narrow stairway. At the top a hallway was fitted as some kind of waiting room. The nun knocked on a door marked 'Prioress' in gold lettering. 'Come in,' shouted a cheerful voice, and the old woman herded Mirabelle and McGregor through, as if they were errant children.

Inside, the room was sunny, with a view over a large kitchen garden behind the quad, with hens pecking in a run along one side. Behind an untidy, ancient mahogany desk another nun stood up to greet them. She was younger than the one who'd shown them the way.

'Ah, Superintendent McGregor, isn't it?' she said. 'And . . .'

'This is my fiancée, Mirabelle Bevan.'

'You're getting married? How lovely. The solicitor didn't tell me that. And you're planning to settle here?'

'Not exactly,' McGregor admitted. 'But we would like to spend some time at Shore Cottage. Weekends and holidays. It's so peaceful.'

The nun cocked her head to one side. 'Weekends? I see. Well, we're not averse to that at the Little Sisters of Gethsemane.'

'I'm glad to hear it,' McGregor replied.

'Please, take a seat.'

The chairs were carved from heavy dark wood. Mirabelle felt as if she was sitting on a throne. 'It's beautiful here,' she commented. 'How old is the convent?'

'The current building is from the mid-Georgian period, as is the house you're purchasing. The order, however, has been here since medieval times. The nunnery was built on the pilgrim route to St Andrews. We're still on that route, of course, though the pilgrims are long gone and the train from Edinburgh takes visitors as far as Leuchars in an hour or so. The sisters are hospitallers.'

'Like the Knights Templar?'

Mirabelle could swear Mother Superior blushed. 'We're not warriors, Miss Bevan. That would certainly not be fitting. We're healers here – perhaps you have heard of our most famous medicine. Gethsemane Salve?'

Recognition lit Mirabelle's eyes. 'Oh, yes,' she said. 'For cuts and scratches?'

'It also heals burns,' Mother Superior added. 'We've been manufacturing the salve for over eight hundred years. It was used during the Crusades.'

'The tin has a cross on it, doesn't it? Like the one outside, at the gate,' Mirabelle said.

Mother Superior smiled. 'Our cross dates to the medieval period and originally sat within our walls but when the nunnery was rebuilt in the 1750s it was re-sited at the entrance, to welcome those who visit us here. I understand you're retired, Mr McGregor, but what do you do, Miss Bevan?'

'I run a debt-collection agency,' Mirabelle replied. It was rare anybody asked but, then, this interview was a test, she supposed, and by being here she had submitted to being judged. 'Though now I oversee matters,' she added. 'I'm not in the office day-to-day.'

'Mirabelle is also a bit of a sleuth,' McGregor cut in. 'That's how we fell in love. She solved one of my cases.'

Mirabelle felt it would be showing off to point out that she had solved more than one. 'We are both retired now, in effect,' she said.

The nun took this in. 'Tell me, when will you be married?'

'The week after next,' Mirabelle replied, with a smile. She had never expected to be so pleased about the wedding but she found she was excited at the prospect of being Mrs McGregor. Mirabelle McGregor. It had a nice ring to it. Her friend Vesta deemed it an improvement.

'Which church?' the nun continued smoothly.

'We are to be married by the registrar in Edinburgh, Mother,' McGregor said.

'A registrar's office?' The nun sounded shocked.

'Yes. We met in a church, actually. Well, in a graveyard. There was a funeral, you see. The thing is neither Mirabelle nor I . . . after the war . . . We both had a rough time of it . . .'

Mother Superior got to her feet. 'I have to be frank. In that case, we cannot have you,' she said. 'I'm sorry. But you must be married in the eyes of God. In a church. Otherwise you would . . . well, you'd simply be fornicators, Mr McGregor.'

Mirabelle did not trust herself to speak immediately. Especially not to point out that in this woman's view they were fornicators already and, which she would probably find worse, unrepentant ones.

'We can help,' the nun continued earnestly. 'We could organise a wedding service for you here. In the chapel. As our new neighbours. It would be my pleasure. But I cannot approve you, I'm afraid, if you are intending to live in sin. Perhaps you would like to reconsider.'

'Yes,' said McGregor, though his tone was far from positive.

The nun paused. 'You will need time to think about it, I should imagine,' she said, as she moved towards the door, the interview clearly over. She opened it. Outside, the old nun was waiting. 'See Mr McGregor and Miss Bevan out, would you, Sister Mary?'

Sister Mary smiled.

'I'm really very sorry,' Mother Superior added. 'Do let me know.'

* * *

Walking back downstairs, Mirabelle was surprised by how much she felt like a naughty schoolgirl. McGregor squeezed her hand.

'Have you been with the order long?' He tried to make conversation with Sister Mary.

'It is forty-one years since I took my vows,' the nun said.

'Do you help with the production of the salve?'

She nodded. 'We all do.'

'I wonder,' Mirabelle said, 'could we peep inside the chapel?'

The singing had stopped now – the rehearsal was over. Sister Mary looked dubious. 'I'm not sure that it's appropriate,' she said.

'It's only,' Mirabelle added, 'that Mother Superior suggested we get married there.'

'Ah.' This reassured the nun. 'Yes, of course. We have several weddings – over the summer especially.'

'Really?'

'It pays for our keep and couples seem to like the chapel – it's more private than a parish church.'

Inside, the air smelt of dusty prayer books and beeswax. Behind the altar a long stained-glass window portrayed a woman in a purple wimple and robe embroidered with flowers, a baby in her arms.

'That's St Enoch,' Sister Mary explained. 'She was expelled by her father after she was raped. A visiting prince came to her chambers against her will and forced himself upon her. She is the mother of St Mungo – that's the baby. He in his turn is patron saint of Glasgow.'

'Expelled?' McGregor repeated. 'If I remember correctly she was thrown into the Forth, was she not?'

'Indeed.'

'So he tried to murder her?'

'It's a very pretty church,' Mirabelle said quickly, not wanting to get caught up in the rights and wrongs of what had happened to a medieval saint. 'I can see why couples choose to marry here. The flowers are lovely.'

'We have a flower garden,' Sister Mary elaborated, with enthusiasm. 'Most of it is given over to growing lavender for the salve, but these *sullivantii* are extremely hardy and we like them for the chapel.'

'Are they daisies?'

'Of a sort. They remind me of the sun.'

Mirabelle nodded. The nun was right.

'And what is this?' McGregor asked, pointing to a short sword mounted on the wall, to the right of the altar.

'Oh, that is the sword the order was named for. It is the blade that was used to cut off the ear of the high priest's servant. In the Garden of Gethsemane. It is our most precious relic.'

McGregor's mouth opened. 'But that sword would be over two thousand years old.'

'Yes. It's Roman,' Sister Mary confirmed. 'A conservator from the National Museum comes every year to inspect it.'

'And you are the Little Sisters of Gethsemane,' Mirabelle said, making the connection.

'We heal wounds. We make hurts better,' Sister Mary said.

'Gethsemane Salve,' Mirabelle added. 'I see.'

Outside the gates, McGregor apologised. 'I'm sorry,' he said. 'I thought it was only a formality. They've been here for centuries, I suppose, behind that wall. Welcoming visitors.' He cast his eyes in the direction of the cross. 'It seems so medieval, doesn't it?'

'So the entail was a curse of sorts.'

'I suppose. We can find somewhere else. Once the new bridge is built Fife will be more accessible and there are some pretty cottages on the other side of the firth in the fishing villages along the East Neuk. Or at the other end of the village there's a few places around Society House – the big estate past the rail bridge.'

Mirabelle smoothed her fiancé's tie. 'Oh, no,' she said. 'I like Shore Cottage. I don't believe in a church wedding, but it is pretty in there. We could get married at the registry office and come here for a blessing afterwards. Do you think that would satisfy Mother Superior?'

'Really?'

'I'm not wearing white,' Mirabelle added. 'And I don't regret the reason it would be inappropriate, though we had best not tell them about that.' She had yet to buy her dress, but the day after next her friend Vesta was arriving from Brighton and the two of them were going shopping. Vesta's wedding dress had been vibrant purple satin, like a film star's. Mirabelle felt she was going to choose a more restrained tone – a dusty pink chiffon perhaps, or a cool blue marquisette.

'Mother Superior didn't say anything about what you were to wear,' McGregor leaned in to kiss her. 'You can have whatever colour you like, darling. She seemed rather young to be in charge, don't you think? And quite inflexible.' His eyes narrowed. 'Though she had the measure of you. You harlot,' he said.

'Fornicator,' Mirabelle snapped back. But she kissed him.

Chapter Two

Come, pensive nun, devout and pure

McGregor's flat on Heriot Row had no telephone. They kept discussing installing one but the truth was that Mirabelle preferred not to be disturbed by calls and, besides, there was a waiting list to get a trunk line and neither she nor McGregor wanted to make a party arrangement with one of the neighbours, which, they were both sure, would feel intrusive.

Mirabelle had taken to eating breakfast in front of the long windows that looked down on the private park that served the houses along Queen Street on one side and Heriot Row on the other. While McGregor rose early and drove to the golf course at Liberton to play a round with two old school friends and a retired superintendent from the Lothian force, Mirabelle indulged herself with a pot of inky coffee and a basket of warm rolls with apricot jam from the greengrocer's on Dundas Street. A lady of leisure now, she read *The Times* from cover to cover, browsed the *Scotsman* and watched her neighbours walk their dogs in the garden – throwing sticks, stopping to greet each other as their pets scampered across the grass, or fumbling to find their keys as they went in and out. People were good-humoured here early in the morning.

In Brighton dog-walkers ignored each other on the pebble beach until at least ten o'clock.

When she had finished eating, she usually walked up the hill to George Street and rang her office from the phone box on the corner. It had been almost a year now – her agreement with Vesta was that Mirabelle would stay on as managing director for eighteen months. But day-to-day Vesta was enjoying being in charge. The talk over the last several phone calls, however, had not been about debt collection, but Vesta's trip north. She was coming almost a week before the wedding, to be followed by her husband, Charlie, and toddler, Noel, in time for the big day and a holiday. Mirabelle had taken a house for them at Portobello so Noel could play on the shore and paddle in the sea. 'He's in for a shock that not every beach is stony,' Vesta had beamed. 'I hope he likes sand. He'll be able to build castles.'

Today, Vesta's new secretary answered the telephone brightly. The office at McGuigan and McGuigan had been in a state of expansion since Mirabelle's departure. Business in Brighton was booming, and Vesta had taken on a second debt collector as well as a red-haired glamourpuss called Marilyn, who had the knack of chiming the name of the company and asking if she could help in such a way that the caller felt they ought to unburden themselves immediately. This new professionalism surprised Mirabelle every morning. 'Hello. Mirabelle Bevan here,' she announced. 'Is Vesta in?'

Marilyn put her through to the office next door, where Vesta now resided behind a modern glass-topped desk with comfortable leather chairs for visiting clients.

'We have a job on,' Mirabelle announced.

'You haven't changed your mind?' Vesta ventured nervously. Even though Mirabelle had fully committed to

Alan a year ago, she had been admittedly skittish in their relationship up to that point.

'We're going to have a church blessing.'

'Really? I thought you didn't believe in that kind of thing.'

'It's a long story. I'll tell you when you get here. But it occurred to me that if we're going to do it in a church, my outfit might merit a veil. Only a small one!'

Vesta chuckled. The first thing Mirabelle had said to her when they originally discussed her wedding outfit was that she did not want to dress up like some kind of doll. She wanted something she could wear again. 'You will look beautiful, whatever you choose,' Vesta cooed. 'I can't wait to get up there.'

'Also, I have a house to show you.'

'A house?'

'A weekend place.'

'You're not coming back, are you?'

It was beginning to feel that way. Mirabelle had always assumed she would never leave Brighton but last night they had discussed selling her apartment on the front. She'd always be able to visit the south coast, she told herself. McGregor still owned a guesthouse near the pier, after all. Their very own hotel.

'How are the figures?' She changed the subject.

'Up,' Vesta announced proudly. 'Though I must say, there was a lot of trouble over the weekend with fighting in the streets. A policeman was injured.'

'I saw that in the paper.' Mirabelle had recognised the officer's name. McGregor had been a superintendent at Bartholomew Square station for years.

'There were crowds of them, Mirabelle,' Vesta complained. 'Tearaways! Those Harrington jackets make the men look aggressive before they even get started on the beer. The minute the sun comes out, mods and rockers pour off the trains from London ready for a barney, and swarms more arrive on motorbikes. The main road into town is a nightmare. I wouldn't blame you not wanting to come back. It's fine where we live, but along the front it's mayhem. And the women look like criminals. People are staying away from the centre at the weekends. Brighton is changing.'

Mirabelle peeked at George Street through the glass of the phone box. The haar made it seem like a sepia photograph. Three cars were parked outside a cashmere shop where a mother and daughter were staring at the window display, discussing ply widths. On the next block she could just make out two advocates turning the corner towards Princes Street, their robes swishing as they hurried across town to the High Court up The Mound. One of the neighbours had complained recently, when she ran into him on the stairs, about the upcoming Edinburgh festival. 'The town goes into uproar every summer,' he said. 'It's been thirteen years. You'd think they'd have had enough but they're staging a parade along Princes Street this year and there's the Highland Games at Murrayfield, which would be enough on its own but now all of a sudden there are plays in every theatre in the city. And the church halls. No single person could get round it all. The whole thing's got out of hand.'

Mirabelle had smiled politely and did not tell him she had booked tickets to see the Military Tattoo at Edinburgh Castle and a Shakespeare play at the Royal Lyceum Theatre. Still, it was hardly mods and rockers. She made a mental note of how calm Edinburgh seemed compared to what Vesta was describing. Another reason, perhaps, to move north. 'We're looking forward to you coming,' she said.

'I've started to pack. Maybe I should bring some paint samples, if you're shopping for the new house.'

'What would I do without you?' Vesta had helped Mirabelle to refurbish her flat after there had been a fire some years ago and had made the process much easier. She had a way with fabrics and seemed to understand what Mirabelle wanted.

After she had hung up, Mirabelle picked up a packet of coffee on her way back down the hill and was surprised, turning the corner, to see an old nun emerging from a small pale blue car parked at her front door. The vehicle was so boxy it looked like a child's toy.

'Hello,' Mirabelle greeted her.

'Good morning, Miss Bevan,' the nun said.

'I'm sorry. I didn't catch your name.'

'I'm Sister Triduana. Named for the saint.' She smiled. 'She put her eyes out rather than succumb to marriage,' she added. 'Mother sent me.'

Mirabelle decided not to comment upon the saint, which left her options limited. 'I've never seen one of these on the road before.' She gestured towards the car.

'My cousin sent it for the convent. Our old Crossley packed up in the spring so I wrote to ask for help. The Mini's the latest thing apparently. She's jolly good, actually. She gets fifty miles to the gallon.'

Mirabelle's surprise must have shown because the nun's expression softened. 'I drove ambulances during the first war,' she explained. 'When my brother died in the fighting, I signed up. They posted me to Serbia. I found my vocation afterwards. It seemed to marry the things I was interested in – faith and medicine. Mother mentioned that you lost your belief in the last war.'

'I suppose I did,' Mirabelle said. 'I was never terribly devout.'

'Oh, neither was I.' Sister Triduana grinned. 'When I think back on it – the parties! Now it feels quite wicked.' She waved her hand in the air to waft away her past self, as if the memory was comprised of cigarette smoke. 'I was a flapper,' she whispered conspiratorially.

Mirabelle grinned. 'Can I help you?'

'Ah. Yes. He doesn't have a telephone but Mother got Mr McGregor's address from his solicitor. She asked me to fetch him. She'd like a word.'

Mirabelle decided to come clean. 'Alan and I discussed it last night and we'd like to take up Mother's kind offer to get married in the chapel. We like the house greatly and, well, it's very pretty at the convent and you'll be our new neighbours. Who better to help us celebrate?' She worried momentarily that the nun would realise she and McGregor were living together here and resolved not to call the flat on Heriot Row 'home', though that was what it had become.

Sister Triduana's expression flickered. 'A wedding. Yes. Lovely,' she said. 'But that's not why Mother sent me. It's because Mr McGregor used to be a policeman. We need his help. It's somewhat delicate . . .'

'He's playing golf this morning, I'm afraid. I can have him ring the convent when he's finished. He usually takes lunch in the clubhouse and gets back here around two o'clock. He's retired, you see.'

Distress showed on the old nun's face. 'Two o'clock,' she repeated. Three hours, it seemed, was too long.

'Is there something I can help with?'

Sister Triduana shook her head. 'I fear we need a detective. Somebody we can trust.'

'I've often helped Alan with cases,' Mirabelle offered. 'Why don't I nip up and leave him a note, and I'll come back with you?'

Sister Triduana acquiesced and Mirabelle disappeared through the main door. When she came out again, the nun started the car and Mirabelle ceased to wonder what had happened at the convent and concentrated on the roaring of the Mini's engine as Sister Triduana took off. As a wartime ambulance driver, the old woman's grasp of road safety had clearly been sketchy and she accelerated at quite a pace, which increased when she hit the straight run of Queensferry Road. Mirabelle found herself gripping the edge of her seat. 'I did some rally driving in 1919,' Sister Triduana shouted over the engine. 'After the war. My cousin, Leda, and I were a team. In France. We drove the Grand Prix.'

'The cousin who bought this car?'

'We were partners in crime in those days.' The nun beamed, the tyres screeching as she turned off towards South Queensferry. 'I have a dispensation to write to her. She's Lady Leda now – married Sir Edmund Ferrier. They live near Nottingham.'

'Did she find her faith too?'

'Oh, Leda had faith all along and a strong urge towards motherhood. She and Edmund have six children. We joke that we make up for each other in the grand scheme of things.'

Mirabelle thought she might find her faith again if she had to sit in a car driven by Sister Triduana for much longer. 'Do you get out a lot?' she asked.

Sister Triduana nodded. without taking her eyes off the road. 'I visit a poor old soul in South Queensferry from time to time,' she said.

Mirabelle did not reply that whoever the nun was visiting could hardly be older than she was, though Sister Triduana's reactions were clearly those of someone half her age.

'We know all our neighbours,' Sister Triduana continued. 'We have a duty to them. The Little Sisters of Gethsemane is not a retreat. We are connected to the world.'

As they whizzed past the naval base and the works for the Forth Road Bridge Mirabelle caught a glimpse of the shanty town built around the site, workers living on top of what must be, even in this warm weather, a great deal of mud. A ragged group of children were paddling in the shallow water of the firth. No wonder McGregor hadn't wanted her to see it before she viewed the house, she thought. The sheer mess of the place would have put her off – washing hanging up to dry among the trees and a ragtag of open-doored caravans and poorly erected army-surplus tents. She felt almost shell-shocked as the old nun passed at speed.

After another minute of driving through the woods, she cornered sharply and pulled into what must have been an old stable block behind the convent, where an elderly Crossley motor was parked, its radiator cover showing beneath a patched tarpaulin. Sister Triduana clearly thought nothing of the speed at which she had travelled and Mirabelle noted drily that the new house wasn't necessarily twenty-five minutes from town as McGregor had said. With a nun at the wheel it could easily take only ten to drive the ten miles.

Entering the compound through a wooden side gate, Mirabelle followed the nun past the flower garden Sister Mary had mentioned the day before, awash with bees. Beyond this a series of khaki Nissen huts stretched in a row. 'What's in there?' she asked.

Unsurprisingly, Sister Triduana didn't slow her pace. 'We moved the manufactory into those. The old building needed repairs and it was more cost-effective,' she said. 'They're well placed for loading out of the back gate.'

'So this is where you make the Gethsemane Salve?'

The nun nodded. 'People often think it's made somewhere else, but we produce everything in the convent – the tins as well as the salve. We have taken a vow to heal people, you see. To look after those around us.'

Mirabelle raised an eyebrow. 'How many nuns live here?' she asked.

'We're seventy now. In the old days there were at least a hundred sisters, but these days younger nuns go into nursing or teaching. The contemplative life is less popular for novices. I can't blame them. I had my stint, helping out in the world. I was almost forty when I came here.'

Mirabelle calculated that that put Sister Triduana at around eighty years of age. She looked well for that. Sprightly, even. It seemed strange to think that the nuns had had lives before they had retreated. That they had had homes and families and friends. Where had they all come from? Had they been teachers and nurses? Or were they all daredevils like Sister Triduana? She didn't like to ask. 'That seems like a lot of work. How many tins do you produce?' she asked.

Sister Triduana turned down a path onto the other side of the kitchen garden, which Mirabelle recognised as the view from Mother Superior's office.

'A thousand a week,' she replied blithely. 'Gethsemane Salve sells all over the world. It's particularly popular in South America. I organise the shipments. I don't work in the factory any more. Not with my old bones.'

'I see.' Mirabelle made a quick calculation – the nuns must be well in profit, yet both yesterday and today they had talked of making money. Perhaps they had charitable commitments.

Sister Triduana led Mirabelle up the stairs to Mother Superior's room where she knocked briskly and opened the door. 'Mother,' she said.

The younger nun looked up.

'I'm afraid Superintendent McGregor is out,' Mirabelle explained, as she saw Mother Superior had been crying: her eyes were pink. She removed a large white handkerchief from her pocket and blew her nose.

'What has happened? Are you all right?' Mirabelle asked.

'Quite all right,' Mother Superior said. 'You may leave us.' She dismissed Sister Triduana promptly and gestured for Mirabelle to sit down.

Through the open window onto the quad, Mirabelle could hear singing. Chanting, almost. It came, she supposed, from the chapel.

'Perhaps it's for the best,' Mother Superior said. 'You are a woman, after all. Yes, I can see you're a person who might take a sidestep as well as one forward, and we certainly need one of those. I'm afraid we require your absolute discretion, Miss Bevan. I felt as if the superintendent had been sent, but perhaps it was you.'

'Sent?'

Mother Superior raised her eyes. 'By Him.'

Mirabelle sank onto the large mahogany seat and wondered what she was hoping she would sidestep. 'Whatever has happened?' she asked.

'There has been an accident . . .' the nun started. 'One of our sisters has been gathered to God.'

'Do you mean someone is dead?'

Mother Superior looked tearful. Mirabelle waited as she took a moment to compose herself.

'She was a novice. Our only novice, in fact. Sister Monica. Newly arrived five months ago. She was working at the vats where we make the salve and she appears to have fallen in and not been able to recover her footing. She drowned. But when we came to lay out her body . . .'

'Yes?'

The nun got up and went to close the window. 'We can't have the police here, Miss Bevan,' she said. 'It isn't appropriate. And that's when I thought of Superintendent McGregor. I mean, you will be neighbours – that's what you want, isn't it?'

Mirabelle agreed.

'And we would always expect to be able to trust our neighbours. That is, to count on their discretion.'

Mother Superior appeared unable to continue.

'It must be such a shock,' Mirabelle encouraged her. 'Please, when you laid out Sister Monica's body, what upset you? What did you find?'

Mother Superior shuddered. 'I'll show you,' she said. 'Follow me.'

Mirabelle fell into step. Mother Superior, she thought, could not be much past forty: a very young woman during the war, only a few years older than Vesta. Inside the nunnery, the passageways were austere, painted white with dark wooden skirtings and framed prints on the wall, faded with age and depicting crosses on hillsides or saints shown with different sizes of halo. They passed through a well-supplied kitchen, where a huge pot of green soup bubbled on an old range and two nuns, their sleeves rolled up as they worked over the sink, were peeling carrots with vicious-looking kitchen knives clasped in their cold pink fingers. Mirabelle felt acutely aware of her high heels on the flagstones and was glad that today she had chosen a deep red wool jersey dress, its bateau neckline and soft lines more demure than that of the figure-hugging, slinky burnt-orange sheath she had worn the day before.

The sound of singing was close now and she calculated they were in a room beyond the chapel, which they seemed to have reached without going outdoors. The nunnery was a labyrinth, with haphazard passages connecting all its functions. Mother Superior made the sign of the cross and motioned Mirabelle ahead into a room lit with candles. On a long, high table, a body was laid out with one of the sisters sitting at its head, praying as she fingered a rosary. Mother Superior motioned for the nun to leave. Mirabelle's eyes were drawn to the dead novice, whose starched white robes and pristine wimple made her look angelic. Usually a young girl like this would be laid out in a simple linen shift, she thought. Perhaps nuns did things differently.

'Poor thing,' she said. 'When would she have taken her vows?'

Mother Superior's lips tightened. 'We are fortunate that she did not do so.'

Mirabelle's brow creased. 'What do you mean?'

The nun did not reply, only reached out and picked up the novice's robes by the hem, pulling them upwards. She met Mirabelle's eye. 'I have no idea how this happened,' she said.

Mirabelle brought a hand to her mouth. Beneath the novice's robe the body was that of a young man.

Chapter Three

Opinions are made to be changed

Mother Superior had a tray of tea sent to her study but neither she nor Mirabelle touched it. They sat in silence before the nun spoke.

'I do not know if we have been harbouring an invert, Miss Bevan,' Mother Superior said eventually. 'I do not know what this person wanted with us. It could have been anything. What I do know is that the story can go no further. And for that reason, I cannot call the police, but I thought of you and the superintendent. It is imperative we find out what they were doing here. Who on earth they were.'

Mirabelle sighed. 'Yes,' she said. 'I see.'

'In return, I will approve your purchase of Shore Cottage,' Mother Superior continued. 'And we will happily pay your expenses. A fee, perhaps?'

'Don't you have to report a death? Surely it would be normal for a post-mortem examination to be undertaken.'

'The convent's doctor will complete a death certificate. We are subject to certain exemptions here – a laxity of which, in this case, we will take advantage. We have our own grave-yard, down by the water.'

'I see. Well, it would be helpful to know how he . . . she . . . that is to say . . .' Mirabelle faltered.

'I think we should continue to call Sister Monica by the name she used here. I have been struggling with that myself but it seems the most discreet course of action.'

'Yes.' Mirabelle gathered her thoughts. 'It would be helpful to know exactly how Sister Monica died. You said she was found in a vat of salve, but a post-mortem examination would ascertain whether she was dead before she fell in, which is a possibility. Perhaps she had a heart attack or a stroke. She was young, but nonetheless . . . And, of course, it's possible that she was pushed.'

'There is no sign of that,' the nun said quickly. 'Why would you think such a thing?'

Mirabelle was not entirely sure how to put it. 'When one is accustomed to investigating murders, one suspends assumption where one can,' she said, weighing her words. 'We must be open to all possibilities and discount them according to the evidence. If there is bruising on Sister Monica's skin, for example, it might indicate that force was used. She was here under a false pretence, after all. Perhaps somebody found out.'

Mother Superior nodded slowly. 'Dr Alexander will be able to tell us, I'm sure. I telephoned her. She will be here shortly. I also called the bishop.'

'What did he say?'

'He concurred with me that we must keep this secret but that we are bound to find out what we can. He is concerned it may be a matter of industrial espionage.'

'What do you mean?'

'The recipe of the salve is secret and would be valuable to other manufacturers. Companies that work for profit and not necessarily for good.'

'Who here knows the recipe?'

'It is passed from Mother Superior to Mother Superior,' she said. 'When I am close to death, my sisters will choose my replacement and I will entrust the secret to the new Mother. It has been done in that way for over eight centuries, Miss Bevan.'

Mirabelle considered this. For a start, if she were a pharmaceutical company she would not send a young man to steal the convent's secret. The war had endowed Civvy Street with a great deal of women who had skills suitable to do the job. 'I'll bear that in mind,' she said. 'I would like to speak to the doctor when she arrives. First, though, may I inspect Sister Monica's room and the place her body was discovered – in the manufactory?'

'Of course.'

'It would also be helpful to know what she did here. I mean, her occupation.'

'All novices work in the salve sheds,' Mother Superior said. 'It is the creed of the sisterhood. It is the first thing everyone learns. I did it myself. Eighteen months of tempering fat and bone into gelatin is an excellent test of faith. The salve smells floral but only after the base is made.'

'When did you come to the nunnery?' Mirabelle asked.

'It seems a long time ago. I took my vows during the war. I had sat my university degree and a master's but He called me, you see.'

'During the war,' Mirabelle repeated. This would make Mother Superior older than she had originally estimated. She tried not to peer across the desk. Mother Superior laughed.

'The contemplative life has some advantages,' she said. 'Prayer and Gethsemane Salve are both excellent for the skin. As is the Scottish weather. We had an Italian nun visiting some weeks ago. She was the same age as I am and her skin was almost desiccated. I will be fifty years of age next spring.'

Mirabelle made a mental note to buy a large tin of Gethsemane Salve and use it daily. The prayer and contemplation would not be so easy.

Mother Superior rang a bell and Sister Mary was directed to show Mirabelle Sister Monica's cell and the vat where the novice's body had been discovered.

'And anything else Miss Bevan requires, Sister,' Mother directed airily.

They set off in silence, Sister Mary striding out. It struck Mirabelle that the old nun did not look as if she was hurrying though Mirabelle had to walk at double pace to keep up with her.

Sister Monica's room was on the first floor of the accommodation block – a solid-looking, barn-like stone structure that ran parallel to the garden. 'Our cells are all the same,' the nun explained, as she opened the door. 'We do not have possessions, apart from our robes.'

'Not even a Bible?'

Mary shook her head. 'If a sister wishes to read there's a library,' she added with enthusiasm.

In Sister Monica's cell, the small casement window was open, a slice of bright sunshine falling onto the wooden floor the only decoration. The room could not have been more than eight feet wide by ten feet long and furnished solely with a single bed down one side and a washstand on the other, a sliver of soap resting on a terracotta tile. There wasn't much that could harbour any indication of Sister Monica's story.

'Is there no fire? No heater?'

Sister Mary let a smile escape her. 'Oh, no,' she said. 'You are wise to observe that. In winter the water freezes most mornings but the chill makes us hurry to the refectory and the chapel and get on with our duties.'

Mirabelle silently hoped that during the winter months each nun had more than the cotton sheet and thin brown woollen blanket that were tucked neatly in place around Sister Monica's mattress.

'Do you know where she came from?' she asked.

'We don't talk about that kind of thing. Life before, I mean. Once a sister arrives, that she chose to join us is all that matters. We wash up like the tide on the shore – accepted as we are. You can talk about it if you want to, of course, but nobody would make a nun do so.'

Mirabelle considered Sister Triduana's candour in the Mini. The conversation had been the nun's choice and she seemed to have no regrets about her decision to come to the convent or, for that matter, about her life before. But others might have joined the Little Sisters of Gethsemane for more difficult personal reasons. She wondered what sorrows might have brought these seventy women together – faith, in her experience, being not only a matter of religion or philosophy, but also of comfort in the face of tragedy. Some might have served in either or both world wars.

'Did Sister Monica have an accent?' she asked.

'I think she was English. She sounded quite like you, in fact.'

London, Mirabelle thought. Oxford, maybe. And more upper class than lower. 'So she wasn't local?'

Sister Mary shrugged. 'When I was at school in Aberdeen they gave us three of the tawse if we didn't speak English properly. She might have come from anywhere, really.'

Mirabelle looked out of the window. The nuns evidently grew their own food as well as medical ingredients, and a long bed of potato plants stretched as far as the Nissen huts from this side of the building. Two women, their dark robes hoisted above wellington boots, were digging a patch, shaking soil off the potatoes and placing them in a huge burlap sack.

'What happens to your things?' she asked.

'Things?' Sister Mary sounded mystified.

'Everyone must arrive with . . . clothes. Money to pay for travel or food?'

'Ah. Yes. We are robed here. I cannot recall meeting Sister Monica before she took her vestments. Her clothes would have been given to charity. Any money goes into the convent's funds.'

Mirabelle nodded. She seemed to know this from somewhere, but could not recall how. 'It must be recorded,' she said.

'Yes.'

'I would like to see the record for Sister Monica, please.'

It made sense that the administration office for the nunnery was close to the front gate – the first door up the path that she and McGregor had used when they came in. A ginger cat lazed in the sunshine on the threshold.

'He's a mouser,' Sister Mary explained. 'You may as well have a lion as a pussy cat but then we'd have more mice.'

The office was unlocked and there was nobody inside.

'In the old days,' Sister Mary said wistfully, 'the convent used to admit patients and receive tithes. Long before my time,' she added. 'These days, there are fewer comings and goings.'

'Patients?' Mirabelle repeated.

'We had a hospital. People came to the sisters for help, you see, when no other help was available. Many centuries ago this place was on the pilgrim route.'

'Mother told me about that.'

'Where Sister Monica is laid out was part of the old hospital,' Sister Mary added. 'The mortuary. It is the only room still in use.'

She directed Mirabelle to a large leather-bound book propped on the desk's slope. 'That's the register.'

Mirabelle opened the tome and the musty smell of infrequently turned pages rose towards her. Inside, the writing was in black ink, though leafing through the pages she realised the last few entries covered a good decade. Towards the beginning of the register, the ink was so old it had faded to a dark rust on the thick leaves. The book had been started in 1842.

Surveying it, Mirabelle could see that for most of the nuns a full name and contact address had been taken. Women arrived from across the country and often changed their names when they got here. Sister Mary, she noted, was from near Aberdeen, as she had said – a village called Strichen – and her name was not Mary, but Norma Flegg. Her endowment, although from 1918, was somewhat larger than Sister Monica's – over two thousand pounds held in shares. Mary either did not realise Mirabelle was checking her record, or did not care. She stood impassively by the doorway, waiting, still as a statue.

Flicking forward, Mirabelle noted that the ink on the entry for Sister Monica was dark and fresh. Monica Smith, she read with a silent sigh. On 14 January, she had arrived in clothes that were donated to a charity in Edinburgh – a skirt and sweater, boots, handbag and coat all long gone and notated by item rather than by label so there was no record of any shop the girl might have patronised. She had had the sum of fifteen shillings and sixpence in cash in her purse, which had, as Sister Mary suggested, been donated to the nunnery's funds.

'Sister Monica did not give a next of kin or an address,' Mirabelle pointed out. 'I think she is the only woman not to do so, at least more recently.'

'That doesn't surprise me,' Sister Mary replied drily. 'I mean, given the circumstances. What we have . . . found.'

Mirabelle squinted. The writing was not entirely clear and she had some difficulty making out the words written in a spidery scrawl in the column reserved for observations. Mirabelle kept meaning to get her eyes tested but the idea of having to procure spectacles was not appealing. She was sure that Sister Mary would (rightly) disapprove of her reticence as a matter of vanity. 'What do you suppose that says?' she asked, pointing to the words.

Sister Mary approached the desk. She had no problem with her eyes. 'I think it says, "She cried."'

'Ah.' Mirabelle nodded, making it out. She wondered if someone sent to spy on the convent would display that kind of emotion and decided probably not. If Sister Monica's tears had been genuine, that is. On balance, though, she reckoned, it was most likely that whoever the girl had been, she had come to the Little Sisters for personal reasons, which, once she had been identified, would narrow the focus of the investigation quite considerably.

'I can imagine her crying,' Mirabelle said. 'Did you have any cause to doubt her? Did you suspect anything?'

Sister Mary's face remained impassive. Was it the habit and the wimple that made nuns so difficult to read? Certainly it stopped a woman passing a hand over her hair or distracting attention by checking a watch or fiddling with an earring. Mirabelle did not like the idea that it was her hairstyle that made her most like herself, or the clothes she chose to wear. On the few occasions she had had to don a uniform she was sure she had still been recognisable.

'We accept our sisters, Miss Bevan,' Sister Mary said. 'We are enjoined above everything to be kind to each other. And that is how we behaved towards Sister Monica. Wrongly, it seems,' she added.

'I'd like to speak to the nun who wrote this entry,' Mirabelle said. 'But perhaps first I could see the vat where the body was found.'

The manufactory yielded as little as Sister Monica's cell. The vat was a wide, gleaming bronze cylinder seven feet across and four feet in depth. All anybody would have to do to avoid drowning would be to stand up, Mirabelle thought, though she recalled reading that it was possible to drown in eighteen inches of water. She decided she would check the cadaver's head for bruising in case the nun had cracked her skull but, that aside, she could see no obvious reason for the accident.

'We heat the salve,' Sister Mary explained, showing Mirabelle a set of valves that required to be opened for gas flames to ignite beneath the vat's metal base. 'It used to be a wooden fire but the nunnery dispensed with that a long time ago. The gas makes the heat more regular, you see.'

It struck Mirabelle that the Victorian gas outlet was likely more dangerous than the vat itself, though that was not how matters transpired. To one side two wooden paddles were propped against the wall with two small wooden boxes for the nuns to stand on.

'And you stir it by hand,' she checked.

'It takes two of us.'

'But Sister Monica was alone when she died?'

'When the vat is in use, the salve is stirred for an hour by two sisters. You have to keep it moving or it will congeal, making its texture inconsistent. We consider the duty a blessing. A meditation. Afterwards, it is left to cool.'

Mirabelle made a mental note to check the identity of the second sister who would have been the last person in all likelihood to see Monica alive. Either that, or the novice's murderer.

Mirabelle imagined trying to recover her footing in a vat of warm, slippery gelatin. The panic. The heaviness of the nun's robes as the thickening salve weighed her down. Yes, it might be more difficult than she had first imagined simply to stand up.

'Do you know what Sister Monica wore on her feet?' she asked.

Sister Mary shrugged. 'We wear flat shoes,' she said, her eye on Mirabelle's blade-thin heels, 'but there are boots and shoes, even clogs and sandals in the store. Sisters choose for themselves.'

'This vat is clearly not in use today.'

'No,' the old nun said reverently. 'The bishop will bless it before we use it again.'

'When will he come?'

'As soon as he can.'

'But normally it would be in use?'

'Certainly,' Sister Mary confirmed. 'Every day except Sunday.'

Mirabelle did not like to point out that Sister Monica's death had held up production. She wanted to ask if they would manage their thousand tins of salve this week. Sister Mary did not elaborate, and when a bell tolled in what sounded like the distance, the nun motioned Mirabelle towards the door.

'That's lunch,' she announced. 'You wanted to speak to the sister who admitted Monica, did you not?'

The refectory was busy. The large pot of green soup that Mirabelle had seen bubbling earlier in the kitchen had been brought through, carried on two squared wooden poles. Three nuns were putting out stacks of wooden bowls as the women filed in and took their places in silence at the long tables. It was strange to see so many nuns together. Mirabelle wondered what the collective term might be for such a gathering. A flock? No – she recalled – a superfluity. Yes, that was it. Too many nuns.

'Will you join us, Miss Bevan?' Mother Superior asked, motioning towards one of the benches.

'I'm not hungry. Thank you,' Mirabelle replied.

Sister Mary's eyebrows rose. 'Hungry,' she repeated, as if the notion was entirely foreign.

'The Little Sisters of Gethsemane eschew all worldly appetites, Miss Bevan,' Mother Superior explained. 'We eat only to fuel our endeavours. However, we do not judge those who are led by their desires. The cloistered life is not for everybody.'

This last comment was directed at Sister Mary – a barb against her judgement of the convent's guest. 'Forgive me,' the nun apologised.

'Not at all,' said Mirabelle.

As the soup was ladled out, the nuns waited patiently. It looked like slop, Mirabelle thought, and felt glad she wasn't to have any. Sister Mary led her to one of the benches in the middle of the room.

'This is Sister Catherine.' She introduced a nun with startling blue eyes and thick dark brows over a heavily lined face. 'She admitted Sister Monica to the order.'

'Hello, Sister,' Mirabelle said.

'Saint Catherine died on the wheel for her faith,' the nun replied, and Mirabelle had to stifle a smile that each nun felt compelled to recite the story of the woman whose name she had taken.

'When Sister Monica arrived, you noted she cried.'

Sister Catherine nodded. 'She did, poor soul.'

'Do you know why?'

'Many of us are here because we lost somebody or because we were put in an impossible position,' she said. 'Because it is not always possible to continue in the world. I assumed that was the case for Sister Monica. It is not the first time I have admitted somebody who was upset.'

'What was she wearing? Can you remember?'

Sister Catherine considered this question. 'Her skirt was on the short side, I recall, but that has become the fashion.'

'Do you know where she came from?'

The nun shook her head. 'I asked in order to write it in the register but she simply burst into tears so violently she was unable to catch her breath. She kept saying, "Please let me in. I have to be with my sisters." It took a long time to calm her down. I took pity on her. I will do my penance now.'

'Penance?'

'For my error.'

'Your kindness, you mean?'

'I was not kind to the rest of my sisters.'

'You had no idea, then?'

'None. Though that is not to say Sister Monica's soul was profane. That she meant us harm. Perhaps an angel has visited us,' Sister Catherine added.

Mirabelle tried to ignore the smell of the soup, which was not pleasant. It did not surprise her that both Sister

36

Catherine and Sister Mary were completely disinterested in eating. Questioning them was more trying than the cryptic crossword. She appeared either to be dealing with people who had an overabundance of judgement or none at all. 'Do you know how Sister Monica got to the nunnery that day?'

Sister Catherine's brow furrowed. 'It was cold,' she said. 'Though at the end of January this year there was a good deal of sunshine. Our cherry trees flowered out of the blue. But Sister Monica arrived before that. There had been snow – yes, it must have been after New Year. The second week of January, perhaps. She had a train ticket in her possession. She got off at Dalmeny station, I imagine, and walked. She arrived in the afternoon. I think it was two or three o'clock. Lunch was over but I made her a cup of tea. Her nose was pink with the cold and she didn't have gloves. I recall I found that strange – she was well dressed otherwise, you see.'

'Do you remember if the ticket showed where she had come from?'

'I'm sorry,' Sister Catherine said. 'It would have gone to be burned with the rubbish, but the child must have come through Edinburgh if she came from the south. All the trains do. From the north there are more options – any of the Fife stations or Aberdeen perhaps. Inverness, even. She was so upset it wasn't possible to make conversation.'

The nuns became suddenly still as Mother Superior rose and gave a benediction. They intoned the Amen together. Mirabelle motioned for Sister Catherine to eat with the others. It was, she noted, the most silent canteen she had ever been in – even the sombre staff facilities during the Battle of Britain had had more life.

'Please,' she said to Sister Mary, who continued to wait politely in case Mirabelle required further assistance. 'You should have lunch. Fuel,' she added. 'And, in the meantime, I might nip back to Sister Monica's cell for another look.'

Sister Mary hesitated but Mirabelle smiled as if she was encouraging a small child to sit down to tea in the nursery. 'I can find my own way. I don't want to interfere with your duty.' She cast her eyes heavenwards and the nun acquiesced.

Along the corridor, cutting back to the accommodation block, she realised the nunnery felt oddly familiar already. Mirabelle had attended an all-girls' school and afterwards had finished in Switzerland. Dormitories and refectories had been a feature of her younger years. Still, something about the Little Sisters of Gethsemane irked her. Arriving at Sister Monica's cell, she lifted the jug of water from the washstand and checked beneath the mattress to see if anything was hidden. One by one she tried the planks that made up the floor and the plain skirting surround, but nothing had been loosened. On her knees, she ran her hand down the hollow metal legs of the bed frame, lifting them one by one to check if something was secreted inside. As she came to the last, she heard the door open behind her and jumped.

'Sorry,' said an attractive blonde in a navy tweed suit and a well-fitted green silk blouse, set off with a string of pearls. 'Jeanette Alexander.' She held out her hand. 'I'm the convent's doctor. I didn't mean to scare you.'

Mirabelle's heart was racing. She told herself off for being excitable as she shook Dr Alexander's hand and gave her name.

'Well, Miss Bevan, I don't blame you for taking a fright. It's creepy, isn't it? A bit like school but not like school at all. As if you're being watched all the time.'

'That's it,' Mirabelle agreed, appreciating the other woman's frankness. 'Exactly.'

'What were you looking for?'

'There are some things Sister Monica must have had. A razor, for a start. I don't know where she hid it.'

'She?'

Mirabelle nodded. 'Mother Superior said it would be best to stick with that, for discretion's sake.'

'I see. Well, the thing I'm interested in is his reason, not his razor. Had the man lost his mind?' the doctor replied. She sounded angry.

'Did you ever meet Sister Monica?'

Dr Alexander shook her head. 'They're nuns. They don't make a fuss. I'm called in rarely, mostly to attend a death.'

'Or an accident?'

'Once one of the nuns got badly burned in the kitchen. The old dears had applied their salve, of course, but after a day or two it was clear stronger medicine was required. But I'm not here often.'

'Have you seen the body?'

'Not yet. Would you like to join me? Mother Superior said on the telephone that I'm to answer all of your questions.'

'I may have several.'

'We should get on with it, then.'

They quit the cell and walked in silence back to the room where Sister Monica's body was laid out. Dr Alexander dismissed the nun in attendance. 'There's no need for you to witness this,' she said. 'Sister Monica will be safe with us but there will be some cleaning up to do afterwards.'

The nun disappeared in the direction of the refectory as the doctor laid her bag on the table and snapped on the electric light overhead.

'Candles are all very well,' she said, 'but we need to see properly. How did you get involved in this? Mother said you're a detective.'

'I used to be. Sometimes,' Mirabelle replied. 'I'll be getting married here, in the chapel, in . . .' she paused to count '. . . ten days.'

Dr Alexander laughed. 'A blushing bride, then. The sisters are quite something for recruiting people. Did she intimate that God sent you?'

Mirabelle nodded. 'Shall we get going?' she suggested.

'Certainly.' The doctor briskly donned a long-sleeved pale green surgical robe and handed another to Mirabelle. Then she expertly removed Sister Monica's vestments and laid them on the chair where the nun had been praying. Mirabelle cocked her head. The way the garment's hem swung was wrong, as if it were weighted. She ran her fingers along the seams.

'I think something's sewn inside,' she said.

Dr Alexander turned away from the body and removed a pair of scissors from her bag. 'Here.'

Mirabelle carefully cut the seam where it disappeared into the novice's hem. From inside, she pulled out a small piece of metal attached to a round yellow tag with a black number on it – seventeen.

'Is it the razor?' the doctor asked, peering over.

'No.' Mirabelle laid it on her open palm. 'It's a key.'

The doctor grinned. 'Well done, Detective.'

'Now I need to figure out what it's a key to,' Mirabelle pointed out, slipping it into her pocket. It was, she reckoned, too small for a proper door, more the kind of key that would fit a box or a locker, and it was modern – unlike the nunnery or anything she had so far seen inside it.

The doctor's examination revealed less than the nun's habit. Sister Monica was, by her estimation, over eighteen and under twenty-five years of age. The throat was blocked with gelatin so the novice had drowned in the salve and, though there was no definitive sign of a fight, there was an injury on the back of the skull. The doctor, however, was unable to say if Monica had lost consciousness and fallen into the vat or whether it had been the other way around. Mirabelle had a sudden vision of the novice floundering in the warm gooey salve, desperate for breath. Slipping. Falling. Banging her head. Yes, it might have been that way. But then again, it might not.

'Did somebody hit her?' she asked.

'I cannot swear there was no force used,' the doctor said, with what was now accustomed frankness, 'but there is no proof of it. It might just as well have been an accident – falling in, trying to get out and cracking the skull. Either's likely.'

Examination of the internal organs showed no indication of a heart attack or stroke. 'He was a drinker, though,' the doctor pronounced, 'a heavy drinker at that.'

Mirabelle peered into the body as the doctor passed judgement on the liver.

'On the young side for this kind of damage,' she said, 'but there's no doubt about it. There are signs of recovery but the injury is pretty extensive.'

'That's interesting,' Mirabelle said. 'There's been no indication that Monica drank.'

'There'd be little opportunity in here. The communion wine would be noticed if it went missing. As far as I'm aware there is a noggin of brandy in the medicine cabinet in Mother Superior's office – no more spirits than that in the whole place. He hadn't had a drink in the hours before death. That's not the reason for what happened.'

'Do you think Monica gave up drinking when she arrived?'

'Perhaps that was what prompted the fellow's faith – if this whole thing wasn't a charade, that is.'

Towards the end of the doctor's examination, Mother Superior joined them. Her eyes passed solemnly over the bloodied body, open at the torso, as if such a sight was natural. 'Can you tell if she was . . . I mean, is there any notion that she may have been . . .' the nun stammered.

'I cannot tell from examination of the body whether a person was homosexual, Mother, if that is what you are trying to ask,' Dr Alexander replied briskly.

Mother Superior shook her head. 'It is not exactly that . . .' she said. 'I mean, a . . . homosexual would surely have joined a monastery.'

Mirabelle sighed. There was, in her experience, no saying what a person might do on account of their strongest and most secret desires. Sister Monica might have come to the nunnery to get away from men entirely. Certainly, Mirabelle was coming to the view that it was more likely the young novice had arrived on a personal quest. Something worth giving up the world for.

'Mother, do you know which sister Monica worked with last? It was her job, was it not, to mix the salve with another nun?'

'Sister Mary,' Mother replied. 'That was why I asked her to show you round. Did she not say?'

Mirabelle shook her head, as if it was of no consequence, but it was an interesting omission. 'Thank you,' she said.

'This fellow is an enigma,' the doctor announced. 'I am pronouncing accidental death. By asphyxiation. Drowning.'

Mother Superior looked relieved. 'We will continue to call her Sister Monica, Doctor,' she added. 'That was her wish as far as we know, and it is ours too.'

Outside, in the courtyard, Dr Alexander lit a cigarette. In the laying-out room, three nuns were washing Sister Monica's body and dressing her in her robe once more. Mother Superior had gone to telephone the bishop to inform him the post-mortem examination was complete and the death certificate in hand. The ginger cat slunk in the direction of the Nissen huts as the doctor inhaled strong Turkish tobacco deep into her lungs.

'That wasn't your first dead body, your first post-mortem, either. Was it? Were you medical during the war?' the doctor asked.

'Not exactly,' Mirabelle said.

Dr Alexander beckoned her closer. 'The old dears are quite worldly in some ways. It's unusual they don't know what's going on. But in matters . . . Well . . . I can put it more frankly for you than I did for Mother and say that Sister Monica was not a sodomite,' she whispered. 'If that's any help.'

Mirabelle raised an eyebrow. 'Thank you.'

'It would be easier, wouldn't it, if there had been obvious violence? Or a heart attack? An accidental drowning seems somehow dramatic. Unnecessary, almost. If somebody wanted to murder Sister Monica . . .' the doctor paused, finding it difficult to use a female name for the novice '. . . if they simply wanted to kill her, they could have sneaked into her cell when she was sleeping and used a pillow. It would have been easier and attracted less attention.'

'You don't think it was an accident?'

'There's no definite sign it wasn't. The thing is, they

won't want an inquest. And if I declare anything other than natural causes or accidental death, that's what there will be. You need to be the inquest, Miss Bevan. Do you understand me?'

Mirabelle nodded. 'I'll do my best to get to the bottom of it,' she said. 'It seems wrong to bury the body without knowing who they were and exactly how they died. But you're right. An inquest is out of the question as far as Mother Superior is concerned. It would almost be unkind.'

A troubled expression flickered across Dr Alexander's face. 'It makes no sense.'

'Not yet,' Mirabelle agreed. 'Still, we know that she was dedicated to whatever she was doing here. We don't know how long she intended to stay in the convent but she must have given up a good deal to do so. Alcohol, for a start. Pulling off this deception would have taken determination, planning and a good deal of effort. It seems to me that there has to be a connection of some kind. Why did she come here? It can't be a coincidence.'

'It's the ultimate intrusion,' the doctor said, as she ground out her cigarette under her shoe, which was far more sensible than the heels Mirabelle was wearing. 'Maybe he was just a thrill-seeker.'

'Perhaps,' Mirabelle said doubtfully. Doctors, she noted, like policemen, tended to think the worst of people. 'Or maybe Sister Monica genuinely intended to take her vows. But whether she came for that or another reason, it was a personal decision. To be here, I mean. Rather than any other nunnery. If I can uncover the connection, it'll all unfold.'

'If it's to do with one of the nuns, I doubt you'll find out anything they don't want you to. I've been the doctor here since I came home from the African campaign in 'forty-three.

It's blasphemy to say it, but this place is like a harem, though one for the greater good rather than some sultan's pleasure.'

Mirabelle was suddenly struck by an image of God as the only man who was welcome inside the convent's walls. 'I might need an insider on my team,' she agreed thoughtfully. 'I can see that.' What she did not add was that she had had an idea of how to acquire one.

Chapter Four

Where there is mystery there must also be evil

'I play eighteen holes on the hill and you manage to get yourself tangled up in a case while I'm gone. A shocking one at that. It's completely inappropriate. They ought to call in the constabulary,' McGregor said, as the couple dressed for dinner.

'So far there's no evidence of foul play,' Mirabelle pointed out, holding up one arm for him to fasten the emerald bracelet she inherited from her grandmother and patting her hair with the other hand as she inspected herself in the mirror.

'A young man hiding in a nunnery dies as a result of an accident? I mean, there's plenty of foul play in that sentence alone . . .'

'But nothing illegal, Alan. They have no obligation to call the police.'

McGregor considered this as he closed the safety catch and kissed Mirabelle's hand. 'That's true,' he admitted. 'Borderline morally, but true.'

'Well, then. The nuns are going to be our neighbours. We should help.'

'The dead man may have a next of kin who ought to be informed.'

'When I find out who he is, we'll certainly inform them.'

McGregor sat on the end of the bed as Mirabelle applied her lipstick in the mirror. 'It's intriguing, though, isn't it?' he said.

This was an admission, she thought, that he had given up on any kind of complaint about the Little Sisters. She smiled. 'Did you win today?'

McGregor shrugged. 'I'm not sure anyone ever wins at golf. I'm three over par and still getting back my form.' He had tried to find a course to play in Brighton when they lived there but had given up only a few months after he arrived in 1951. The station had been permanently busy and the hours were too long to accommodate a hobby that required a regular eighteen holes.

'You'll be a scratch player again before you know it,' Mirabelle said, with a smile.

At the Roxburghe Hotel on George Street they sat at the bar on high stools upholstered in green velvet as the Italian barman mixed Camparis. The newly decorated walls of the bar were almost the same colour as the drinks. Mirabelle relaxed to the sound of Dave Brubeck playing in the background as McGregor ordered cold roast beef with salad and chips for both of them, and they sipped from frosted highball glasses. It could be Soho, she thought. As plates of rare Aberdeen Angus sliced so thinly they were almost transparent were placed on the bar, McGregor noticed his solicitor, Mr Wallace, steering a mousy-looking woman in an old-fashioned black dress into one of the booths that were separated from the main body of the room by painted fretwork and silk ivy. The lawyer raised his hand in greeting. As he approached across the patterned carpet, he wafted a cloud of whisky fumes.

'The Little Sisters of Gethsemane,' he got out by way of greeting. 'I hear they were charmed by you, Miss Bevan. Well done. We anticipated they might be difficult about the new owners of Shore Cottage.'

'Really? Why?' Mirabelle asked.

'Nuns!' Wallace replied, as if this was an explanation. And then, 'They don't like men, do they? We knew we'd need to find a married couple to take the house at least. If not a spinster.'

Mirabelle met McGregor's eye. Wallace clearly wasn't acquainted with Sister Monica's demise. 'I admit I'm fascinated by them. What else do you know about the order?' Mirabelle asked. 'It seems quite the operation.'

'Oh, they're wily old birds,' the solicitor exclaimed, bringing his forefinger to his nose and tapping it as if he was sharing a secret.

Mirabelle did not reply and this encouraged him.

'Gethsemane Salve,' he added, pointing at her. 'Centuries of the stuff. It works too – a veritable cure-all. It's made them one of the wealthiest orders in Britain. Buckfast Abbey's got nothing on our sisters.'

'One of the nuns told me they host weddings in the chapel to raise funds,' Mirabelle said.

Wallace giggled. 'They're not short of money,' he said. 'Not at all.'

'Have you met any of the nuns?'

'Only Mother Superior,' he admitted. 'We look after legal matters for the diocese. I met her at the Bishop's Palace.'

'Mother Superior's one of the younger nuns, isn't she?'

'She was a tutor before she took holy orders,' Wallace confided. 'Classics. They're a force to be reckoned with, those women.'

'I noticed that most of the nuns are rather elderly. When we visited there was a dearth of novices, I must say. I wondered what might draw someone to joining such an order, these days. It seems quite the commitment.'

'Well, that is the bishop's main concern,' Wallace said, lowering his voice. 'I mean, nowadays young women join the FANY or the Wrens or whatever. They go to teach in Africa. Help build hospitals for charity and so forth.'

'Africa, yes,' Mirabelle said thoughtfully.

'The point is, they don't need to be part of the Church. I expect the Little Sisters may sell on the business at some stage. Gethsemane Salve could be made in a proper factory at just as much profit and the money used to fund their charitable concerns. They'd be able to get on with praying and whatnot. Good works. In the next decade or two they'll have to consider it. They won't have enough hands.'

An Italian waiter arrived and offered a tray of mustard to Mirabelle and McGregor with a flourish.

'I mustn't keep you.' Wallace gave a little bow before returning to his table.

The waiter brought the chips and salad and opened a bottle of Chianti, which McGregor tasted and approved.

'We could honeymoon in New York,' he said, as he tucked in.

Mirabelle smiled. He was suggestible, and the music was catchy. 'In a series of jazz dives, you mean?'

'In a five-star hotel. There must be a good one.'

'At least one, I imagine.'

They had not booked anything yet, and as Vesta and Charlie would be in town, they wouldn't go anywhere for at least a week after the wedding.

'I've heard it's nice there in September,' McGregor said. 'It would be an adventure. The autumn trees upstate are famous. We could hire a car.'

'The doctor says that Sister Monica was a heavy drinker,' Mirabelle replied, her eyes straying to Wallace's table where a bottle of champagne was being poured into crystal saucers. The waiters were ignored by the couple, who were so deep in intimate conversation that they were almost joined at the lips.

McGregor sat back and regarded his future wife. She clearly wasn't interested in a honeymoon – an indication that this case was serious. 'I could get Wallace to introduce me to the bishop if you think it would help,' he offered.

Mirabelle kept her voice low. 'Perhaps. There has to be a connection, doesn't there? A young man arrives at a convent and enrols as a novice. It can't have happened out of the blue.'

'The natural question is, how did he know about the Little Sisters of Gethsemane?' McGregor said.

'That's definitely where I have to start,' Mirabelle agreed. 'It seems most likely "Monica" had previously come into contact with the convent because of something personal. If that's the case, there's a strong chance he knew one of the nuns.'

'And that means somebody inside the convent knew him,' McGregor continued.

Mirabelle nodded, lifting the glass of wine to her lips. 'But none of the nuns have come forward to identify the body. And not only that – one of the sisters must have been living in a situation for the last five months where she knew there was an interloper in her community. A man.'

Mirabelle's eye rested again on Wallace's table. 'Do you think it's an affair?' she said thoughtfully.

'I think she's his secretary.' McGregor followed her line of sight.

'Not them.'

'Monica was in his early twenties – is that right? How young is the youngest sister?'

'Perhaps one of them is his mother.'

'That seems more likely. Saint Monica was a mother, wasn't she? A good mother.'

Mirabelle searched her memory. 'Saint Augustine's mother, I think.'

'Yes, that's it.'

'All right. Let's say this young man came to the convent to find his mother. And instead of knocking on the front gate and just asking to see her, he puts on women's clothing and enrols as a novice. It still doesn't make sense.'

McGregor speared a chip with his fork. 'What it adds up to is, if he came to see somebody – one of the nuns – she's unwilling. She didn't want to see him in a normal way. And now she doesn't want to admit the connection even if it means that Monica goes unidentified. I mean, presumably somebody outside the convent cares that he's dead and they'll never know. That's quite something to have on your conscience, don't you think? For a nun?'

Mirabelle pondered a moment. 'It seems likely that many of these women don't want to see anybody from the outside world. Stands to reason – you'd think that's why they went there. But if your child were to come for you, surely . . . Even if your brother were to come. A nephew. A friend. The idea that one of those women could be a mother and have left their child . . .' Her brow furrowed. 'It feels wrong.'

McGregor put down his cutlery. His expression softened. 'Does it bother you that we won't have children?'

'No,' she said simply, sounding surprised. 'Not at all.'

'Good. Is this case going to become more important than our wedding?'

Mirabelle smiled again.

'Ah. I see. I know my place. What time is Vesta arriving tomorrow?'

'In the morning. She's taking the sleeper. I've arranged to go down for her at nine. To Waverley.'

'And you'll buy the dress and order the flowers?'

'All that kind of thing.'

'Ten days,' said McGregor.

Mirabelle sliced a sliver of pink beef and applied bright, peppery mustard. 'Nine days,' she said. 'I'm going to solve this case before we get married.'

'At least that means I stand some chance of getting away on a honeymoon,' he replied with a sigh.

Mirabelle swallowed the mouthful. Her lips tingled from the mustard. She leaned across to kiss him.

'That's more like it,' he said. 'Why don't I organise a visit to the Bishop's Palace? We can interview him together. The order might not be as sequestered as you're assuming. The Church is a global concern, you know.'

Mirabelle didn't doubt it, but there was nothing more she could do tonight. 'Let's skip dessert and go home to bed as soon as we've finished the wine,' she whispered.

Outside, the moon hung low along George Street, the parked cars casting navy shadows onto the pavement as they walked arm and arm towards Heriot Row. The sky was so bright, the streetlights seemed redundant. The gate of the gardens opposite the house creaked as a late-night dog-walker slipped onto the illuminated grass and his dog disappeared into the black bushes like a shot.

'I love you, Mirabelle Bevan,' McGregor said. 'You're going to be a beautiful bride.'

'I love you, Alan McGregor,' she replied. 'And I'm sure you're also going to look nice.'

Chapter Five

Our deeds disguise us

The concourse at Waverley station was thronging with passengers as the train arrived from Glasgow in a cloud of steam. A boy standing on a wooden box held a copy of the *Scotsman* over his head and shouted the headlines as he did good business, selling copies of the paper from the canvas bag over his shoulder, which seemed almost as big as he was. Vesta was easy to pick out coming from the direction of one of the rear platforms in a perfectly fitted lime-green summer dress and matching hat, with a huge white leather suitcase wheeled on a trolley by a uniformed porter. She jumped up and down with excitement as she spotted Mirabelle rounding the corner under a hoarding advertising Bell's whisky. The women flung their arms around each other. The porter looked away.

'Might you find us a cab, please?' Mirabelle directed him, as she linked arms with Vesta and the man cleared a path through the crowd towards the line of glossy black cabs that descended the slope from Waverley Bridge.

The driver loaded Vesta's suitcase into the front as Mirabelle tipped the porter. 'Where have you come from, miss?' the driver asked in a friendly tone.

'Brighton,' Vesta said. 'I got the sleeper from London.'

'But where are you really from?'

Mirabelle sighed. She'd forgotten how people reacted to the colour of Vesta's skin.

'Bermondsey,' Vesta said patiently. 'I was brought up in London.'

The man took a breath, about to contest this, but Mirabelle said: 'Take us to thirty-two Heriot Row,' she said. 'Please.' And guided her friend into the back seat.

'Oh, you're right in the middle of everything,' Vesta declared, as they glided along Princes Street past the castle and up Hanover Street. 'It's beautiful, isn't it?'

'It's quite different from Brighton, especially the Old Town.' Mirabelle pointed towards the castle. 'But you're right. I like it here.'

'You said you'd booked us a place by the sea?'

'From next week. It's a sweet little house in Portobello right off the promenade. And very well appointed. There's a television and a large refrigerator. For now, though, I thought you'd stay with us.'

'We have all this shopping to do.'

'We do. But there is something else,' Mirabelle admitted. 'I need a favour.'

'Anything,' said Vesta, contentedly.

Mirabelle thought her friend had better hear what it was first. 'I'll tell you when we get in and we've had a cup of tea.'

The driver carried Vesta's suitcase up to the first floor and Mirabelle unlocked the door. Vesta explored the apartment – gasping at the long-windowed drawing room that overlooked the gardens, then tutting at the old-fashioned kitchen and gloomy bathroom while Mirabelle made a pot of tea and brought it through on a wooden tray. 'I keep thinking I should do something with the place, but we're not sure if we're going to stay,' she said.

Vesta collapsed onto the comfortable sofa and leaned back to stare at the cornice and the elegant chandelier that hung from a chipped Robert Reid ceiling rose. The ice-blue wallpaper was at least fifty years old, faded but pretty with pockmarks in places round the windows. McGregor said he and his cousin used to practise shooting their catapults in this room when they were kids.

'You've been up here for more than a year, Mirabelle.'

Mirabelle shifted. 'We came down at Christmas.'

'I'm not complaining. But you might have, I don't know, put up some tiles in the loo. Renovated.'

Mirabelle poured the tea. 'I might,' she said doubtfully.

'So, what's this favour?' Vesta asked, picking up her teacup and taking a shortbread biscuit from the plate.

'How do you feel about nuns?'

Vesta moved forwards on the sofa. 'I don't know any personally. There were nuns in Bermondsey. The Poor Clares, I think.' She shuddered. 'When bananas came back at the greengrocer's a cluster gathered outside.' She paused.

'A superfluity,' Mirabelle corrected her.

'I remember them eating the bananas, sitting in a row on one of the benches on Bermondsey Street,' Vesta finished, with a smile. 'Strange-looking women. It's stayed with me – so, as you're asking, I think they're creepy. Why?'

'Alan bought us a house just outside town. A holiday place. And there is a convent nearby – our nearest neighbour. One of the nuns died a couple of days ago. A novice.'

'A young nun, you mean?'

Mirabelle nodded. 'In her early twenties and in mysterious circumstances. The thing is, I can't work out how to get the nuns to speak to me. The Mother Superior has asked me to investigate but I'm such an outsider. I keep thinking if only I had somebody on the inside . . . someone I could trust. Someone they would trust too . . .'

Vesta choked on her tea. 'Oh, no,' she said, with a cough.

'It would only be for a few days,' Mirabelle replied quickly. She got to her feet and disappeared out of the room, coming back with a habit and wimple on a sturdy wooden hanger. 'Mother Superior gave me this. It's your size,' she said. 'They know what I look like, Vesta, and, besides, I'll be moving in nearby. I can't do it myself.'

'That,' Vesta indicated the robe, 'doesn't have a size. Besides, we're supposed to be ordering flowers and finding you a wedding dress . . .'

'That won't take long. You can choose whatever you like . . . I don't care.'

'A full-length white gown with a full veil and a lily bouquet?' Mirabelle paused.

'I wouldn't do that to you, don't worry.' Vesta laughed. Mirabelle smiled. She had missed the sound of her friend's laugh. 'But you're getting married. I want it to be lovely for you,' Vesta continued. 'God, Mirabelle . . .'

Mirabelle put down her teacup. 'I know,' she said. 'But the thing is, this nun wasn't a nun. She fell into a vat of the salve they make at the convent and drowned. She knocked her head somehow. And when they came to lay out the body, well, she was . . . a he. He'd been living in the convent for five months and none of the other nuns had noticed.'

Vesta's brow furrowed. 'You mean . . . ?'

'The novice was a young man.'

'I don't understand. Why had he . . . why would anyone?'

'That's what I want you to find out. Sister Monica – that

was the name the young man used – must have gone to the Little Sisters of Gethsemane for a reason.'

'The Little Sisters of Gethsemane as in Gethsemane Salve?'

'The convent makes a thousand tins a week. It's impressive, actually.'

Vesta finished her biscuit and licked an errant smear of sugar from her forefinger. She got up and touched the wimple. 'That is intriguing,' she said. 'It's nice cotton – rather too starched to be comfortable, I should think.'

Mirabelle grinned. 'I've arranged with Mother Superior that you will arrive as Sister Joseph. You'll be there to learn how the manufactory works – your order intends to make soap. I thought that would give you a good reason to ask questions. The sisters aren't exactly chatty, though it isn't a silent order. They seem very productive – they grow their own food and the ingredients they use to make the salve. You could consider it a kind of working holiday. It'll only be a day or two.'

Vesta considered a moment and then nodded. 'All right,' she said.

'I have everything planned,' Mirabelle continued. 'I'll ring every morning at ten o'clock and you'll be with Mother Superior in her study. It shouldn't take long. If we can find out why Sister Monica came to the convent, it would be a huge step forward. It's the key to the whole thing.'

'Saint Joseph was Jesus's father, wasn't he?'

'Oh,' said Mirabelle, 'you're going to fit right in.'

Vesta changed into the habit in the guest bedroom, hanging her green dress on the rail where it looked slightly mournful on a satin-covered hanger swaying in the otherwise empty wardrobe.

'Mother said she would see to it you were accommodated in Sister Monica's old room. I searched it but you never know.'

'Find anything?'

'This,' Mirabelle scrabbled around in her handbag and withdrew the key. 'It's my only clue so far. She had concealed it in her robe. I don't know yet what it's for.'

Vesta cocked her head to one side. She looked strange in the wimple, stark without the hair framing her face and stocky without a tailored waist to show off her figure. 'You don't recognise it?'

'No,' Mirabelle admitted.

'It's a locker key. They have those keys exactly for the lockers at Brighton railway station, though the tags aren't yellow – they're red. The numbers are in the same font. Haven't you used the lockers?'

'No,' Mirabelle said.

Vesta picked up another shortbread biscuit and bit into it decisively. Mirabelle did not like to say that it might be her last biscuit for a while. She had a sudden vision of Vesta being presented with a wooden bowl of thick green soup and decided to make sure she took a packet of biscuits with her, perhaps some cheese, too. There were a few things in the kitchen cupboard she could secrete in a bag.

'You need to check the railway station and the bus station, I suppose,' Vesta continued. 'That would be a good start. I could come with you, if you like. Is it on our way?'

Mirabelle was about to answer that the convent wasn't far and she'd deal with the station herself, when the front door opened.

'Vesta!' said McGregor delightedly. He would normally kiss Vesta on the cheek by way of greeting, but he held back. 'My goodness. You look . . .'

Vesta drew a cross in the air. 'Sister Joseph,' she said. 'I look like Sister Joseph.'

'Bless me. I have certainly sinned,' McGregor replied, as he took a piece of shortbread off the plate. 'So she talked you into it?'

Mirabelle drove. It took far longer than it had when Sister Triduana had been at the wheel, through the West End and out of town along Queensferry Road. It had been so sunny of late that people were complaining their gardens needed rain, though the wheat fields were a stunning gold under the clear, blue sky. As the firth came into view, with the thin outline of the Fife coast across the water, Vesta clapped her hands. 'Oh, it's lovely,' she said. 'And the convent is out here?'

'Right on the water,' Mirabelle confirmed.

'Can we look at the house you've bought?'

Mirabelle cut off at South Queensferry past the little harbour and the shanty town at the bridge works, where today a team of workers were hoisted on a platform drilling something into the shore, taking advantage of the tide being out. She turned down the track, dappled in shadows. Shore Cottage was as pretty as she remembered. The women got out and wandered around the side of the house, into the garden.

'It's a fancy holiday place,' Vesta said. 'I thought it was supposed to be a cottage.'

'A four-bedroom cottage. I suppose, compared to the other old buildings round here, it seems small enough to merit the name, though there are some actual cottages at the other end of the village. Do you think Noel will like it?' Mirabelle teased. Vesta's toddler was the arbiter of everything in her household. 'We could teach him to sail,' she added.

They wandered through the trees and discovered a short

stretch of beach, with rock pools at one end, the jetty and the wooden boathouse McGregor had mentioned at the other. 'This is glorious,' Vesta said. 'It feels absolutely private.'

'I wonder if we'll buy a boat,' Mirabelle mused. 'For day trips and picnics.'

They made their way back to the garden where a sandy-haired middle-aged woman, with a thin slash of red lipstick that exactly matched the roses on her floral apron, appeared framed by the back door. Her body seemed if not plump then on the cusp of being so.

'Can I help you, Sister?' she said.

Mirabelle and Vesta felt strange, as if something had shifted. Nobody normally spoke to Vesta first when Mirabelle was with her.

'Sister Joseph came to meet me on behalf of the convent,' Mirabelle said. 'I'm the new owner.'

The woman stepped back a fraction. 'Oh, ma'am,' she said, 'I'm Mrs Grieg, the housekeeper.'

Mirabelle held out her hand. 'You've done a lovely job on the place, Mrs Grieg. I hope you might continue to look after it for us when we get the keys.'

'Aye.' Mrs Grieg nodded enthusiastically. 'Thank you.'

'I'm thinking of making a few changes to the decor. Might I show Sister Joseph inside?'

Mrs Grieg ushered them in. 'I've never met you before, Sister,' she said.

'I'm from another convent. I've come to see the manufactory,' Vesta replied smoothly. Mirabelle stifled a smile. Vesta's tone was different from usual: she didn't sound as bubbly. The persona of Sister Joseph was setting in.

'Are you from Africa then?' Mrs Grieg asked. 'We donate to the African mission. The wee Black babies, poor souls.'

This would have been a step too far for Vesta to bring off and she knew it. When perpetuating a cover (or, as it might otherwise be known, a lie) it was always best to stick as close to the truth as possible. Mirabelle had taught her that.

'I'm from Bermondsey. The Poor Clares,' she replied. 'It's lovely to be here. Out in the country.'

'They won't give you the recipe, will they?' Mrs Grieg sounded concerned. 'The Gethsemane Salve?'

'That won't be necessary,' Vesta assured her. 'My sisters and I will be making soap. I'm here to learn the administration required to run a manufactory. That's all.'

'Can I fetch you ladies anything?' Mrs Grieg offered.

'A tray of tea would be marvellous, if you can stretch to it,' Mirabelle said, adding in a whisper as Mrs Grieg closed the door behind her. 'The Poor Clares? Where did you get that from?'

'I have to come from somewhere,' Vesta replied. 'I've seen it on a sign near where my mother lives.'

Mirabelle got up. 'Come on,' she said, 'I want to show you the rest of the house.' When they came down again Mrs Grieg had laid out tea in the sitting room. The sun played across the thick carpet, highlighting the swirls of pale pink, green and cream.

'That's kind.' Mirabelle thanked the woman. 'It's good to be able to get a feel for the place. Have you worked here long?'

'I looked after Miss MacDonald for thirty years,' the housekeeper admitted.

'You must have been terribly upset when she died.'

Mrs Grieg neither confirmed nor denied this. 'She went into the Royal Infirmary in Edinburgh at the end,' she said. 'I knew she wouldn't come home again. She said she wanted to see Christmas one last time for the carols and that. And she did before they took her in, as if a doctor can really help a woman of that age. She was dying and she knew it. I work three mornings a week at the big house,' she added. 'But I could have looked after her here. We'd have managed.'

'The big house?'

Mrs Grieg gestured in the direction of the road. 'The Farquharson-Sinclairs,' she said. 'They don't have ladies' maids any more but I do the shoes and the ladies' wardrobes – sewing buttons and darning. The stains!' She raised her eyebrows disapprovingly, as if stains were a measure of misbehaviour. 'You wouldn't believe it.'

'I look forward to meeting them – my new neighbours,' Mirabelle replied.

'Miss Grace is away, of course,' Mrs Grieg added. 'Italy.' She sniffed pointedly and pursed her lips. 'For nine months or near enough.'

Vesta took a sip of tea. 'Mrs Grieg, I don't believe you're being entirely charitable,' she said.

The housekeeper looked sheepish. 'I'm sorry, Sister. It's only if a young girl in the village behaved like that . . . got caught out, I mean, well, she wouldn't get sent to Italy, that's for sure.'

Mirabelle put down her cup and saucer. While she would not be happy with the housekeeper discussing her business so freely with people who were effectively strangers, it was useful in this situation. She decided to deal with Mrs Grieg's capacity for gossip on another occasion and, for now, simply exploit it. 'Is there any indication of the man with whom Miss Grace . . . dallied, Mrs Grieg?' she asked.

The housekeeper's lipstick formed a thin red line, like a wound that might never heal. 'I'm not privy to that,' she admitted, 'but Miss Grace isn't getting married, is she?

They won't let her keep the baby, I shouldn't think. The parties at that house! People said in the village that all those people arriving for the weekends would only be trouble. Well, her mother knew early on, is all I'll say. She was sent off as soon as she began to show. And now the girl's in Italy and not a ring on her finger.'

'Poor Grace. I shall pray for her,' Vesta said piously.

Mirabelle tried not to look surprised. 'Well, *I'm* getting married,' she said. 'Before we move in here. We're going to have a service at the nunnery. In the chapel. I will be Mrs McGregor.'

Now it was Vesta's turn to look surprised.

Mrs Grieg's thin red line turned upwards at the ends. An unexpected dimple appeared in her cheek. 'How lovely, ma'am,' she enthused.

'Perhaps you'd like to attend. We don't know many people in Edinburgh.'

'Thank you, ma'am,' Mrs Grieg said.

'And if you hear anything about Miss Grace's lover, I'd like to know. We're neighbours now, and it's always best to be informed, don't you think?'

Mrs Grieg seemed to accept this. She bobbed a half-curtsey and left the room. Vesta relaxed into her seat in a most un-nun-like fashion.

'I can't see how that could be connected, do you?'

Mirabelle shrugged. 'Not really. I mean if Sister Monica was the father, he should have gone to Italy, shouldn't he? And instead he infiltrated a convent peopled by much older women – albeit nearby – and stayed on long after the girl had gone.'

'Poor Grace Farquharson-Sinclair,' Vesta said. 'I can't imagine.' She laid her hand on her stomach.

'You're married to Charlie,' Mirabelle pointed out. 'Nothing like that will happen to you.'

Vesta beamed. 'Yes. I'm a married nun with a very naughty four-year-old son.'

'In the medieval period, I'm sure that wasn't unheard of,' Mirabelle added knowledgeably.

Vesta finished her tea. 'You're the only person I can think of who would ever lead me astray by committing me to a religious order. Well, we'd better get on with it, I suppose.'

'See if you can have a chat with Sister Mary when you arrive. She was the last person to see Sister Monica alive, as far as I can make out. They were working in the salve sheds together. She didn't want to talk to me about it.'

Vesta looked suddenly concerned. 'Right,' she said. 'Mirabelle, are you sure I can pull this off?'

'You did very well with the . . .' Mirabelle gestured in front of her '. . . pious air and all of that.'

Vesta grinned. 'Let's just hope the nuns think so too.'

Chapter Six

Where there is no novelty, there can be no curiosity

Pulling away from the convent, Mirabelle checked the figure of Vesta in the rear-view mirror as her friend stood at the high gate with a small, battered leather case in her hand that contained her toothbrush, toothpaste and some groceries that Mirabelle had salvaged from the kitchen cupboards at Heriot Row. The heavy wooden door opened. As Vesta stepped inside, a single magpie landed in a monochrome flutter on the wall and Mirabelle felt unexpectedly concerned. 'One for sorrow,' she murmured, and saluted the bird in the rear-view mirror, feeling foolish for being so superstitious. At McGuigan and McGuigan Debt Collection, Vesta had faced several tricky debtors far more dangerous than the Little Sisters of Gethsemane but, somehow, Mirabelle didn't like to drive away. She felt as if her friend were being incarcerated behind the convent's high, rough-hewn walls as if it were a prison. Mirabelle told herself to stop being silly and changed gear.

Turning back onto the main road, past the building site, the car seemed too silent so Mirabelle switched on the radio. The general election in October was being discussed, something about Harold Macmillan. She wound down the window and allowed the brisk breeze to refresh her as she speeded into town. At Haymarket station, she parked the car and slipped inside, asking a porter about lockers and showing him the key she'd found. 'There are lockers at the left-luggage office at Waverley,' he said. 'You could try those.'

Outside, she sat back in her seat and considered a moment before sparking the ignition and driving back to Heriot Row. In the flat, McGregor was lying on the bed propped up on a large pile of pillows and reading a hardback copy of *Naked Lunch*, which he had bought the week before at Baumeister's on George IV Bridge. He put down the book, open pages to the bedcover.

'You'll break the spine,' Mirabelle objected. She picked up a scrap of paper and inserted it as a bookmark.

'Vesta did it, then?' he said. 'Good for her.'

'She did. And I met our new housekeeper at Shore Cottage. Mrs Grieg.'

'What's she like?'

'Indiscreet.' Mirabelle removed the key from her pocket. 'I thought I'd see if this fitted the lockers at Waverley. Want to come?'

They walked up Hanover Street and eastwards along Princes Street, away from the castle, with the sun high in the cloudless sky behind them. Two children were playing with hoops in the east gardens as glassy-eyed seagulls looked down. Holding hands, Mirabelle and McGregor turned down the slope into Waverley, past a queue of black taxis, engines chugging, as the couple continued onto the concourse. A cluster of four or five porters in uniform were waiting for a train, sharing cigarettes and laughing. As they passed, the man from earlier recognised Mirabelle.

'Meeting another friend off a train, ma'am?' he asked, tipping his cap. 'Is there a conference at the university?'

Mirabelle held up the key. 'I've something to pick up.'

'The lockers are round the corner,' the man replied, pointing the way.

As they turned off the main plaza, Mirabelle wondered momentarily why there might be lockers as well as a left-luggage office but she supposed the office might not always be open. Opposite platform twenty, they stood in front of the array of little doors looking for number seventeen. 'Go on,' said McGregor, and she tried the key. It turned. 'Bingo,' she breathed, as she looked over her shoulder to make sure nobody was watching. Inside, there was a brown leather briefcase.

'Get what you were looking for, did you, ma'am?' the porter said, appearing behind them out of nowhere.

Mirabelle jumped. 'Yes. Thank you,' she said.

'Sure you're not meeting a train?'

'Not just now,' she replied.

The man stepped back, waiting. McGregor stared blankly back at him. 'Do you mind?' he said.

'You'll manage it all right?' the porter checked. 'Not too heavy?'

'Yes. Yes. We'll be fine. Thank you,' Mirabelle waved him away.

He backed off. She pulled out the briefcase.

'Come on,' said McGregor. 'Let's look at it in the café.'

The café smelt of bacon rolls inside. There was some banquette seating at the back. McGregor ordered two cups of tea. Once they had sat down, Mirabelle emptied the contents of the briefcase onto the seat between them. First was a well-thumbed copy of *Punch* magazine from early January, on its cover a drawing of Christmas trees put out in the rubbish in front of a grey terrace of London houses.

'To read on the train,' she said.

Next: a brown leather wallet containing a surprisingly large amount of cash to leave in a railway station, even in a locker – £24 15s 2d. McGregor counted it, rifling the well-made leather wallet and finding, in addition, part of a photograph that had been cut to exclude something or somebody. They peered at it together. The print was of two children and had been taken sometime during the war. The girl was thirteen, perhaps, the boy only five or six. Both carried gas masks. Mirabelle squinted at the image. 'If it's a person who's been cut out, they're most likely a parent,' she said, turning her attention back to the briefcase.

Caught at the bottom, in the thick folds of leather, a single key on a plain leather fob was dislodged and fell onto the seat next to her. It was an extremely standard-looking house key, she thought, cursing their luck.

'No driving licence. No business card,' she said, with a sigh. 'We still don't know who he was. And a key like this could be for anything.'

McGregor picked up the photograph again and examined it more carefully. 'This is interesting,' he said.

Mirabelle took a sip of her tea. 'What?'

'That's Hampstead.' He laid the photograph on the table. 'On the Heath. That's the orchard. There aren't many fruit trees left and the ones that are still there are old. But that's where it is, I think. The lie of the land and that apple tree – it's quite famous. Our boy is from London.'

Mirabelle squinted at the photograph again.

'You need glasses, old girl.' McGregor grinned.

She shrugged, but he was probably right.

'Trotter's on Castle Street – that's where my uncle used to go. We should get you booked in.'

Mirabelle suddenly felt the judgement of the Little Sisters of Gethsemane upon her. Her soul rebelled against spectacles. She was vain.

'I can't believe you missed that.' McGregor sounded chuffed. 'We went there once. Don't you remember?'

Mirabelle was bemused that he recalled the layout of some old trees and the crest of a hill, but McGregor often surprised her. 'All right,' she said. 'I'll make an appointment tomorrow after I've checked on Vesta.'

'I can make a couple of calls,' McGregor offered, indicating Sister Monica's erstwhile possessions. 'Missing persons in London – men in their early twenties with possible connections to the Hampstead area.' He stirred some sugar into his tea. 'Of course, the other thing we should think about is how long this briefcase has been in the locker.'

Mirabelle picked up the copy of *Punch*. 'Since he put it there, I suppose,' she said. 'Before he went to the convent.'

McGregor grinned. 'Yes. January. But they don't leave railway-station lockers in use for six months. People forget things – they'd end up with no lockers at all. Usually they're cleared out from time to time.'

Mirabelle slowly replaced everything in the briefcase. 'So he must have paid extra to leave it there? Made an arrangement?'

McGregor nodded. 'I'd say so.'

She cursed herself for not thinking of this. McGregor's policeman's brain was strong on logic. Though that meant they were a good team.

'Most likely he knew how long he'd need the locker for,' she reasoned. 'It means he didn't intend to stay at the convent for ever.'

'Exactly,' McGregor said with a grin. 'Come on.'

He led the way. They abandoned the tea, the bell on the café door sounding as they stepped once more onto the smoky concourse. The briefcase felt heavy in Mirabelle's hand as they turned into the left-luggage office. The place was deserted. A locked mahogany counter blocked access to the storage shelves. McGregor rang the brass bell. The note echoed.

'Quiet in here,' he said.

Then, from behind the shelving, a thin man appeared in a dark uniform the same colour as his greying hair. A cigarette hung from his lip as if it was a permanent fixture. Mirabelle thought he looked as if he was entirely constructed from ash.

'Yes, sir,' the man said, with a mock cheeriness that was not reflected in his appearance. 'Can I help?'

'Lovely day,' McGregor started.

The clerk agreed, though Mirabelle noted there were no windows in the left-luggage office.

'I came to pick up something from the lockers for my nephew,' McGregor said. 'Locker seventeen. He asked me to see if he owed anything extra.'

'Extra, sir?'

'For the locker. He took longer than he expected.'

'Your nephew, sir?'

'Yes. Locker seventeen.'

'I'm sorry. The lockers are self-service. Your nephew must be mistaken.'

'He's not mistaken,' McGregor said.

'You just put in a penny. I can show you,' the man continued, pulling back the brass bolt on the counter and lifting it up.

As they turned towards the door Mirabelle spotted the porter from earlier loitering uncomfortably opposite the office on platform twenty. As the clerk passed them, leading

71

the way back to the lockers, the man began to walk away from the main body of the station, pushing his trolley ahead of him. There was, she noted, no train on platform twenty and, she would guess, from the dearth of people nearby, none expected.

'Him,' she said.

McGregor put his fingers to his lips and let out a shrill whistle. He lifted his hand to hail the porter, but the man, so keen to engage them earlier on, kept walking.

'Number seventeen? That locker is vacant,' the clerk said.

McGregor and Mirabelle ignored him. They began to run up the platform, Mirabelle ahead of McGregor, despite her heels and the heavy case. The porter abandoned his trolley and disappeared behind three wooden wagons in a siding. McGregor jumped onto the track, Mirabelle behind him now. She considered removing her shoes. The porter was nowhere to be seen as McGregor rounded the first of the wagons. He pointed in the direction of a thin passageway flush to the stone wall. They ran into it and up a steep run of worn stone steps onto another platform where several smartly dressed passengers were waiting for a train. A much younger man in uniform approached them officiously. 'Do you have a platform ticket?'

'A porter came out ahead of us. Have you seen him?' McGregor said.

'You can't be on this platform without a proper ticket, sir,' the young man repeated, more aggressively.

'I'm a police officer. Did you see a porter come out ahead of us?'

The man stood back. 'No,' he said.

The train was approaching the platform now, steam descending thick as a raincloud, the chugging of the engine heavy on the air.

'What's that way?' McGregor asked, pointing up some steps.

'The exit to Market Street.'

It seemed the most likely route out of the station. Mirabelle and McGregor scaled the steps and turned onto the street but the porter was gone. A drunkard in a stained and torn mackintosh dozed in a doorway beside a long flight of stairs that led up a smoke-darkened pend to Cockburn Street. A van was unloading boxes of Granny Smiths into the fruit market. McGregor offered the drunk sixpence and the man stared at it as if it was a vision.

'Did you see someone come out of the station before we did?' McGregor asked.

The tramp's eyes were glazed and his skin grubby. 'Whit?' he said.

McGregor repeated the question and the fellow picked up an empty Sweetheart Stout can and shook it. 'Every bastart coming out of there ignores me.'

McGregor sighed. He handed over the coin and put his arm protectively round Mirabelle's shoulders. 'We'll find him,' he said. 'It just might take a couple of days.'

Chapter Seven

Truth will rise above falsehood as oil above water

Vesta followed Sister Mary from shed to shed and feigned interest in the cleaning techniques used on the convent's ancient copper vats and, the ginger cat notwithstanding, what to do to protect the shelving against mice.

'It must be satisfying,' Sister Mary said, 'helping in Africa. Mother receives letters from patients who have been cured, you know. But it isn't the same.'

'I'm from London,' Vesta parroted. This kind of thing was getting worse, she thought. It had become more frequent since the *Windrush* arrived, flooding London and the south-east with people from the Caribbean. Her mother complained about the new immigrants. 'They're penniless,' she said disapprovingly, as if it was the fault of the Black men sleeping rough on benches in west London parks that they had not been able to find accommodation or employment. 'They're giving us a bad name.'

At first, Vesta had thought that there simply being more Black people would make it easier – more normal – but that wasn't proving the case.

'Where is your order exactly?' Sister Mary asked cheerily.

'Bermondsey,' Vesta replied, thinking of the nuns on the bench eating bananas.

'You will do good work among the poor in Southwark, Sister.'

'You know Bermondsey?' Vesta asked.

'I'm from Aberdeen,' Sister Mary said, 'but my aunt used to live in Greenwich. We visited when I was a child.' Greenwich was on the same side of the river, though miles further east and a different world with its wide Georgian streets, fancy stucco terraces and pretty villas. 'My uncle was in the navy,' she added. 'He was stationed at the Royal Naval College. I think he taught something – navigation, I expect,' she said vaguely. 'My aunt volunteered at a soup kitchen in Poplar. She took me with her once.'

Encouraged by Sister Mary volunteering personal information, Vesta decided to push for more. 'I understand there is to be a burial tomorrow. One of your order. I was sorry to hear of it.'

The nun nodded. 'After a fashion,' she said. 'You will join us in mourning, won't you?'

'What was she like?'

Sister Mary paused, as if considering how much Vesta might know and how much it was appropriate to tell her. 'Sister Monica was a novice. She died in the manufactory. It was an accident.'

Vesta looked concerned. 'I had no idea,' she lied. 'I assumed it was an older woman. Someone who had been here a long time.'

Sister Mary sighed. 'Each sheaf will be gathered in its season. That's what the Bible says. Still, a few of our older sisters will not be with us for much longer, I fear. Gone on the tide. Sister Bernadette is ninety-six and mostly confined to her cell. She came to the convent in 1879. She told me once that she had brought a novel by Émile Zola that had only just been published. It concerned a priest, though I have not read it. It is still in the library, I expect. For her first thirty years in the order Sister Bernadette had a maid. Lots of nuns who came in the old days were ladies. That was the way of it before the Great War. '

'She must have been very young.'

'She had a calling from the time she was a child. She was here when Queen Victoria died, through the First World War and the General Strike. It's inspiring to think of such a retreat. A sister becoming part of history in the service of God. It's what we all pray for, isn't it? I wish I had known earlier in my life that it was my destiny to take my vows.'

'Why?' Vesta asked.

Sister Mary shrugged. 'To live my whole life here, not only part of it.'

Vesta smiled. 'And this poor dead novice will not have that experience.'

'He did not want it for her,' Sister Mary pronounced. 'He called her to him.'

Vesta tried to look pious again. She thought it best to allow a long pause.

'How did the accident happen?' she asked, after a good thirty seconds. 'Could anything have been done to avoid it?'

Sister Mary led her into the next shed. 'It was here,' she said. 'The bishop will rededicate this room after the funeral. There are already measures in place to guard against accidents. Two sisters must mix the base together and leave it to set.'

'That's what she was doing when she died?'

76

Sister Mary shook her head. 'She mixed the salve with me. She was supposed to help in the kitchen afterwards.'

'But she didn't leave?'

'No.'

'Why?'

'I have no idea.'

'Where did you go after you had finished?'

'I left Sister Monica to wipe down the paddles. I went to check on the still – the lavender oil. Will you make your own oils, Sister Joseph? For the soap?'

Vesta nodded.

'Not lavender, though,' she said, feeling creative. 'We grow . . . rosemary and we have bee hives,' she added. One of her mother's neighbours had a hive at the bottom of his garden. He had planted banks of lavender for the bees and rosemary as well.

'Honey? In Bermondsey?'

'We have only three hives but they are fruitful.' Vesta shrugged off the lie as casually as she could, but Sister Mary hadn't finished.

'Rosemary soap,' she mused. 'That's unusual. I've heard of rose and lily, of course, but rosemary . . .'

'It's a clean smell,' Vesta said vaguely. 'And cleanliness is next to godliness,' she added.

'Well, if you will be making oil, I must show you our still.'

'Thank you. So you were the last to see the novice, then, Sister Mary?'

She did not reply. 'This way,' she said, leading Vesta into another shed where a huge still scented the air with such a strong smell of lavender that it turned Vesta's stomach. She breathed through her mouth and felt suddenly warm as if she had walked into a patch of unbearably dense sunlight.

'The flowers are delicate,' Sister Mary said, as she strode ahead without noticing Vesta's difficulties. 'Distillation is a complicated process.' She indicated a large wooden barrel. 'The blooms must be bruised gently to open the petals. Then they are treated with steam and alcohol. The oil we make is of an extremely high quality. It is intense.'

'High quality,' Vesta managed to repeat from behind.

Sister Mary turned. 'Are you all right, Sister?'

Vesta steadied herself against a stack of wooden boxes.

'Here.' The nun offered her arm. 'It's shocking, I know. Poor Monica. It is not pleasant to think of her dying. If only I hadn't rushed in here that day perhaps it would never have happened. The cycle was nearly done, you see, and I wanted to check it. If I had been slower, I might have been able to stop her falling in. Or perhaps I would have been able to pull her out. I have prayed about that but it was in God's hands. He gathered her to Him.'

'You didn't hear anything?' Vesta asked between breaths. The sheds were close together and the corrugated iron did not swallow sound. Surely the nun would have shouted for help, she thought, feeling woozy. She wondered if she had eaten something bad, but then, what could it possibly have been? She had had tea and toast on the train. Tea and shortbread with Mirabelle. More tea at Shore Cottage. Perhaps, she thought, she hadn't eaten enough, but the thought turned her stomach once again.

Outside, the bell sounded. 'Dinner,' said Sister Mary. 'Perhaps that will help.'

As the nun turned, Vesta caught a whiff of sweat from the old woman's robes and almost gagged. She burst into the sunshine and declined the offer of further help, instead walking as far away from Sister Mary as she could.

'I need fresh air,' she said.

'The air here is marvellous. All God's treasures. Fresh, as you say. Some days we can smell the salt from the firth. We're not far from the water.'

Now she'd mentioned it, Vesta could just make out a vague scent of seaweed. She tried not to think about it as Sister Mary led her into the refectory where the air hung heavy with boiled vegetables. Vesta recoiled.

'Oh dear,' she said.

'You're ill,' Sister Mary said. 'Tell me how to help.'

Vesta nodded. 'God,' she muttered under her breath. Sister Mary raised an eyebrow. 'God help me,' Vesta recovered herself. 'I might retire. I think I should lie down.'

'I can come with you, if you like.'

'No. Please eat. You must be hungry.'

Vesta went back outside into the sunshine. She tried to measure her pace, nodding greetings as she passed more sisters making their way to the refectory. Clasping her hands in front of her, she breathed deeply as she went down the hallway back to her cell, where she shoved the battered bag she'd brought under the bed so that she could climb wearily on top of the blanket. The thin mattress was extremely uncomfortable but it wasn't that she was cursing as she counted the days of the last month on her fingers and realisation set in. How could she not have noticed? It had been six weeks, maybe seven now. Things had been so busy at work and then there had been Mirabelle's wedding to consider. She retched. And smiled. Charlie would be delighted. They had talked about this – a little sister or brother for Noel. A little sister, Vesta hoped. Her mother would be over the moon. Only two days after Noel's birth she had been talking about 'the next baby'. 'I've waited so long to be a grandmother,' she had said. Vesta's oldest brother hadn't married – it looked like he never would.

Carefully Vesta reached under the bed and opened the case, hoping Mirabelle had packed a handkerchief. The smell of the cheese rose from inside, catching her unawares, so she had to rush to the bowl beneath the pitcher of cold water left for her to wash. Finally she was sick. She looked around. There was no toilet in here in which to dispose of what had come up. She sighed, opened the door to the deserted hallway and wearily carried the bowl to the bathroom at the end of the corridor. The room was larger than she had expected and contained a vast enamel bath and a large sink as well as a stack of thin, greying linen towels. Vesta poured the bowl's contents down the lavatory and flushed. She rinsed the bowl in the sink. Exhausted, she slumped onto the cool terracotta floor tiles. 'Now I'm a pregnant nun. Thanks, Mirabelle,' she whispered.

When she was expecting Noel, Vesta had slept fourteen hours a night and eaten jam sandwiches, mostly, for the first month. And chips. She hadn't been able to face much else. But that wasn't going to be easy at the Little Sisters of Gethsemane, even with the help of Mother Superior.

Vesta pulled herself onto her knees, deciding she would just have to do her best. She was about to haul herself upwards again when the door opened.

'Oh, Sister,' said a bright-eyed nun. 'Are you all right?'

'I feel ill,' Vesta admitted.

'I will pray with you,' the nun offered cheerfully, dropping to her knees. 'He will help.'

Vesta sighed. She clasped her hands and wondered how long she should wait before suggesting that lying down in her cell might be a more efficacious solution. Time elongated. She couldn't say if the nun next to her prayed for a minute or ten. It was all just murmuring. The woman smelt, she noticed, of carbolic soap, which Vesta did not find nauseating. She wondered if she ought to have said that the Bermondsey nuns were going to manufacture that. At length, the nun whispered, 'Amen.'

'I should lie down,' Vesta ventured.

The nun offered her arm and Vesta took it.

'Oh,' she exclaimed, at the end of the corridor, 'you're staying in Sister Monica's old cell.'

'You knew Sister Monica?' Vesta asked.

The nun nodded and bit her lip. 'She was a tremendously kind person.'

Vesta opened the door but could not forgo the opportunity to find out whatever she could. 'It seems such a tragedy,' she said, in as encouraging a tone as she could muster.

'She is with God,' the nun intoned, as if she did not quite accept this version of events.

'It was a horrible accident, by the sound of it,' Vesta said gently. 'Poor Sister Monica.'

The other nun's eyes suddenly appeared fiery. 'I hope it will teach people – He giveth and He taketh away. We must measure our actions.'

'What do you mean?'

The nun's eyes dropped to the floor where she examined the long wooden boards. She was wearing brogues, Vesta noted, tied with ragged laces.

'Sister Monica argued with Sister Evangelista,' the nun said. 'I saw them in the kitchen garden on the day before Monica died. The poor thing was very upset.'

'What was the argument about?'

The nun's eyes filled with tears. 'I don't know,' she said. 'I couldn't hear what they were saying. They were by the raspberry canes. Sister Evangelista is always so ... bossy. I shouldn't have told you. I'm sorry. I'm sure it's nothing to do with what happened.'

'Did you tell Mother?'

The nun shook her head. 'Please, forget what I said.'

Vesta looked longingly at the uncomfortable bed with its starched sheet and thin blanket. 'Nonetheless, I'd like to meet Sister Evangelista,' she said. 'I'm sure she wouldn't hurt another nun but it's not good for one of us to have the guilt of an argument like that on her conscience. We should try to help her.'

The young nun seemed to calm at this suggestion.

'I'm sure it's nothing,' Vesta added. 'I mean, everyone loses their temper sometimes.'

The nun looked unsure about the veracity of this. Vesta sat down on the bed for a second. She wasn't sure that she was capable of this job any more, but she wouldn't be able to speak to Mirabelle until tomorrow, and perhaps Sister Evangelista could tell her something useful. She imagined asking Mother to order her a taxi and returning to the spare bedroom in the Heriot Row flat where she would sleep and sleep and Mirabelle wouldn't trouble her with food – except buttered rolls with honey, perhaps. Maybe tomorrow.

'Does Sister Evangelista have a particular job?' she asked.

'She looks after the kitchen. And some of the older nuns.'

'Do you know where she is?'

'Oh, yes,' the nun replied. 'We can't possibly speak to her. That's the thing.'

Chapter Eight

A fiddler, and consequently a rogue

Mr Wallace the solicitor came through with an invitation to the Bishop's Palace to the south of the city at Churchill. Mirabelle had never visited that part of Edinburgh, with its sandstone Victorian villas and leafy gardens. As McGregor pulled up at the lights on the main road Mirabelle peered through the windscreen. 'Is that . . .?'

'It's called Holy Corner. Four churches. One on each corner, or close enough.'

Mirabelle grinned. Scotland outdid itself with its profusion of churches and complicated denominations. Over the winter, going back and forth from McGregor's Highland estate before its sale, they had passed through tiny villages in Perthshire that had two churches at opposite ends of the only road, no more than twenty cottages between them.

'Gosh,' she said. 'It's called Churchill, isn't it? That must be why.'

'Churchill is there.' McGregor motioned ahead. 'That's the hill.' He smiled. 'There's another church just over the crest.'

'I can see why the bishop chose to live here,' Mirabelle added drily.

When the lights changed, McGregor turned left along Chamberlain Road where trees in late blossom overhung the pavement. 'It's pretty,' Mirabelle commented, as McGregor rounded a pocket park fenced with iron railings, before continuing through the open gates of the palace, which, Mirabelle noted, despite its domed copper roof, was more in the way of a mansion house. The building was surrounded by a pretty garden with a path that led to a private chapel of the same pinkish stone, with jewel-like stained-glass windows, located against the high back wall.

As McGregor parked the car, a plump older woman appeared in the main doorway to greet them. She wore a cream bouclé suit edged in thin black brocade, which reminded Mirabelle of upholstery material. Her hair was dyed brown and rather stiffly set so that it looked almost like a helmet. Around her neck she wore a pair of spectacles on a delicate gold chain. As McGregor parked the car, the woman propped the spectacles on her nose. Mirabelle made a silent decision that if she needed glasses she would not employ this method of keeping them handy.

'Mr McGregor,' the woman greeted the superintendent, only nodding at Mirabelle. 'And who is this?'

'My fiancée,' McGregor replied. 'Mirabelle Bevan.'

The woman nodded again. 'I am Mrs Munro,' she introduced herself. 'The bishop's secretary. Did you have far to come?'

'Not at all,' McGregor said. 'Only from town.'

'Ah – I thought perhaps you were visiting us from . . .' here Mrs Munro paused as if the word tasted strange in her mouth '. . . Glasgow.'

'Glasgow? Not at all.'

'I must have picked that up incorrectly from Mr Wallace.'

84

'Indeed.'

'I'm very relieved. We do not like to vie for funds with Glasgow, which has its own . . .' she paused again as if she could hardly bring herself to say the word '. . . bishop.'

'Funds?'

'Mr Wallace explained you have lately returned to Scotland and would like to show your support for the Church.'

McGregor did not correct her as they moved through the front door. Mirabelle's heels clicked across the impressive black-and-white-tiled floor, echoing through the high-ceilinged entrance. Several paintings in gilded frames depicted religious figures – St Catherine on the wheel and St Valentine pierced through the heart.

Beyond the hall they were admitted to the bishop's study. A walnut desk with an inlaid ox-blood leather top was furnished with a modern-looking telephone and an old-fashioned ink-blotter. Behind it an ornate brass cross had been brought to a high shine. Mrs Munro fetched a tray laid with a decanter of sherry and small Victorian glasses in the shape of thistles. 'The bishop will be through directly,' she said, and left the room.

Mirabelle sank onto a chair upholstered in buff damask in front of a small Rococo marble fireplace, which was set with a precariously balanced unlit pile of logs. McGregor stood in front of the fire. A pewter mug held a cluster of paper spills, ready to light the logs. They both felt self-conscious. Mirabelle examined the eyes of the paintings as if the medieval icons might be watching her – St Mungo and St Columba, she guessed.

After a minute, the bookcase shifted and a hidden door opened into the room. A small man with rosy cheeks, wearing a black cassock and a purple zucchetto entered jauntily. He held out his hand, which was adorned with gold signet rings bearing carved cabochons of different colours. 'Mr McGregor . . . and you must be Miss Bevan. Mother Superior told me about you. Most impressive. Well, well. I'm glad to meet you both,' he said, making for the tray that Mrs Munro had laid out. 'Sherry?' he offered, and did not wait for them to acquiesce before pouring three glasses, then looking round as if he was bemused. 'I generally have *cantuccini* with my evening sherry but it appears not to be the case today,' he said, as if he was accepting a test of will that God himself had thrust upon him.

McGregor and Mirabelle took their glasses. Mirabelle sipped. The sherry tasted of raisins.

'Your secretary appears to be of the opinion we are here as donors,' McGregor said, before lifting the glass to his lips.

'Ah, yes. Mrs Munro is loyal but we saw no reason to upset her.'

'Would she be upset?'

'She might have been. She has helped with administration at the convent from time to time and I saw no reason to either worry her or potentially spread gossip. If Mrs Munro were worried, she would likely confide in somebody and, frankly, the fewer people who know about this, the better. You have bought Shore Cottage, Mr McGregor?'

McGregor nodded.

'When do you marry?' the bishop asked smoothly.

'Nine days.'

'I will be glad of it. Mr Wallace intimated that you are currently living in a flat on Heriot Row.' He said this with distaste, though did not explicitly add that Mirabelle and McGregor were living in sin.

'It's a family flat. We haven't decided where we might move once we're married, have we, Mirabelle? One thing at a time, eh?' McGregor replied cheerily.

'And, Miss Bevan, you spent some time at the convent yesterday. Did you find anything that might reveal our interloper's identity?'

'No. It seems Sister Monica fooled everybody.'

The bishop sat down behind his desk. 'I see.'

'However,' Mirabelle added, 'we have located a briefcase the young man brought with him, before he . . . became a novice. It contained this.' She reached inside her clutch bag and pulled out the photograph. The bishop peered at it.

'The orchard is on Hampstead Heath,' McGregor added. 'The photo was taken during the war. The gas masks . . .'

The bishop nodded. 'Yes.'

'And my associate, Vesta, as I'm sure you know, has entered the convent as Sister Joseph,' Mirabelle added. 'I felt the nuns were more likely to open up to one of their own. Vesta is easy to talk to.'

'Yes, I was uncomfortable about that. We are not the Gestapo, Miss Bevan. We are not the Secret Service. Undercover nuns. I cannot pretend the idea sits easily with me.'

'You are welcome to ask the sisters directly why Sister Monica was in the convent. I am almost sure that one of them knew her. It seems manifest that she went in to make contact with that person. Vesta was the best way I could think of to find out who it is because, despite Sister Monica's death, none of the nuns have come forward.'

'And you have no idea what "Sister Monica's" reason might have been for doing what she did?'

Mirabelle put down her thistle glass on a side table. 'I'm inclined to believe it was personal. I considered industrial

87

espionage – somebody seeking the formula for the salve the nuns manufacture – but in that case an interested party would surely have sent a woman. It makes no sense to take the extra risk of putting in a young man. I'm convinced Sister Monica went there under her own steam and must have done so through desperation and at some personal cost.'

The bishop took a few moments to consider this. 'Yes,' he said. 'I can see what you're saying.'

'Personal reasons are the most difficult to uncover, of course,' Mirabelle added. 'Though it has occurred to me that this scheme of Sister Monica's would surely be a last resort. I'm positive that the young man must have tried to get in touch in other ways. I understand the nuns require permission to correspond with people in the outside world.'

'Yes. Mother Superior would only rarely withhold permission, if ever.'

'In what circumstances might she exercise her judgement?'

The bishop turned the glass in his hand. 'Unsuitable correspondents of one kind or another. Or if a family member was hostile.'

'Hostile?'

'It happens. Not every parent is happy when their child decides to take vows. And the reverse is true as well. I have advised upon several such cases. Sometimes there comes a point when it is better simply to cease dialogue.'

'Might there be a list of requests by potential correspondents?'

'I shall ask Mother Superior to share it with you.'

'Thank you.'

The bishop finished his sherry. 'Perhaps I can give you a quick tour of the palace,' he suggested. 'We have some interesting paintings. A Christina Robertson from her time at the Russian court in St Petersburg and two portraits of clergymen by Allan Ramsay the Younger.'

'Jacobite clergymen?' McGregor said, with a grin.

'I believe so,' the bishop confirmed. 'The eighteenth century is fascinating, isn't it? The Stuarts were Roman Catholics but their followers were a broad church, so to speak. Episcopalians who believed in Divine Right were not happy to see the Stuarts passed over for the crown. In that respect the Pretender was a unifying force,' he said with a sigh, as if he was nostalgic for an issue that brought together divergent denominations.

The couple followed the old man into another, grander, reception room with several comfortable sofas ranged around a much wider green marble fireplace. 'This is another Ramsay. It is the wife of the Reverend James Forbes,' the bishop said with a flourish, indicating a portrait of a lady wearing an enormous hat and pulling a long white ostrich feather elegantly through her fingers. 'It was painted in the 1730s. Clergymen might have more than one profession in those days, and Forbes was also a lawyer. Isn't she lovely?'

'What was her name?' Mirabelle asked.

The bishop motioned into the ether. 'It is lost in time.'

'What a beautiful room.' Mirabelle changed the subject. It irked her that men's names seemed never to be the lost ones.

'This is where we host interfaith meetings,' the bishop continued. 'There is a Jewish community in Edinburgh, nearby. Also a Muslim community. Recently we even had Hindu guests – the holy man was fascinating, though he found the Scottish weather wearing. And this is Lord Robert St Clair.' The bishop indicated another portrait, this time of a solemn-looking man in a black suit with a white lace collar.

'His descendants will be your neighbours at Shore Cottage. The Farquarson-Sinclairs, as they are known now.'

Mirabelle's eyes lit. 'I heard a piece of gossip about Miss Grace.'

'Ah. Yes. I know of it. It is never good news when a young lady's reputation fails. I must say, her mother was quite distraught. Ruari Farquarson-Sinclair will be standing for election, you see. That's the girl's father.'

'This year?'

'Indeed.'

'Is that why Grace was sent so far away . . . Italy, wasn't it?'

'You are well informed, Miss Bevan. That is the trouble, is it not, these days, when the grand houses only employ staff part-time?' The bishop's eyes twinkled. He was, Mirabelle noted, a wily old goat beneath his bluff good humour.

'If only someone had been employed part-time to look after Sister Monica,' she ventured.

'Ah, indeed,' the bishop agreed. 'But you will get to the bottom of it, I'm sure.'

Mirabelle silently hoped Vesta was having better luck.

Outside, the light was beginning to fade. The bishop showed them to the door. Their footsteps crunched pleasingly on the gravel as they walked to the car, turning and waving at the old man, who stood framed in golden light, like an ecclesiastical vision.

At the steering wheel, McGregor pulled onto the road. The streetlights here were old-fashioned, sweeping down Strathearn Road ahead as he turned north along the loan towards Bruntsfield Place.

'They're showing *Pillow Talk* at the Gaumont,' he said. 'They say it's great fun.'

'Doris Day and that actor . . .' Mirabelle said vaguely.

'Rock Hudson,' McGregor confirmed. 'Do you fancy it? We could have popcorn instead of dinner,' he suggested. 'Very American.'

Mirabelle looked over her shoulder but the Bishop's Palace had fallen out of sight. 'He knows more than he's saying,' she said.

McGregor agreed. 'Senior churchmen are diplomats. Politicians, really. In my experience,' he added.

Mirabelle wondered how much experience McGregor could reasonably have had. She couldn't think of a single case in Brighton that had involved somebody senior in the Church. Still, he was probably right.

He pulled the car to the kerb at Tollcross and gestured towards a small shop near the crossroads. 'We're almost out of tea,' he said.

Mirabelle stared out of the window as he disappeared inside. The doors of the King's Theatre were open and a few people were milling about in the warm light of the foyer before the evening performance. She squinted as a woman in a red Burberry raincoat stalked past the billboard, which announced the Scottish premiere of *The Birthday Party* by Harold Pinter. One of their neighbours at Heriot Row had seen the play in London and declared it 'turgid as hell'.

The woman noticed Mirabelle. She paused and raised a hand. Mirabelle wound down the window. 'Mrs Munro,' she said. 'Might we offer you a lift?'

'I'm on my way home,' the bishop's secretary replied, gesturing along Gilmore Place. 'I always walk. It's not far.' Her coat, Mirabelle noted, matched exactly the tidy slash of her lipstick. She suddenly wanted to mess up the older woman's hair, as if this might free her, somehow.

Mrs Munro seemed unhappy, as if she had been packed away too tightly.

'Are you going to the theatre?' Mrs Munro asked.

'No. Mr McGregor is in the shop.'

'It's handy, that Johnny Awthings. I sometimes run out of lemons.'

Mrs Munro hovered awkwardly. Mirabelle waited.

'Is there something on your mind?' she asked, after a good minute had lapsed. 'The Little Sisters of Gethsemane, perhaps?'

Mrs Munro's lips pursed momentarily, her perfect lipstick forming orderly dips and swells, like a line of pomegranate seeds that glowed against her white, powdery skin. 'Those women are saints. It doesn't sit well,' she started. 'This death. I am afraid that . . . it wasn't an accident.'

'What makes you think that?'

The older woman's lips wrinkled, as if to prevent more words being indiscreetly uttered. Mirabelle decided to try a different tack.

'The bishop mentioned you've helped at the convent,' she said. 'Administration, was it?'

Mrs Munro nodded. 'Stocktaking,' she said. 'They used to do it all themselves but the convents are dying. It's a long, slow death but the world has changed.'

Mirabelle had a vision of Mrs Munro as a well-upholstered avenging angel, in her bright Burberry jacket. She seemed angry.

'Something just doesn't sit right. It hasn't sat right for a while,' she managed to get out.

'At the convent?' Mirabelle asked.

The woman looked as if she was in a trance. 'The convent, yes,' she said, 'but poor Grace. She was a lovely child.'

'Do you mean Grace Farquarson-Sinclair?'

'They should have strung up the fellow. They should have closed it down. Men like that . . .'

'Men like what?'

'The Irish,' Mrs Munro mouthed. 'Those navvies. What do we need another crossing for? The ferry is perfectly adequate. It's the men who are the cause of all our sorrows. The wars. The violence. That poor girl. She'll never recover.'

Mirabelle's mind raced. 'Do you mean that Grace Farquarson-Sinclair was raped?' she asked. 'By one of the men working on the new bridge?'

The words seemed to stun Mrs Munro. Mirabelle cursed silently that she had cut in. It might have been better to let the woman keep ranting and try to piece things together afterwards.

'I've been asked by the bishop to look into Sister Monica's death,' she said gently. 'I'd be grateful for anything you can tell me.'

Mrs Munro drew back and Mirabelle turned to see McGregor coming out of the shop with a packet of tea marked 'Tender Leaf' and a white paper bag that probably contained toffees.

'Mrs Munro,' he greeted the secretary. 'Can we give you a lift?'

'It's only around the corner,' Mrs Munro said, bringing herself under control once more. Mirabelle thought she was doing remarkably well, given how she felt about men. At the palace Mrs Munro had greeted McGregor so cordially.

'If you're sure,' McGregor said, completely unaware of the woman's views. He opened the car door and dropped the shopping onto the back seat before getting behind the wheel.

'Good evening,' Mrs Munro said, and turned away.

Mirabelle gestured to McGregor to wait. She got out onto the pavement. 'Mrs Munro,' she called urgently, her heels clicking as she followed the woman towards the corner. 'Please.'

But Mrs Munro's gaze fell on McGregor through the windscreen. 'You go on,' she said. 'Your man will be waiting for you.'

'Let him wait,' Mirabelle objected.

Mrs Munro's eyes were hard. 'I shouldn't have said anything. Without knowing, it's just gossip.'

'Please. Help me,' Mirabelle repeated.

But the older woman's eyes narrowed as McGregor turned on the engine. 'He's getting impatient,' she said, and turned to walk away.

'I got treacle ones,' McGregor said, offering Mirabelle a toffee as she got back into the car. 'If we hurry we can park on Torphichen Street and make the late showing. With luck we'll catch the newsreel.' Mirabelle crossed her legs away from him. 'What was that about?' he asked, as he pulled away. When she told him he pronounced Mrs Munro a 'man-hater' and Mirabelle couldn't deny it but she had a creeping feeling that, even though she couldn't discern exactly what the bishop's secretary had been talking about, something darker and knottier than she had expected might have happened at the nunnery. Or nearby. Mrs Munro, she thought with a shudder, might have become almost hysterical but that didn't mean she was wrong.

Chapter Nine

Tears are the silent language of grief

The following morning haar curled round the buildings on Mirabelle's route to the telephone box, and a fine mist-like rain that McGregor called 'smirr' and Mirabelle called 'drizzle' permeated the air, soaking her clothes without seeming wet. Nobody on George Street was carrying an umbrella, she noted, and that must have been because umbrellas afforded little protection in this weather when the water seemed to seep in more than it fell from the sky. Yes, that was it, she decided, as she dialled the number to get through to Mother Superior's office.

'McGuigan and McGuigan . . . oh,' Vesta's voice chimed.

'It's me,' Mirabelle said. 'I hope you're doing a better job than that of being undercover.'

The crisp sound of Vesta biting into a slice of toast emanated down the line. Mirabelle had skipped breakfast for the first time since she had arrived in Edinburgh – her first case since then, too.

'Are you all right, Vesta?' she asked.

'Yes. Blooming,' Vesta sounded immensely pleased with herself. 'I'm reading the log of communication requests between the sisters and the outside world. Mother Superior has been most understanding.'

'Did anyone request to communicate with Sister Monica?'

'No,' Vesta said, and another crunching sound indicated that the toast was going down well. 'If a letter is received with or without permission, it's logged. Sister Monica didn't receive anything. Or send anything out either.'

'McGregor and I talked about this yesterday,' Mirabelle said. 'See if you can find someone who made repeated requests to communicate with a nun. Going into the convent in disguise probably wasn't Monica's first shot at making contact.'

Vesta paused. 'I'm looking,' she said. 'I haven't seen anything like that yet.'

'So you haven't found anything worthwhile?'

'Well, yes, actually, I have . . .'

Mirabelle moved the handset from her left hand to her right and turned to look the other way along the street where, quite unexpectedly, a patch of sunny blue had opened in the sky above the headquarters of the Royal Bank of Scotland on St Andrew Square.

'Thank goodness,' she said. 'Sister Monica is turning out quite the enigma. I can't say I've found out anything useful here, to be frank.'

'Oh, yes. Sister Monica,' said Vesta, as if she had only just remembered. 'She had an argument with one of the other nuns the day before she died. Sister Evangelista.'

'And what has Sister Evangelista to say about that?'

There was a short pause as Vesta sipped what Mirabelle imagined must be a cup of tea. 'Nothing,' Vesta said. 'She isn't allowed to speak until the end of the week.'

'What?'

'She's retreated into the anchorite's cell.'

'What?'

'The anchorite's cell. Nuns used to go into it permanently but now it's only used periodically. It's absolutely tiny. Apparently there's hardly room to lie down. You're locked in and the sisters bring you porridge once a day, which is served through a slot in the door. They can't speak to you and you aren't allowed to talk to them either. It's a vow of silence. Sister Evangelista asked permission from Mother Superior the evening before Sister Monica died – to retreat, I mean. She hasn't even been told that Sister Monica is dead. She can't come out until her allotted days have passed. That's the arrangement.'

'And can't Mother Superior do something to get us in?'

'I'm afraid not. It seems they take the anchorite's vow very seriously.' There was another crunch. 'Several of the sisters correspond with men incarcerated in Peterhead Prison, you know,' Vesta said cheerfully. 'And the men write back. Sadly the log doesn't itemise what they say to each other. I also worked through the convent's accounts. The nuns are doing very well – I mean, there are hardly any expenses and they have been going for a long time. But they're millionaires, really. I guess the pennies add up. Are you coming to the funeral later?'

Mirabelle leaned against the glass wall of the box. 'Yes,' she said. 'One o'clock, isn't it? We ought to ignore each other.'

A man wearing a bowler hat and striped trousers stopped at the door of the telephone box. He glared at Mirabelle in an ungentlemanly fashion and pointedly looked at his watch.

'I have to go,' she said. 'I'll speak to you later.'

'But—' Vesta started, as if she had something else to say, but Mirabelle had already hung up.

★ ★ ★

97

Back at the flat Mirabelle fished out the black dress she had bought in Benzie and Miller in Fraserburgh the year before for the funerals of McGregor's cousin and his wife, Eleanor. So much had happened in only a few months, she thought, as she pulled up the zip and scrabbled in the wardrobe to find a pair of black kitten heels – the lowest she had apart from a pair of dark tan walking shoes that were wholly unsuitable for anything other than climbing a Munro. It was warm for gloves, but she felt the occasion merited a pair of wrist length at least and a hat – she had a black straw with a pale grey ribbon, which she ran over with a damp sponge to freshen it. Things in Heriot Row always seemed to get dusty, because they were living in the middle of town.

McGregor had taken the car to the Braids for his daily match, so she walked up to the taxi rank on Hanover Street and stared out of the window as the driver took the now-familiar route towards South Queensferry and past the site of the new bridge. What had Mrs Munro meant about Grace Farquarson-Sinclair? Was the girl's rapist still working on the site? Checking her slim gold watch, Mirabelle saw she had almost an hour to spare. She might as well use it. 'Could you drop me at the big house?' she asked the driver. There was no harm in introducing herself as a new neighbour and seeing the lie of the land.

The sign at the gatehouse announced St Clair's Vale, and up the driveway the taxi deposited Mirabelle promptly at a set of long double doors painted, unusually, in dark blue rather than black. Though built at the same time, the house was far grander than Shore Cottage, with a wide portico and floor-to-ceiling windows on the lower and upper floors. The Vale faced the direction of the nunnery, she thought, as she gathered her bearings, and from the upper floors there must be a view onwards to the firth.

As the taxi disappeared she rang the doorbell, which was answered at length by a handsome young butler, who took her name and led her through the high-ceilinged, flagstoned hallway into a drawing room at the rear of the house, with an open view over a rose garden and a long pond around which several wrought-iron seats with yellow cushions were arranged in the emerging sunshine. You never could tell what the weather would be like in Scotland. Rain one minute and bright the next. As Mirabelle peered she saw the cushions were made of oilskin – wise, given the weather.

'Isn't it lovely?' said a woman's voice and Mirabelle turned and took in a tall, ash-blonde beauty resplendent in a pair of tapered white trousers and a boat-necked peach blouse, set off by a lavish turquoise necklace. 'Belinda Farquarson-Sinclair,' she introduced herself. 'It's awfully nice to meet you – you're our new neighbour, aren't you? My goodness, you look as if you're going to a funeral, Miss Bevan.'

Mirabelle looked down at her outfit. 'I am,' she said. 'One of the nuns passed away the day I came to view Shore Cottage and they're burying her today. I thought I would attend.'

'You are good,' Mrs Farquarson-Sinclair said and coolly removed a cigarette from an onyx box on a side table. She motioned, offering one to Mirabelle, but Mirabelle declined as the other woman raised a matching onyx lighter and lit up, inhaling deeply. 'I'm awfully glad to meet you,' she said. 'You're marrying a Robertson, aren't you?'

'Alan McGregor,' Mirabelle admitted, 'but, yes, his family are Robertsons.'

'Terrible business,' Belinda declared, settling down on a comfortable pale pink sofa and motioning for Mirabelle to join her. 'Did you know Eleanor Robertson?'

'Yes. I liked her.'

'Awful business,' Belinda repeated. 'I suppose you know all about it.'

'I was there,' Mirabelle said. She didn't want to go into what had happened the previous year. McGregor might have inherited the estate but they'd both have given anything for the Robertsons to be alive, and for Eleanor not to have been a Russian spy and, for that matter, a murderer. Belinda Farquarson-Sinclair could know only the half of it. The whole affair had been hushed up by the Foreign Office. Still, Mirabelle had discovered early on that the upper classes in Scotland all knew each other and most of each other's business.

'I love it here,' she said. 'We're excited about moving in. How long do you think it'll take to build the bridge?'

Belinda spread herself glamorously across the cushions, as if for a fashion photo, and took another draw on her cigarette, blowing the smoke towards the ceiling. 'For ever,' she drawled. 'I bet it'll feel like that anyway. They say 1963 at the least. The whole thing is so untidy, a terrible muddy mess, and it'll be worse over the winter but it'll make it easier for people to get to Fife. Still, as I said to my husband, who the hell wants to go to Fife? Can I be nosy and ask, are you planning to have children?'

'Children?'

'Once you're married.'

'I doubt it,' Mirabelle replied. 'You have a girl, as I understand it.'

'She's travelling. We have two boys at school.' Belinda glossed over her own family scandal. 'I must say I'm glad to meet you. I had assumed you would be a younger woman, if you don't mind me saying.'

'Not at all.' Mirabelle smiled. 'I had a career, you see.'

'A career? How exciting.'

'The nuns are fascinating, aren't they?' Mirabelle veered away from talking about her time as a debt collector. Mrs Farquarson-Sinclair, she was sure, would not consider the chasing up of outstanding payments a suitable occupation for a lady.

Belinda stubbed out her cigarette, her square-cut diamond engagement ring slipping half an inch down her elegant finger as she did so. 'I'm glad the nuns didn't put you off,' she said. 'I'm sure some people would feel they did not want the eyes of God upon them, over the garden wall, so to speak.'

'Miss MacDonald didn't feel that way.'

Belinda laughed. 'Old Bang Bang. Heavens, no. Didn't you know she was a nun? She lapsed, as it were. I'd never heard of that before – nunnery drop-outs. She was still on good terms with the convent. The old girl was pretty devout. She attended Sunday service at the Gethsemane chapel. Bang Bang MacDonald – I don't expect we'll ever see her like again.'

'Bang Bang?'

'Do you know, I can't remember the old stick's real name. She was handy with a shotgun, though, I must say. She took potshots at rabbits. Almost killed the postman once.'

'And she had been a nun? At the convent? Here?'

'Decades ago. Before I married my husband. I bet the solicitor didn't tell you that when he was selling you the property. Anyway, her family didn't want the house after she died. I don't blame them. Nuns are a bit spooky, aren't they? I'm sure they can see your soul. I had a tutor who was a nun when I was a girl – ghastly.'

Mirabelle considered for a moment before pushing on. Belinda, after all, had been astonishingly frank so far, verging on the intrusive. She wondered if she had had a drink or two.

'I heard about your daughter. I'm sorry. It must have been difficult.'

Belinda stiffened. 'Grace was foolish. It only takes a moment of being foolish for a girl.'

Mirabelle bit her lip. The pregnancy wasn't Grace's foolishness if a man had forced himself on her.

Belinda stubbed out her cigarette with some violence. 'I'll thank you not to pass on the story. I suppose one can't stop these things getting out.'

'Is she all right?'

Belinda got up and walked to the window. 'She's a mystery, actually. I couldn't get anything out of her. She feels guilty, I expect.'

'And there was no prospect of the chap . . .'

'I think we have ascertained that the chap was unsuitable – one assumes so anyway.'

'Do you mean you don't know who he is?'

'She wouldn't say, Miss Bevan. And perhaps that's for the best. Gosh, I wasn't expecting this conversation. One generally ends up chatting about the garden when people come to call.'

Mirabelle smiled. 'I'm sorry. You seemed so much more direct than most people.'

'I've often heard it said that I'm brusque.'

'Well, I don't listen to half of what people say and I don't believe the other half,' Mirabelle said brightly.

'I'm glad to know that.' Belinda smiled. 'People really are frightful. It's as if they're determined to think the worst. What time is the funeral? I can have someone run you over, if you like.' Her eyes fell to Mirabelle's shoes. 'It'll be muddy on the track after the rain last night,' she added.

★ ★ ★

The bishop held a service in the chapel. All incomers from the outside world were seated in a row at the front – Dr Alexander in a charcoal grey dress with a wide skirt and tan leather belt that looked almost frivolous compared to the sensible navy suit she had worn to attend to Sister Monica's body. Beside the doctor sat two stony-faced priests, who had accompanied the bishop. Behind them row upon row of nuns in identical habits stretched towards the arched doorway. Vesta was the only one who stood out. Both she and Mirabelle studiously ignored one another.

As a small choir of nuns sang a requiem of 'In Paradisum' a capella, Mirabelle's mind wandered. She couldn't help wondering how the gossip about Grace Farquarson-Sinclair had reached Mrs Munro's ears and if it was true. Belinda was right: people loved to believe the worst, especially when the subject of gossip was a woman and, for that matter, a woman in an elevated social position. But it was also true that sometimes when something awful happened to somebody they loved, people didn't want to believe it. Was Belinda protecting herself from the full force of her daughter being badly hurt? Poor Grace, she thought, and hoped that the girl was being looked after in Italy.

Sister Monica's coffin was carried to the grave by the priests and four of the sturdier nuns, led by the bishop, and followed by everybody else in an orderly monochrome procession against what was now the bluest of skies. The sun had come out, the view to Burntisland and Aberdour clear across the firth from the graveyard, which was littered with centuries of crosses, carved stone angels and plain curved gravestones covered in lichen. Wild sea holly grew haphazardly alongside a few banks of lavender. The bishop intoned a final prayer and called Mother Superior to the head of the grave where she took a handful of earth and threw it into the chasm. It landed on the lid of the coffin with a thump.

'Sister Monica had not been with us long,' she said sadly. 'We know little about her, but she was part of our community and will rest with us here. She liked this place – the water and the sky. Acceptance is the creed of the Little Sisters of Gethsemane. We lay the fault where the fault lies. We make things right. Sister Monica must answer to God for her sins. Here on earth, it is our duty to accept her. She is one of us in perpetuity now.'

Mirabelle scanned the faces of the nuns. One or two were crying, raising handkerchiefs to mop their tears, but most simply looked sombre. Vesta noticed the weepers too – she would ask questions later no doubt. Mirabelle had hoped one of the nuns might break down and reveal something – a connection or an admission. But the bishop closed the service and the nuns left in a ragged formation, Vesta giving Mirabelle a sly wink as she turned to go. As the last sister disappeared up the path, a flock of seagulls swooped across the water and the youngest two priests removed spades from behind a nearby mausoleum. They waited reverently to one side while Dr Alexander and Mirabelle loitered at the grave. The doctor lit a cigarette.

'The bishop is going to rededicate the manufactory now.' She raised her eyes towards the gate. 'Have you worked out what Sister Monica was doing here yet?' she asked.

Mirabelle shook her head. 'Not nearly. You haven't ever come across Sister Evangelista in your practice, have you?'

The doctor inclined her head. 'I have,' she said. 'Mother Superior called me to help her last year. Why?'

'She had an argument with Sister Monica the day before she died. What help did she need?'

'I can't say. The sisters are patients. They're entitled to confidentiality. Is it important?'

The women paused. Mirabelle did not challenge what Dr Alexander had said but neither did she answer her question. The doctor motioned her to follow and together they turned up the path as the priests moved forwards and started to shovel earth into the grave. Halfway towards the gate, Dr Alexander took a deep draw of her cigarette as if she had made a decision.

'I should tell you. Evangelista hurt herself,' she whispered. 'She cut herself all over. I never saw anything like it. It looked as if she had been in a car crash or a bomb had gone off, as if glass had splintered into her skin. It was just before Christmas. They wouldn't have called for me but a couple of the wounds became infected. She might have died without antibiotics. She'll always have scars. Does that help?'

'I don't know,' Mirabelle admitted. 'It's all jigsaw pieces still. Nothing seems to fit. What do you think happened? Did she do it herself? Was it a religious conviction, like ascetics beating themselves?' She had read about that somewhere, though she couldn't remember where.

The doctor shrugged and ground out her cigarette underfoot. 'There was nothing in the cuts – no gravel or glass as you might expect if there'd been an accident. It might have been self-inflicted. Honestly, cutting is more common than people like to think – in younger women especially. For a nun, I suppose it might have a religious connotation. Part of the philosophy here is to bear suffering for the sake of God. There's no reason the food has to be so awful, for a start. Maybe she got it into her head that she needed to bear the pain, because it must have stung. Has he been any help?' She cast her eyes towards the convent.

'The bishop? He wants to get to the bottom of it but there isn't a lot he can do.'

Dr Alexander raised her eyebrows. 'I see,' she said.

'If there's anything else . . .' Mirabelle tailed off, but the doctor shook her head.

'I need to get back. I have a surgery in an hour.'

Before she left, Mirabelle knocked on Mother Superior's door and entered. The nun looked up. 'Miss Bevan,' she said. 'Any news?'

Mirabelle sighed. It felt as if people were expecting a miracle. 'I was hoping I might have a chance to speak to Vesta.'

'She offered to help in the salve shed,' Mother Superior said. 'I can have somebody fetch her if you like.'

Mirabelle considered this. 'I don't want to arouse suspicion. Just let her know that I'll ring her in the morning as usual. I hope she comes up with something. Frankly, I'm drawing a blank.' But as she said it, she thought that wasn't quite true. It was just everything seemed so disconnected. 'I'm missing something,' she added.

'I will pray for you, Miss Bevan,' Mother Superior said. 'For all of us. You will get to the bottom of this. I have absolute confidence. That is, after all, why you were sent to Shore Cottage.' She raised her eyes in deference to a higher power.

'Thank you,' Mirabelle replied. 'I wonder, would you call a cab, please? I need to get back into town.'

The cab was going to take forty minutes, the dispatcher said. It was rush-hour in Edinburgh and the convent was too remote for a taxi to be waiting nearby. Rather than hovering in Mother Superior's office, Mirabelle bypassed the salve sheds and wandered along the shoreline. Sister Monica's grave was filled now and the graveyard deserted, save for two gannets swooping over the water in search of their dinner. A mine-sweeper from the naval base glided by in the distance as Mirabelle stopped and peered at the grave. Something was peeking through the flattened earth, a spike of green, though nothing could have taken root yet. She took off a glove and brushed aside the soil to reveal a sprig of rosemary tied with a thin piece of yellow ribbon. 'Rosemary is for remembrance,' she said out loud, then looked behind her. There was nobody. 'Who wants to remember you, Monica?' she asked, as she reburied the herb.

This investigation felt like a huge responsibility. Nearing the water, she could see the boathouse at the cottage. Taking the inland road, the house seemed further away from the convent but now she realised its proximity. The boundary line between the convent and the cottage, she supposed, must be marked by the burn that tumbled down the slope and into the firth. Mirabelle followed the rushing water and stood staring in the direction of the bridge works. Sister Monica had liked it here, Mother Superior had said in her eulogy. Mirabelle considered jumping the burn, which was only a couple of feet wide, and walking through the copse of sycamores that shielded her new home, but she decided her kitten heels would not survive the adventure. Instead she turned inland and followed the gushing water back towards the convent till she came to the place where it spilled out of the earth, at the edge of the graveyard. It was pretty, like a fairy waterfall. She squinted, noticing something glinting through the water. Something gold.

Nobody was nearby. Carefully Mirabelle perched on the bank and manoeuvred to see what was catching the light but the water was too fast. Holding the base of a trailing ivy in one hand to steady herself, she reached out, drenching her glove and one side of her coat in freezing water. Was it a rock? No. Too regular a shape for that. She felt her way until she had hold of the object and pulled it out, splashing her dress. Then she laughed, recognising it – a Kemel's Coffee tin, lodged on a stone that acted like a little shelf. It couldn't have been there long – there was a camel on one side and on the other some words obscured by a line of rust, commemorating the 1958 Grand Prix.

Mirabelle tipped the contents onto the bank – a cutthroat razor, a mirror no more than three inches square and a small wooden drum of shaving soap. 'Bingo,' she said. 'You used the burn to shave. You came here every day.' Scooping up Sister Monica's things, Mirabelle discovered another item in the bottom of the tin. A key. 'Not another,' she said despondently. This time the key was older – too large for a modern lock and slightly rusted – so not for a modern door. As far as she had seen, there were no locks in the convent, not on the cell doors or even on the lavatory. The front gate was secured by a medieval-looking bar, which had to be hauled in and out of place from the inside. This key, however, must open something. She looked round at the graves but there were no gated mausoleums. What did Sister Monica want to unlock? she pondered. Another question to add to her long list. She sighed, as she turned up the path to wait for her taxi at the cross by the door.

Chapter Ten

Friends are the siblings God never gave us

The next morning Mr Leech, the optician, wore the thickest glasses Mirabelle had ever seen as he tested her eyesight. She was not particularly worried that she couldn't read the smaller print, but he kept tutting as she halted on the second or third line of the chart. 'Hmm,' he said, and placed an optical lens over her left eye.

'Is everything all right?' she asked.

'Astigmatism,' he said mysteriously, and changed the lens, leaning forwards as she told him what she could see. 'Only slight,' he pronounced.

In the showroom between smart white smooth columns the glass-topped cherrywood cases displayed spectacle frames and McGregor sat reading a magazine without difficulty while he waited for her.

'What's the diagnosis?' he asked.

'I need reading glasses,' Mirabelle admitted. It was hardly a revelation. She picked a pair of tortoiseshell frames off one of the stands, tried them on and peered into a mirror mounted between the display cases. McGregor looked on, amused.

'Men don't make passes at women in glasses,' he said with a grin, and Mirabelle put down the frames.

'They make me look like a swot.'

He laughed. 'You are a swot. Let's face it. You have a first-class degree. From Oxford. You're the cleverest woman I know.'

'Well, I don't want to look that way,' she snapped, and immediately regretted it. It probably didn't help that she had lain awake the night before, going over what Mrs Munro had said, regretting not asking Belinda Farquarson-Sinclair more questions and wondering if Vesta might manage somehow to get some answers from Sister Evangelista. The key from the tin was now nestling in her bag. McGregor had pronounced it impossible to say what it might open. 'It's absolutely generic,' he complained.

At the desk she paid her bill and said she would come back to choose some frames. They emerged onto George Street in the sunshine, past the car showroom. As they rounded the corner, the view of Fife reminded Mirabelle of the graveyard the day before. She felt suddenly tired.

'The nunnery is extremely close to the house, you know,' she said. 'I hadn't realised. The graveyard banks the boundary at the end of our little wood. It's not as remote as I thought.'

McGregor took her hand. 'Do you feel odd about living next door to a graveyard?'

This hadn't even occurred to her. 'No,' she said.

'A week today we'll be on our way to the Registrar's Office,' he added.

'Yes.' She had completely forgotten about the wedding.

'Mrs McGregor,' he added, with a grin. When this didn't elicit a response he changed the subject. Over the years the superintendent had learned to accommodate Mirabelle's need to solve all kinds of puzzles.

'What has Vesta turned up?' he asked patiently, and Mirabelle checked her watch with a gasp.

'Damn!' she said. 'I should have called ten minutes ago.'

She rushed to the phone box and scrabbled in her purse for change as he waited on the corner. The telephone in Mother Superior's office was answered that morning by a male voice with a broad Scottish accent.

'Aye,' the man said. 'Who's this?'

Mirabelle hesitated, trying to figure out what on earth might be going on. 'Is that the Little Sisters of Gethsemane Convent?' she asked. 'Mother Superior's office?'

'It is. Who am I speaking to?'

'I wanted to talk to Sister Joseph. I'm from her order,' Mirabelle added.

'Can I take your name?' the voice enquired.

'Sister . . . Angelica.' She picked the moniker out of thin air. The man did not question it. She wondered momentarily how Saint Angelica had died or even if there was a Saint Angelica. There must be.

There was a scuffling sound as the man put his palm over the phone. 'Which one is Sister Joseph? Do you know?' he said.

Another male voice answered in a more sedate tone. 'She's the Black woman, sir. The one who was sick . . .'

'I'm sorry. Sister Joseph is indisposed. I'll pass on a message,' the man said.

'Indisposed?' Mirabelle's stomach turned over. 'What do you mean?'

There was more rustling and the phone was handed to someone else.

'This is Sister Mary,' said a more familiar voice.

'Is Sister Joseph all right?' Mirabelle began to feel confused with all the sisters. I'm a nun, she thought. Just remember that. It's a part to play.

'She's fine,' Sister Mary said breezily. 'Only she's been ill. She ate a sandwich on the train and it seems the fish paste wasn't right. You'd think she'd have tasted if it was off, but she didn't. Poor thing, she's had an upset stomach since she got here. Perhaps I can help with your enquiry, Sister Angelica. Is it about the soap?'

'Yes. The soap,' Mirabelle confirmed, feeling that this conversation was becoming more involved than she might like. Vesta had never eaten a fish-paste sandwich in her life – she abhorred the stuff.

'I meant to ask Sister Joseph which order she came from,' Sister Mary said warmly. 'Where are you calling from?'

Mirabelle searched her memory. 'The Poor Clares,' she said. 'We're the Poor Clares. In Bermondsey.'

There was a pause. 'I thought the Clares wore brown robes. You're Franciscans, aren't you?'

Mirabelle began to panic. 'Is Sister Joseph not wearing hers?' she asked anxiously. 'What colour does she have on?'

The nun dissembled, not wanting to get Joseph into trouble. 'I expect Mother insisted she wear the same as we do. Black,' she said, and sniffed, pausing. 'I'm sorry,' she added. 'It's just with the police here today . . . we're rather . . . stretched. May I ask Sister Joseph to ring you back?'

'The police? What are the police doing at the convent?'

Sister Mary sniffed again. 'I shouldn't say.'

In the background the male voice sounded insistent. 'I need the phone, Sister. Now.'

'Of course, Inspector Rennie,' Sister Mary replied, and the telephone clicked.

Mirabelle walked back onto the street. McGregor was staring at Italian leather notebooks in the stationer's window. 'Do you know an Inspector Rennie on the force?' she asked.

'Here? No. Why?'

'He's at the nunnery. I think something has happened. Vesta couldn't come to the telephone. They said she's ill.'

McGregor pulled the car keys from his pocket. 'Well, we can't have that,' he said. 'Come on.'

They walked quickly back to Heriot Row where the car was parked, or, as McGregor deemed it jokingly, 'abandoned' because it was Mirabelle who had last used it. He fired the ignition and made heavy weather of straightening the wheels and steering the vehicle onto the road. Mirabelle ignored this and sat running through the possibilities. She scarcely registered the picturesque silhouette of Edinburgh Castle as they passed it on the other side of Princes Street. She had sent Vesta into a closed community where there was likely a murderer in hiding. Had that person felt threatened? Had they lashed out? If anything happened to Vesta she would never forgive herself.

Then she noticed that this was not the route they usually took to the nunnery. She gazed down Queensferry Street past Rankin's fruit shop, with its colourful boxes of bananas and oranges on display, as McGregor continued along Shandwick Place.

'We're better to go to the source, don't you think?' he said.

Mirabelle had a sudden vision of God sitting behind a desk like the bishop's in an office somewhere in the West End. 'What do you mean?'

'Torphichen Street nick,' he replied. 'Here it is.'

The station was round the corner from the Gaumont cinema. McGregor parked at the door and ushered Mirabelle inside. A steel-grey sergeant stood at the front desk, as in every other police station Mirabelle had ever been inside. The hallway smelt of filing cabinets and bleach. 'Yes, sir?' the man said.

'I'm Superintendent McGregor, retired,' McGregor introduced himself. 'I wonder if you might check if Superintendent Scott could see me. It's a matter of urgency.'

'Yes, sir.' The sergeant disappeared behind an opaque glass screen.

'I've been meaning to come and see Gene Scott for a while,' McGregor said.

In a minute or two they were led through a door and up a set of stairs to a pale green corridor comprised of offices. The sound of typewriters chimed in concert. Up here the hallway smelt of talcum powder and sweat. Superintendent Scott stood up as they rapped on the door and entered his office. He shook McGregor's hand enthusiastically across a highly polished desk with exceptionally neat piles of paper spaced evenly across its surface.

'I hear you've been turning in par at the Braids,' he said.

Another golfer. Mirabelle didn't see the point. Her father, once pressed to a round at Richmond Park, had said he'd rather walk the eighteen holes without having to whack a ball around. 'That way at least you can take a dog,' he'd said.

McGregor introduced Mirabelle, and Superintendent Scott offered them whisky 'or,' he added, 'some tea, perhaps.'

'Tea would be nice,' McGregor replied, not pointing out that it was early in the day to be hitting the hard stuff.

'What can I do for you?' the superintendent asked, as he sat down and motioned them to do the same.

'The Little Sisters of Gethsemane at South Queensferry. You have a man there today. Rennie, is it?'

Scott cast his eyes to the ceiling. 'He's from Glasgow,' he said. 'Transferred a couple of months ago. I swithered sending him to a nunnery but he's the most senior officer I have available. He's extremely competent and it is murder. Has he caused some kind of problem?'

'Murder?' McGregor said.

Scott lit a cigarette and took a deep draw. 'One of the nuns was killed this morning,' he added.

Mirabelle went pale. 'Which nun?' she asked, beginning to panic. Just not Vesta, please, her mind raced. Not that. Had Sister Mary been trying to be diplomatic?

Scott regarded Mirabelle carefully. 'What do you mean, Miss Bevan?'

'Who was murdered, Superintendent Scott?' Mirabelle's tone was insistent.

'Are you familiar with the convent?'

'We are about to get married there. We are buying a house nearby.'

'I see. Well, congratulations.'

Scott's gaze was rock hard. He was a man without anything to give in the seams. You could see that from his suit, Mirabelle thought, perfectly cut but entirely without flourish. Exactly what was required and no more, with such tidy piles of paper on his pristine desk. There was a stand-off as they sat in silence for a few moments.

'Mirabelle is concerned because she knows some of the sisters,' McGregor pressed. 'She's worried for a friend.'

Scott took this in and softened. 'I'm afraid the Mother Superior was killed early this morning,' he said.

Mirabelle relaxed because Vesta was safe, and then, taking in the superintendent's words, felt a wave of guilt at her relief.

'Mother Superior?' she repeated. She'd seen the nun only the day before. At her desk. In the pink. It didn't make any sense.

'Was she drowned?' McGregor asked.

Scott looked quizzical. 'Drowned? Why would she be drowned? No – she was . . . I don't like to say it in front of a lady. She was stabbed. It was a slashing, really. The poor woman was practically beheaded.'

Mirabelle let out a gentle 'Oh!' in exclamation.

'It happened in the chapel,' Scott added.

'Beheaded?' McGregor repeated. In all his time on the job he couldn't think of a murder where a victim had been beheaded.

'Sorry. That was dramatic. This thing has a biblical feel,' Scott said, as a female police officer knocked on the door and brought in a tray with tea and a plate of Huntley & Palmers biscuits. She laid it on the desk with a clink. 'Thank you, Constable,' Scott said, and stubbed out his cigarette. 'It was a frenzied attack. Her throat was slit. It wasn't a beheading. I shouldn't have put it like that.'

None of them felt like tea but Scott poured three cups anyway and added a shot of whisky to his own. 'How well did you know the Mother Superior?' he asked.

McGregor nodded as if answering was a decision. 'We're getting married at the convent, but we'd only met her once or twice. She was a nice woman. What was the weapon that killed her?'

Scott raised his eyes to the ceiling. 'That's our first problem. The Sword of Gethsemane. We've had the bishop on to us already. He called it "a major historical artefact". The National Museum oversees its upkeep. I told the old man we'd be holding it as evidence and he wasn't best pleased. The museum is sending someone to make sure we don't damage the thing. I mean, really. Who keeps that kind of weapon just hanging around? It's two thousand years old!' Scott sighed. 'I suppose I'll have to go down and have a look. I shouldn't have dispatched Rennie. It's more of a diplomatic incident than a regular murder.'

'We'll come,' McGregor added. 'Perhaps Mirabelle will be able to put the nuns at ease. You'll get more out of them.'

Scott seemed to accept this.

Back in the car, alone with McGregor, Mirabelle crossed her legs. 'You didn't tell him about Vesta.'

'Not yet,' McGregor admitted.

'Or Sister Monica.'

'We can tell him when we get there, if Rennie hasn't uncovered it yet.'

She didn't like to say anything, but these omissions were exactly the kind of thing McGregor used to object to when Mirabelle was working on his cases. It felt good that this time they were on the same side, she thought, as he pulled past Haymarket station and cut through the West End onto Queensferry Road.

Twenty minutes later they turned off for the nunnery and Mirabelle realised she felt as if she had been sedated. The death of Mother Superior was difficult to take in. Outside, at the Celtic cross, three police cars were parked haphazardly against the verge and an ambulance was stationed at the side gate, its back door ajar.

A group of children from the building site had assembled at the side of the road. 'What's going on, mister?' one of the kids shouted, as they got out of the car.

McGregor motioned them away. 'You shouldn't be here,' he said. 'Move along!' Then he turned to Mirabelle.

'They'll need to remove the body for a proper post-mortem examination.'

'Why do they have to do that? Her throat was slit,' Mirabelle whispered blankly. 'Even I could tell you what she died from.'

'Regulations,' McGregor said sagely. 'The procurator fiscal. In Scotland the process is different. It's more rigorous. They'll bring her body back. They'll be able to bury her when the police have finished.'

The convent's gate opened smartly when they rang. It was manned by a policewoman who struggled with the huge bar as McGregor introduced himself and said he was with Superintendent Scott, who was on his way. The woman accepted this and didn't ask about Mirabelle.

'We know where we're going,' McGregor told her and they walked up the cobblestoned path and across the courtyard towards Mother Superior's office. The place was deserted, eerie almost. The sound of communal prayer drifted towards them from the refectory – women's voices chanting in unison with an undertone of weeping. A male police constable stood guard at the chapel door. McGregor nodded at the man and they continued through the doorway and up the stairs.

Mother Superior's door was wedged open with two heavy, leather-bound books. There was nobody inside. The desk looked tidier than when they had been there the other day, as if somebody had been putting the convent's papers in order. McGregor stared out of the window over the gardens. 'They'll pray all day, I should think. A thing like this. All week, perhaps. Imagine locking yourself up in here for years and then . . .'

Mirabelle didn't reply for a moment. The nuns weren't exactly locked in. The convent's boundaries were like a sieve.

'For it to happen twice,' she said, 'one dead nun after another, they'll be terrified. I would be.'

She turned her attention to the tidied papers – an electricity bill among a stack of other invoices and confirmations for wedding bookings, including cheques and a postal order. She pulled out a sheet of paper so thick it could have been vellum. 'Look at this,' she said, reading.

'What is it?'

'A petition against burying Sister Monica in the graveyard.'

'Who signed it?'

Mirabelle squinted at the names.

'Give it to me,' McGregor said with a smirk. 'Sisters Mary and Bernadette,' he read out. 'I don't know any of the other names.'

'We should speak to the nuns who signed it first,' Mirabelle said.

Scott appeared in the doorway behind them. 'Which nuns?' he asked.

McGregor handed him the paper.

'And you think that a nun stabbed the convent's Mother Superior to death over a difference of opinion about a gravestone?'

There was an awkward silence. Behind him a brief hammering sound wafted up the stairs and two more men appeared at the door.

'Sir,' said one – a wiry detective with a tidy blond moustache, wearing a buff suit and a well-tailored raincoat. As he swept in, the smell of tobacco preceded him.

'This is Detective Inspector Rennie,' Scott said. 'Rennie, this is Superintendent McGregor, retired. What progress have you made?'

Rennie sighed but his gaze was intense. It was as if he

could see right through you, Mirabelle thought. 'Early days, sir. Some of the sisters correspond with lifers. At Peterhead prison mostly but one in Barlinnie. I've rung to find out if any of them got out recently. None wrote to Mother Superior, but still.'

'Oh, that's all we need,' said Scott.

Rennie's dark gaze landed on McGregor, then lingered more languorously on Mirabelle. He had more flair than Scott – that was apparent from his clothes. There was something of the mod about him, but not quite. 'She's a good idea, sir,' he said, motioning towards Mirabelle. 'We'll need more female officers for this one.'

'Miss Bevan isn't an officer.'

'Oh, yes? What is she doing here, then?' Rennie asked.

Mirabelle cleared her throat. 'I'm a private detective,' she said. 'I'm here because this isn't the first murder in this nunnery.'

Scott sat down in Mother Superior's chair. 'What do you mean?'

Mirabelle discovered that she was rather enjoying knowing more than any of the real policemen. She picked up the petition that Scott had discarded. 'This novice died three days ago in suspicious circumstances. And . . .' she paused '. . . she wasn't a novice, not really. She had lived in the convent for several months and nobody suspected her.'

'Suspected her of what?'

'He was a bloke,' McGregor said. 'A young man.'

Scott, Rennie and the other officer hesitated, then burst into gales of laughter.

'A man? It's like one of those *Carry On* films,' Rennie said, his face twisted into a gleeful, ghoulish grin. 'You're joking.'

'An invert, more like. Maybe one of the nuns did do

it after all . . . Sick bastard. And the Mother Superior let this bloke be buried here as . . .' Scott checked the petition '. . . Sister Monica.'

'The novice's sex is irrelevant,' Mirabelle said firmly. They were like naughty schoolboys – children, practically.

'Looks like the nuns didn't feel that way,' Rennie quipped.

'Well, these nuns in particular didn't feel that way.' Mirabelle pointed at the names at the bottom of the petition. 'But, honestly, I agree with you. I doubt any of them tried to . . . how did you put it? . . . behead Mother Superior in the chapel. Do you know what time the murder took place?'

Rennie shifted. 'She went to early prayers.'

'Matins,' Mirabelle corrected him. She wasn't sure how she knew the name.

'Matins, aye,' Rennie continued. 'And breakfast. But nobody had seen her since about six thirty this morning until the body was found.'

'And when was that?'

'A little before nine.'

'Who found her?'

'Some Black nun who's visiting from a convent down south. Mother Superior had been letting her use this office. Anyway, she went into the chapel, I don't know why, and discovered the body. She ran up here immediately and dialled 999.'

Mirabelle and McGregor both shifted. 'I'd like to speak to this nun,' Mirabelle said.

Scott sat back in his chair. 'Have you finished with her, Rennie?'

'As far as I could go. She started vomiting,' the inspector said.

No wonder, Mirabelle thought. Poor Vesta. It must have been a shock. 'Perhaps I could talk to her. I'm sure a woman's touch will be helpful.'

'A woman's touch,' Rennie repeated. 'Maybe.'

'Where is she now?'

'She went back to her cell.'

'I know where the dormitory block is. I'll see if she's feeling well enough to answer more questions.'

Mirabelle didn't wait for a reply and none of them stopped her. Leaving McGregor with the men, she cut downstairs and along the corridor, speeding up as she went so that she was almost running by the time she got to the accommodation block. Upstairs, in Sister Monica's cell, Vesta was sitting alone on the bed, her cheeks wet with tears. The room smelt vaguely of sour milk.

Mirabelle flung her arms around her friend. 'I'm sorry,' she said. 'What an awful thing to happen.'

Vesta heaved up a sob from somewhere deep in her gut. 'There was blood everywhere,' she gasped. 'I've never seen anything like it. It was so still in there, almost peaceful, and she was just lying by the altar with the sword cast to the side. It was like a tableau. She was still warm, Mirabelle. I checked her pulse but she was gone.'

Mirabelle didn't want to come out with the platitudes that people normally divested themselves of after shocking experiences. It wouldn't be honest to tell Vesta the memory would fade or that it must be for the best. Scenes of carnage from wartime remained as fresh in her mind as the day she had walked into them and none for the best, not one of them. The dreams sometimes caught her unawares even nowadays.

'Do you have any idea who might have done it?' she asked.

Vesta sniffed. 'How could I possibly? And, Mirabelle . . .'

She was about to say something more, but Sister Mary appeared in the doorway holding a cup of tea. 'Here,' she said. 'I thought this might help. Miss Bevan, what are you doing here?'

'I came with Superintendent McGregor. When I heard who had found Mother Superior's body, it seemed to me that Sister Joseph shouldn't be left alone,' Mirabelle replied smoothly.

'Of course,' Sister Mary said.

Vesta sipped the tea.

'Sister Mary, who will take Mother's place?' Mirabelle asked.

The nun looked impassive. 'The bishop is sending somebody to look after things in the meantime,' she said, 'but we will vote. We sisters choose our mother superior. It has always been that way, though of course it normally happens before the sitting mother passes.'

Mirabelle remembered Mother Superior's explanation. 'So . . . would a nun have to agree to stand for election?' she asked.

'Oh, no.' Mirabelle detected the merest blush on the old woman's cheek. 'The bishop will decide on two candidates he feels appropriate and we will choose between them. It wouldn't be right for a sister to put herself forward.'

Vesta placed the cup on the floor with a bleak expression, and Mirabelle got up and opened the window to air the room. 'She was a wonderful woman. So forgiving. So accepting. I only met her the other day but she was kind. And she seemed extremely efficient in the convent's business,' she said.

Sister Mary's eyes filled with tears. 'I'm sorry,' she apologised. 'It's the shock.'

'I noticed that you disagreed with her. About burying Sister Monica in the graveyard.'

Sister Mary sniffed, pulling herself together. 'The graveyard is for nuns. Sister Monica wasn't a nun. That had become clear. It was hardly a normal state of affairs.'

'Not normal. No. I suppose not.'

Sister Mary picked up Vesta's empty cup. 'Some of the other sisters felt the same. But the body is buried now and we have another funeral to consider – a more important one. Our mother superior is gone on the tide. And we must lay the fault where the fault lies, as is our way. Then we will move on.'

Mirabelle caught that phrase again. Mother had used it at Sister Monica's funeral. She supposed nuns were accustomed to flowery language. She watched Sister Mary's face, which continued serene.

'Move on? But the murderer must still be here,' Vesta said.

'Here?' Sister Mary sounded shocked. 'That's not possible. My sisters and I are the only ones here. I had better get on, if you don't mind looking after Sister Joseph, Miss Bevan?'

'But how would somebody get in? And why would they want to kill—' Vesta continued.

'That is enough,' Sister Mary said, cutting her off.

The old nun turned and left the room. Vesta lay back on the bed, with one hand on her stomach. 'I can't see any of them doing it, if I'm honest,' she said, 'but why would somebody from outside want to hurt Mother? Also, Sister Monica died less than a week ago so this is the second death in no time and probably the second murder. One motive would be difficult enough to find, but two? It's got to be the same person – the same reason, at least. Something worth killing two nuns for . . . '

'You're right,' Mirabelle said. 'It isn't an easy place to move about unnoticed and it's likely the two deaths are linked. Are you all right to stay inside a bit longer? We might need you here.'

'I just want to sleep,' Vesta said, closing her eyes. 'I feel exhausted.'

Mirabelle thought of how people had such different ways of coping. After the harrowing experience Vesta had just undergone, she doubted she'd be able to sleep. She herself had spent most of the war as an intermittent insomniac. But Vesta's breathing was already smooth and sleepy. Perhaps it was better that way, Mirabelle thought, as she got up and left the cell, closing the door behind her.

Chapter Eleven

But once to die

In the courtyard the police constable refused to allow Dr Alexander to enter the chapel where the body lay. Mirabelle emerged onto the cobblestones to the doctor protesting in the most strident terms.

'I'm the woman's GP,' she insisted. 'I attend to all the nuns. I was sent by the bishop.'

'I'm sorry, miss,' the constable replied, blocking the doorway. 'It's Inspector Rennie's orders and he's in charge.'

'Don't call me "miss". I'm a doctor,' Dr Alexander snapped.

'Hello,' Mirabelle hailed her. 'What's going on?'

'This officer won't let me see Mother Superior's body,' Dr Alexander said. 'The bishop asked me to issue her death certificate.'

'I expect the police don't want the scene disturbed,' Mirabelle replied. The constable on the door looked grateful at this intervention, but didn't add anything to confirm it.

'I don't understand what's happening,' the doctor said, with a sigh. 'Two bodies within a week.'

'Well, exactly,' Mirabelle said. 'I was just saying that the deaths must be related, but how they're related is another matter. And, of course, Inspector Rennie will be playing catch-up because Sister Monica's death is news to him.'

'Could we have done something more? Ought we to have reported what happened to Monica?'

Mirabelle shook her head. It was often the way with the best people – they tried to take responsibility wherever they could, even for something as perverse as a murder.

'Have you found out anything more?' the doctor pressed her.

'No,' Mirabelle admitted. Her discovery that Monica had shaved in the burn didn't seem like much by way of progress, and though she had another key in her possession, she had no idea what it was for.

'Why don't you come up to Mother Superior's office? I can introduce you to the detective in charge,' she said, but when they got to the top of the stairs, there was only another constable sorting through the papers on the old desk. McGregor, Rennie and Scott had disappeared. The only evidence that they had been there were three of Superintendent Scott's half-smoked cigarette butts stubbed out in a saucer in a swathe of ash.

Lingering in the hallway, Dr Alexander stared through the window opposite the office door, looking down on the constable guarding the chapel. 'I am her doctor, you know,' she said.

There was no measure in pursuing that. It was a police case now. Mirabelle took a seat in the hallway on the short bank of chairs set out for nuns to wait. She motioned the doctor to sit next to her. 'We can watch from up here. That way we'll know when they bring her out.'

'I saw the ambulance,' Dr Alexander said, and put down her bag.

Mirabelle decided to ask more questions. Through the open door of Mother Superior's office, she noticed the policeman slowed slightly, as he listened to their conversation without looking up.

'I visited the Farquarson-Sinclairs yesterday. I wonder what they will make of this,' Mirabelle started.

'You'll be a neighbour soon, too,' the doctor said. 'If this doesn't put you off.'

Mirabelle didn't reply directly. There had been murders as close to her old flat in Brighton as this convent was to Shore Cottage. 'It's such an odd place, a convent,' she said. 'Flinging yourself into religious devotion.'

'I think most nuns look on it as joining a community,' Dr Alexander replied. 'People think of it as a retreat, but it's not really. It's just a different way to relate to the world. To help.'

'Do they often know each other before they decide to come? It seems such an odd life to choose out of the blue.'

'Some do. A couple of sisters are related, if you see what I mean. I suppose people tend to move in ways that are familiar. My father was a doctor. I don't expect I'd have read medicine if I hadn't had a glimpse into his life. Some of the women are sent here through the bishop or connections in their own parish. Everything is a kind of club, isn't it?'

'When the bishop got in touch to ask you to sign the death certificate, what did he say?'

'It was his secretary.'

'Mrs Munro?'

'Yes. She said the bishop would like me to issue the death certificate to keep things consistent. The Church is always keen on things being done in the usual way.'

The door opened at the foot of the stairs and, after

a moment, McGregor appeared at the head. Mirabelle introduced him to the doctor and they shook hands.

'They'll be bringing out the body in a minute,' he said.

'Were you allowed in the chapel?'

'Yes. The attack was spur of the moment, from the look of it. It's carnage in there. I can't see how anyone could have planned it. The sword is extremely keen for such an old blade. Turns out the National Museum maintains it.'

'It's Roman,' Dr Alexander said. 'It's a Roman army sword.'

'All our suspects are currently praying,' McGregor continued. 'Rennie has made it clear he has difficulty in differentiating one nun from another. He won't allow me to sit in on the questioning.'

'How about me? He seemed to go for the idea of a woman's touch,' Mirabelle tried.

'Not you either.'

Mirabelle sighed. Below them, two ambulance men emerged, carrying a stretcher draped with a tidy grey blanket. They set off across the courtyard.

'There she goes,' McGregor said.

'Where will they take her?' Mirabelle asked.

Dr Alexander stood up to get a better view. 'The city morgue. It's in the Old Town. Near the university.'

'Very Burke and Hare,' McGregor said.

'Sometimes I think Edinburgh can't get away from that,' the doctor mused, as she bent down to pick up her case.

'What do you mean?'

'Its history. Stiff upper lip. Medical excellence. The Enlightenment. All very worthy. I suppose we're all bound by our history, aren't we? Well, that's that,' she said, with resigned air. 'I'd better get back to work.'

They watched her go.

'This is one time we can't follow the money and there's no jealous husband involved, unless you count . . .' McGregor cast his eyes upwards. 'And none of the nuns want to speak to us. I'll be amazed if Rennie gets anything out of them.'

Money and love as motives were always a policeman's assumptions and not without reason, though several of the cases Mirabelle had solved over the years hadn't involved either of those things.

'They're so removed from everything in this place,' she said wistfully. 'Maybe somebody did get in and do it.'

'And get out again unnoticed,' McGregor said doubtfully.

Mirabelle wondered what Bang Bang MacDonald might have said. She sounded a practical sort – just what they needed right now – and the one person who knew the workings of the convent intimately but could also judge it from the outside. She wondered if the old woman had ever seen Sister Monica tarrying by the burn. From the house, that must just be possible from the vantage of the upper floor. Though she would have died around the time the novice trudged from Dalmeny railway station to the convent in the freezing cold. Something flickered in Mirabelle's mind, like a flash of electric light in the dark.

'They're going to fingerprint the sword and they'll take all the sisters' fingerprints too.' McGregor drew her attention back to the immediate procedure. 'But there was a lot of blood. It'll make it difficult.'

'You don't think they'll get much, then?'

He shrugged his shoulders. 'The fingerprint guy was doubtful. He said they've started holding evidence because you never know in time. Things are changing on the science side. The reality is they'll never let the police hold the Sword of Gethsemane in some evidence store, murder weapon or not.

It's probably the most famous piece of military equipment in the world. Scott said to the bishop he thinks in future they should keep it in a glass case for safety.'

'Glass can be smashed,' Mirabelle pointed out.

'I think, as far as we're concerned, we should just let Rennie get on with it. For us, in here it's probably all down to Vesta. Is she all right?'

'She's shocked but she agreed to stay. You're right. We need to see if we can pursue anything on the outside,' Mirabelle said, thinking it through.

McGregor shifted. 'I have an idea. I made a couple of enquiries. Do you want to follow them up with me?' He checked his watch. It was almost lunchtime but there were no cooking smells coming from the convent's kitchen, thank goodness. The nuns were probably going to fast, Mirabelle concluded. Vesta wouldn't like that.

'Want to come with me?' he asked.

'Oh, yes,' she replied. 'Whatever you say.'

They got up to leave. The policewoman on the gate straightened as she opened the door, like a military guard. Outside, the children at the turn-off were seeing who could keep up a hoop for longest. It looked as if they were betting on it. Mirabelle squinted, as a piece of silver glinted in the sunlight, handed between plump fingers.

'It's the Cooperative centenary. They get metal badges from the milkmen,' McGregor said. 'It's the hand of St Cuthbert.'

'How do you know about all these saints?' Mirabelle asked.

'Maybe it's a Scottish thing. Cuthbert was a Scot, I think. A healer.'

She didn't question him further. She seemed to know things too. 'I suppose we pick things up, whatever we believe,' she said.

As they swept back onto the road, three little boys were climbing one of the trees. 'I'm sure that's dangerous,' McGregor commented, but they didn't stop.

Back in town he swung off at the east end of Princes Street and parked on St James Square. The houses were similar to those on the smart streets around Heriot Row but had fallen into disrepair, with some absolutely derelict. 'They're going to refurbish this whole place. Bulldoze it and build something modern,' he said.

Looking up, Mirabelle noticed a woman in a grubby upper window staring down at them in the sunshine. She was wearing a cheap, old-fashioned dress, her hair tied up in a cotton scarf.

'It seems quiet,' Mirabelle observed. 'Why are there no children?'

'There was a double murder over the main road a few years ago,' McGregor said. 'They got the guy – he was hanged – but most parents don't let their kids out any more in this part of town. I can't say I blame them. Maybe I should have dropped you off in the West End. Are you sure you want to come?'

'Of course.'

'All right,' McGregor said.

Across the main road there was a pub in the basement down a set of worn stone steps. The frontage was crusted with dust from the road and there didn't appear to be any sign of the place's name, only a damaged McEwan's beer insignia – a smiling Cavalier drinking a pint with a hole smashed in it. Round the corner an older boy wearing tattered grey shorts sat on a ground-floor windowsill drinking a bottle of lemonade through a straw. Brave fellow, Mirabelle thought, and slipped her arm through McGregor's.

'Don't make eye contact with anyone,' he said, and opened the door.

It was dim over the threshold. The floor was flagstoned and high tables were placed the length of the room at right angles to the bar, behind which a man, shirtsleeves rolled up and thin, white hair combed back, looked up as they entered. On the bar, there was one beer tap and behind it a single bottle of blended whisky attached to an optic.

'We've no ladies' facilities,' the barman said with a sniff, looking them up and down.

'Two drams, please,' McGregor said.

As the barman turned to fetch the drinks, Mirabelle loitered. There were three occupied tables in the gloom: each with a man drinking alone. McGregor walked ahead and stopped at one. The drinker shifted, turning away. 'They said I'd find you here,' McGregor said and, peering, Mirabelle recognised the porter's uniform and then his face. Without taking his eyes off McGregor, the man lifted a half-finished pint of beer to his lips.

'You're police, aren't you?' he said, and sipped.

'Used to be.'

The porter glanced at Mirabelle. 'I didn't cop her.'

'Well, she copped you.'

The barman set out two drams and pushed a ceramic jug of water along the bar. Nobody moved, only listened as McGregor continued.

'We want to know about the lad who tipped you to keep that locker up. He paid you, didn't he?'

'What if he did?'

'Tell me about him.'

'He was English. About twenty years old. Dressed smartly. Like a toff.'

'He didn't give you his name?'

'Naw.'

'When did he say he'd be back?'

'He didn't. He said it might take a while.'

'What might take a while?'

'His business. He wanted me to stop them clearing out the locker while he was gone.'

'Why didn't he just put it in Left Luggage?'

'Late train,' the porter said. 'The office closes at six sharp. I don't know.'

'And he said he'd be back – after a while?'

'Aye. Why?'

'He's dead.'

The porter lifted the glass to his lips once more, hunching over it protectively. 'He said he'd pay me the other half when he came to pick up the case.'

McGregor smirked. 'Looks like you're out some money, then, unless you've something worthwhile you can tell me. Why did you run?'

The porter shrugged. 'Habit.'

They both waited.

'I think you didn't want the clerk at Left Luggage to find out you'd taken money.'

'Mebbe,' he admitted.

Silence descended once more.

'Well, if there's nothing else . . .' McGregor turned. He laid a coin on the bar and poured a splash of water into each of the whiskies. 'Cheers,' he said, lifting a glass. Mirabelle and he downed the drinks and were turning to go when the porter called them back.

'I could do with another beer.'

McGregor paused before laying a coin on the bar to pay for it. The barman set about pulling a pint from the tap.

'The lad gave me a quid and said there would be another quid in it when he came back,' the porter said.

'You'd have to have something good for it to be worth that much to me.'

'Aye. Well, he did say one thing.'

'And what was that?'

'That it might be the summer before he was back again. Which is now, I suppose. And that by then she'd be long gone.'

'Who? What did he mean?'

'I don't know,' he said. 'He'd had a drink on the train. You know how posh bastards get when they've had a couple. Everyone's their friend.'

'Posh?'

'English.'

'By then she'll be long gone? He said it just like that?'

'Aye. Sad, almost. Like he was figuring something out.'

McGregor peeled a pound from the roll of notes in his pocket and put it down. The porter laid his hand over it and the money disappeared like a magic trick.

'Cheers,' he said, raising the pint glass.

Outside they crossed the main road.

'It's the pregnant girl, isn't it?' McGregor said.

'I don't know,' Mirabelle replied. 'I'm not sure if that's possible. Grace Farquarson-Sinclair was sent to Italy three months ago by my reckoning. That's March. Mrs Grieg said she was just starting to show then, which means the baby would have been conceived before Christmas, perhaps even as early as Guy Fawkes night. Sister Monica arrived in the middle of January. If it's Grace's baby he was referring to, he knew about it before Grace's parents did.'

'Maybe he's the father.' McGregor took the car key from his pocket. 'Maybe it wasn't rape after all, and Mrs Grieg was right about those house parties at St Clair's Vale. Your doctor friend should be able to confirm the timings. Why don't you ring her?'

Chapter Twelve

Suspicion is the companion of mean souls

Dr Alexander's surgery was the front room of her house – a well-kept stone affair at the west end of South Queensferry high street, opposite the old church. The front garden was a riot of colourful blooms, patches of orange chrysanthemums vying in the beds with overgrown pink hydrangeas, deadly nightshade bushes and bright yellow lilies, like spears of light. The smell of the water drifted up from the shoreline on the warm afternoon air, a heady mix of seaweed and salt mingling with a vague floral scent as Mirabelle walked up the path and knocked on the door. Talking in person almost always elicited more information than speaking on the telephone, as she'd told McGregor when she dropped him back at the flat.

'Hello,' the doctor greeted her, as she opened the door. In the background the sound of classical music floated from the study – Beethoven's Piano Concerto Number Four. A good choice, Mirabelle thought. Concertos were more to scale than symphonies. She always found the sound of a full orchestra too large for a domestic setting. The doctor had good taste.

'Are you busy, Doctor?'

'Jeanette, please. And I'm always busy.' She laughed and stood back to allow Mirabelle to enter.

The surgery was tidy, though three large half-drunk cups of tea sat at the edge of the doctor's desk. Jeanette turned down the volume on her record player and discreetly closed the file she had been reading. Mirabelle noticed that the small, open fire was stacked efficiently with wood and chunks of coal, ready to take a match. The summer in Scotland was unreliable and it was best to be ready for anything.

'Can I get you something?' the doctor offered.

Mirabelle shook her head. 'I have a couple of questions. I'm afraid they're about Grace Farquarson-Sinclair. I assume the family are your patients.'

'I can't discuss health records. I'm sorry. What I said about Sister Evangelista after the funeral might have given the wrong impression. I shouldn't have said anything.'

'I'm glad you did.'

'Was it helpful?'

'We're working on it.'

'Well, I can't tell you anything more, I'm afraid. How would you like it if your doctor told other people your private information?'

'These are specific questions. Nothing too personal, just timings. It would help immensely.'

'You mean Grace's baby?'

Mirabelle nodded.

'And you think this has something to do with what's going on at the Little Sisters of Gethsemane?'

'Potentially. Some evidence has come to light. Only an offhand comment but it merits investigation.'

Jeanette Alexander sighed. She sat at her desk and motioned for Mirabelle to take the chair opposite. 'What is it?'

'Alan, my fiancé, turned up a man who spoke to Sister Monica at Waverley station when he got off the train – before he changed into Monica. He said something odd about "She'll be long gone." He meant by the summer. By the time he'd finished at the convent.'

The doctor pulled forward one of the cups of cold tea and wrapped her fingers round it. 'What does that mean?'

'I don't know, but it tells us he thought he'd be in the convent until the summer – whatever he was doing was going to take several weeks. It also tells us that he intended to get out again. But I have no idea to whom he was referring.'

'You wondered if he meant Grace?'

'Yes.'

'When did he arrive?'

'The second week of January.'

Jeanette Alexander considered this. She brushed a strand of blonde hair over her ear. 'I didn't see Grace until February. I remember because it was Valentine's Day – the fourteenth. I thought that was ironic.'

'Did she tell you who was the father of her child?'

She shook her head. 'She didn't want to talk about it and I didn't push her. You said you were only concerned with the timing.'

'Fair enough. So, to be clear, Monica arrived a month before Grace confirmed her pregnancy. Though there is nothing to say he hadn't been there before that. In fact, if anything, it's likely. After all, he must have known about the convent before he arrived.'

'Maybe,' said the doctor. She pushed away the cup of tea. 'Besides, why would he go into the convent if it was Grace he was interested in?'

'I don't know,' Mirabelle said. 'When is Grace's baby due?'

'Next month, I think. Possibly the month after.'

'So the child was conceived . . . in October or November? Is that correct?'

'It's not an exact science.' Dr Alexander laughed. 'Especially when the mother doesn't want to tell her doctor any details about the conception.'

'And the doctor doesn't push her to,' Mirabelle added.

The doctor let this go.

'Mrs Grieg thinks that the father is one of the Farquarson-Sinclairs' house guests but I've also heard a rumour that Grace was hurt. That she was attacked by one of the workmen from the bridge.'

'I don't know who the father is, Mirabelle. There will always be a good deal of gossip in these situations. That I can tell you.'

'But Grace was upset?'

'Of course she was. An unmarried girl getting caught out like that. She's young too. She was confused and afraid. I think in the circumstances the Farquarson-Sinclairs have behaved reasonably but they might not have. I don't understand what you're getting at.'

'I'm trying to work out what he meant,' Mirabelle explained. 'If Monica said something about "she'll be long gone" to someone he met the night he arrived, who was he talking about? If I can ascertain that, presumably the woman he's referring to will be able to identify him. Do you think it might be Grace?'

'I don't know. Look, I can see the information would be useful but it's not my job to pry – actually, for a girl in Grace's situation quite the reverse. It's my job to care for her. Half the time unwanted pregnancies come about because young women don't know what to do to stop it. And then they have no idea what to expect while they're pregnant. Everything in our society is set up to punish a girl if she steps out of line and to keep her as ignorant as possible. That's the truth.'

'So when you saw Grace in February exactly what happened?'

'I confirmed she was pregnant, which she had guessed. She was having dizzy spells but I said they would most likely pass. Then I told her what was likely to happen – when she would grow bigger, what she could expect by way of symptoms. That kind of thing. Basic information.'

'But not when she was due?'

The doctor sighed. 'All right,' she said, giving way. 'She couldn't tell me exactly when she conceived. She was very vague about it.'

'So, not a rape, then? More of an ongoing relationship.'

There was something intensely practical about Dr Alexander. Now she raised her hands as if surrendering. 'I don't know. People deal with trauma in different ways. Time can concertina memory. Shame makes people forget. I didn't press her because her trust was more important than that information. I didn't know they were going to send her away – I might have had to look after her to term. I offered to speak to her parents, but she refused. Look, I have to get on,' she said, as if the shutters were coming down. 'I hope that's helped. I'm sorry, but in good conscience I can't add anything more. I've betrayed the poor girl's confidence enough as it is.'

Outside, Mirabelle stood on the street. What Jeanette Alexander had said was interesting but it wasn't conclusive. As she tarried, two women carrying shopping baskets passed her, eyeing her dress and then the car. The doctor was right about the judgements women face, she thought, as she got back in. Ahead, seagulls swooped over the firth – she could see them through the trees. It was warm today. She took her sunglasses out of her handbag and put them on before starting the ignition and trundling along the road in the direction of the bridge works. As she approached she made out a familiar figure – a woman ahead of her on the road in a red jacket, carrying a leather suitcase. Mirabelle stopped the car and got out. 'Mrs Munro!' she called, and waved, picking her way through the dried mud. Mrs Munro turned abruptly. She looked as if she was lost – an older, stranger version of Little Red Riding Hood venturing into unfamiliar territory from her Tollcross home.

'Goodness,' she said, with a glance at Mirabelle's high-heeled shoes. 'I don't know how you're managing in those, Miss Bevan.'

'Are you going to visit the convent?' Mirabelle asked.

'Not so much visiting as going to work. The bishop sent me to look after Mother Superior's office,' Mrs Munro said. 'There was some talk of dispatching a priest but I'm used to it there. They'll elect a new Mother soon enough.'

Below, on the building site, children from the caravans stopped what they were doing and pointed at the two women. Then the workmen noticed them. A wolf-whistle issued from the crowd and a few low, uncomfortable laughs. Both women ignored them. Mirabelle's eyes fell to Mrs Munro's suitcase. 'You're moving in?'

'It seemed the most sensible thing. Going backwards and forwards to town is time-consuming. Besides, the bishop wants to feel he has eyes and ears on the place after all this trouble.'

'I was thinking about what you said . . .'

'Please don't.'

'This site,' Mirabelle continued.

Mrs Munro snorted. 'Living like animals,' she said.

'Is that how people out here feel? I wondered about . . .' she gestured '. . . the neighbours?'

Mrs Munro considered this for a moment. 'Mr Farquarson-Sinclair sold land to the project. Mind you, if he hadn't it would have been bought compulsorily. The truth is the benefit of the bridge will be to Fife and Perthshire more than anybody round here.'

'And Miss MacDonald? Do you know what she thought of it?'

Mrs Munro considered again. Her powdered face looked unnatural in the sunshine. 'I think she was excited about her view. Two bridges – a red one and a silver and white. Though she'd have preferred a more traditional design, I imagine. She'll never see it now, of course. Are you looking forward to moving in?'

'Yes,' Mirabelle said, her tone more enthusiastic, she realised, than she felt.

Mirabelle did not ask how Mr Munro felt about his wife moving into a convent, albeit only for a few days. Neither did she comment that the bishop had objected to Vesta going in, as if she was some kind of spy, while now, effectively, sending a spy of his own.

'It's been such a difficult time,' Mrs Munro added. 'I want to apologise for my behaviour the other evening. I was terribly tired. It's been busy at the palace and I found the death at the convent most upsetting. I hope you can discount what I said. It was conjecture and most inappropriate.'

Mirabelle smiled. 'Of course,' she said. 'These are indeed trying times. Who do you think did it, Mrs Munro? Do you have a theory?'

The other woman pursed her lips so that the line of pome-granate seeds appeared. 'It can't be anyone in the convent,' she said. 'That's the main thing. Before Sister Monica came nobody had joined for many years. So much violence all at once. It doesn't make sense that such a thing would suddenly happen. Maybe the young man brought somebody with him – someone who followed from outside.'

Mirabelle did not say anything to counter this. It seemed a reasonable assumption that Sister Monica had known one of the nuns, but the idea that someone from outside the convent could have had murderous intent towards the novice and Mother Superior seemed unlikely. 'I suppose you might come to some understanding when you're staying there,' she said drily.

'I shall be very busy,' Mrs Munro carried on. 'I'm to complete the accounts and sort out the filing system. All work has stopped, you see, so it's an opportunity to catch up and take stock.'

Mirabelle hesitated. 'Oh, yes,' she said. 'Mother Superior mixed the salve, didn't she? She was the one with the formula.'

'I'll sort that out,' Mrs Munro replied briskly, as if she was being sent to deal with an unruly child.

'They usually elect a new mother superior before the old one dies,' Mirabelle added, thinking aloud.

'There's never been a mother superior murdered before or one who died so suddenly,' Mrs Munro confirmed. 'But the Little Sisters of Gethsemane have been an institution for more than eight hundred years. The order has survived plagues and wars and famines. I'm sure it will survive this.' She glanced back at the road. 'Well, I'd better get on,' she said, as if Mirabelle was keeping her.

'I could give you a lift,' Mirabelle offered, looking back towards the car.

'Oh, no! Not at all!' Mrs Munro made it sound as if the suggestion was an eccentric one. 'I'm fine,' she insisted.

Mirabelle watched as the bishop's secretary disappeared round a bend in the track. From the site, the sound of concrete mixers floated towards her. Beyond, to the north, there was a beautiful view. The tide was high and the water seemed endless. Even with the bridge works, it seemed such a peaceful place. She should know better by now, she thought. There was no such thing. Up the hill a man in an ill-fitting suit and a pair of long wellingtons approached the gate of the site but did not walk through.

'You all right, miss?' he asked.

'Mirabelle Bevan.' She held out her hand. He looked as if she had offered him a cold fish.

'It's a building site, miss,' he said. 'Best not to hang around.'

'I'm moving in up the road. To Shore Cottage,' Mirabelle tried.

'Heard about us, have you?'

'What do you mean?'

'I'm one of the surveyors. I know the locals aren't happy about the site. They hate the men living here like circus folk, but there aren't enough proper houses out this way and they need to be close. My lads get blamed for everything.'

'Everything?'

The man's eyes hardened. 'A boat got taken a couple of weeks ago. A farmer gets tatties nicked out of his field. The locals are annoyed cos the kids are going to school in the village and they've had to take on an extra teacher. They don't complain about the naval personnel at HMS *Lochinvar* even though they get drunk and start fights. It's always our men who get the blame. I'm sick of it.'

Mirabelle shifted from foot to foot.

'Look, I don't mean to take it out on you but what I'm saying,' he continued, 'is don't listen. Our lads work hard here and most of them are family men. I don't know why you're here, but if you've any problems, tell me. I'll sort it out.'

Mirabelle paused. 'You're asking me not to call the police,' she said flatly.

The man nodded reluctantly. 'We had them here today already. Twice. A nun got killed.'

'I know,' said Mirabelle. 'Two nuns.'

The surveyor grunted. 'Well,' he said, 'I'm asking you to move along.'

'Do you have any men here convicted of assault? Against women?'

The surveyor's eyes widened. 'Did one of the nuns get . . . hurt that way?' he asked, more gently.

'No,' Mirabelle said, thinking of Grace's pregnancy. 'I'm looking into something else. From last year.'

'And you think one of my lads attacked a woman?'

'I don't know,' said Mirabelle. That was the problem.

'If it turns out it was someone here, you won't get any resistance from me to bring charges. We don't harbour rapists or murderers,' he said with determination. 'But nobody springs to mind.'

Mirabelle turned back towards the car. If only it were that simple. 'Thanks,' she said.

She took a moment and then started the engine. It felt as if what had happened in the convent was fanning out along the track. Beyond the Church's jurisdiction. Mrs Munro had been dispatched to control matters. Mirabelle smiled. The bishop's secretary could be as determined as she liked, but if Mother Superior had taken the formula to her grave (or to the mortuary, at least), there seemed little she could do about it.

The nuns grew their own ingredients, which meant the exact formula could not be reconstructed from orders delivered. It made the telling of it more difficult. She wondered if some of the older nuns might have an idea, Sister Mary or Sister Triduana or the one who was confined to her cell – the nun who was ninety. Then she thought of McGregor always following the money, and here the livelihood of dozens of women was potentially seeping down the drain. Not that nuns were supposed to care about that kind of thing. Still, she thought, probably at least part of the income went to the diocese. Yes, that made sense. Still, it remained far more likely that the murderer was one of the nuns, no matter Mrs Munro's opinion or that the men from the site were being blamed for petty theft and disturbing the peace. Grace was another matter. In any case, she concluded, no wonder the bishop was interested enough to want someone of his own on the inside.

Chapter Thirteen

Quiet as a nun breathless with anticipation

When Vesta woke up after a couple of hours, she felt considerably better and the police were just leaving. They allowed the sisters to clean up the chapel. Vesta offered to help but the nuns wanted to perform this service for Mother Superior themselves and clearly considered it an honour. Sister Triduana dutifully filled two small flasks from the pool of Mother Superior's blood that had collected on the flagstones, while Sister Mary stood at the lectern and intoned prayers over the army of nuns with their mops and brushes and cleaning rags.

Vesta shuddered when Sister Triduana brought the blood into Mother Superior's office and put the vials in the corner cupboard. 'We may want relics,' she said reverently.

Vesta wondered if they intended to start proceedings to beatify the dead woman. As a child she had once attended Sunday service at a church in Lambeth where a skeleton studded with precious gems was encased in a bronze and glass coffin. She'd been staying with a school friend.

'Gruesome,' her mother had called it, when she got home.

Vesta's family's Sunday service was Baptist and full of music, but the memory of the skeleton stuck in her mind.

She hoped Mother Superior would be given a proper burial. She hadn't known her for long but she had seemed a woman more suited to a return to the soil than one who would want to be stripped of her flesh and kept on show. The vials of blood seemed an especially ghoulish touch – though, given she couldn't keep down much other than toast and tea, Vesta recognised it might seem different if she weren't pregnant.

'You must have had a terrible shock, Sister,' Sister Triduana said.

'Don't mind me,' Vesta reassured her. 'I can look after myself. I don't want to intrude.'

The old woman accepted this at face value and returned to the chapel.

Vesta made more toast in the convent kitchen and another cup of sweet tea and took them back to Mother's office. Nobody was interested in where she was, or what she was doing. Once the chapel was cleaned, some of the nuns started praying in a continuous rotation, the sound of which formed a rhythmic backdrop as Vesta put her cup on the desk. She opened the window a crack to let in a breath of fresh air and stared at the vegetable garden below. The sound of hens clucking wafted upwards, in a strange kind of syncopation with the prayers. It was idyllic here. The Little Sisters had been a short, sharp shock at first, but this morning when Vesta woke up, before she found Mother's body, she realised she had acclimatised. Her life in Brighton was busy. Between looking after the house, seeing to Noel and Charlie and running the business, she rarely had ten minutes to herself. Staying here had made clear how complicated her days had become and how much simpler things could be. She found she didn't miss her comfortable suburban house, with all its modern conveniences, and the endless round of choices she had to make over what to eat, what to wear and what to do. The convent's set routine reminded her of childhood – a time of simpler expectations. She wondered if Sister Monica had found herself seduced by that as well. If Vesta hadn't found Mother Superior's bloodied body, she would have considered her stay here enlightening.

Vesta bit into the toast with a satisfying crunch. She no longer felt sick if she didn't think about more complicated food than she could stomach. However, with the manufactory closed and the sisters engaged in prayer, her investigation had more or less ground to a halt. As she licked the vestiges of butter from her fingers she began to search the office. So far, beyond the four sisters who had objected to Sister Monica's burial, there had been no indication of anything of interest: only some accounts and several letters from the mother superiors of other convents. It pleased Vesta that these women living in isolation around the world were in correspondence, sending parcels and sharing ideas. She hadn't been confident of her cover when she arrived, but now she saw it made perfect sense. Of course a nunnery hoping to start a commercial concern would send a representative to another nunnery already engaged in one.

She fingered the petition on top of Mother Superior's pile of papers and once more noted the names of the nuns who had signed it. Then she caught sight of a movement through the office's open door and out of the hallway window beyond. A smart woman wearing a well-cut cream coat and a chic mauve hat was picking her way across the cobblestones towards the chapel. At first, the woman reminded her of Mirabelle, but she was taller and paler. Vesta got up and trotted down the stairs, emerging into the courtyard just as the woman reached the chapel door.

'Excuse me,' she called. 'Can I help you?'

The woman turned. 'Who on earth are you?'

Vesta paused. Here she was, dressed in a nun's habit in a convent, and a woman who looked like she ought to be attending Ascot was questioning her presence.

'I'm Sister Joseph,' she said, and held out her hand.

The woman sighed. 'I can't keep up. Are you from one of the foreign missions?'

'No,' Vesta said wearily. 'I'm from Bermondsey.'

The woman looked confused.

'London,' Vesta elucidated.

'Well, what are you doing here?'

'I'm a nun. In a convent,' Vesta replied. 'What are you doing here?'

The woman drew herself up. 'I'm Belinda Farquarson-Sinclair. I live at St Clair's Vale.'

'St Clair's Vale?' Vesta queried.

'I'm a neighbour. This is our parish church near enough. I've come to pray.'

Mrs Farquarson-Sinclair could not have looked less like she intended to pray and Vesta was about to say something discouraging when Sister Mary emerged from the chapel.

'Belinda!' she exclaimed, and flung her arms around the woman's frame before collecting herself. 'It's been a long time,' she added.

'I thought I ought to come,' the woman said. 'I nipped through the back gate. It seemed right to light a candle or something . . . under the circumstances.'

'You should. Of course.' Sister Mary stepped aside to usher her through the chapel's door.

'Can I help you?' the old nun asked Vesta, once they were alone.

'I didn't know if Mrs Farquarson-Sinclair ought to be here. I came down when I spotted her.'

'Oh, Belinda used to come to us as a little girl,' Sister Mary said. 'For religious instruction. She married her cousin and they live nearby. She's not devout, really. I've hardly seen her in years, but the Sinclairs go back a long way with the convent.'

'Really?'

'Mother taught her her first Latin,' she said nostalgically. 'I don't suppose that happens so much in urban orders,' she added sadly, as if the Poor Clares of Bermondsey were disadvantaged by the hubbub of city life and a lack of intimacy with the hoi polloi.

'I don't suppose it does,' Vesta agreed. 'Well, I'm just working in Mother Superior's office, looking at how your shipments are placed.'

'Of course,' Sister Mary said.

Vesta took a breath. 'You know, I couldn't help noticing that you had petitioned Mother about poor Sister Monica's burial. It was on her desk.'

Sister Mary's eyes flashed. 'Not you as well,' she snapped.

'I'm sorry. What do you mean?'

Sister Mary was clearly struggling to control her temper. 'That woman asked me about it too. The clothes horse moving into Miss MacDonald's house. The one living in sin with the policeman.'

'Mirabelle Bevan?' Vesta tried not to smile. 'What did she want to know?'

'As if any of us would murder anyone. I disapprove of burying a man among us, that's all.'

Vesta noticed Sister Mary had used the present tense. She clearly still disapproved of Sister Monica's interment. 'I can't blame you,' Vesta said. 'You weren't the only nun to sign it.'

'Yes. Four of us. We are the older sisters so I suppose we're the most traditional, though you might argue we ought to be the ones best schooled in acceptance. I wish we hadn't sent the stupid thing. It didn't make any difference. Now the police clearly believe that Sister Monica's death had something to do with poor Mother. It's a travesty.'

Vesta waited a moment. 'Well, two deaths in not many more days. It does seem—'

'Mother Superior had nothing to do with Sister Monica,' Sister Mary burst out. 'She would not have involved herself in any kind of subterfuge. It's just not possible. Some madman breaks in and takes her life, and because of that miscreant, it makes it look as if . . .' The old woman started to cry.

Vesta reached out and hugged her. 'Please,' she said. 'I'm sure the police will get to the bottom of it.'

Sister Mary sniffed. 'Well,' she said, drawing a large, crumpled white handkerchief from her pocket and blowing her nose loudly, 'I certainly hope so. But if they try to cast aspersions on Mother, then they will have us to deal with, the Church too. That much I can tell you, Sister.'

'Of course.' Vesta squeezed the older woman's hand. 'Look, I'll just keep out of the way. I have a good deal of office experience, you know. Why don't I organise Mother Superior's desk so it'll be ready for whoever takes over?'

Sister Mary nodded. 'That would be helpful.'

She was turning to go back upstairs as the sound of the bell ringing at the gate reached them. The nuns moved together down the path and Vesta manhandled the heavy bar as Sister Mary opened the door. The old nun's face took on a serene expression. There was Mrs Munro in her red Burberry raincoat, clutching a large, battered leather case.

'Ah, Sister Mary. And you must be Sister Joseph,' she hailed

153

Vesta, as she stepped over the threshold. 'The bishop sent me,' she announced proudly.

'Mrs Munro. Nice to see you again,' Sister Mary said. Vesta thought the nun didn't sound at all welcoming. She was nowhere near as delighted to see the bishop's secretary as she had been to see Belinda Farquarson-Sinclair.

'Terrible times,' Mrs Munro added, seemingly not noticing Sister Mary's frosty tone as she bustled over the threshold. 'I'm here to look after Mother's office. The bishop thought it would be helpful.'

Sister Mary looked from Mrs Munro to Vesta and back again as Vesta replaced the bar on the gate.

'Sister Joseph can show you,' she said curtly. 'She has a good deal of office experience. I must go back,' she added, glancing up the path towards the chapel.

'It's such a lovely sound, the sound of prayer, isn't it?' said Mrs Munro.'

'Lovely,' Vesta replied. 'If you'll just follow me.'

Upstairs in the office, Mrs Munro glanced disapprovingly at the remains of Vesta's toast, which sat at the head of a small trail of crumbs that led to the chair where she had been sitting.

'May I fetch you a cup of tea, Mrs Munro?' Vesta offered.

'Yes, Sister,' Mrs Munro chimed. 'That would be lovely. Just milk for me.'

Vesta picked up her cup and plate. She walked back down to the kitchen and put the kettle on to boil as she helped herself to a slice of bread this time, with a thin smear of jam. When the water boiled she made a fresh pot, put two cups on a tray and went back up to the office. Mrs Munro had installed herself behind the desk, in Mother's chair. She was reading a file that Vesta knew contained correspondence with the electricity board. The papers in front of her, however, had been moved. Vesta put down the tea.

'Thank you,' Mrs Munro said.

'It's a bit of a mess,' Vesta replied, as she flicked absent-mindedly through what had been left on the desk.

'I'll whip it into shape in no time,' Mrs Munro said cheerfully.

Vesta stopped as she leafed through the scatter of papers a second time. No, she thought, it definitely wasn't there. But it had been. The vellum with the nun's petition about the burial had gone.

'Can I help?' she offered. 'I can do accounts and I've refiled the whole of our office at the Poor Clares. I didn't know Mother Superior myself, you see, so I'm not exactly bereaved and I'd like to be helpful.'

'Not at all,' Mrs Munro said. 'It's kind of you, Sister Joseph, but I'll get to grips with this lot. That's why the bishop sent me.'

Yes, Vesta thought, but how much of it will still be here by the time you've finished? Still, there wasn't much she could do if Mrs Munro was insistent.

'All right,' she said, 'I'm here if you need me.' She picked up her cup and slipped out of the room.

Outside, Belinda Farquarson-Sinclair was coming out of the chapel.

'Ah, Sister,' she said, as if Vesta had been summoned at her command. 'I'd like to make a donation in honour of Mother Superior's death. I thought something to go to the African missions. Something to benefit women, if that's possible. Would a hundred pounds cover it?'

'That's tremendously generous . . .' Vesta started. She was about to add that she wasn't involved in the African missions

155

but Belinda had whipped a cheque book and gold fountain pen out of her handbag and was already writing. 'I'll make it out to the Poor Clares, shall I?'

'I'll see it gets to the right place,' Vesta replied, thinking that this woman did not appear the least bereaved. If anything, she seemed quite cheery.

Mrs Farquarson-Sinclair tore off the cheque and waved it in the air so the ink would dry. She looked as if she was waving a flag at a festival. Then she presented it to Vesta with some reverence. 'I think the work you're doing is just marvellous,' she said. 'The poor little Black babies.'

Chapter Fourteen

That which appears white is really black
if the Church so decides

The next morning, having elicited very little from Vesta, who had taken her usual call with Mrs Munro at her shoulder, Mirabelle decided to return to the Bishop's Palace to dig over old ground. Two little boys of about ten years of age on blue bicycles were racing round the pocket park across from the open palace gate when she arrived. Mirabelle's taxi driver rolled down his window and shouted at them to keep out of the way and they disappeared up Greenhill Road, like flashes of sunlight, dodging between the shadows of overhanging trees. Mirabelle tipped the driver and walked up the driveway, checking her reflection in the glass around the door before ringing the bell. In due course, a young cleric answered and peered at her through tortoiseshell spectacles, clasping his hands in front of him, as if in prayer.

'Yes?' he said, an Italian accent immediately apparent.

'I'm Mirabelle Bevan,' she announced. 'I'd like to see the bishop.'

'The bishop is busy,' the priest said dismissively, his accent even stronger.

'He'll want to see me,' Mirabelle said with confidence. 'It's about the Little Sisters of Gethsemane.'

The priest showed her into the library and disappeared. A warm slice of golden sunlight cut into the room through the long window. It was the same shape, Mirabelle thought, as the light that had fallen onto the floor of Sister Monica's simple cell on the first day of her investigation, but the decorations at the palace were far more ornate. Mirabelle stared at the portraits and tried to remember each man's name. When the bishop arrived he greeted her with a cheery 'Good morning, Miss Bevan,' and the priest followed him with a tray of coffee. 'We drink it rather strong,' the bishop apologised. 'It's a habit I picked up on my travels. I hope you don't mind.'

'Not at all,' Mirabelle assured him.

'Sugar?'

'No, thank you.'

The bishop added three lumps to his own small cup. 'In the Middle East they always add sugar,' he said. 'There's a little place in Jerusalem that's run by an Arab – a Muslim, actually – and his coffee . . .' he motioned to signify its excellence. 'He used to serve it with roasted peanuts whereas we only have shortbread, I'm afraid.' Mirabelle took a finger from the plate.

'That will be all.' The bishop dismissed the priest, who bowed formally and left.

'Well,' he said, settling into his seat with anticipation, as if Mirabelle had arrived at the palace with rare gossip, 'I'm glad the police have left the convent. Their presence was distressing the sisters. What have you come to tell me?'

Mirabelle took a sip of the coffee. It was, as the bishop had intimated, extremely good. 'I'm not here to tell you anything. I'm here to ask.'

'I see. What would you like to know?'

'First, why have you sent Mrs Munro to the convent?'

'Rose? She's there to look after Mother Superior's office.'

Mirabelle put down her cup. 'If you aren't frank with me, it's going to make things more difficult. You aren't concerned about whether the convent's invoices are in order. Are you?'

'No.' The bishop did not add anything to his admission.

Mirabelle waited. 'It would also be helpful to know more about Grace Farquarson-Sinclair,' she tried again.

'Really?'

'Have you ever met her?'

'Yes. The family are not devout but they are traditional. They admit Our Lord at Christmas and attend my private carol service here.'

'Miss Farquarson-Sinclair's condition must have been a disappointment.'

'There are few families in which a sixteen-year-old unmarried girl being with child would not be a disappointment, Miss Bevan.'

'Do you have any idea who the father is?'

'That doesn't matter. Grace will give birth in Italy and the child will go to a good Christian home. The girl will be able to make a decent marriage in time. I don't see what this can possibly have to do with either Sister Monica's death or Mother Superior's murder. You have no need to concern yourself with Grace or her baby. All will be well. There are plenty of married ladies who can't have children, especially among those who leave it late in life to take their marriage vows.' He eyed Mirabelle as if to intimate that this might be her situation.

Mirabelle ignored the implication. 'It isn't helping that there are no records of the nuns' lives before they took their vows,' she said.

'That is the point of the cloistered life, Miss Bevan. The world does not follow a nun when she devotes herself to God. It is a fresh start. A rebirth.'

'It makes the convent an excellent hiding place. What do you think Sister Monica was doing there?'

'That's why we enlisted your help. If I knew . . .'

Mirabelle sighed. 'I shall tell you what I think.'

'Please do,' said the bishop.

'First, Rose Munro has been sent to secure the formula for Gethsemane Salve. Institutions like the Little Sisters or, for that matter, your diocese are generally excellent at preserving their interests. It makes no sense that the formula for a product as profitable as the salve would be held by one person – especially given the precarious position of nunneries over the centuries.'

'Precarious?'

'Not in more recent history, I grant you, but plenty of nuns have been slaughtered in past times. The formula is in the convent somewhere and my guess is that Mrs Munro has been tasked with finding it.'

The bishop put down his cup and made an arch of his fingers. He nodded. 'All right,' he said.

'Does the diocese take a cut of the salve's profits?'

'It's called a tithe.'

'And that's your interest in the convent?'

'My interest is in the sisters doing God's will, Miss Bevan. And in their welfare.'

'How much is your tithe worth?'

The bishop sighed. 'The salve is profitable, I'll give you that. The sisters are not a mendicant order. They are of the world in that respect and have not taken a vow of poverty, though individually they own no property. They support many charitable endeavours with the money they make. They do good.'

'And they support you too.'

Mirabelle waited again but the bishop was not somebody who felt he had to fill in awkward silences. She decided to push on.

'Second,' she said. 'I don't know whether Grace Farquarson-Sinclair's pregnancy is connected to Sister Monica's arrival at the nunnery. But it might be. What I do know is that after what one assumes has been decades if not centuries of life at the convent, and the surrounding area, being extremely stable, there is suddenly a rash of activity. Of violence.'

The bishop nodded again. 'That's certainly true. The last uproar at the Vale was before the new house was built, when the Sinclairs lost their sons at Culloden.'

'When was that?'

'1746. The lands and titles went to a cousin of the main line. Rather in the way it has with your fiancé and the Robertson inheritance.'

'Two hundred years ago,' Mirabelle said.

'It's a long time . . . and no time at all. It depends whether one is mortal or, as you have already pointed out, whether it is a concern. An institution, you called it, did you not?'

'Do you know if any of the nuns has a past that they ran away from?'

The bishop smirked. 'They're nuns not saints, Miss Bevan. I imagine many of them joined the order to escape the world, one way or another.'

'Did Miss MacDonald?'

The smirk widened into a smile. 'Ah – the previous occupant of your holiday home? She was an extraordinary woman, difficult but admirable. She was probably one of the most independent people I have ever come across and I include ascetics in that consideration. Hermits.'

'Belinda Farquarson-Sinclair called her Bang Bang.'

The bishop let out a laugh that sounded like a yelp. 'I heard they called her that. It means they were fond of her, I suppose. Giving her a nickname.'

'Why didn't she stick with her vows?'

'The cloistered life is not for everybody. I myself would not like to be part of a closed community.'

Mirabelle's face betrayed her surprise.

'There is a difference between being a priest and a monk. I am part of the world in a different way, Miss Bevan. We all have our calling.'

'When Miss MacDonald decided to live at Shore Cottage, she didn't go far, did she?'

'I suppose not. It was in her family. It's a lovely house in a good situation. That's what attracts you to reside there, does it not? I also understand that, while she was not in orders, Miss MacDonald remained devout.'

'She attended the nuns' chapel. She was fond of Christmas, too, by her housekeeper's account.'

'Well, there you are.'

'Why did you engage me for this task?'

'I didn't. Mother Superior engaged you. In fact, as I understand it, she intended to engage your fiancé.'

Mirabelle leaned forward. 'The nuns will choose a new mother superior next week from two candidates that you will nominate. Who will you pick?'

The bishop nodded. 'It is a concern, I grant you. And not one I was prepared for. The outgoing mother superior was relatively young. I had not anticipated her death would precede my own.'

'Her murder,' Mirabelle corrected him.

'How is your friend getting along?' the bishop asked, changing the subject. 'Vesta, isn't it?'

'She found Mother's body. She was the one who called the police.'

'I didn't know that. Is she all right?'

'She was extremely upset but she has agreed to stay at the convent for the time being.'

'That's brave,' the bishop commented. He paused. 'I haven't yet decided which nuns would be best suited to the situation of Mother Superior,' he admitted. 'But I have been considering it.'

'Sister Mary?'

'Perhaps. She is an able woman though, to my mind, somewhat inflexible. You think I'm up to something, Miss Bevan? I am an old man and it has been a long time since my actions have given anybody cause for suspicion. But, then, I suspect you are someone who is always looking for ulterior motives.'

'Only because I so often find that people have them.'

'Beware of that. It may be helpful in some situations, I grant you, but never, I should think, in a marriage.' He got to his feet. 'If you'll excuse me, I hope you find out what Sister Monica was doing at the convent. I would very much like to know. Now I have business to attend.'

Mirabelle sat back, frustrated, as he left the room and the Italian priest returned, silently escorting her to the door. There was little chance of hailing a taxi there in the suburbs, so she began to walk towards Bruntsfield Place. At the top of Greenhill Gardens the links opened before her and the castle came into view. Edinburgh was such a scenic city – you never could tell what vista would arise round the next corner or over the crest of a hill. Up till now she had enjoyed living in Scotland because it was so different from her life in Brighton, though now here she was on the trail of a murderer once more and this case was a tough nut to crack. 'It's one of the nuns,' she whispered under her breath. 'It has to be.' But she wasn't sure of it.

She shuddered, despite the warm sunshine, remembering that she had agreed to get married in the chapel in only a few days. It didn't seem right to take vows at the site of such a violent murder. As she strode across the links in the direction of the Meadows, she remembered that she had yet to buy her wedding dress and see to the flowers. It felt almost surreal in the face of these deaths – making a vow to a joint life and moving into Bang Bang MacDonald's old house, without understanding what had happened. Was she becoming sentimental? Or superstitious? Perhaps that always happened to brides. 'I'll put a sprig of rosemary in my bouquet,' she decided, thinking of Sister Monica's grave and wondering who wanted to remember the novice so much they had buried a herb of remembrance in the soil. Yes, she decided, there was that to work out as well.

Chapter Fifteen

The envious die not once, but oft

Back at the flat on Heriot Row, as Mirabelle let herself in she was surprised to hear a woman's laughter coming from the drawing room. She removed her hat and gloves and opened the door. Inside, McGregor was sitting on one of the comfortable chairs opposite an attractive blonde in her late twenties. They were sipping from crystal glasses each furnished with a golden pool of whisky. The blonde was dressed in a well-tailored, baby blue mohair suit, short-sleeved with a small diamond pin on the collar, which, surprisingly, she had paired with cream leather shoes that had rather too sensible a heel, in Mirabelle's view, and a heavy gold signet ring on her smallest finger that must have been made for a man.

'Ah. Darling. This is Wendy.'

Wendy stood up and offered Mirabelle her hand. 'Wendy Lamont,' she introduced herself.

'We met at the clubhouse,' McGregor added. 'Wendy's the women's champion. She has the best follow-through I've ever seen.'

'You're a golfer,' Mirabelle deduced, her tone surprisingly frosty. It had been a trying day. She hadn't had anything to eat apart from the bishop's shortbread and now it was long past lunchtime. She had hoped to hail a cab on Melville Drive but nothing had passed, and eventually she had decided to walk home in the hope that this would jog some kind of breakthrough in the case as she thought things through, but the nuns' murderer continued to be elusive.

'Isn't everyone a golfer in Edinburgh?' Wendy said lightly. 'It's just glorious at this time of year up on the hill. The view of the city is marvellous. Alan said I might be able to help, Miss Bevan.'

McGregor held up the decanter of whisky and Mirabelle shook her head. 'Help?' she repeated. 'I could certainly use some of that. I've been thinking about the physical strength required to almost decapitate somebody and it is quite considerable. Sheer fury will take you so far, of course, but you need strength too.'

Wendy's eyes widened. 'What?' she said.

McGregor's mouth widened into a grin. He poured Mirabelle a whisky despite her protestation. 'You obviously need this,' he said, handing her the glass. 'I asked Wendy to help because she's a fashion writer, Mirabelle.'

'I have a column in the *Scotsman*,' Wendy added. 'And sometimes *Country Life*.'

'You need a gown. For the wedding,' McGregor reminded her gently. 'Mirabelle is working on a case. A murder,' he tried to explain. 'She gets terribly distracted when she has a case on her hands. You'll have to excuse her.'

'Gosh,' Wendy said, sounding relieved. 'It's not often they put a woman on the crime desk. Which paper are you working for?'

Mirabelle sipped the whisky. The taste of peat and dried fruit opened in her mouth, providing some refreshment.

'I don't write about crime. It's not really a job – more of a hobby, really,' she admitted, and McGregor let slip a laugh.

'A hobby,' Wendy repeated, averting her gaze, which now moved from the chipped ceiling rose towards the door and escape.

'Mirabelle is a private detective,' McGregor explained. 'I used to be a policeman. She's helping the constabulary with a case.'

Wendy's eyes were now glued to her glass. She swirled the whisky round it. 'Gosh,' she said, sounding relieved. 'That's exciting.'

'Two women are dead.' Mirabelle's tone continued frosty. 'It's not that I had forgotten about buying a dress for the wedding, it just didn't seem important,' she added.

'Well, you will definitely need a dress for the day, won't you? Important or not,' McGregor said. 'I was trying to help.'

'It's good you want to help. I was beginning to think all you cared about was golf,' Mirabelle snapped cattily.

'That's not fair!'

Wendy put down her drink on the leather-bound side table. 'I'm sorry,' she said. 'I didn't mean to intrude. I'd better go.'

'You aren't intruding,' McGregor insisted.

Mirabelle suddenly regretted what she'd said. 'Please don't go.' She added her voice to McGregor's. 'The truth is it's been a lot of pressure. It's a terrible case – a horrible murder. And I was supposed to shop for the dress with a friend but she can't just now.'

'She can't because you roped her into this mess, Mirabelle,' McGregor added. 'You sequestered her.'

'Yes. It's rather taken over,' Mirabelle admitted. 'Then I came home and you were here and, well, you're rather attractive.'

Wendy's stare softened into a cheeky grin. 'He's a dish, your fiancé,' she said. 'But he's not my type. I promise. My cousin got married last year and she was an absolute nightmare. She turned into a grumpy grouse for three whole months and she's a darling, really. Impending matrimony puts a gal under a lot of pressure.' She checked her dainty gold wristwatch. 'Time is marching on. It's almost three. I know a little boutique in Thistle Street. If we go now they'll definitely fit us in.'

'Yes,' said McGregor. 'You're supposed to be enjoying this, Mirabelle. Go on.'

Thistle Street was so narrow it remained in shadow even on the sunniest summer day. The women rounded the corner and Wendy removed her sunglasses, propping them on her head as they strode through the shade along the thin pavement. Being out in the real world without the weight of responsibility for anyone's murder almost felt like a relief, Mirabelle thought, even if it was only momentary. At the far end of the block a group of children were playing tag, squealing as they chased each other onto Thistle Street Lane and then back into the street.

About halfway along, Wendy rang a bell and a young girl opened the door. She was dressed in a brown linen shift with pins stuck through the collar. 'Good afternoon, Grazyna,' Wendy said. 'Is Katja in?'

The girl stepped back, and Mirabelle and Wendy entered a small entrance area painted pale grey. Two smart antique chairs freshly upholstered in matching steel grey fabric were placed against the wall over which there was a painting of an orchid. The girl disappeared through another door and Wendy took a seat. 'Katja is from Poland. Her husband was in the air force during the war. That's how she ended up here. She's the best seamstress in the country, in my view. You didn't want off the peg, did you?'

Mirabelle sat down in the second chair. 'I don't mind off the peg or on it but I don't want white. Or cream,' she said decisively.

'Certainly not. A lady of your experience,' Wendy replied, with a glint in her eye.

Mirabelle smiled. It was nice to be here but, still, it didn't seem right shopping without Vesta, though McGregor had a point, she supposed, and she was warming to Wendy.

'You have a good figure,' the girl added. 'Dream model, really. What did you have in mind?'

'Chiffon, I think,' Mirabelle said. 'But nothing too sweet, if you know what I mean. As you say, I'm past forty. How old are you, if you don't mind me asking?'

'I'm twenty-eight.'

'You seem . . . mature for your age.'

Wendy laughed. 'I don't know if I'm mature. This is the oldest I've ever been. I suppose we'll have to see what happens.' She paused. 'Taupe is chic and you can accessorise it so many ways – pale pink if you want to go that way, and it is summertime, or black if you want to look more . . . sombre. Or French.'

'My grandmother was French. From Paris.'

'I can see that in your bone structure.'

The door to the rear opened and an older woman joined them. 'Miss Lamont,' she greeted Wendy reverently.

'Katja, this is Miss Bevan. She's getting married and she needs a non-wedding dress.'

Katja cocked her head. She motioned for Mirabelle to rise and examined her as if taking her measurements by eye.

'Chiffon, we thought. A mid-taupe with lots of ruching. A boat neck – would that be right?' Wendy continued. 'Something along the lines of Maggy Rouff or one of the other Parisian designers with a small atelier. We're looking for chic, you understand. Three-quarter length?'

Mirabelle nodded. Rouff was one of her favourite labels. She never wore Chanel, these days, because of what Coco had done during the war. She couldn't understand how people had forgotten about it so easily. 'Exactly. Rouff,' she agreed. 'Not Chanel.'

Katja wrinkled her nose. 'I can't bear that scent,' she said. 'It stinks of collaboration.'

'Quite,' Mirabelle agreed. 'I usually wear Yardley. You know where you are.'

She could see the dress now in her mind's eye – a luxurious design worn with long kid gloves, and extremely high heels. Perhaps she would take Wendy's advice and accessorise in black.

'I'm afraid we have a rush on. We need it in a week.' Wendy gave an apologetic grin and the Polish seamstress froze. 'Mr McGregor, Miss Bevan's fiancé, says he's happy to pay if you need extra help so it'll be ready in time.'

Katja paused, taking all this in. 'Come!' she announced, as if this was a challenge and she was accepting it.

The women followed her into the back room where Grazyna and another young woman were sitting at a bench stitching next to the window. A radio was playing music but the volume was so low it sounded almost as if the tune was coming from another room, somewhere far off. Grazyna jumped to her feet and took Mirabelle's jacket while Katja produced a measuring tape and, without writing anything down, wound it round Mirabelle's bust, her waist, then her hips, and moved on to taking the vertical measurements for the bodice and the hem. Wendy lit a cigarette and leaned against the wall, next to a long, gilt-framed mirror. 'Silk chiffon,' she said. 'Of course. And an underskirt. You might want to use a little satin. I mean, I don't need to tell you, do I?'

Katja didn't confirm or deny anything. She was engrossed in what she was doing. Mirabelle thought, as the seamstress moved her arm this way and that, that she'd never been measured so thoroughly. 'I had thought of a veil,' she said. 'We're having a blessing in a chapel and . . .'

'No,' Wendy said firmly, as if she was speaking to a small dog. 'Flowers in the hair will be much better. I know a chap.'

At the window the third woman nicked her finger and went to wash her hands at the free-standing enamel sink. She took a tin of Gethsemane Salve from the shelf and efficiently dabbed it on the wound.

'Ah, you use the nuns' medicine,' Mirabelle commented.

Katja looked up from her measuring. 'It is very good,' she said. 'It's the marigold. You can smell it. Excellent for the skin. We have this in Poland.'

'Marigold,' Mirabelle repeated. She hadn't noticed. 'Gosh, I thought it smelt more of lavender.'

'Yes. Lavender,' Katja agreed. 'To cover the smell of the marigold. The sisters are wise, no? Marigold smells . . .' She made a face, the necessary vocabulary deserting her.

Mirabelle smiled. Mother Superior's secret was not so secret, it seemed, though there must be other ingredients too.

Outside, Wendy kissed Mirabelle's cheek and Mirabelle thanked her.

'Will you come back to Heriot Row for a drink?'

'It's not like me to turn down a drink but I have to change for dinner,' the girl said, and checked her watch. 'You learn to drink a lot, you know, on the fashion desk. I'd best get going. We're starting early tonight.'

'A date?'

'A friend.'

'I'm sorry I was . . . grumpy,' Mirabelle apologised.

'Let me know when your fitting is arranged and I'll come along, if you like,' Wendy offered. 'You have shoes, don't you? Or do you want something new?'

Mirabelle grinned. 'Oh, don't worry. I have shoes.'

As she walked back down the hill in the afternoon sunshine Mirabelle felt suddenly sad. She and Vesta would have had more fun choosing her dress, but it wasn't only that. The deaths at the Little Sisters had consumed her, like every other case had during the course of her career. Her fascination with murder separated her from the people around her, even McGregor. In less than a week she would be taking her marriage vows and she had felt jealous just because a younger woman was sitting in the drawing room. She had snapped at her fiancé rather than trusting him. She'd have hoped and expected she'd behave better than that.

'It's the case,' she muttered, trying to excuse herself. She could hardly have turned it down. Two people had died after all. So she had forgone the fun of arranging the wedding and planning changes to the interior of Shore Cottage. And now Shore Cottage felt dismal. As if it was involved in all this: as if it was tainted. She wished momentarily that she and Vesta were walking along the front at Portobello. She missed the sea, not seeing it in the distance as she did in town here but it being close enough for her to hear the waves breaking on the shore, like she could from the long windows of her flat on the front in Brighton. She steeled herself. Solving cases was a compulsion – an ongoing one that got in the way of her living a normal life. A happier one. She would apologise to McGregor, she decided. She'd make it up to him.

Back at Heriot Row, however, she heard a man's voice in the drawing room as she closed the front door. The tone was not McGregor's. She collected herself before breezing in this time.

'Hello, darling,' McGregor said. 'You remember Inspector Rennie, don't you?'

The inspector got to his feet. 'Miss Bevan.' He gave a small nod. 'It's a beautiful place you have here.'

Mirabelle did not comment. The flat was grand but old-fashioned.

'Do you live in town, Inspector?' McGregor asked.

Rennie smiled. 'I stay at Marchmont. A few of the detectives live in tenement flats on that side of town. Unmarried men. It feels like a cliché, bachelors ordering a pie in the pub or fish and chips for dinner, but it's handy for Torphichen Street and we congregate in Bennett's after work, halfway home.'

'It's a good boozer,' McGregor said, and turned his attention to his fiancée. 'Did you get fixed up?'

Mirabelle poured herself a tonic from the drinks tray. 'I went to get fitted for my wedding dress,' she explained. 'How's the case coming along?'

Rennie shrugged. 'We can't get anything out of the nuns,' he admitted.

'Yes. Tricky.' Mirabelle wasn't sure what else to say. She had also tried and failed. So far.

'There's something almost hysterical about the nunnery. Like *The Devils of Loudon*,' Rennie added.

'What?'

'It's a novel by Aldous Huxley,' the inspector continued apologetically. 'It's set in a French convent and the nuns go mad. As if they're possessed. It's a thing, isn't it, mad nuns, like that film, *Black Narcissus*? But at the Little Sisters it's just the opposite. They're too controlled. Not in their grief – several were crying after Mother Superior's body was discovered – but more in how they talk about their lives. You'd think they'd want to find the killer but they won't tell us anything. I can't decide if they know something they aren't saying or if they have no idea and don't want to think about it. I've been a Huxley fan since I was a kid,' he admitted apologetically. '*Brave New World*. I know they're only novels but I thought the stories might help me understand them. I was wrong.'

Mirabelle smiled. Rennie was unexpected. It seemed the taste exhibited in his well-cut suit extended to the reading of books. It was a pursuit in which most policemen did not indulge. She checked her snobbishness – there was no reason his accent would preclude him from an interest in the arts. She would never have thought that way in Brighton, but here in Edinburgh the neighbours along Heriot Row were judgemental, to put it mildly. And Superintendent Scott too, she remembered. Saying that Rennie was from Glasgow as if that might sum him up. She mustn't let that kind of thing rub off on her.

'I'm sure the nuns won't talk to you because they think of their silence as loyalty,' she said.

'Maybe. So you think they know something?'

'They must. I can't see how they wouldn't – even if they don't know what it means. They've been there hiding from the world for ages and suddenly it bursts in on them – all the wickedness there is.'

'We're focusing on finding the identity of the young man,' Rennie continued earnestly.

'Monica?'

He nodded. 'Aye,' he said. 'Monica. That's got to have something to do with this whole business. But there's precious little to go on. We're coordinating with Scotland Yard. They're working through records of missing men of the same age from the London area but so far we haven't found a match.'

'If you've people to throw at it I have an idea or two,' McGregor offered.

'Go on.'

'Mirabelle and I tracked down the porter who helped Monica when they arrived. The fellow came up from London on the evening train but didn't get to the Little Sisters until lunchtime the following day.'

'Oh, yes,' Mirabelle said, her brain running ahead. Mother Superior's murder hadn't pushed Sister Monica out of her mind exactly, but the violent nature of what had happened meant the novice's death had taken second place. Now she focused. Rennie was right. Of course he was. Sister Monica's murder had been first so if they could find her or his identity, and what she or he had been doing there, it might be the key to what had happened to Mother. McGregor motioned her to continue. 'So where did Sister Monica stay that night?' she reasoned. 'That merits investigation. We ought to have thought of it.'

'January the thirteenth,' McGregor added. 'If we can find out where he stayed, we can also check shops nearby. I assume he brought with him the clothes to become Sister Monica but you never know – perhaps he forgot something and needed to buy it. Stockings. Lipstick. Something like that. And that brings us to the next question.'

'What?' Rennie asked.

'He had to change somewhere. Checking into a hotel as a man and checking out as a woman would be bound to get him noticed. It would be risky though not unheard of to use a public toilet for the same reason. It's possible that he might have known somebody in the city, stayed with them, and if he did that, it means they know who he is but not necessarily that he's dead. In the circumstances that person might want to come forward, don't you think?'

'That means going public,' Rennie mused.

'Is that a problem?' McGregor asked.

'The bishop,' Rennie said grimly. 'He's been on to the super several times. He wants everything to be done as discreetly as possible.'

Mirabelle thought for a moment. Light dawned. 'Monica didn't know anyone here. She couldn't have. Not someone she could have stayed with anyway or she'd have left the bag there rather than taking the locker, don't you think?'

'You're right,' McGregor said. 'Of course he would.'

'And there's another thing that's been on my mind,' she continued.

'What's that?'

'What happened to the clothes? They must be somewhere. She didn't leave them with the briefcase. But when Monica put the case into the locker at Waverley he was dressed as a man and the next thing we know he turns up at the Little Sisters as a woman. What happened to the male clothes? Presumably she was aware the female clothes would be given to the poor. So what did she intend to wear when she left the convent and came back for the briefcase? How would he become a man again when he'd achieved whatever he went into the convent to do?'

'Perhaps he didn't think that far ahead,' Rennie said. 'You'd be surprised how many criminals do things that are completely illogical. Maybe he threw the clothes away to get rid of them. On the spur of the moment.'

Mirabelle shook her head. 'It was thought through. It must have been. For this kind of deception to be successful, it couldn't have happened without thorough planning. Monica secreted a razor in the nunnery. He left his briefcase because he knew he'd be coming back. The male clothes are somewhere. They must be.'

Rennie finished his drink. 'You're very good,' he said to Mirabelle.

McGregor raised his eyes. 'Oh, she's only starting. It'll drive you crazy, trust me.'

Mirabelle ignored this comment.

'I'll start the men on hotels and guesthouses – near Waverley to begin with,' Rennie said, getting to his feet. 'Thank you, Miss Bevan.'

McGregor saw him to the door. When he came back into the drawing room Mirabelle was at the window, looking down on the inspector as he made for his car.

'I'm sorry about what happened earlier,' she said. 'It's not that murder used to bother me less, but more recently . . . it seems particularly senseless.'

'It's since Eleanor died last year,' McGregor said, winding his arm round Mirabelle's waist and nuzzling her neck. 'I feel that way too. It's just not a job I want any more. I want you all to myself, now it's only the two of us.'

She considered this. Maybe he was right. 'I felt so jealous suddenly, Alan.'

'It's a compliment. And unusual of you to miss something so obvious.'

'What do you mean?'

'Wendy Lamont is a dyke, Belle. Not, I'll grant you, one walking round in men's clothes, smoking cigars, but she has no interest in me. Couldn't you tell? She lit up when you walked in. I'm the one who ought to be jealous.'

'Oh,' Mirabelle said, and the word sounded almost like a question.

'You're the only woman who matters,' McGregor said, kissing her neck. 'I thought you knew that. I think I'd better prove it, don't you?' He took her hand and led her through the flat in the direction of the bedroom.

Mirabelle went willingly. She tried not to think about Sister Monica. Or Mother Superior. But she couldn't help it. Could two of the nuns be lovers? she wondered, and shuddered because most of them seemed too old, but then she felt sure she and McGregor would always have this between them, no matter how grey they became, how wrinkled. She tried not to judge people but so often it came down to that in cases – understanding how people felt. Knowing them.

McGregor pulled the curtains in the bedroom. The late-afternoon light illuminated the pattern, blowsy pink roses casting a gentle glow over the room.

'Come here,' he said, sitting on the bed.

And she stopped thinking about murders and nuns and the purchase of property and did as he asked.

Chapter Sixteen

Deceit: guile, chicanery, duplicity

Mirabelle walked up to the telephone box on George Street bright and early the next morning. She hung about on the corner, not wanting to ring too soon in case Vesta wasn't ready and she had to speak to one of the nuns. She took her sunglasses out of her bag and put them on – it was bright again today. McGregor had insisted on cooking breakfast: boiled eggs with buttered soldiers as if she was a child, and a pot of tea on a tray in bed. She had to admit she felt a good deal better. Yesterday, as the afternoon had worn towards evening, they'd stayed in the bedroom and cracked open a bottle of champagne, which they consumed with a tin of game soup and some pâté before sitting at opposite ends of the gargantuan bath, dripping hot water in slowly and talking until the sky darkened. McGregor wasn't golfing today but he'd decided to go to Torphichen Street to find out if Rennie's men had made progress overnight. While Edinburgh was home to several hotels and guesthouses, the initial search area was small enough to be covered relatively quickly.

A lady firmly grasped the hand of a little girl she was pulling along the street. 'There's nothing to be frightened of,

Audrey,' she insisted. 'Mr Campbell is an excellent dentist. He knows what he's doing.'

Mirabelle smiled sympathetically at Audrey, who was putting up as much resistance as a small girl might without bursting into tears.

Checking the clock outside the bookshop, she slipped into the telephone kiosk and dialled the now-familiar number. Vesta answered on the second ring.

'Mirabelle?'

'Yes.'

'I'm not supposed to be in the office,' Vesta hissed. 'Mrs Munro is an absolute harridan. She's taken over the whole place. I swear she's as bad as Stalin. I tell you what, though,' there was the sound of drawers being opened and closed, 'she's done quite the number here. The filing is in excellent shape and the stationery store is far tidier. She's removed a few things. That petition against Monica's burial for a start. And I can't find the log of correspondents.'

'Where is she now?'

'Calming down the rumpus. I say rumpus but they're nuns. It's more a steely silence and some crying in the corridor. They're having a meeting.'

'What's happened?'

'Didn't you hear? The bishop has chosen a candidate to be mother superior.'

'Who did he pick?'

'Sister Triduana.'

'Gosh, she's a bit old, isn't she?'

'That's what she said.'

'Who's the other candidate?'

'That's what the crying is about. He said that in the circumstances he felt there wasn't anyone else to put up, and

Sister Triduana ought to be appointed without an election. The nuns are furious. This will be the first time since the foundation of the order that they haven't chosen the mother superior themselves.'

Mirabelle considered this. 'Sister Triduana will be good at it, though, I should think. She's a sensible kind of person.'

Vesta didn't comment. 'They're meeting in the refectory,' she said. 'I've heard whispers they're going to start a campaign for Sister Mary to be on the ballot. She gave a speech after matins this morning about the importance of self-determination. I think she might be succumbing to the sin of ambition.'

'I'm not sure ambition is a sin,' Mirabelle rejoined. 'Not in the Bible.'

'Well,' said Vesta, 'I'm no closer to finding out any-thing useful.'

'What have you been doing?'

'Mostly seeing to some of the older nuns. They're nice old women. Two of them are sick and confined to their cells most of the time so I take up their meals and have a chat. Sister Evangelista used to do it but she's still in the anchorite's cell. They want to pray quite a bit, of course,' she added.

Mirabelle considered this. 'Vesta, do you think the formula for the salve is there? In the office?'

Vesta sighed. 'I don't know. If it was, I'd imagine Mrs Munro has it now. I could ask my old ladies, if you like.'

'Do.'

'The meeting is coming out,' Vesta said. 'I can hear them. Mrs Munro will be back any moment. I'd better go.'

The telephone clicked. Mirabelle leaned against the wall of the kiosk. She'd chosen a pale gold summer dress this morning and her customary pair of heels in a light tan. The skirt was fitted and it felt tight as she rested against the glass. It was as if she was at one remove from this case. The truth was that McGregor was in a better position to keep tabs on what the police were up to and Vesta was best placed to keep an eye on the nuns. She considered walking to Trotter's to choose her glasses, but she didn't want to. Instead, she wandered back to Heriot Row, running over the detail of Sister Monica's arrival in Edinburgh, Grace's pregnancy and wondering to whom the formula of Gethsemane Salve was most valuable. She realised she should have asked Vesta if the nuns grew marigolds. She'd like to see if Katja was right, though in her experience the Poles who had come to Britain during the war were highly practical and not prone to mistakes. The whole thing felt like an impossible knot.

Standing between the car and the front door, she realised she didn't want to go back into the flat. Nowhere really feels like home, she thought, as she pondered Shore Cottage and the pretty road beside the water. Bang Bang MacDonald had lived there for twenty years or more. She must have liked it. Mirabelle wondered what the old woman's first name was. She should check, she thought. And it would be interesting to know if her body had been buried with the Little Sisters or somewhere else. This thought seemed to prompt her. She didn't have anything to investigate this morning but she could look into the old woman's illness and, for that matter, her death. She suddenly recalled Mother Superior sitting behind her desk. The nun had said she wanted someone who could step sideways to investigate on the sisters' behalf. This would be a sideways move, the best Mirabelle could come up with, but, she told herself, she ought to do something.

She drew the car key from her purse and slipped into the driver's seat, starting the engine. It idled a moment while she made the final decision to follow her curiosity. Dr Alexander had been the old woman's physician but Mirabelle knew she wouldn't divulge anything more; her enquiries into Grace's pregnancy had made that clear. So Mirabelle turned the car south and drove across Princes Street, past the castle and towards the hospital that backed onto the Meadows. She pulled up outside George Heriot's School and straightened her hat using the rear-view mirror. Then she got out and climbed the steps into the comforting shade of the Royal Infirmary's black-and-white-tiled hallway.

Some of the nurses looked like nuns, she thought, as she passed a gaggle of young women in blue uniforms wearing white caps, like wimples, her heels clicking along the corridor until she reached the office. She knocked on the door.

'Good morning.' The woman behind the desk was wearing an ill-fitting grey suit and considered Mirabelle over the top of her spectacles, demonstrating almost exactly why Mirabelle was not eager to choose frames at Trotter's.

'Hello,' Mirabelle started. 'I wonder if you can help me. I'm looking for a patient. She died in January.'

'We don't keep death certificates in the hospital, madam,' the woman said. 'You need to go to the Registrar's Office at the east end of Princes Street.'

'I rather hoped,' Mirabelle ventured, 'that I might be able to speak to the lady's doctor.'

'That's most irregular. Are you a relation?'

Mirabelle shifted. 'It's a long story,' she said, with an apologetic slip of a smile. 'The deceased owned the house I'm moving into.'

'Infectious diseases go to the cottage hospital,' the woman said, 'if that's what you're worried about.'

'It's not that.'

The woman pursed her lips. 'Well, what is it?'

'I'd just like to know more about her.'

'We don't accommodate that kind of thing, madam.'

'But cause of death will be on the certificate?'

'That is a matter of public record. Certainly.'

Outside the office, the hallway seemed longer than it had when Mirabelle came in. The hospital was older than the one in Brighton and solidly built. Mirabelle sank onto a seat in front of the long columns of names that made up a brass war memorial on the wall. Through an open window, the sound of the school playground floated on the summertime air. It must almost be the holidays. She considered a moment. Bang Bang MacDonald's death certificate was unlikely to tell her anything useful. It was human contact she was looking for – someone who'd known the old lady, if only fleetingly. A glimpse of something personal. Miss MacDonald had been familiar with the nunnery – so familiar she'd decided to leave it. Maybe she'd said something – last words that would prove prescient.

Determined, Mirabelle got up and returned to the doorway where a board with directions was hoisted on a pillar. She followed the signs for the geriatric ward on the first floor. Upstairs on one side of the corridor, the rooms had a view across the Meadows in the direction of the Bishop's Palace. Mirabelle removed a handkerchief from her handbag and drew it to her face. She knocked on the office door at the head of the ward.

'Come!'

Inside, another stern-looking woman, this time wearing a sister's uniform, sat at another desk. The main difference that Mirabelle could discern was that this nursing sister did not wear spectacles. 'Yes?'

Mirabelle sniffed. She would have to lie if she was to have

any chance of getting the information. 'I understand that my mother's great friend died on this ward in January,' she said. 'My mother is unwell and could not come herself. We only just found out. We've been away, you see. I wonder if you might be able to reassure me. My mother would like to know that she didn't suffer. Miss MacDonald of Shore Cottage, South Queensferry. We didn't even know she was ill.'

The stern woman shook her head. 'I'm sorry,' she said. 'We don't give out patient details to people who aren't family members. I'm sure you understand. Perhaps you could get in touch with your friend's minister, or her family if she had any. That would be the usual thing.'

Mirabelle sniffed and drew herself up. 'Please,' she persisted. 'It would make such a difference.'

'I'm sorry.' The sister got up and called one of the nurses from the ward. 'Nurse McLeod,' she said, 'please could you see this lady out.' She looked Mirabelle up and down. 'She may require a cup of tea before she goes.'

The nurse was young and her face was flecked with freckles. A shock of thick ginger hair was held in place under her cap by the agency of a number of hairpins. 'Are you all right?' she asked, as she led Mirabelle away.

'I hoped to speak to somebody who had nursed a friend of my mother's. She died in January and we only just found out.' There seemed little point in keeping up the charade but it was difficult to backtrack.

'I'm sorry,' the girl said, and unlike the two older women, she sounded as if she meant it.

'I'm sure lots of patients die on this ward,' Mirabelle said. 'It must be one of the more difficult placements.'

Nurse McLeod nodded solemnly as she halted at the stairwell. 'I thought it would harden me but I still cry,' she volunteered. 'Quite often, actually. And I don't even know the patients. Not really. They're such fond old dears.'

Mirabelle stopped. This was an opening. She grasped the nurse's hand. 'Her name was Miss MacDonald. She lived in South Queensferry,' she said.

The girl's green eyes widened. 'You mean Bang Bang?'

Mirabelle laughed. 'She didn't bring the shotgun with her, did she?'

'I wouldn't have put that past her. But no. That's what he called her. She was always Miss MacDonald to me.'

'Who called her?'

'Her nephew,' the girl said. 'He came to see her before she passed. From London, I think.'

'I didn't know that,' Mirabelle replied. 'I'm glad she had somebody. Which of the MacDonald boys was it?'

The nurse shrugged shyly.

'They're a good-looking family,' Mirabelle added encouragingly.

The girl smiled. 'He was dishy,' she admitted.

'And he came in the middle of January. The thirteenth or fourteenth, I imagine.'

The nurse paused. 'He just made it. She died the next week. Would you like a cup of tea?' she offered. 'Sister said it might be advisable.'

In the canteen Mirabelle sipped a green cup of pale tea while Nurse McLeod described a man who fitted Sister Monica's description as near as Mirabelle could reckon it. Then the girl talked about Bang Bang MacDonald's demise. 'She was very ill,' she said. 'There wasn't much we could do. The doctor told him that. The two of them sat there crying. I didn't hear what they were talking about. Saying goodbye, I expect.'

'It sounds rather intense.'

'Sometimes it's just like that,' the nurse admitted. 'Families having their last moments.'

'She had faith, didn't she?'

'Oh, yes. Definitely. That makes it easier, I should think. I hope this comforts your mother.'

Mirabelle had a sudden flash in her memory of Mother Superior. 'Yes,' she said vaguely. 'Could you tell me, did any nuns visit her before the end?'

Nurse McLeod's eyes narrowed. 'Nuns? Oh, yes. There was a lady who came. On the last day, I think. I don't know her name, I'm afraid.'

Mirabelle put the cup back onto its saucer. Usually she would press for a description but a nun was nothing but a nun in a person's memory. Besides, the fact Sister Monica had been here meant she had further investigations to be getting on with. The key from the Kemel's Coffee tin was burning a hole in her pocket now she had an inkling of what it was for.

'She wasn't in pain,' Nurse McLeod said. 'It was quite peaceful at the end.'

'Thank you,' Mirabelle replied. 'You've been very helpful.'

Back at the car she checked her bag for the key before starting the engine. At Shore Cottage she rang the doorbell but there was no reply. Mrs Grieg must be at the Vale, Mirabelle thought, and tried the key in the door. It fitted. Inside, the roses had scattered their petals across the hall table. Mirabelle glanced only fleetingly through the sitting-room window with its view of the bright water before going upstairs. Mrs Grieg had cleared some of the cupboards and there was nothing in the bathroom save a bottle of bleach under the sink. In the main bedroom the chest of drawers was empty and had been freshly lined with strips of wallpaper and muslin bags of dried lavender. The wardrobe creaked as Mirabelle drew it open but it was empty too.

The second bedroom, however, hadn't been cleared and, hanging there, she found what she was looking for. A grey, well-tailored suit in winter-weight tweed, the label declaring it was made by 'R. Rosen, tailor. Highgate', and a pair of black Oxfords with mud on the heels. She surveyed the room. 'You stayed here on the thirteenth,' she whispered. 'Right here. You weren't in a hotel at all. You knew Miss MacDonald. You knew her well enough to cry when you visited her at the infirmary.' Turning back towards the wardrobe, she checked the contents of the pockets – a lighter and a packet of cigarettes (no case, she noted) and, inside the jacket, a membership card to a poker club in Holborn in the name of Paul J. Thompson.

With this in her hand she ran down to the hall table and lifted the phone, asking the operator to connect her to Torphichen Street police station. The officer who replied couldn't find Inspector Rennie or Superintendent Scott and had never heard of McGregor but Mirabelle left a message anyway. Then she opened the back door of the house and sat on the step, staring towards the water.

Paul J. Thompson had been here. This was where he had changed. But not where he had left his briefcase. Yes, that was a puzzle. Still. He'd known Bang Bang MacDonald, which meant in all likelihood he'd been familiar with the nunnery before he came, just as they had assumed. Had Thompson known what he was about to do, Mirabelle wondered, when he sat weeping at Bang Bang's bedside? He must have. 'It's all linked,' she said out loud. 'It's not about the nunnery, it's about someone inside it. The connection is what's important – between Bang Bang and Sister Monica and maybe one or more of the other nuns.' She had suspected something of this nature but here was the proof, or the beginning of it. Beyond the trees in one direction the untidy view of the bridge works was superseded by the rust-red rail bridge glowing in the sunshine beyond the village. In the other direction the Little Sisters' graveyard jutted into the firth.

Mirabelle got up. She closed the door behind her and made her way through the shady trees towards the burn where she'd found the Kemel's Coffee tin after the funeral. It felt like a place where two worlds met – Paul Thompson on one side became Sister Monica on the other. Bang Bang MacDonald was a nun to the east of the rushing water and a private citizen on the west. The nunnery wasn't a locked room. It was wide open right here where nobody overlooked it. Paul Thompson could have got in and out of the convent whenever he wanted to. He had the key for Shore Cottage and a change of clothes. As long as he wasn't missed, he would have been able to move relatively freely. Where might he have gone? she wondered. And who might he have brought with him to the empty house? Maybe he'd known Grace Farquarson-Sinclair after all.

At the limit of the burn Mirabelle gingerly jumped over, looking up towards the nunnery in case she was spotted, but the buildings were obscured from view. It seemed such a peaceful place for something so dark to have happened. The earth on Sister Monica's grave had begun to settle. Now she knew the novice's real name, it felt wrong that it wouldn't be marked on the stone cross that would eventually be raised there.

'Paul Thompson,' she said out loud. St Paul was one of the apostles, as far as she could remember. 'Paul J. Thompson,' she said again, and wondered what the J stood for.

Chapter Seventeen

Nothing is so aggravating as calmness

Vesta carried the tray carefully upstairs and balanced it on her knee so she could open the door. Inside the cell, Sister Bernadette was dozing, propped on a pile of pillows encased in heavily starched linen. The nuns in the laundry added starch to everything, even the handkerchiefs, which, with the weeping and wailing of the last few days, had led several of the sisters to become dry-skinned and red-nosed. Vesta laid the tray on the side, glad that she didn't have to eat the vegetable soup.

'Sister.' She roused the old nun, who opened rheumy eyes and took a moment to focus.

'Ah,' the old woman said, struggling to sit up. 'Sister Joseph. You're still with us.'

'Still here.' Vesta smiled cheerily.

'Me too,' Sister Bernadette added. 'Some nights I think He will take me. But he never does.'

'Now now, that's not something to worry about.'

Sister Bernadette clasped her hands. 'We must pray,' she announced.

Vesta waited reverently while the old woman muttered a benediction, then joined her in an 'Amen' before balancing the tray on Sister Bernadette's bony lap.

'Sister Evangelista will be back to look after you soon,' she said. 'She comes out of the anchorite's cell tonight. The deaths will be a shock, of course, but at least she'll be able to attend Mother Superior's funeral. I'm looking forward to meeting her.'

'Sister Evangelista does not add as much salt as you do,' the old woman said, bringing the spoon to her mouth.

'I'm sorry. Did I overdo it?'

Sister Bernadette shook her head. 'It's delicious,' she replied, which in Vesta's view was definitely an overstatement, salt or not. The day before, she had brought the old lady some bread with butter and jam, and she had been as shocked as if the plate had been loaded with lobster thermidor from the Ritz. Not that Vesta wanted fancy food right now. More than anything she would have liked chips served piping hot with salt and vinegar and a buttered roll. The thought momentarily distracted her.

This was the third day she had been serving Sister Bernadette's meals. The nun ate unimaginably slowly and quite without relish but, Vesta thought, at least that allowed her to make conversation during her visits. Not that Sister Bernadette gave much away. Still, Vesta was no quitter. She'd keep trying.

'Did you ever meet Sister Monica?' she asked.

Sister Bernadette put down her soup spoon. 'I did not,' she said. 'Not as such.'

'What do you mean?'

'I was carried down to the chapel at Easter to pray with my sisters. Sister Monica was among us then.'

'I see.'

'My eyesight is not good. Not any more. For faces, I mean.' She squinted at Vesta. 'I can still see light and dark, so it's easy to recognise you. You're the only darkie we have, Sister Joseph.'

Vesta's jaw stiffened but she let this pass. 'I would like to know more about Sister Monica. I feel as if she must have been taken for a reason,' she said. Sister Bernadette tutted loudly and Vesta cocked her head. 'Did I say something wrong?'

The old nun regarded the soup spoon as if meditating upon it. 'Sister Evangelista didn't like the girl,' she confided. 'I said to her that it wasn't right to admit such a thing but she got herself into quite a state about it. We own nothing in this world. We are quite without possessions saving the love of our sisters. Understanding each other, as we do. Accepting each other.' The old lady commenced again on the soup. 'Not that the body should have been buried here. I agreed with Sister Mary about that.'

'But why didn't Sister Evangelista like Sister Monica? I don't understand,' Vesta persisted.

Sister Bernadette gave a little shrug. 'She seemed to be . . . challenged by the girl. She thought she was some kind of troublemaker.'

'Do you mean that they argued? Someone mentioned that to me.'

Sister Bernadette moved the spoon through the soup as if carefully assessing this notion. 'It may be the case at the Poor Clares that sisters discuss each other's business. Each other's behaviour. But here it's considered a sin,' she said at last.

Vesta apologised and sat down in the chair next to the bed.

'Perhaps you could read to me,' Sister Bernadette suggested.

The book on the table looked like a Bible, but when Vesta opened it, it was the novel by Émile Zola, which Sister Bernadette had brought into the convent with her as a novice. Its pages were well thumbed, Vesta thought, as she flicked through. 'Start anywhere,' the nun directed. 'But be warned. You may be shocked. Monsieur Zola made a vow to "live out loud", you know, and he kept it. He hides nothing. Nothing at all.'

Almost an hour later, Vesta took the tray down to the kitchen and washed the bowl and spoon in the sink. The contents of the novel had been entirely unshocking, as far as she could tell, but Sister Bernadette was a relic of a bygone age when socialism was a dirty word and unmarried men and women could not be left in a room alone together. She sighed and propped the clean dishes on the edge of the sink.

There were another three hours before she was required to do anything else and several more before Sister Evangelista would come out of her confinement. Even then, it seemed to Vesta, having withdrawn from the world for a week, the nun might be shell-shocked and awkward. Either that or thirsty for company. She smiled. No, that was not how she would be. These women were a different breed. They seemed most comfortable being solitary in a crowd, as if hiding in plain sight. At first Vesta had expected the nuns to behave like a family – they were called sisters, after all – but quickly she had concluded that the community was like no family she knew. The women conformed and were distant at once. It was a strange state of affairs and not as jolly as she had anticipated.

She wondered how old Sister Evangelista was and if Sister Monica's youth had troubled her. It seemed unlikely. Had Evangelista guessed the novice's secret? Or was she the reason Sister Monica had come to the Little Sisters in the first place? What had the women argued about? Outside, the weather was bright today and through the window Vesta watched two red squirrels running up and down the trunk of a horse-chestnut at the limit of the kitchen garden. The convent was quiet. Production had recommenced on the salve and there was a constant prayer vigil in the chapel to honour Mother Superior's memory, three sisters at all times. The nuns were taking it in shifts. Mrs Munro remained ensconced in Mother Superior's office.

'I have to do something,' Vesta mumbled under her breath, as she decided.

Quietly, she sneaked back along the corridor to the accommodation block. The rooms weren't marked by name but she knew Sister Evangelista's cell was on the same floor as Sister Bernadette's, which narrowed her choices to nine rooms. Mirabelle always said being methodical got the best results so Vesta started at the end of the corridor, knocking before she opened each door. The cells were identical, apart from the view from the windows: onto the garden on one side and the firth on the other. The sisters, it seemed, were keeping the convent's rules with no personal possessions and only some dirty washing piled in the corners here and there – socks, pants, a rather worn sanitary belt and in one cell a Bible that looked as if it had never been opened. One by one, Vesta checked for loose floorboards and skirtings. She ran her hand under the furniture to see if anything was taped out of sight. In a room more than halfway along on the seaward side, she found three notes hidden under the mattress, simple pieces of tatter-edged paper with no address and no name either to the recipient or from the sender. Each piece of paper was folded and stored without an envelope. 'Got you.' She smiled as she leaned against the bedstead to read.

I will wait at the gate to the graveyard at 10. We won't be overheard there. If you will speak to her we can sort out everything. You owe me that.

and

Don't think I won't go to Mother if I have to. Everything has changed for me. You have to be honest.

and

I'm begging you not to make this more difficult. I have the right to know. Don't you understand what torture this is? Please stop ignoring me.

She read the words twice, noting the tone of desperation, then stowed the papers back in their hiding place and slipped along the corridor. Sister Bernadette had fallen asleep again, but as Vesta opened the door she stirred.

'Is it time for tea?' the old nun asked.

'Not yet,' Vesta replied cheerily. 'With Sister Evangelista coming out of the anchorite's cell today I thought I might change the linen on her bed. I like to be useful. It's this floor, isn't it?'

Sister Bernadette gave a shallow yawn. 'Two doors along on the other side. She has terrible nightmares. I hear her scream.'

Vesta nodded. It was the right room. 'Thank you,' she said.

'Sister Evangelista is so untidy.' She was only half awake, if that. She fumbled among the bedclothes for her rosary, like a child grasping a teddy bear in the night.

'Untidy?' Vesta pushed.

'The other day her robes were splashed with salve. She smelt of the garden. I used to dig in the garden. I like root crops. You know where you are with potatoes and carrots. Root crops get on with each other. Especially beetroot. You can plant them anywhere.'

Vesta pulled the covers up to Sister Bernadette's chin and retreated.

The corridor felt colder on the way back downstairs than

it had coming up. She recalled the correspondence book in Mother's office. Sister Evangelista had had permission to write to a murderer in Peterhead called John Healey and one of her relations. Had that been a man? Vesta couldn't remember and the book was now in Mrs Munro's keeping. The names of the various nuns' relations were jumbled in her head – someone's aunt called Lily Ensom in Putney, brothers and uncles elsewhere in London, sundry cousins in Manchester and Dundee, and a woman in Cyprus. It wasn't that it hadn't seemed important as she read the names but nothing had stood out because no one had been called Monica.

Cursing her memory, she went over the content of the notes once more, turning past the kitchen block from which she could smell baking bread. Outside, walking towards the sea, she watched as seagulls swooped elegantly over the water in the distance and two yachts headed towards the open waters of the North Sea. Vesta wondered where they were going as she reached the limit of the lavender field and turned along the path towards the water. If the notes she'd found had come from Sister Monica, she had certainly sounded insistent, and another nun was involved too. *If you will speak to her we can have it out.* Did Monica mean Mother Superior? Presumably not, given she'd threatened Sister Evangelista with Mother Superior's intervention. The whole thing felt as if Sister Evangelista had been held to ransom. This didn't make sense. It was Sister Monica, after all, who had had the biggest secret. Surely.

The air was warm and smelt of the flowers that were being attended by bobbing bees. It ought to have been an idyllic day. Vesta suddenly thought of her garden at home in Brighton. The plum tree at the bottom of the lawn would fruit soon. After Mirabelle's wedding, perhaps. Noel liked plums. He liked all fruit, but plums were his particular favourite. She touched her stomach. Would this new baby be the same? Vesta was different from her brothers. If the child was a little girl perhaps she'd be like her: plump and mostly happy. Efficient, with a love of being in charge. Vesta remembered her schoolbag, always packed early on a Sunday afternoon while her brothers had to be rallied by her mother right up till bedtime. 'How difficult can it be to get your things together?' she'd enjoined them. But the boys never seemed able to. Noel showed worrying signs of a similar organisational deficit. He was a child who ate all his sweets at once and left his panda where it fell. Poor Panda had been retrieved by turns from the local butcher, the playpark and, once, from the back seat of a bus.

Beyond the lavender, the path disappeared into a copse of trees where the anchorite's cell was built from stone, like a hermitage. In winter the trees protected it from the worst of the cold, in summer they offered shade – the anchorite's only worldly comfort. Vesta hesitated a moment before striding purposefully through the little wood, coughing to announce herself. 'Sister Evangelista. I'm Sister Joseph. I had to come. I have questions. It's very important. And I have some bad news, I'm afraid.' No sound came from the cell. Vesta took a step closer. 'Sister Evangelista,' she tried again, a little louder. 'I know this is unconventional. I wanted to wait, but the thing is, I found the notes in your cell and I need to speak to you.' She realised her words echoed the insistence of Evangelista's correspondent, which it might be assumed had driven her to the anchorite's retreat in the first place. 'I'm sorry,' she said. 'I don't mean to pry. It's only that it's very important.' Vesta bit her lip. That had come out in the same tone and still no response. 'Sister Evangelista,' she said, stepping closer.

The opening in the door was only a few inches high, just wide enough for a book, a candle or a plate of food to be passed through it. Like a letterbox. 'Sister Evangelista,' Vesta repeated. 'Please.' She bent down and peered into the darkness. It took a moment or two for her eyes to adjust. 'Hello,' she said, 'hello,' and blinked. The little cell was absolutely black inside but she could just make out a hunched figure against the wall. Still, if the nun had been wearing her wimple, surely Vesta would have been able to see the starched white linen. The figure inside wasn't moving and the cell was completely dark. 'Are you all right?' Vesta asked. 'I'm going to come in,' she announced. Still nothing. Vesta felt the moment merited some kind of prayer. Perhaps the sisters were getting to her. She allowed a moment's silence, then lifted the latch.

Inside, the tiny cell smelt of moss and stone. A makeshift burlap mattress was propped against the wall: not a figure at all. It must be a damp place to sleep, Vesta thought, and stepped inside, trying to imagine spending a week there, alone in the darkness apart from the single slit of light. It was colder than she had expected. She shuddered at the thought. Why would anyone choose to do that? What good could possibly come of it? Then she turned her attention to where Sister Evangelista might have gone.

Chapter Eighteen

When anger rises, think of the consequences

In the graveyard, Mirabelle heard the nun before she appeared, which gave her a chance to hide. It was lucky the gate was creaky, she thought, diving behind a blackthorn bush as the nun opened it. Mirabelle watched through the branches as the woman paused, taking in the view before turning towards the burn. She seemed distinctive: younger than most of the nuns and stocky. Mirabelle tried not to prick herself on the jagged leaves as she manoeuvred, keeping the nun in sight as she headed past the gravestones, straight for the little waterfall where the Kemel's Coffee tin had been hidden. The nun tried three times to retrieve it from the rushing water as if it might have slid along the ledge. Then she fumbled in the stream, in case it had fallen. Finally, when she realised it had gone, she sank onto the bank, her habit soaked, and began to cry. Leaving it a moment, Mirabelle emerged from behind the bush. 'Hello,' she said. 'Are you all right?'

The nun sniffed and eyed Mirabelle with disdain. 'Who are you?'

'Mirabelle Bevan.' She held out her hand. 'I'm your new neighbour. Well, about to be. My husband and I have bought Shore Cottage.'

She paused. It was the first time she'd called McGregor her husband and he wasn't yet. Why hadn't she said fiancé? 'We're not actually married,' she admitted, cursing herself for sounding like a schoolgirl. 'The wedding is next week – we're planning to have it here, actually. In the chapel. Did you come to visit a grave?'

It was clear that this wasn't the nun's intention but it seemed a good way to start a conversation. The nun shook her head, then noticed Monica's freshly dug plot behind her. 'Oh,' she said.

'I came to Sister Monica's burial,' Mirabelle continued. 'The bishop gave a lovely sermon.'

The nun gasped. 'Monica?' she said.

'Weren't you there?' It hadn't been this nun, Mirabelle thought, who had left the rosemary, then.

The woman scrambled to her feet. 'I have to go,' she said. She cast a glance towards the nunnery, then set off wearily, as if the gentle slope upwards was as steep as Mount Everest. Mirabelle followed her. 'Sister,' she called but the nun didn't turn. She laid a hand on the nun's arm. 'I don't mean to intrude but you seem upset.'

The nun shook her off. 'I need to speak to Mother Superior,' she snapped. 'Leave me alone.'

'Mother? Don't you know?' Then the penny dropped. 'You're Sister Evangelista.'

Her habit was so wet it hung heavily around her frame, as if it were slumped in exhaustion against her. Her eyes were rimmed pink. 'What do you want?' she snapped.

'I'm afraid Mother Superior is dead. She was murdered two days ago.'

Sister Evangelista's face twisted but she didn't cry. 'You seem to know a lot about my sisters' business,' she said.

'Mother asked me to take an interest—' Mirabelle started.

'In her own murder? What do you mean?'

'In Sister Monica's death.'

'Why would she do that?'

'Because Sister Monica wasn't what . . . Mother expected.'
Sister Evangelista froze.

'But you knew that,' Mirabelle continued, as she realised.
'Was that why you fought with her? It would help a great deal
if I could talk to you about it.'

The nun pulled away. 'Get off me,' she said, and stormed further up the hill. Mirabelle followed once more. 'Get away!' Sister
Evangelista hissed, and glanced in the direction of the main
gate. 'You shouldn't be here. The Little Sisters of Gethsemane
is a place of refuge. It's private.' Then she turned up the cobbled path into the courtyard and disappeared into the chapel
where the chanting of the sisters engaged in the vigil for Mother
Superior faltered, then resumed. Mirabelle paused in the courtyard. Above, Mrs Munro's face appeared in the window. She
fumbled to open the casement and peered down, her lips pursed.

'Miss Bevan,' she said disapprovingly. 'What are you
doing here?'

Mirabelle sighed and gestured towards the doorway to
the building, entering and climbing the stairs. At the top,
Miss Munro had the air of a schoolmistress about to cane an
errant pupil.

'I need to speak to the bishop,' Mirabelle said. 'I've got a
name for Sister Monica. I know who he was. I've passed it on
to the police but the bishop really ought to be told.'

She pushed past Mrs Munro into Mother's office. Vesta
was right: the place looked a lot tidier. A vase of *sullivantii*
sat on the now clear desk next to a jagged crystal bowl of
powdered lemon bonbons.

'Sister Evangelista is involved somehow,' she added, through the open door. 'We knew one of the nuns must have known Sister Monica's identity and it foxed me as to why that nun hadn't come forward. The anchorite's retreat explains it.' Now, she thought, even though that mystery had been solved, Sister Evangelista's response had raised several more questions. Had the nun been on her way to Shore Cottage? And, if so, why? Was her distress about Sister Monica the only thing on her mind, or was she troubled about something else? 'She didn't want to talk to me,' Mirabelle added. 'She went into the chapel.'

'Sister Evangelista?' Mrs Munro said. 'But she's not due out of the anchorite's cell until sunset. Stay here,' she added, and disappeared downstairs.

Mirabelle sank onto the chair behind the desk and eyed the bonbons. She wondered if McGregor had got her message yet. The sooner he knew, the sooner Scotland Yard would be informed and Paul Thompson's relations could be told. They must be worried half to death. Given it was unlikely they had colluded in his plan to enter the convent, as far as they were concerned he had probably been missing for five months. She removed a sweet from the little bowl and popped it into her mouth. It was utterly delicious. Still, she preferred the way Mother Superior's office had been before: untidy yet more relaxed.

She was considering her old office at McGuigan and McGuigan and whether Vesta refurbishing it might have made it less welcoming to clients, when she was disturbed by the ungodly sound of shouting from the courtyard followed swiftly by the crack of glass shattering. Mirabelle jumped to her feet and ran to the window in the corridor, which remained ajar. The rumpus appeared to be coming from the chapel from which Mrs Munro suddenly emerged. She ran back upstairs, her heels trip-trapping on the stone treads. Mirabelle couldn't help thinking she had the air of a panicked hen.

'What's going on?' Mirabelle asked, but before Mrs Munro could answer, one of the chapel's stained-glass windows seemed to crumple as part of an oak pew crashed through and landed on the cobbles in a shower of glass, the end shearing off and splintering with an almighty crack.

'My God!' said Mrs Munro, and ran to pick up the telephone. 'That's it. I'm calling the bishop.'

Below there were screams as nuns appeared from the manufactory, the kitchen and the garden to see what the noise was about. Another pew was launched through a second window, with a second ear-splitting crash.

'Is it Sister Evangelista?' Mirabelle asked, but Mrs Munro was jabbering into the handset.

'I can't stay here. I can't and I won't,' she was shouting. 'They're impossible. I knew things were bad but I hadn't realised how far the lack of discipline had gone. I'm coming back to the palace,' she announced, and replaced the handset, smartly picking up her handbag as she pulled on her coat.

'These nuns are out of control. The bishop is most displeased,' she said. 'He'll certainly take action. No doubt about that.' And she took off down the stairs.

Out of the window Mirabelle watched Mrs Munro's red Burberry bypass a tangle of black and white nuns assembled outside the chapel as she picked her way across the glass-strewn cobblestones towards the front gate. 'You've always been a clype, Rose Munro,' one of the nuns spat, in an ungodly fashion. 'A real Goody Two Shoes.' Mrs Munro did not reply and the nun moved back into the group, glaring resentfully at Mrs Munro's retreating figure.

'What on earth is this about?' Mirabelle asked, into the silence of the corridor. She felt glad that, though the nuns felt they were doing God's work, none of them had thought to look upwards. Below, Sister Mary appeared from the direction of the manufactory and started organising everyone. Dustpans and brushes were fetched. Nuns disappeared into the refectory and Sister Evangelista walked out of the chapel crying, flanked by another sister with her arm around Evangelista's shoulders. Sister Mary was furious. Mirabelle leaned in to hear what she was saying through the open window.

'What on earth have you done?' Sister Mary snapped at the younger nun.

Sister Evangelista sobbed. 'Everyone is dead. I didn't do it! I swear I didn't.'

'We know that, my dear,' Sister Mary said, in a more comforting tone.

'The men want the formula, don't you see? That's all they're after. Well, they can't have it. I won't have everything spoiled again.'

Then from the direction of the kitchen, Sister Triduana appeared and asked what was going on. Sister Mary turned on her. 'She just found out about Mother,' she said, 'and the boy. That's all.'

'Gethsemane is supposed to be a retreat from the world,' Sister Evangelista moaned, and fell to her knees. 'We're supposed to be safe here. And now everything is rotten, like the snake in Eden.'

'Get up, girl,' Sister Triduana snapped. 'I can't see how you having a breakdown is going to help anybody. And this is sheer vandalism.' She gestured towards the shattered glass and wood. 'What were you thinking?'

Sister Mary interposed her body between the two nuns. 'You don't care about us, do you? Is that why he chose you? You filthy stooge. You'd let him take it all – the only proper occupation we have now and you'd let him do whatever he wants with it.'

Sister Triduana's response was immediate. She lifted her fists and struck Sister Mary hard with, Mirabelle had to admit, an excellent right hook. Her months on the front lines had clearly taught her a thing or two that she hadn't forgotten in the intervening decades.

Sister Mary reeled. A slim trickle of blood slid from her nose. 'You'll never be Mother Superior. Nobody trusts you,' she sneered. 'What are you going to do? Punch your sisters' lights out whenever they ask a question? There are a lot of questions, Sister.'

Sister Triduana's eyes filled with tears. 'He calls us,' she spat. 'It is a duty. The world has changed, Sister. What was I supposed to do?'

'What would He have done?' Sister Mary roared. 'Do you think He would let them get away with this? This convent is a place for the humble and the good. It is a place where we lay the fault where the fault lies. Where men do not have the advantage. Do you think He would have let the bishop take our birthright? After almost a thousand years? He didn't tolerate moneylenders in the Temple and He wouldn't tolerate this.'

Sister Triduana reached out towards her. 'There are seventy of us now, Sister. In ten years we'll be lucky if we're forty. We have to do something.'

'We may have to. We . . . may have to,' Sister Mary said, as if she was thinking this proposition through. 'But Mother Superior? What of her? How can we possibly make these decisions when she is gone? Killed. Here. In the way that she was. And we still don't know who did it.'

Sister Evangelista began to moan, a high keening sound, as she crumpled.

Sister Triduana's cheeks flamed. 'We owe all our devotion to Mother,' she said. 'We can agree on that.'

Sister Evangelista continued to cry, loudly.

'Pah!' Sister Mary seemed unconvinced. 'Take this poor woman up to her cell and stay with her,' she ordered the pale, silent nun, who still had a steady hand on Sister Evangelista's quivering shoulder. 'We must recover ourselves from the rot that has overtaken us here. All of us as sisters. We will make it right as we always have.'

Mirabelle moved away from the window and sat on one of the chairs set out for the nuns to wait on. She wondered what Inspector Rennie would make of what she'd just seen. It was close to the hysteria he'd described in Huxley's book but it was easy to dismiss upset women as hysterical. Too easy. She'd seen it during wartime and since the peace as well. Some things didn't change. Below, everything became quiet except for the clink of smashed glass and splintered wood being tidied. A few minutes later the singing started once more in the chapel. The bishop had a full-scale rebellion on his hands, she thought. Sister Mary was clearly in charge now. And none of the nuns had realised that she was still here. Yes, she decided, that was an advantage.

Chapter Nineteen

Some virtues are only seen in affliction

Mirabelle hid in Mother Superior's office until the nuns had eaten dinner. Vespers and compline were late, it seemed, during high summer – bedtime services rather than in the evening. Still, the nuns did not seem to be concerned with the imminent sunset. She would have liked to get hold of Vesta as she waited, but she judged it too dangerous to risk looking for her and, though she kept an eye on the windows over the courtyard and the garden, she did not catch a glimpse of her friend. As soon as it was safe to do so, she'd find her.

The evening light glowed golden now and a pale ghost of the moon appeared in the vivid blue sky, like a reflection of the summer sun. Out here, she thought, you'd be able to make out the stars over the water once it got dark. In Edinburgh the stars were few and far between, the streetlights obliterating all but Orion and sometimes the planet Venus: the brightest light in the night sky. She wondered what McGregor was up to. If he had got her message and Paul Thompson's family had been located and informed. Perhaps they would have some inkling of why he had come here. Surely they would want to help get to the bottom of what had happened.

At eight o'clock the nunnery's bell tolled and the nuns began to congregate in the refectory. Sister Mary appeared from the chapel, as if she had been in prayer, readying herself. Mirabelle waited until everybody was assembled, then crept along the corridor until she reached the passageway between the kitchen and the refectory where she halted outside the closed door to listen. Inside, the Lord's Prayer was being intoned in chorus. After the Amen, Sister Mary started to make a speech, but Mirabelle couldn't hear what she was saying. Annoyed by the thickness of the door and that there was no keyhole to look through, she sneaked outside, keeping close to the stone wall and crouching below the windowsills as she crept along the herbaceous border towards the refectory's only open window.

Sister Mary was by now in the middle of what sounded like an involved speech. 'These are challenging times,' she was saying. 'But for the Little Sisters of Gethsemane action has always been as important as prayer. So as we pray together as sisters, we must also take action together. Many of us came here seeking stability, yet now is a time of change. Many of us came seeking safety and yet here, manifestly, some of us have been in the greatest of danger. It is not up to us to choose. It is for Him to decide.' It sounded, Mirabelle thought, as if Sister Mary was building up to something. 'Our convent has faced great challenges over the centuries and we have, through the ingenuity and determination of our sisters, always flourished. We have done our best to make things right in the world. We must be ingenious again now for the sake of our faith and our sisterhood. We must stand together against the dominion of men. It is going to be difficult. It will take honesty and humility and determination. We must pray for the Lord to guide us in this challenge, which He, after all, has set.'

There was a banging noise, which Mirabelle realised was the nuns thumping the long tabletops. Perhaps it was considered inappropriate for them to clap or cheer. She peered over the sill just in time to see Sister Triduana get to her feet. The old nun walked to the head of the room with steady purpose as the banging subsided and Sister Mary stood back. The crowd settled. Sister Triduana paused dramatically. She clasped her hands in prayer and fell to her knees. 'I ask your forgiveness,' she said. 'I have wronged you. All of you, my sisters.' The old lady began to weep. 'Sister Mary is right. We must stand together. We must stand honestly. We must . . . confess everything to each other and root out anything between us that is not holy. Mother Superior may be gone but the Church is our mother too. And yet there has been such corruption. Such evil. As Our Lord stood against the moneylenders in the Temple and the high priests where he saw they had done wrong, we shall stand for right, and I shall stand with you if only you can forgive me.'

It was a stirring speech but the nuns didn't bang a vote of confidence for Sister Triduana on the tabletop. Mirabelle hazarded another peek over the sill. There was an uncomfortable shifting among the women and a younger nun stood up. Sister Mary nodded in her direction and the nun cleared her throat. Mirabelle hunkered down again but was distracted by a movement on the other side of the garden. It was Vesta. She waved to attract her friend's attention but Vesta didn't see her and continued along the path. Mirabelle hissed, 'Pssst!' Vesta looked upwards as if the sound had come from above. Perhaps, Mirabelle thought, living like a nun had affected her perception of what was possible or indeed likely. 'Pssst!' she hissed again, and waved. Vesta peered towards the herbaceous border as she realised Mirabelle was crouched behind a thyme bush. She smiled, began to move towards it and stopped. Above Mirabelle's head a face appeared. Sister Mary looked down with condescension.

Mirabelle scrambled back onto the path and brushed down her skirt. 'Yes. Hello,' she said, sounding flustered.

'You've been snooping again, have you? How long have you been here, Miss Bevan?'

'I came this afternoon,' Mirabelle said, as several other faces appeared behind Sister Mary's.

'I don't recall you arriving.'

'I walked from Shore Cottage. If you cross the burn beside the graveyard . . .'

'Ah. Yes. Not exactly trespass, though as I understand it you are not yet the owner of Shore Cottage.'

Mirabelle tried not to look sheepish. She suddenly wished that as well as leaving a message for McGregor about Paul Thompson's name she had stated her whereabouts. 'The thing is, Mother Superior asked me to look into Sister Monica's death,' she said in her defence. 'And now she's dead too, I'd like to help if I can.'

This did not have the effect she had hoped for of mollifying the nuns. The women behind Sister Mary began to whisper among themselves.

'I've been helping the police with their enquiries,' Mirabelle added, to no better response.

'And what have you found out?' Sister Mary asked.

'Today I uncovered Sister Monica's real name.'

'And? What is it?'

'Paul Thompson,' Mirabelle announced. 'He may have been related to Miss MacDonald. He visited her in hospital before she died and stayed at Shore Cottage the night before he entered the convent.'

Sister Mary nodded, taking this in. 'Well, you've done your job, then, haven't you? Just as Mother asked.'

'No.' Mirabelle couldn't help the word coming out as if it was an exclamation. 'Mother asked me to find Sister Monica's identity, but she also wanted to know why she came to the convent. Why she died.'

The younger nun who had been about to speak let out a loud sob and Sister Evangelista pushed forward with a furious expression on her face, as if she might climb through the window. 'Sister!' Sister Mary chastised her. 'Control yourself.'

Mirabelle decided to push what was undoubtedly a pressure point. It seemed the only way forward. 'There was something off about Sister Monica's death,' she said. 'Dr Alexander found a wound on the back of her head. It may have been sustained when she fell. Or she may have been hit when someone lost their temper.' Mirabelle couldn't help remembering Sister Triduana's sterling boxing skills demonstrated only that afternoon. Still, that was a leap. The link between Sister Evangelista and Sister Monica seemed more pressing, and Sister Evangelista was clearly a hothead. She kept the stocky nun in her sightline. 'Given what happened afterwards – what happened to Mother Superior, I mean – well, it certainly merits investigation,' she added.

'You can't hang about here, spying on us, Miss Bevan,' Sister Mary said crisply. 'I don't see why you'd want to. We sisters are in the habit of dealing with our own problems. You are not welcome any more than the police are. I couldn't be plainer.'

Mirabelle sighed. This wasn't the first time she'd been accused of spying during the course of her career. Neither was it the first time she'd persisted with a case in the face of a full police inquiry. 'Yes, you're not complying with the police investigation either. Are you?' she snapped. 'Which, for all your talk of humility, is quite arrogant, if you ask me.' It had been a long day. A long week, if it came to that. 'You're not above the law, Sister Mary. Temporal or spiritual.'

Her accusation seemed to rouse the nun. 'No. But we are subject to a higher power,' she rejoined. 'We consider what is morally right first in all things. That and our sisters.'

'It sounded the other way around from the speech you just gave.'

Sister Mary's eyes narrowed. 'How can you possibly understand? When Cromwell came to Scotland we hid,' she barked. 'The villagers claimed one sister each as an aunt, a grandmother, a maid. Our sisters gave up their habits and entered the world. We razed our crops that year so they wouldn't find us. We left our real home.'

'Cromwell . . .' Mirabelle stuttered. 'But that was in the seventeenth century. What on earth has that got to do with all this?'

'The Little Sisters of Gethsemane survive,' Sister Mary said. 'We survive everything. The Crusades. The Rough Wooing. Cromwell. The Jacobite uprisings. Hanoverian repression. The monks of Arbroath Abbey did not make it through the Reformation, even. The abbey is a ruin still, yet here we are. Sisters together. He protects us. And as long as we sisters survive, the Church survives. No matter where we are, we are together, and we do the right thing, no matter what the social convention or how difficult that might be.'

'Where does one of you being a murderer fit into your philosophy, Sister?' Mirabelle rejoined.

Sister Mary's jaw hardened. 'Wherever He wishes it to,' she said.

'You can't mean that.' Mirabelle sounded shocked. While the nuns had hardly been helpful, she had never once thought in the last few days that they weren't talking because they were on the side of the murderer.

Sister Mary didn't budge. 'I'm sorry, Miss Bevan, but we need to get to the bottom of this ourselves. Whatever it may be. You have stumbled into our order's private business and you are not welcome. Sister Triduana,' Sister Mary said, 'would you take Miss Bevan to the sacristy and lock her in? As a show of faith?'

Mirabelle let out a hoot of disbelief. The ridiculousness of the idea that these old women in their unwieldy robes might best her. 'And what do you think that will achieve?' she asked.

'It will give us time,' said Sister Mary. 'I give you my word that we won't hurt you, but we need to make our own decisions.'

From the side door, Sister Triduana appeared at the top of the path, striding towards Mirabelle with purpose. By the time Mirabelle had grasped that she was serious, she had only a second or two to get out of the way, further into the garden. I mustn't look at Vesta, she thought. I mustn't let them know we're together. But Vesta was striding towards the nun, and struck Sister Triduana on the shoulder. Her response was immediate: 'This is none of your business, Poor Clare,' she snapped, and roughly pushed Vesta off. Mirabelle began to run. It wasn't easy over the uneven ground, especially in unsuitable shoes. The fitted skirt restricted her stride so she pulled it over her knees. If she could make it back to the graveyard, she thought, she could jump the burn and run at full pelt to the car. She was younger than Sister Triduana and relatively fit. She had not, however, counted on the fact that Sister Mary had chosen Sister Triduana for a reason. A glance behind revealed that, to her surprise, the old nun was gaining on her and was about to launch herself in some kind of rugby tackle. Mirabelle speeded up, but it was no use. Sister Triduana came at her with a singular determination and brought her down at the edge of the lawn, pinning Mirabelle's arms behind her back. Her surprise must have shown.

'I was often left in charge of the officer's mess in the old days,' Sister Triduana explained, as she pulled Mirabelle to her feet and marched her towards the chapel.

The sacristy contained the only stained-glass window not to have been broken by Sister Evangelista's earlier outburst. The shattered glass from the other windows had been swept into a wooden crate, which was placed in the corner next to the two broken pews stacked on top of each other. Apart from this the room contained an oak wardrobe, a tiny mahogany table and an uncomfortable matching chair. The intact window, Mirabelle noted, was too small to escape through. It depicted an image of the baby Jesus in a manger with a blue swathe of glass beneath it, as if the manger were floating on water. That's odd, Mirabelle thought. Bethlehem was inland, near Jerusalem. There was no body of water there.

Sister Triduana lit a lamp and balanced it on the table. 'You've only yourself to blame,' she said.

Mirabelle knew that prisoners ought to try to befriend their captors but she was too cross for that. 'I blame you,' she said very definitely.

The nun affected a serene air that was entirely out of place given her tackling skills. 'I'll fetch you a hymnal to read, Miss Bevan,' she said. 'I'm not going to tie you up,' she added. 'Nothing like that.'

'I should hope not.' Mirabelle did not yield. 'Kidnap is quite sufficient a charge without compounding your crime by restraining me.'

'I didn't take you for melodramatic, Miss Bevan. Not until now,' Sister Triduana said, as she returned with a hymnal, which she laid on the table.

Mirabelle eyed the door. Like every other in the convent, it did not have a lock. Triduana appeared to read her mind. 'I'll bar it,' she said, in a matter-of-fact tone. 'I'm sure Sister Mary will let you go tomorrow. We need to find our feet. That's all.'

The nun left and the sound of a pew scraping across the flagstones emanated from the chapel as the old woman hauled it into place. Mirabelle waited until it was quiet and tried the door, pushing against it as hard as she could. There was no moving the barricade, which appeared to be wedged firmly under the handle. This was positively medieval, she thought, cursing her luck though the sacristy was no kind of oubliette – they'd have to come and get her at some point. Carefully, she climbed onto the table so she could peer through the glass of the flaming orange manger. The sky was darkening now, the sun melting into the sea. 'I'm trapped in a stone box,' she said, and sat down.

It was dark when she opened her eyes and the lamp was failing. She had fallen asleep with her head on the table and as she sat up her back ached. She wondered what time it was, and then there was a sound at the door. It wasn't the loud scraping that had accompanied Sister Triduana blocking the exit, but something more gradual. Mirabelle looked round. There was little in the room with which she might defend herself. Then she realised she was sitting on the best piece of furniture for the job. She jumped to her feet and took up the chair in both hands, poised to attack whoever was coming in. The noise continued and eventually the door opened a crack.

'Mirabelle,' a familiar voice hissed.

'Vesta!'

'Can you get through this gap?'

Mirabelle put down the chair and eyed the slim opening, which was no more than six inches wide. Vesta was habitually an optimistic sort of person. 'I don't think so,' she whispered.

There was the sound of further scraping and the thick wooden door shifted another six inches – all the difference. Mirabelle levered herself into the space and squeezed through. Beyond the door, the chapel lay in absolute darkness and it felt cold now the windows were gone. Through the vacant arched frames, Mirabelle could see the moon, low and full over the courtyard.

'Thanks,' she said.

'I had to wait until they'd gone to bed,' Vesta explained.

'I thought they might lock you up too.'

'They confined me to my cell but they don't lock nuns in. We're supposed to do what we're told. I said the Poor Clares were opposed to all kinds of violence. Sister Mary said we were a younger order, whatever that means. They don't know we're connected.'

Together the women pushed the pew back across the door and crept outside into the chill evening air.

'I can let you out of the gate,' Vesta offered.

'Aren't you coming with me?'

Vesta shook her head. 'I should stay. They'll send me home soon – well, back to Bermondsey. But not now. They as good as said they need the weekend to sort things out. Besides, it's Sunday the day after tomorrow – or today now. I shouldn't think nuns travel on the Lord's Day. Do you?'

Mirabelle took her friend's hand. 'You should come,' she said.

Vesta shook her head. 'If I get more time on the inside I might be able to figure out at least one of these murders,' she replied, sounding determined.

'Not if they confine you to your cell.'

'They have to let me pray. I'll be allowed into the chapel. Who knows? Maybe the bishop will turn up for a showdown about the formula for the salve.' Vesta grinned. 'I'd like to see that.'

It seemed so peaceful here despite everything. As they walked towards the gate Mirabelle could have sworn she could hear water – though maybe it was only the burn. The smell of garden roses scented the night air. 'It's beautiful, isn't it?' Vesta pulled back the bar and Mirabelle stepped through the door into the outside world.

'Be careful,' Mirabelle said.

Another of Vesta's finest grins beamed at her. 'Don't worry about me,' she replied, and the gate closed.

Outside, an owl hooted in the woods as Mirabelle picked her way down the track towards Shore Cottage. The trees cloaked the path in darkness and made the air seem even chillier. It had been some day, she thought, and there was so much to uncover. Despite everything she still had no idea which nun had murdered Mother Superior, though it seemed the sisters knew. As she reached into her pocket for the car keys she realised she had left her handbag in Mother Superior's office. She cursed herself for not checking before she left the convent – sloppy thinking. She briefly wondered if she could hot-wire the engine, knowing perfectly well that she had no idea how to. Still, her pocket contained the key for the cottage. There was that at least, she thought, as her fingers closed around it. And inside she would be able to call a taxi.

At Shore Cottage, she breathed out for what felt like the first time in hours as she switched on the kitchen light. The clock on the wall read just past one. Mirabelle sank onto one of the chairs with a sigh. Her shoes were muddy and there were streaks of dust and stains of green sap from the plants in the herbaceous border on her pale gold frock. She wasn't sure she would be able to get them out. The taxi office would be closed by now, she remembered, and the buses and trains were finished for the day, even if she walked into South Queensferry past the building site, the naval yard, Dr Alexander's surgery and the old church at the edge of the village. More than two miles. McGregor would probably be worried, but there was no easy way to reach him and it would take all night to walk home. Sniffing, she scented toast on the air. She must be imagining it, she thought. She was just hungry. She'd get something to eat tomorrow when she made it home.

Slowly she got up and moved into the hallway without switching on the light. This was where Paul Thompson had stayed and now she would stay here too – at least until it was possible to call a cab, once the sun was up. The bedrooms were made up, she recalled gratefully. She was about to climb the stairs when something or somebody moved in the sitting room. A flash of black and white in the moonlight cast through the window. Mirabelle's heart raced as she peered into the room, shadows from the trees falling onto the patterned carpet. Had one of the nuns followed her or had Sister Evangelista sneaked out of the convent as she had clearly been planning to do before she smashed up the chapel? In the dark it was easy to panic. Was there a ghostly nun? Had Mother somehow returned?

Her fingers shaking, Mirabelle reached along the wall beside the door to feel for the light switch, but there wasn't one. Gingerly she entered the room, which now appeared empty. She reached towards the table lamp but before she could switch it on, the black and white entity launched itself towards her from behind and she tumbled onto the swirling carpet. There was a tangle of monochrome and the flash of a face that was far too pale. Mirabelle screamed and fought, and then the light clicked on. Mrs Grieg, in a maid's uniform, was sitting on her chest with her hair wound in rollers and cold cream smeared on her face.

'Miss Bevan. Oh, no!' she said. 'I'm sorry.'

The housekeeper pulled back and Mirabelle sat up feeling shaken but relieved.

'Are you all right, miss?' Mrs Grieg asked, putting out a hand to help Mirabelle to her feet.

'I think so,' Mirabelle said. 'What on earth are you doing here?'

Mrs Grieg looked bashful. 'I sometimes stay,' she admitted. 'There's a maid's room behind the kitchen and it's handy for the Vale. Miss MacDonald never minded.' She looked down. 'Mrs Farquarson-Sinclair insists on uniforms. Below stairs and all. It's old-fashioned, I know. You frightened the life out of me.' Mrs Grieg paused. 'What are you doing here?'

Mirabelle sighed. 'I got caught up at the convent. I left my car keys in Mother's office and I can't go back to get them, not at this time of night,' she said, thinking she could hardly tell Mrs Grieg exactly what had transpired at the Little Sisters of Gethsemane. She wasn't sure herself, yet. 'I thought I'd sleep here and ring a taxi in the morning. I know I'm not really the owner,' she finished.

Mrs Grieg waved this fact aside, as if it were a mere formality, and did not ask how Mirabelle had obtained a key to the house. She could hardly complain, after all.

'That's going to need to be soaked, miss, when it goes in the laundry.' Mrs Grieg gestured at Mirabelle's dress.

'Yes.' Mirabelle recalled the smell of toast in the kitchen. 'I don't suppose you might be able to make me something to eat?' she asked.

At the table, Mirabelle sipped a strong cup of tea and nibbled a passable corned-beef sandwich with a smear of horseradish as the clock's hands ticked towards half past one. Mrs Grieg stood at the sink, washing the bread knife over and over. 'I saw that Mr Thompson left a suit upstairs,' Mirabelle said casually.

Mrs Grieg didn't turn. 'Aye,' she said. 'I wondered about that. I have no idea what to do with it. I tried to get in touch to return it but he didn't reply to my letter.'

'What was he like? Paul, wasn't it?'

'The Thompson bairns have been coming here since they were in primary school.'

'Thompsons?'

'Miss MacDonald's nephew and nieces. She taught them to sail and to shoot. They lived in London, you see,' Mrs Grieg added, as if this explained all deficiencies in the children's wider education.

'I understand that Mr Thompson visited Miss MacDonald in the Royal Infirmary before she died.'

'She'd have liked that. It's better when you get to say goodbye properly, isn't it? She deserved a proper send-off.'

'What do you mean?'

'She was a good aunt to them.'

'How many Thompson children are there?'

Mrs Grieg laid the bread knife on the side to dry. She turned and wiped her hands on a tea-towel. 'Three,' she said.

'The others will be terribly upset, I imagine. First their aunt dying and now their brother.'

Mrs Grieg's right eyebrow raised. 'What do you mean?'

'Paul Thompson was found in the nunnery. He died there.'

'What?'

'Mr Thompson was the novice. Sister Monica.' Mirabelle let this information sink in. Mrs Grieg was indiscreet but Mirabelle no longer felt any need to shield the nunnery from scandal. 'Anything you know would be extremely helpful, Mrs Grieg. The police are stumped.'

'Oh, my. He must have been desperate,' Mrs Grieg said breathlessly. 'As if I'd know anything about something like that.'

'Do you know anything, though?'

The housekeeper made a harrumphing noise. 'I don't know what he thought he was doing. I mean, if he wanted to see them surely he could simply have arranged a visit. They're an odd family, right enough.'

'What do you mean?'

'Those wee girls had religion from too young an age. It was never natural. They used to hold prayer vigils in a tent in the garden. Wee shrines set up in the hall upstairs when they came to visit.'

'Religion? What do you mean?'

'Two nuns in one family? Three, if you count Miss MacDonald, though she lapsed. And now the boy following them in. Oh, it's very odd.'

Mirabelle put down the sandwich. 'Do you mean Miss MacDonald's nieces are nuns? In the convent? Here?'

'Didn't you know?' Mrs Grieg smirked. 'Mr Wallace said you were some kind of detective.'

Mirabelle ignored this jibe. 'Do you know which nuns?'

she asked, but she already had a strong suspicion about one of them at least.

'Och, it's a funny name.' Mrs Grieg narrowed her eyes and sucked her teeth, as if she was trying to wring inspiration from Shore Cottage itself. 'Very flowery. Is it . . . Sister Eglantine or something like that?'

'Sister Evangelista?'

'Yes. That's it. And Sister . . . Oh it's a much more ordinary name. The saint who looked after the cross. She was Roman, I think. I don't keep with all that Catholic nonsense. Are you a Catholic, Miss Bevan?'

Mirabelle shook her head and scoured her memory. 'Do you mean the Emperor Constantine's mother?' she said slowly. 'Keeper of the cross? St Helena?'

'Sister Helena,' Mrs Grieg confirmed. 'That's it. Like the island where they put Napoleon. Oh, I haven't seen the girls in years. Like most of the sisters they never go to the village. Sister Triduana gets the shopping now and then. Just wee things they need. And Sister . . . oh, what's her name?'

'Mary?'

'Yes. Nice old dear. You see the older nuns about the place sometimes. But not the young ones.'

Mirabelle stood up. This information was important. 'I have to speak to Mr McGregor. Do you know anyone with a car who might be able to drive me back to town?'

Mrs Grieg paused. She looked at the clock on the wall. 'Mr Crichton, the newsagent, has a car. A natty wee Morris,' she said. 'Or they have vehicles at the naval base. I'm sure they wouldn't mind obliging a neighbour. If it's an emergency.'

Mirabelle remembered seeing the newsagent through the window of his shop, which was hung with advertisements written on cards that offered dressmaking skills and piano lessons. He had looked a kind sort of person and, besides, she naturally shied away from getting anyone naval involved. Things had got out of hand when she worked alongside servicemen in the past.

'Could we rouse the newsagent, do you think? Would he mind?'

'There's little the Crichtons wouldn't do for a sum of money.' Mrs Grieg snorted. 'If you don't mind paying, that is.'

'Not at all,' said Mirabelle. 'Mr McGregor will have cash when we get there. Please, can you show me the way? The request might be better coming from someone he knows.'

Mrs Grieg removed her apron. 'Aye, all right,' she said. 'I'll fetch my coat.'

Chapter Twenty

Simplify, simplify

'The murderer is the other sister. Helena,' Mirabelle said decisively. 'It has to be. And Evangelista was trying to protect the girl. Evangelista has a temper. That much is clear. One way or another they're in it together.'

'But she'd have to be delusional. Deranged . . .' McGregor said quietly.

It was, by now, after three in the morning and McGregor and Inspector Rennie, who had been summoned via Torphichen Street, were slumped in comfortable armchairs in the drawing room at Heriot Row. A pot of strong coffee had been brewed and Mirabelle had drunk a sufficiency. She found that she didn't want to sit down and instead was pacing, like a caged animal, up and down in front of the empty fireplace.

'I am still lacking a motive, Miss Bevan,' Rennie said level-headedly. 'Though I'm not saying you're wrong. In the morning I'll take these nuns into custody myself. We'll question them both – Evangelista and Helena. I'm sure we'll get to the bottom of it.'

McGregor added a spoonful of sugar to his cup and stirred thoughtfully. 'Actually, there are a lot of potential motives knocking about but none of them sit well,' he said.

Rennie smirked. 'You want sense from the criminal classes? Crime never makes sense. I'd have thought you'd know that, sir.'

Mirabelle didn't say so, but she disagreed. Crimes always made sense. Murder might be violent and misjudged but once you understood the perpetrator, you usually understood why they had done it.

'Well,' she said, 'there's clearly a lot going on. The nuns are exercised about the formula for their salve. They have a battle ongoing about control of the convent: this election and so forth. And then it seems likely that there's some kind of family feud among the Thompsons. Is it about their inheritance, do you think?' She bit her lip. A dispute over an inheritance between nuns seemed highly unlikely but she kept seeing Sister Evangelista's face, determined and furious, as she almost flung herself at Mirabelle through the refectory window. 'Also, I can't see how Mother Superior fits in. Why kill her, for Heaven's sake?'

Rennie lit a cigarette. 'If it's about the Thompsons, as far as I can make out the only two left alive are these nuns, so if the murders are a Thompson affair, the killer really has to be one of those women.'

'You haven't turned up any other suspects?'

Rennie took a deep draw. 'It seems the Little Sisters are the end of the Thompson line. There's a house in Hampstead and Shore Cottage as well as a portfolio of stocks and shares. The father died last winter. On Christmas Eve, in fact. Presumably Monica would have inherited: Paul, that is. Perhaps now the Church will take everything.'

'What about the mother?'

'She died during the Blitz. She was a Wren as far as I can make out. What did you do during the war, Miss Bevan?' the inspector asked casually.

225

'Oh,' said Mirabelle, 'I was a secretary.'

McGregor regarded his fiancée sideways. He no more wanted to discuss the war than she did, but Mirabelle had done a great deal more than filing during her years with the Special Operations Executive.

'So what we have is a family where the mother died in the Blitz,' Mirabelle summed things up, 'and the father presumably brought up the three children – two girls and a boy – in London, though they visited their aunt in Scotland, of whom we can assume they were fond. Paul Thompson was, anyway. He cried when he visited Miss MacDonald in hospital. At some point the girls went into the convent, at a relatively young age, we might assume. They were always devout and the Little Sisters, anyway, has a close connection to their family through their aunt. Which means the boy was left alone with his father – the youngest. Last year he was left completely alone, if you think about it. The father died just before Christmas and the aunt pegged out right after the father. In January. All Paul Thompson was left with by way of family were his sisters, who, it seems clear, did not want to speak to him. We have no idea why.'

'I can see how it might throw a fellow off, right enough.' Rennie stubbed out his cigarette. 'I can charge them, you know. The nuns. For locking you up. That's kidnap, Miss Bevan.'

Mirabelle shrugged. 'What would be the point? I'm fine. I'm only sorry I sent you on a wild-goose chase checking hotels when Paul Thompson stayed at Shore Cottage.'

'It's an investigation, isn't it? It either runs in a straight line and it's over quick, or you need to circle around it. Like a tiger hunt.' Rennie grinned. 'And it takes longer.'

Mirabelle raised an eyebrow. 'Well, we're still circling,' she said. 'I find it hard to believe that a young man would be so thrown by the death of two older relations that he'd dress in a nun's habit and infiltrate a convent in order to get close to two women who had no interest in him. Because that was what he did. When he arrived at the Little Sisters he burst into tears. "I have to be with my sisters," he said, and the nun, Sister Catherine, who admitted him, didn't understand what he meant. She thought he was talking about the other nuns. But really it was Helena and Evangelista. One of whom probably killed him in the end.'

'Cries a lot, doesn't he?' McGregor said thoughtfully. 'At his aunt's bedside. On admission to the Little Sisters of Gethsemane . . . It's unusual. Most men would rather die than cry in front of anybody else.'

Mirabelle raised an eyebrow again. Sometimes McGregor was a dinosaur.

There was a sharp rap on the door of the flat. Mirabelle thought they really ought to have a telephone installed as soon as they could, party line or not. The lack of one was proving most inconvenient. 'That'll be one of the neighbours, I should think,' McGregor said, checking his watch as he went to answer it. 'Not that we have been dreadfully noisy, but still.'

When he came back he was followed by a constable in uniform.

'Sir.' The young man tipped his hat at Rennie. 'The sergeant thought you'd want to see this.' He handed over a buff file.

'Couldn't it wait?'

The young policeman half shrugged. It was the middle of the night and the pubs were long closed. There was little for the force to do on the graveyard shift other than catch up on paperwork and patrol the streets in the hope of catching burglars in the act. Rennie opened the file.

'Can I offer you a cup of coffee, Constable?' Mirabelle asked.

The man moved his weight from foot to foot. 'No, thank you, miss. No coffee for me.'

'Tea, then?'

'I'd love a cup of tea.'

She disappeared into the kitchen and switched on the kettle. She wondered if it was all the coffee she'd drunk or that she'd fallen asleep for a couple of hours in the sacristy but she didn't feel tired. When the water boiled she brewed the tea and took it through. McGregor had moved to the window and was staring in contemplation at the dark, silent city.

'There are milk and sugar on the tray,' Mirabelle showed the constable, who promptly emptied the contents of the milk jug into his cup, added three lumps of sugar and stirred before slurping the tea loudly.

'I need to get my car back,' McGregor said.

'I left my handbag in the convent,' Mirabelle added.

Rennie put back the papers, closed the file and laid it on his lap. 'Curious,' he said.

'What's that?' McGregor turned.

'The father. He died here. James Albert Thompson. There's a report from the fiscal.'

'He died in Edinburgh?'

'The death certificate says cancer.'

'Was he in hospital?'

'No. That's odd, isn't it? People generally die at home of a heart attack or a stroke but not of cancer. Someone ill enough to be on the point of death would normally be in hospital.'

'Who was the doctor?' Mirabelle asked. 'Who signed the death certificate?'

Rennie opened the file again. 'J. Alexander,' he read out loud.

Mirabelle bit her lip. 'Oh dear.'

She hesitated because she didn't want to elaborate but it seemed churlish not to tell the inspector. 'That means there's a possibility that what we have is a serial killer – a third death. Do you know where James Thompson died exactly? Does it say?'

The constable put down his empty cup with a clink on the tray. Rennie looked annoyed. 'A serial killer? What do you mean?'

'Jeanette Alexander is the convent's doctor,' Mirabelle explained. 'Her practice is in South Queensferry. I have known her to take instruction from the Mother Superior and the bishop. Not fraudulently, but to facilitate matters. Make things easier. And we have three dead bodies located there or nearby. In fact, four if you count Miss MacDonald, though admittedly she died in the Royal Infirmary. It would be foolish not to consider the possibility that the deaths are linked and, given that we know two were likely murder, it makes sense to call the third into question.'

'Killed? By whom? A rampaging killer nun?' Rennie snapped. 'Unlikely.'

'Where did James Thompson die?' McGregor echoed Mirabelle's question.

Rennie sighed. 'Shore Cottage,' he admitted. 'But you can't be murdered by cancer. There was a proper post-mortem. Undertaken at the city morgue.'

'I think we have to look at it . . .' Mirabelle started, crossing her arms.

Rennie held up his hand to stop her. 'I'll have somebody speak to the pathologist tomorrow,' he said, 'to put your mind at rest, Miss Bevan. You've been a tremendous help. But I doubt it'll turn up anything. We need to be practical here – focus on what's most likely.' He got to his feet. 'As I said, we'll question Sister Evangelista and Sister Helena tomorrow. That's where the interest is. And we'll do it on our turf, not theirs. Early doors.'

'I'd like to come with you to the convent in the morning, Inspector,' McGregor said. 'I need to pick up my car and I can fetch Miss Bevan's handbag while I'm there.'

'And make sure I'm doing what you think I should be doing,' Rennie added, with a twinkle in his eye. 'All right,' he conceded. 'I'll give you a lift. Half past eight? But, Miss Bevan, you have no police background and you've already been kidnapped as a result of this investigation. You need to stay away, do you hear me? Leave this to me.'

Mirabelle nodded solemnly.

Rennie checked his watch. 'I'll get four hours' sleep if I get my head down.' He handed the buff file back to the constable. 'I'll drop you at Torphichen Street on my way, Officer,' he said.

Mirabelle and McGregor stood side by side in the long window and watched as Rennie and the policeman got into a car below and drove off. Edinburgh was all but silent at this time of night and the sash and case window was open a crack at the top so they could hear the engine long after the car had turned the corner. McGregor put his arm round Mirabelle's shoulders and kissed her neck.

'He wouldn't have agreed to take both of us,' he said.

That was probably true.

Silently they changed into pyjamas, McGregor's striped cotton and Mirabelle's slick peach satin, before slipping into bed. McGregor fell asleep immediately with his arm curled round her but Mirabelle lay staring at the ceiling. Despite the warmth of McGregor's body she felt bereft. Mirabelle had pursued all kinds of criminals over the years, from gangsters to bent coppers, from spies to lovesick youngsters barely beyond childhood, but something about what had happened at the Little Sisters of Gethsemane chilled her. Beyond the nuns' routine, their habits and their business concerns, there was a dark heart in those woods at night and in the cemetery that led down to the firth. There seemed too many connections between the people involved and none of them healthy. Rennie didn't want to feel things had got out of hand, but they had patently already done so. Had Paul come to challenge his sisters over their father's death? He had been the end of a line but, still, it felt like a well had been poisoned. Mirabelle immediately told herself off for being melodramatic. Still. It did. And she kept coming back to the idea that something important was missing. There was something they hadn't found out yet. Not even a clue.

Chapter Twenty-one

The cautious seldom err

Vesta woke early. The cells at the convent did not sport either shutters or curtains but it got light around four in the morning at this time of year and the sunrise and birdsong were better than any alarm clock. She stretched and sat up, squinting into the garden, which was already bathed in bright sunshine as she considered what had happened with Mirabelle the night before. It seemed like a dream. Nobody would know yet that she was safely away. Matins was in about an hour and Vesta decided she ought to keep away from the chapel until then, given the nuns would not discover Mirabelle's escape until they checked the sacristy.

She yawned and got up, splashing her face with water from the ewer and slipping out of her white cotton nightgown and into the habit she had been provided with. There was, she thought, something free about these clothes compared to her usual attire. It was a uniform of sorts but more than that – even in uniform women usually felt they had to do their hair. One of Vesta's friends from school in Bermondsey had been expelled from the army cadets for repeatedly undoing her top button. 'But it looks better that way,' she had complained. Not that Vesta normally wore any kind of uniform, but it took her three-quarters of an hour to get ready most mornings and here she was, her face clean and her hair concealed tidily under the wimple. No need for a mirror, even. A nun, after all, was just a nun.

As her stomach grumbled, she left the room and went down to the refectory for a cup of milk and a slice of bread and butter, which she ate at the long table alone. As she finished, two nuns came in and took their places on the lower table. She was about to carry her dirty plate to the kitchen when the old brass bell at the front gate sounded. The nuns froze, then looked at each other.

'I'll fetch Sister Mary,' one said.

They got to their feet.

'I'll go to the gate. Slowly,' the other replied, as she tucked her hands into the long sleeves of her habit and quit the room in such slow motion it was almost balletic.

Outside, in the courtyard Vesta could hear the rest of the order congregating now, rustling habits and the soles of sandals on the cobbles as the nuns emerged from the accommodation block. She joined them. The bishop and three priests in black vestments were emerging into the courtyard, the serene nun ahead of them, setting as slow a pace as she could. About a dozen of the women assembled, curtseying in unison as the party approached. Vesta thought she discerned a flicker of satisfaction on the bishop's face at their submission. He made the sign of the cross.

'I have come for Sisters Evangelista and Helena,' he said. 'I will speak to them.'

Sister Mary composed her expression as she moved to the front of the group. 'Our dear sisters are no longer here,' she said.

Vesta's heart sank. She tried to read Sister Mary's face but the old nun seemed absolutely unfazed. What on earth had happened in the night? Were Sister Evangelista and Sister Helena all right? Was Sister Mary lying or, Vesta worried, suddenly in a flash, were the two younger nuns dead?

'And where, pray tell, are they?' the bishop asked in an affronted tone.

'They are safe,' Sister Mary replied calmly. 'That is all I am permitted to say.'

'Permitted? By whom? I demand, as your bishop, that you tell me.'

Sister Mary's face remained stationary. 'Forgive me, my lord,' she said.

He did not like that. 'Where is Sister Triduana?' he snapped.

She appeared then at the entrance to the dormitory wing and came to stand beside Sister Mary. 'You will have to forgive us all,' she said. 'We have considered matters and, despite everything, we have hope. We take strength from our order. Our sisterhood.'

'Hope!' the bishop spat. 'Any hope you harbour cannot last, you stupid woman. The police will make the same connection I have made when they look into Sister Monica's identity. Sisters Evangelista and Helena will need proper protection. They must be sent abroad, at the least. Besides, it is time to say plainly that this place cannot continue indefinitely in the way it has. Times are changing. The Little Sisters of Gethsemane must change too. You have no purpose any more.'

'We may be old but we are not weary. He will protect us,' Sister Mary said evenly. 'All of us are getting older, my lord.' She eyed him pointedly.

Vesta felt suddenly proud of these women for not being cowed. She wondered what connection the bishop had made when he had looked into Paul Thompson.

'I will take Mother's office,' he said. 'You will be called individually,' he added. He and his cohort swept past the nuns and up the stairs.

Vesta turned to Sister Triduana. 'What happened to Sisters Evangelista and Helena?' she whispered. 'Are they all right?'

Sister Triduana regarded her for a moment. She laid a hand on Vesta's arm. 'Many secrets are hurried away under cover of darkness. For He is wise,' she whispered, and winked cheekily. 'The Little Sisters of Gethsemane, like the Poor Clares, I'm sure, have many friends in the world.'

Vesta smiled. She thought if the two younger nuns had left the convent it must have happened after she had freed Mirabelle and gone up to bed. Before that she had been listening carefully and would have heard the gate had it been opened to spirit the sisters away.

'When?' she asked.

Sister Triduana gave her a sweet from her pocket. 'On God's tide,' she said. 'Do not concern yourself. Go to Sister Bernadette, Sister,' the nun advised, as one of the priests appeared at the entrance to Mother Superior's stair. 'She will need breakfast.'

'Sister Mary,' the priest called, with the tone of the secretary at a dentist's surgery. 'He will see you first.'

Matins was getting under way, rather late, Vesta noted, given that the sun was long risen. She collected a tray and laid out Sister Bernadette's breakfast. On the way to the dormitory block she passed Sister Mary coming down after her interview, as collected as ever.

'He wants to see Sister Triduana,' Sister Mary said to the priest at the bottom of the stair, and the name was repeated, called like the tolling of a bell by one and then another of the bishop's attendants. As Sister Triduana disappeared up one stairway, Vesta climbed another.

'Good morning, Sister,' Vesta said cheerily, as she laid the tray on the side table.

Sister Bernadette was, most unusually, already awake. 'Ah. My dear,' she said, and peered at the tray, which contained a clay beaker of milk, bread, butter and a sliced apple. She eyed the apple with dubiety.

'I could stew it for you if you'd prefer,' Vesta offered.

Sister Bernadette beamed. 'For lunch,' she said, with enthusiasm.

Vesta placed the tray on her lap. 'Sister Evangelista and Sister Helena have gone,' she said. 'In the night.'

The old nun nodded and sipped her milk. 'I'm glad you're here, my dear. It occurred to me only this morning that living through interesting times is often so . . . inconvenient. Irregular hours and so forth. But He would not have sent such times if we were not equal to them, would He?'

Vesta sighed. So all the nuns knew – even bedbound Sister Bernadette. 'How did you find out that they had gone?' she asked. 'Nobody told me.'

'Sister Mary visited in the night. Just before the sky got light. I am the oldest sister, after all.'

'Have you lived through interesting times before, Sister?'

The nun shrugged. 'It is our order's burden.'

'The bishop has arrived,' Vesta added.

'I said he would,' Sister Bernadette replied sagely, and put down her beaker. 'Maybe you should go back to your own order, Sister.'

'I thought it would be best to leave on Monday,' Vesta said reverently. 'It would not do to travel on the Lord's Day.'

The old nun sighed. 'You may be right, of course.'

Vesta stared out of the window across the garden. 'I wish I could help,' she said. 'That's all.'

Sister Bernadette squeezed her hand. 'You got rather caught here, didn't you? You'll be glad to get back to your own work. With the African mission. Far less . . . dramatic, I should think.'

Vesta bit her lip and restrained herself. 'Do you think the bishop has come for the formula to the salve?' she asked.

Bernadette gave a throaty chuckle. 'Undoubtedly. He thinks it is a secret.'

'Well, isn't it?' Vesta said.

The old woman waved her hand as if casting a spell. 'Passed from Mother to Mother. He thought Triduana would give it to him for she is the most biddable of us. You can always jolly Triduana along. It is her particular sin. However, one would think a man such as our bishop would understand the power of a story when set against the likely reality.' She bit into the slice of bread. 'You've sprinkled this with salt,' she added.

'In the absence of jam,' Vesta replied. 'I'm sorry.'

'Sublime.' Bernadette narrowed her eyes and smacked her lips.

'So isn't the formula passed from Mother to Mother?' Vesta pressed her.

Sister Bernadette affected serenity. 'I have said too much.'

'We shall have a formula for our soap at the Poor Clares,' Vesta added. 'That's why I'm asking.'

The sound that the old nun emitted was more a bark than a laugh. 'I hope your soap sells a great deal, but there is a lot of soap in the world. When the first sisters perfected Gethsemane Salve there was nothing like it. A man might die of a wound then – a woman too. In some places in the world today they still do. We kept that knowledge among ourselves so we might use it for good, not only in healing people but in bringing them to God,' she said. 'If there is one thing an older sister comes to understand, it is mortality. Only a fool would leave such valuable information in the hands, or mind, of one person. That would be vanity. Of course, more recently Mother discussed keeping the formula in a bank vault or sealed in a solicitor's safe. Times have changed. But these options were not available to the first Little Sisters of Gethsemane, not for centuries.'

Vesta perched on the edge of the bed. Bernadette was enjoying this. 'Go on,' she encouraged her.

'I have no more to say. Think, girl. Even you know the formula if only you are open to it. I won't tell you any more than that. We have not survived these centuries by telling our secrets, or for that matter the secrets of others.'

Vesta tried to work it out as Bernadette popped the last piece of bread into her mouth and chewed it with relish.

'Did Evangelista kill Sister Monica for the formula? Is that what you mean?'

'No.' Bernadette sounded genuinely shocked at this suggestion. 'Why would Monica matter? He was nothing. It is women who hold the power of creation. He was only a blip.'

'Not to Evangelista, he wasn't,' Vesta objected.

Bernadette sighed and pushed away the tray.

'Tell me,' Vesta begged her.

The old woman shook her head. 'I am sworn,' she said. 'But, I promise you, Evangelista has only acted for the best in all things. If with a somewhat dramatic flair. It is to the good that most men do not listen to women. Do not understand their actions. There, I have said too much as it is. I thought you would see it.'

As Vesta took the tray back downstairs she ran through

what she knew of Evangelista. The nun had fought with Helena over Monica but that made no sense because Vesta still didn't know why Monica had come. If it was to obtain the formula for Gethsemane Salve the young nun had failed, surely. Had Helena sought to help her? No. That couldn't be the case. Before Monica died, Evangelista had already retreated, which suggested she was in some kind of pain or confusion. That she wanted time to think. If the formula was shared among the nuns, she would not have needed any such thing. Her week in the anchorite's cell, however, had not calmed her. The state of the chapel was testament to that.

After Vesta had tidied up she decided she ought to join the rest of the sisters in the chapel. Quietly, she slipped into a pew at the back and noted that the door to the sacristy was open now and the smashed pews had been stacked once more to the side, awaiting repair. She searched the congregation for the figure of Sister Mary, but from the back all the nuns looked almost exactly the same. Nobody, it seemed, was perturbed about Mirabelle's escape. Beyond the broken windows the sky was blue this morning as the nuns chanted. It must be almost nine o'clock by now, Vesta thought. It would take the bishop all morning to work his way through the sisters, questioning them one by one.

'The salve,' Vesta whispered over and over, as if she were praying too. 'The salve and what it's made of.' And then it came to her as clear as the blue sky through the broken window frames. The formula had been on the glass. It was painted alongside the saints. Yes, she thought, all of them had been surrounded by flowers and leaves and crossed bones – daisies on their dresses. Lavender at their feet. That, she thought, was clever, and it meant, as Bernadette had intimated, that every one of the Little Sisters knew perfectly well what the formula was and none of them needed to mention a word to pass it on. It was there in front of them every day, when they made their devotions. In smashing the windows Evangelista had been trying to save the convent. A dramatic gesture against the incursion of the bishop, just as Bernadette had said, and, yes, easily misinterpreted by Rose Munro. By anyone looking on who didn't understand the significance of what had been painted onto the glass.

Vesta's eyes flashed as she continued to solve the puzzle. This meant that the deaths could not have been about the formula at all – not if it was an open secret. As long as one of the nuns survived, there was no chance of losing it, as the bishop clearly feared. The ingredients could be pieced together again and, for that matter, passed on. Already the sisters had collected the shattered images of the female saints and stored them in the sacristy.

She smiled slyly. The women must feel smug, she thought, with the bishop searching so desperately to find out something that had been in front of everyone the whole time. When he had taken the service for Monica's funeral it had shone onto the flagstone floor, lit by the sunshine. Well done, she thought. Well done. And turned her mind again to the murders.

She was just considering whether Mother Superior's death might be illuminated in the light of this new knowledge when one of the priests came into the chapel and touched her lightly on the arm. 'The bishop would like to see you, Sister Joseph,' he said. 'Please, come with me.'

'What does he want to talk to me for?' Vesta asked.

The priest either didn't know or didn't want to explain. 'Please. Come,' he repeated.

As Vesta climbed the shady stairwell she passed another

nun coming down, her face wet with tears. Oh dear, she thought. The bishop must be becoming more insistent. But he couldn't reasonably expect her to know anything about what had gone on. Or about the formula, for that matter. She hadn't known a quarter of an hour ago – she must try to return to that mindset. She paused outside the door of the office before knocking.

'Come in,' an impatient voice snapped.

Vesta took a deep breath to steel herself and opened the door.

Chapter Twenty-two

Discovery is not in seeking new landscapes
but in having new eyes

Mirabelle was not prepared to be left behind in Heriot Row. She dressed sensibly today in a pair of chocolate-coloured ankle grazers with a matching silk blouse and she left before Rennie arrived to pick up McGregor, who leaned against the doorframe as she passed. 'You can't help yourself, can you?' he taunted her.

Mirabelle kissed his cheek. 'I'll see you there,' she said.

She walked up to Princes Street station in the sunshine to catch the train to Dalmeny. The carriages were mostly empty, except for a few sailing enthusiasts heading for the harbours on either side of the firth. It was a lovely day to be out on a boat, she thought, as she slipped into first class and donned her sunglasses. People derided the Scottish weather, but when the sun shone it really was beautiful.

At Dalmeny station she got out and made her way down to the village. It was still early and South Queensferry was making a sleepy start to this sunny Saturday. She raised a hand to wave at the newsagent through the window. He recognised her and waved back. No wonder, she thought. McGregor had given him a five-pound note for driving her back into town so late. She watched as a paperboy with a full sack trudged from house to house delivering copies of the *Scotsman*. The bridge works were closed today and, facing eastwards, the village looked picturesque in the sunshine. She hoped the new bridge wouldn't spoil the place when it opened.

As she continued, she spotted a car parked outside the church. It was a glossy black Bentley that looked as if it had been abandoned beside a yew tree growing over the pavement. Mirabelle wandered over and laid her hand on the bonnet. The engine was warm. She glanced across the road at Dr Alexander's house. The front door was closed and Mirabelle could see through the window that the doctor was not in her surgery. The village felt deserted this morning. There seemed only one place the driver of the Bentley could have gone. There might be no service under way in the church but the door was open.

Following her nose, Mirabelle dodged through the gravestones, past an information board, which explained the history of the parish and its importance to pilgrims making their way to St Andrews during the medieval period. The ferry across the firth had carried them to Fife, leaving from the stretch of water lapping at the church's boundary. It had been for most the last leg of a long journey. Mirabelle wondered if there were any pilgrims, these days. It seemed unlikely.

Places of worship always smelt the same, she thought, as she dodged through the church's open door and breathed in the scent of waxed wood and old books, which hung heavily on the air. At the front, near the altar, a man in a well-cut brown tweed suit was on his knees, praying. Mirabelle slipped into a pew near the rear and waited.

He seemed intent. His pale hair was trimmed tidily and his choice of a green shirt with, she peered, a matching, darker green tie made him look almost timeless. Then, quite suddenly, she was distracted by the sound of a woman screaming outside, in the distance. No, she thought, not screaming exactly – more shouting. The man looked over his shoulder and got to his feet. He was taller than she might have expected, she thought, as she got up too, and together, without saying a word, they strode back outside into the sunshine. There was shadowy movement in several of the village's windows as people strained to see what was going on. Opposite the church Dr Alexander appeared in her doorway as the source of the noise, a woman in a thin cotton dress, so washed out it was difficult to tell what colour it had been, ran towards the village followed by three grubby children.

'Help!' she shouted. 'Help! There's a body!'

Mirabelle cocked her head and realised that the word wasn't body but 'baby'.

'Help!' the woman shouted again, continuing towards South Queensferry high street with the children in her wake.

The man from the church pushed ahead now, past Mirabelle, with a stern 'Excuse me', and strode onto the road. 'What is it?' he asked the woman, intent on taking charge of the situation as he stood in front of her, blocking her path.

'We need the police,' she said, making to move round him.

The man put out his hands and held her in place as if he might shake her. 'What's happened? Tell me.'

The woman squirmed. 'Leave me alone.'

One of the children, a little boy wearing grey shorts and a

short-sleeved blue shirt kicked the man in the shins. 'That's my ma!' he shouted. 'Let her go!'

Dr Alexander ran down her path, and from the direction of the village a policeman appeared, trotting up the road in his shirtsleeves, his hat in his hand and a Golden Retriever in his wake.

The man let the woman go and the doctor pushed in. 'Can I help?' she asked. 'Has somebody given birth at the site?'

'Now, now.' The policeman pulled up. He put his hat onto his head, out of force of habit, Mirabelle thought. The dog's tail was wagging as if it was clockwork. Then, realising how ridiculous he must look, the policeman pulled back his shoulders as if standing to attention. 'Can I help you, madam?' he asked.

The woman was crying now. 'Yes,' she said. 'It's the children. They found a baby buried in the woods.'

All eyes turned to the scatter of children at the woman's heels. The eldest girl stepped forward. 'We were digging,' she explained.

'Digging?' the policeman repeated.

'To make a pond,' the girl said. 'For the ducks. So they won't fly away and we can feed them.'

The policeman didn't question this. 'And what did you find?' he asked.

The girl sighed. 'A wee bairn,' she said. 'Just the bones of it. Wrapped in an old bit of sacking.'

Dr Alexander visibly relaxed. The man from the church took a step backwards. 'God,' he said, 'I thought someone had actually died.'

'If you don't mind, sir,' the policeman said. He turned towards the little girl. 'I'd better take a look, don't you think? Can you show me?'

'Will the dog come? Is it a police dog?' the little boy asked.

The policeman's expression softened. 'He's off duty. But he can come with us, if you like.'

The girl nodded and the party turned back down the road, the little boy taking his mother's hand. 'It was such a shock, Officer,' the woman said, as if she was apologising.

Everyone watched until they were out of earshot. In the flats above the shops, people moved away from the windows and went back to their breakfasts.

Dr Alexander gave a cursory smile. 'Gosh,' she said.

'What on earth do you think happened?' Mirabelle asked.

The doctor shrugged. 'I'm almost certain it's historic,' she said. 'Unbaptised children used not to be buried in hallowed ground. She said it was only the bones.'

'Yes,' the man agreed. 'Unbaptised children end up in Purgatory.'

'You're out early,' the doctor commented.

The man's gaze flicked back towards the church. He looked older than he was, Mirabelle thought, perhaps because he seemed worried. 'We had news last night,' he said, taking a car key out of his pocket. 'I was just . . . well, you know.'

'Is Grace all right?'

'She's fine.'

'Did she have her baby?' Mirabelle asked, cutting in.

The man turned. His hazel eyes narrowed as if he had only just noticed she was there. 'Who the hell are you?' he snapped.

Dr Alexander intervened. 'Miss Bevan has been helping at the Little Sisters,' she said. 'With the recent trouble. Mirabelle, this is Mr Farquarson-Sinclair from St Clair's Vale.'

Mirabelle held out her hand. 'It's nice to meet you. I didn't mean to pry.'

Dr Alexander's smirk betrayed that she clearly didn't believe this. But she didn't say anything. Mr Farquarson-Sinclair's handshake was as firm as you would expect of a parliamentary candidate.

'I've met your wife,' Mirabelle said. 'We're going to be neighbours. My husband and I have bought Shore Cottage.' She bit her lip. She'd called McGregor her husband again. Dr Alexander smirked once more.

'Robertson, isn't it?' Mr Farquarson-Sinclair said.

'His family. Yes. He's a McGregor, in fact.'

This appeared to soothe Mr Farquarson-Sinclair's concerns. 'Nasty business.' He gesticulated down the road. Mirabelle felt unsure whether he was referring to the deaths at the Little Sisters, the skeleton that had just been discovered or the trouble with McGregor's family the year before. It would have been rude of him to talk that way about the tragedy that had led to McGregor selling the family estate, she decided, but for the purposes of the conversation it didn't much matter which of the nasty businesses he was talking about.

'I'm glad to hear your daughter is all right,' she said. 'Please give Belinda my best.'

'Right,' he replied, and returned to his car.

Mirabelle and Dr Alexander stood in the street as he started the engine and drove back down the road. The doctor let out a long breath. 'That's some start to the day,' she said.

'You seem very relaxed about it.'

'Well, *you* obviously can't wait to get married.'

Mirabelle restrained herself from stamping her foot. 'I keep saying Alan and I are already hitched,' she said. 'I don't know why.'

'I imagine the fact that men like Mr Farquarson-Sinclair don't value a woman on her own probably has some bearing,'

Dr Alexander replied. 'He doesn't take us seriously – not even as doctors. When he was ill last winter, he insisted on a second opinion – some man he went to school with who has a practice in the New Town.' Her face crumpled. 'Oh, bother,' she said. 'You really are much too easy to talk to.'

Mirabelle grinned. 'I thought he was older. From the back. In the church.'

'He's probably quite good-looking, really,' the doctor said, as if such matters were ascertained in a laboratory. 'What are you doing out here anyway?'

Mirabelle shrugged. 'Right now I'm trying to figure out why a baby's skeleton being buried in the woods doesn't seem to worry you.'

Jeanette Alexander fumbled in her pocket for her cigarettes. She lit one and took a deep draw. 'Most doctors don't panic. Not once the patient is dead,' she said. 'If there's one thing you learn quickly, it's that.' The observation hung in the air. The doctor let it. Mirabelle adopted an unconvinced expression. After more than a minute of silent scepticism, the doctor let out a gasp. 'Oh, all right,' she said. 'It's not the first time they've found a baby's skeleton in the woods.'

'What do you mean?'

'The nunnery,' the doctor said simply. 'The hospital.' She gestured in the direction of the bridge works.

'Do you mean the nuns had . . . babies?'

Jeanette Alexander laughed heartily. 'I suppose some of them might. But that's not it. I know it looks like a sleepy little village, with its tiny church and the pretty terraces of fishing cottages, but South Queensferry was a real . . . centre. An important place. Hundreds of years ago, admittedly. Not even that many hundreds of years. People were still making pilgrimages into the eighteenth century.'

'You mean the crossing?' Mirabelle asked.

'Exactly. That's why the Little Sisters are here in the first place. It was like being on the highway – everyone went right past the door.'

'And they offered medical help? Gethsemane Salve.'

'They're known for the salve. I mean the salve is what went out into the world. They found half a pot of it buried with a skeleton near Acre a couple of years ago. It's in a museum in Jerusalem now. I suppose many of the pilgrims who came here were ill. That would have been why they made the journey. Medieval medicine couldn't do much for degenerative conditions so people relied on faith. Miracles. I'm sure the nuns would help anyone who needed it, but they were known for helping women in particular. They were early . . . feminists in a way.'

'And the skeleton of this baby?'

'Childbirth was dangerous. It's easy to forget just how dangerous it was. Women still die today but not in the same numbers. Babies too.'

Mirabelle nodded. 'So you think the skeleton . . .'

'It'll be historic. They couldn't bury them in the graveyard either here or at the nunnery if they weren't baptised. It wasn't . . . allowed.'

Mirabelle stared across the road at the graveyard. 'But the mothers . . .'

'Oh, yes. There must be mothers buried there. It's been a sanctified site for a millennium more or less. The ferry went from right there.' The doctor gestured past the graveyard. 'It moved decades ago, of course. There's a service that takes cars across at the other end of the village but the tailbacks are dreadful. That's why they're building the bridge. That church is relatively new by comparison to the cemetery and the nunnery – and St Clair's Vale if it comes to that. It was part of a priory originally – Carmelites, I think. Long gone now. The Little Sisters of Gethsemane are quite the survivors.'

Mirabelle wondered when Inspector Rennie and McGregor might arrive. It was almost nine o'clock. 'Thank you,' she said. 'It's so interesting, isn't it?'

The doctor turned towards her house. 'I'd better get on,' she said.

Mirabelle decided to take a walk through the graveyard. The commemorative stones were mostly not as old as the doctor's story would suggest but the site was relatively small and, she thought, graves could well have been dug on top of each other. She shuddered. The idea of being buried always scared her. It had been one of her worst fears during the Blitz: that a bomb would hit and she'd be buried alive in the rubble. The village might be pretty but it was so steeped in history it almost felt difficult to move. It had formed the place as if the stories of thousands of people were captured in the buildings. So many things seemed to have happened there – pain and illness, suffering and belief.

In the sunshine, she sat down on a mossy stone bench and stared along the coast towards Shore Cottage, which was obscured from view by the trees. That was when she noticed it. It was the stone that first drew her attention – one of few in the cemetery that was not dusted with moss and lichen because it was too new. Curious, she cut through the higgledy-piggledy older graves and stood before it. It said simply, 'James Thompson 1899–1958'. Sister Monica's father, or rather Paul Thompson's – Sister Evangelista and Sister Helena's father too. He had died younger than Mirabelle had imagined. She wondered what kind of cancer it had been. It made sense that they had buried him here. He had died at

Shore Cottage after all: why not inter him close by, near his daughters?

She looked round. Most of the other graves bore inscriptions: biblical phrases about eternal rest and angels. James Thompson had nothing save his name and dates. No, not nothing. Someone had visited the grave. She bent down and dusted off a layer of soil to reveal a posy of rosemary tied with a yellow ribbon. 'Hello again,' she said, picking it up. The rosemary leaves were still lithe. They couldn't have been left more than a day ago, not in this weather. The stalks were tied in the same way as the bunch that had been left on Sister Monica's grave.

Picking her way down the lines of monuments, Mirabelle checked the rest of the little cemetery. At the far end there was a small stone mausoleum dedicated to the Farquarson-Sinclairs. Two of the family dogs had been buried there in 1878, and a ladies' maid who, it said on the memorial stone, 'had given the family good service for 46 years'. The last interment was from 1944. Mr Farquarson-Sinclair's father, she calculated.

Back in the main part of the graveyard, she wondered where Bang Bang MacDonald's body lay. Not here by the look of it, next to James Thompson, who must have been her brother . . . or, she thought it through, her brother-in-law. That would be why they had different surnames. Two burials only months apart in the same family: you'd expect them to be together. Perhaps she's with the nuns, Mirabelle thought, and slipped the sprig of rosemary back onto James Thompson's grave. Then she turned down the road through the woods and began to walk.

Chapter Twenty-three

Some rise by sin, some by virtue fall

Vesta braced herself as if she was about to dive into icy water before stepping into Mother Superior's office. 'Come in!' the bishop called airily. Inside, he was sitting behind the desk, comfortable in Mother's chair. 'Ah . . . Sister Joseph . . . Miss . . . Vesta, isn't it?'

Vesta grinned. He knew she wasn't a nun, which provided her with an opportunity to take charge – at least of what he called her. 'It's Mrs, actually,' she said crisply. 'Mrs Lewis.'

The bishop hesitated. 'Mrs Lewis,' he repeated, as if her name were a riddle or perhaps a question. 'Have you found out anything? Do you know who killed Sister Monica?'

Vesta shook her head. 'I'm sorry,' she said. 'It's difficult to get anything out of the nuns. They don't go in for casual conversation.'

The bishop's lips tightened. He was evidently finding the same. 'Do you know where Sister Evangelista and Sister Helena have been concealed?'

'The nuns didn't include me in whatever they got up to last night,' she admitted.

The bishop held her gaze as if he was examining her soul. 'Very well,' he said at length. 'I want you to fetch my secretary's things. You might as well be useful. Mrs Munro was staying here. She left yesterday without her bags.'

Vesta shifted from foot to foot. 'I see,' she said.

'It isn't appropriate for a man to enter the accommodation block. I want you to pack for her and hand her case to one of the priests. Then you can go. Your services are no longer required.'

'But I don't want to go,' Vesta objected.

The bishop's cheeks flushed. 'What you want is of no concern and less interest. You have been curiously ineffective, Mrs Lewis. Frankly, I can't see the point of Miss Bevan paying your fee.'

'Mirabelle isn't paying me,' Vesta said. 'I'm on holiday. I'm here for the wedding.'

The bishop exhaled furiously. 'Whatever it is. You're dismissed,' he barked.

'Mother Superior contracted Mirabelle,' Vesta continued to make her case, 'and Mirabelle contracted me. I don't work for you.'

The bishop's eyes narrowed. 'How do you think the sisters will take it if they find out you're not really a nun, Mrs Lewis? How do you think they'll react if they discover you've been spying on them? You have no authority here. You're only a woman.'

'What do you mean?'

The bishop coughed. 'Your sex makes you particularly vulnerable. Don't you understand that? The Church requires women to obey its edicts if they want protection. We burned witches not ten miles from this convent. The Little Sisters of Gethsemane lie within my jurisdiction and I am taking charge. You will recognise my authority or things will go badly for you.'

Vesta crossed her arms, then uncrossed them. Mirabelle was better at confrontation, especially with old White men. 'Witches,' she said. 'What nonsense.'

The bishop stared at her as if she were a fool. It felt as if they were at an impasse. Vesta considered continuing to argue. It was not as if he could burn her at the stake. However, she wasn't sure what she'd gain from picking a fight with him. When it came down to it, the priest who had called her upstairs was a larger fellow than the bouncer on the door at the Regent ballroom on Saturday night and she wouldn't pick a fight with him either. The reality was, the longer she could stay inside the convent, the better. She might as well go to the accommodation block.

'You don't have to threaten me,' she said. 'I'll fetch Mrs Munro's things.'

She closed the door behind her and slowly made her way along the corridors that led to the nuns' sleeping quarters. Mrs Munro had been staying in one of the cells on the top floor. 'It has the best view,' she'd said, as she'd panted her way up the stairs. Inside, Vesta pulled the secretary's suitcase from under the bed and removed her things from the washstand. She took down a thin pink cardigan from the hook behind the door and folded it.

She was about to pack it into the case when she caught sight of a pile of papers underneath a tangle of Mrs Munro's stockings and a fresh blouse. On top was the petition against Sister Monica's burial and below that the convent's correspondence log. Vesta opened it. Sister Evangelista had been given permission to correspond with Paul Thompson, she noted. No surprises there. She'd have guessed as much now. She turned the page to Sister Helena, who, it seemed, was in touch with nobody. Putting the log back, she continued down the pile to another small leather-bound book. Opening it, she saw it was a log of the prayers the order had offered up including intercessions for good causes. These were recorded daily and went back for years.

She turned to the previous November and began to read the tiny, spidery writing that crept tidily across the page. The nuns had prayed for James Thompson on his death. The entry called him a sinner, she noted, and for several weeks between that date and the middle of January they had offered devotions for the wellbeing of a Sister Grace. It had been the main thing they prayed for. Vesta closed the log. She had not met anyone called Sister Grace the whole time she'd been at the convent. Did it mean Grace Farquarson-Sinclair? Did the nuns know about the girl's pregnancy? No, it was too early for that, surely.

Her curiosity piqued, she closed the suitcase and carefully picked it up. It was heavy, the leather-bound books adding considerable weight to the thin summer clothes Mrs Munro had brought with her. Vesta manoeuvred it out of the cell and hauled it downstairs slowly, step by step. On the first floor she stopped, considering, then made a detour to Sister Bernadette's cell.

The old nun was still propped up in bed, though she now had a psalter in front of her at which she was squinting. Vesta knew Bernadette wouldn't be able to make out a single word, though she probably knew the book's contents by heart.

'Sister Joseph,' Bernadette greeted her delightedly. Ever hopeful, she peered around Vesta as if a snack might be concealed behind her.

'The bishop questioned me,' Vesta announced.

The old nun closed the psalter with a decisive snap.

'He asked me to fetch Mrs Munro's bag and I looked inside. Might I ask you something?'

'Of course, my dear.'

'Who is Sister Grace?'

Bernadette's face opened into an almost toothless grin. 'She left the order. She was a lovely woman. Very devout. She lived nearby for a long while, though she has been gathered to God now, bless her soul.'

'Do you mean Bang Bang MacDonald?'

The nun let out a laugh that sounded as if it had come from the belly of a far younger woman. 'The gun,' she said. 'Ah, yes. She used to prop it in the doorframe of the chapel when she went in.'

'Her name was Grace, was it?'

'Grace was the name she adopted when she took orders. Her real name was Cressida, I think. Cressida MacDonald – quite a mouthful. I can see why they called her Bang Bang, can't you?' The nun seemed serious suddenly. 'We each choose our names when we come here. Saint Grace was a martyr of the early Church. They cut off her breasts when she refused to abandon her faith.' She shuddered at the thought. 'Bang Bang must have chosen it.'

'I read in Mother Superior's log that the whole order prayed for Sister Grace last winter. Weeks of it.'

'She was ill before He took her,' Bernadette said slowly, as she remembered. 'Poor Grace.'

'Did you know her well?'

Bernadette nodded. 'As well as I might. Why do you ask?'

'I didn't know who she was and I wondered why everyone had prayed for her.'

'Ah – the true work of our order. Our triumvirate.'

Vesta sank onto the chair beside the bed. 'I worked it out,' she said with a grin. 'The windows. The formula. Seven parts of lavender at St Brigid's feet to four parts of bergamot on St

Enoch's dress and two of marigold and the bones to make the gelatin and . . . Is it salt? The little pile in St Triduana's hand?'

Bernadette brought her finger to her lips. 'Sssh,' she said.

'That's very clever – the recipe as a picture,' Vesta said. 'The bishop is sending me away,' she added with a sigh. 'You confided in me and I want to confide in you too. I came here under false pretences, Sister Bernadette.'

Bernadette reached out a thin-skinned, freckled, bony hand and grasped Vesta's fingers. 'We do not demand to know why women come. I always assumed you chose us because of your child, Sister Joseph.'

Vesta's hand sprang involuntarily to her stomach. 'But . . . how could you know that I'm . . .'

Bernadette chuckled. 'Come now. You scent the air like a hunting dog, Sister. Yet you cannot bear to look at the food you bring me. You wish for a little girl, I imagine.'

Vesta sat back in surprise. 'How on earth . . .'

'It's your nature. You are of the Divine Feminine,' Sister Bernadette said in a matter-of-fact tone.

'Do the other nuns know?' Vesta demanded.

Bernadette gave a little shrug. 'I have no idea. You perhaps do not realise because I am old, but I have a great deal of experience,' she added, somewhat smugly. 'Some convents are places to hide from the world. The Little Sisters of Gethsemane is no different in some respects from those places, but we do not hide here. That is the difference. We are sisters not only to each other but to all women.'

'The true work of the order,' Vesta whispered, repeating what Bernadette had said, a glimmer of understanding forming in her mind. A triumvirate must have three pillars.

Prayer. Yes, that would be one. Solidarity with other women. Care for them, perhaps. What might the third thing be? 'This place is a refuge, then,' she said.

Bernadette squeezed Vesta's hand once more. 'I'll give you some advice. You must not be embittered by what has happened to you. There are evil men in the world but also good ones. I believe there are more good than bad, no matter how much evil I see. However awful the circumstances of her conception, your daughter is a gift. All will be forgiven for she is holy.'

It was Vesta's turn to smile. 'I wasn't raped, Sister Bernadette,' she said, thinking of the sparkle in Charlie's brown eyes and the way he held her when she was sleeping. 'I'm a married woman. I'm not really a nun.'

'Ah,' Bernadette said, as if the pieces were falling into place. 'I wondered.'

'Where did I go wrong?' Vesta asked, as a matter of professional interest.

Bernadette gestured airily. 'You don't pray,' she said. 'You're not interested in prayer.'

Vesta laughed. 'No. I tried but I'm not very good at it.'

'I wasn't sure, of course. The first ten years I was here, I did not truly understand the importance of prayer. I considered myself a woman of action. But I have come to see the vital nature of devotion. Prayer is a form of action. Quite as much as anything else.'

'And the work of the order?'

Bernadette gestured again. 'We move with the tide. It is the rhythm of God. I rather assumed you were readying yourself to ask for help. Which we would never deny you.'

'Actually, I hoped to be able to help you. But the bishop wants me to go,' Vesta said.

'Are you pleased to leave?'

'No.'

The old woman cocked her head to one side. 'But it is time, I think. And the bishop will be gone soon. Perhaps then you will return . . .'

Vesta kissed the old woman on the forehead and left the room. Outside, she manhandled the suitcase downstairs and presented it to the priest stationed at the bottom of the stairs that led to Mother's office.

'Here,' she said. 'The bishop asked me to fetch this. It belongs to Mrs Munro. There are papers inside that may be of interest.'

The man picked up the case with one hand and placed it to one side. Vesta cursed having had to struggle.

'I understand you're leaving,' he said.

Vesta neither confirmed nor denied this. Her eyes wandered across the courtyard, towards the chapel.

'It would be best if you don't say goodbye. There's no need to disturb the sisters,' the priest said, his emphasis on the last word almost a scolding, showing that he knew she had never taken vows. 'They are godly women.'

Vesta took heart from the vacant windows. The nuns knew how to keep secrets. How to defend themselves. 'Right,' she said, 'I'll fetch my bag.' He followed her at a distance as she went back upstairs and swept her things into the old case. Outside once more, she set out across the courtyard, down the path in the sunshine. The priest continued to escort her. 'I'm going,' she said.

'I shall bar the gate behind you.'

It seemed strange he did not walk alongside. It was like being trailed by a kind of Brylcreemed ghoul. She stood back from the gate and let him wrestle the bar out of its socket.

Opening the door, Vesta peered onto the tree-lined track. The world seemed suddenly indescribably huge. The priest stood back. 'Goodbye,' she said. He didn't reply and she didn't look behind her, only heard the door close in her wake and the bar scrape back into place. She stopped then and looked both ways. Further down the track a huge black car with a man at the wheel rumbled through the trees. She squinted – it was a Bentley. Charlie always said he'd love a soft-topped Bentley more than a Rolls-Royce or a Jaguar. 'They're almost silent,' he had enthused, when they'd passed one in Soho the last time they'd been in London.

Vesta stepped to the side and let the car pass. The man raised a hand in a cheery sort of wave that did not match his expression. This did not worry her for she was far more set on getting back to Mirabelle. The leaves cast dappled shadows onto the ground ahead, and as she turned in the opposite direction she pieced together everything she'd learned in the last few days up to the moment she'd said goodbye to Sister Bernadette. It felt as if she was unravelling quite the tangle of complicated information. She needed to process it.

As she approached Shore Cottage, Mrs Grieg appeared ahead, a string bag in her hand containing a pint of milk, a packet of fig rolls and a tin of blacking. 'Good morning, Sister Joseph,' she greeted Vesta.

'Good morning.' Vesta decided not to disabuse the housekeeper about who she was. It would only necessitate a long explanation. Through the trees she could just catch a glimpse of the water down at the firth, sparkling in the sunshine. 'Blacking today?' she said, indicating the tin in the bag.

'The stove,' Mrs Grieg confirmed. 'The new houses have electric ovens and they're cleaner but I'm not sure they cook properly. I wonder if Miss Bevan will want to refit the kitchen when she marries.'

Vesta decided not to tell the housekeeper that Miss Bevan was unlikely to cook at all. She wondered whether the oven in Mirabelle's flat on the front in Brighton had been switched on once in the whole time she had lived there. 'Mrs Grieg,' she said, 'might I come in for a while? I need to sit down. Do you happen to have a pen and paper I could borrow? I'm sure Miss Bevan wouldn't mind. I need to make some notes.'

'Of course, Sister Joseph,' Mrs Grieg replied. 'Would you like a cup of tea?'

Vesta's face cracked into a grin. 'Thank you.'

The women turned off the main track.

'There's trouble in the village this morning,' Mrs Grieg said, as eager to share gossip as usual.

'What kind of trouble?'

'A baby's skeleton found in the woods.' Mrs Grieg gestured towards the bridgeworks. 'Some of the children from the shanty found it. Those Micks are as bad as Gypsies.'

'Now, now, Mrs Grieg.' Vesta endeavoured to look pious.

'But they are, Sister,' the housekeeper insisted. 'Blow-ins. Nobody from round here would be surprised at finding such a thing,' she said with a self-satisfied air. 'Screaming and the like.'

'What do you mean?'

'We know. Over the years. The lost souls. Stillborn babies. Unbaptised. They cannot be buried in consecrated ground. Grace have mercy on them.'

'Grace?'

'Saint Grace, Sister. The patron saint of lost children,' Mrs Grieg said, as if speaking to an infant.

It was as if a light went on in Vesta's brain. 'Saint Grace,' she repeated. 'I thought she was a martyr,' she added, picking up her pace. She really needed to write all of this down. 'Patron saint of lost children. Of course. Thank you.'

Chapter Twenty-four

Woman rules us still

Mirabelle kept an eye on the main road but there was no sign of McGregor and Rennie. Nor in the other direction did the local policeman make his return from the bridge works. A man walked his terrier down to the water and bade Mirabelle a bluff 'Good morning' as he passed, his shadow trailing in his wake as the dog jumped enthusiastically into the swell. 'Dougal!' the man shouted. 'Not again!'

After a few minutes, she decided to walk on to Shore Cottage. McGregor, after all, would give her a lift home from there, eventually. This time, rather than follow the path, she cut through the trees, half hoping she would come across the policeman and the party from the site. She was curious about the baby's skeleton. The child had said the bones had been swaddled in sacking and it occurred to her that the cloth might hold a clue to the baby's identity and how long ago it had been put into the ground. It made sense to her that a woman might go on pilgrimage to hide her pregnancy hundreds of years ago, as Dr Alexander had said, but it seemed unlikely that medieval sacking would survive for centuries buried near the damp, muddy foreshore.

The woods smelt of green leaves and mulch, and it was markedly cooler out of the sunshine. Mirabelle was glad she'd worn appropriate footwear as she scrambled over a moss-covered trunk that must have been felled in a storm and continued inland, following the undulation of the hill as it rose. It was so quiet here it was difficult to believe she was only a few minutes outside the capital city. She hoped the new bridge wouldn't disturb the peace. The rail bridge hardly seemed to impinge on the village, except for the occasional rattle of a passing train.

Coming into the sunshine at the base of a wheat field, she put her hand up to shade her eyes and fumbled in her pocket for her sunglasses. Across the field a figure wearing a wide-brimmed hat hovered on the fringes. She was carrying a large basket. Mirabelle squinted and set out to greet Belinda Farquarson-Sinclair, who was wearing a shapeless green dress the colour of camouflage, quite a change from the last time Mirabelle had seen her when she had sported an outfit that might have adorned the pages of *Vogue*. 'Hello,' Mirabelle called.

Belinda looked up and drew a hand to her hat, as if checking her appearance. 'Oh, it's you,' she said. 'It was difficult to make you out. Brown,' she added, her eyes running across Mirabelle's outfit.

'And you in green.' Mirabelle smiled. She peered at the contents of Belinda's basket. 'Are those elderflowers?'

Belinda nodded. 'They grow on the edge of the wood and in the hedgerows. Our cook makes them into cordial. The flowers will be finished soon. I thought I'd pick the last of them.'

'Keeping your mind off things?'

'What do you mean?'

'I met your husband in South Queensferry,' Mirabelle admitted. 'At the church. He mentioned you had had news of Grace.'

'Gosh. You're just everywhere, aren't you?' Belinda sneered. 'At the convent attending the funeral of someone you didn't know. In church, prying into my family's private business. You pop up all over the place.' She paused, biting her lower lip. 'I'm sorry,' she said. 'That was rude of me.'

'It's all right. Mother Superior asked me to look into Sister Monica's death,' Mirabelle added. 'I was prying, you're right, but I was asked to do it. It seems as if a perfect storm is hanging over everything out here. Two nuns dead in a week, to start with.'

Belinda crouched to snap off a small cluster of elderflowers. She put them into the basket. 'I'd better get on,' she said, and turned in the direction of St Clair's Vale.

Mirabelle fell into step beside her. 'I didn't take you for the make-do-and-mend type,' she said.

Belinda shrugged. 'I'm not really. All that seems old-fashioned and rather dull now. We can have whatever we want these days.'

'Can we?'

Belinda didn't reply.

'It's such a fascinating place out here,' Mirabelle tried to put her at her ease. 'Such a beautiful day, too. It's always so peaceful.'

Belinda turned. 'Look, what do you want?' she asked bluntly.

'Mother Superior—'

Belinda cut her off. 'Yes, yes, I know. Mother asked you to look into the death of some nun and now you want the run of the place.'

'In point of fact, it wasn't a nun. It was Miss MacDonald's nephew.'

Belinda rolled her eyes. Mirabelle cocked her head. That certainly wasn't the reaction she might have expected, though it was possible Belinda had already heard about Paul Thompson's infiltration of the nunnery. The story was sensational enough to spread like wildfire once it got out in the village.

'I'm curious about Miss MacDonald,' Mirabelle continued. 'I noticed her brother-in-law's gravestone at the church.'

'You really are incorrigible.'

'He wasn't as old as I expected. The nuns seem to benefit from impressive longevity. I had assumed Miss MacDonald was an old woman. But her brother-in-law was only sixty. Was she older or younger than him?'

Belinda picked up her pace. 'I don't know.'

'How old would you say she was at a guess?' Mirabelle asked.

'Late fifties?' Belinda sounded exasperated.

'It seems they both died quite young, then.'

'I suppose so,' Belinda replied bitterly. 'Some people are weak in the chest or the heart or whatever.'

'Neither of them died of respiratory or pulmonary problems.'

'Oh, do fuck off!' Belinda exclaimed.

'I beg your pardon?'

Belinda stopped dead. 'This is none of your business,' she spat. 'It's nasty – poking about like this into poor Bang Bang's death. She was a jolly nice person. Why don't you just go away?'

'My husband and I have bought Shore Cottage,' Mirabelle said.

'I've a good mind to ask whoever the new Mother Superior is not to give consent to you moving in. I can't imagine having someone like you as a neighbour, Miss Bevan. We don't like busybodies here. We keep ourselves to ourselves. It's the Queensferry way.'

Mirabelle took a step backwards. 'It seems I've shaken you, Mrs Farquarson-Sinclair.'

'Yes,' Belinda snapped. 'Pursuing me over my own land the day my daughter . . . my little girl . . .' She bit her lip again. 'Dammit,' she said, closing her eyes. 'You don't have children. How could you possibly understand?'

Mirabelle blushed. Belinda was right. She didn't understand. The other day this woman had seemed as cool as a cucumber about her daughter's pregnancy.

The sound of a siren cut through the woods, distracting both of them. 'What's that?' Belinda said.

'I imagine it's the police,' Mirabelle replied. 'A baby's skeleton was found near the bridge site this morning. Dr Alexander thinks it's probably historic – medieval perhaps. They used to bury unbaptised children in the woods.'

'Down by the water,' Belinda said wistfully.

'The doctor said that one had been found there before.'

Belinda turned inland. 'I'm going home,' she said. 'I've had quite enough.'

Mirabelle watched her go. As she disappeared between the trees the basket tipped and some of the elderflowers spilled onto the ground, but Belinda didn't stop to retrieve them and Mirabelle thought it wouldn't be helpful to shout to point it out. She decided to cut back to the main track. Turning, she headed towards the shoreline, coming out on a high embankment at the start of the shanty village, where a police car had now parked at the gates alongside two other vehicles.

Mirabelle continued down the hill, past the works. To the right, where the trees met the shore, a crowd had formed. The policeman in his shirtsleeves was directing people to keep back. Children were struggling to see what was going on as two uniformed officers dug in the ground. She strained to make out Rennie and McGregor, who were interviewing occupants of the campsite to one side. Ah, she thought, that's where they got to. Rennie cut off his conversation when a man raised a large camera over the heads of the children and took a picture, a flash bursting like a firework. The inspector was angry. She could hear him shouting, though couldn't make out the words from so far away. Something like 'You can't take pictures of the kids.' Mirabelle's gaze shifted further towards the water where a group of women were praying, along from the excavation. She squinted. Two of the women seemed out of place. She wondered why. They were dressed like the others but seemed separate somehow. As the prayer finished, they crossed themselves in unison.

Inspector Rennie turned and noticed them at the same time; something out of step. He walked over and started to talk to one of them. The other moved backwards into the trees. The journalist with the camera followed and took two pictures of the inspector before one of the policemen could interpose himself in front of the camera. Rennie reached out and pulled the woman away by the arm. The crowd shifted, as if torn between the baby's skeleton being unearthed and the line of questioning unravelling in its midst. Mirabelle wished she could hear what was being said. She made her way past the first line of caravans and into the trees.

By the time she emerged at the crowd, however, Rennie, McGregor and the women were gone. She cursed herself.

She must have passed them in the woods. There were tracks all over the place between the trees.

'Excuse me,' she asked a lady, who was holding onto a little boy. 'Did you see the policemen who left? With a woman?'

'Aye,' she said. 'She was a nun. Nun on the run.' She smiled. 'Can you imagine that?'

'Nun on the run?'

'That's what he said. Why else would a nun leave the convent? With all that's been going on, I don't know what she was doing here. The police have her now, anyway.'

'Did you catch the nun's name?' Mirabelle asked.

'Helena,' the journalist said as he approached. 'Who might you be?'

'I'm a neighbour,' Mirabelle said. 'I live down the track.'

The journalist accepted this and didn't seem to notice the woman eyeing Mirabelle with disbelief. Everyone round here really did know everyone else.

'Do you know that nun?' the journalist asked. 'Helena? You must be familiar with the convent.'

'Only a little,' Mirabelle said uncertainly.

'There's been a lot of trouble recently. Would you say the nuns were crazed, Mrs . . .?'

'I would not,' Mirabelle replied firmly, and did not give her name.

'All right if I get a picture?'

'Certainly not.' She turned away, stepping under cover of the trees.

As she scrambled back up to the track, away from the site, she pictured the two women in her mind's eye. They had been uncomfortable in their clothes. That was what was out of place. It must feel odd after years in a habit to wear a light summer dress. Rennie was a good policeman to pick up on it. Normally, it was the kind of thing only a woman might sense. Staring ahead in the direction of the convent, she realised how little she knew about Sister Helena. Vesta had mentioned Evangelista, and the nun's erratic behaviour meant she had garnered all the attention. It was Evangelista who had indulged in self-harm for whatever reason – religious devotion or otherwise. It was Evangelista who had lost her temper in the chapel and smashed the stained glass. Evangelista who had been seen arguing with Sister Monica. Evangelista whose furious face had appeared framed by the window above Mirabelle's head the previous evening. The other Thompson sister was silent, almost anonymous. That had been a flaw in the investigation: she hadn't realised that until now.

McGregor wasn't going to pick up the car any time soon. Not now. He'd stay with Rennie and sit in on any questioning he was allowed to, so Mirabelle began to walk with some determination in the direction of the convent. She recalled the two women as best she could. It was difficult to say if the second had been Evangelista. Recognising a nun in civilian clothes was near to impossible. The hair and the colour of a dress changed everything, it seemed. However, what was certain was that the woman she'd questioned had talked of only one nun being taken away. So had the journalist. Had the second melted into the woods?

As the Celtic cross loomed ahead, Mirabelle slipped around the side of the convent's high wall. There was no point in knocking on the door – she definitely wasn't welcome. The loading gate was barred today but Mirabelle continued round the perimeter to where the wall became lower on the garden side and there she carefully climbed over, dropping onto a bed of brassicas – white and purple cauliflowers. Glad she had worn such a dark colour, she slid round the perimeter of the garden. As she neared the building complex she could hear the sisters chanting in the chapel. She checked left and right as she slipped inside, along a corridor that she knew would take her in the direction of the old hospital. If she calculated correctly, this would bring her out where she wanted to be – just inside the main gate.

The skirtings were dusty: a good sign that the corridor was little used. She moved silently, on tiptoe, as quickly as she could along the terracotta tiles and through a heavy oak door that creaked loudly as she opened it, making her heart pound. On the other side, the building lay in darkness, an eerie atmosphere, like that of an abandoned stately home. The room where Monica had undergone the post-mortem still smelt faintly of bleach. As Mirabelle passed it, she came into a hallway with a staircase that must have led up to the old hospital wards. She gasped, clearing the banister, as a huge ivory figure of Christ on the cross loomed at her from the top of the stairs, as if it was fluorescent. She almost crossed herself. The nuns must be getting to her. It was important to stay calm.

Crossing the hallway, she tried a door that was only a cupboard containing a musty old mop and half-empty packets of soda crystals. The next door was more fruitful and opened onto the reception area she had visited with Sister Mary on the first day of the investigation. Two long windows shed enough light to read by as Mirabelle pulled herself onto the high wooden stool where a nun would sit to admit a new sister. She ran her hand across the leather binding and opened the heavy front page of the admissions log. 'Damn,' she cursed. She almost wished she'd gone back to Trotter's. She would, she promised herself, once all this was over. Pausing for a moment to try to focus, she turned the pages with a good deal more purpose than she had the first time she'd been here. Now, of course, she had more idea what she was looking for.

Cressida MacDonald had arrived at the Little Sisters of Gethsemane in July 1941. She had given an address in north London and had been wearing what sounded like wartime utility clothing – an A-line skirt and a blouse with a Peter Pan collar. Mirabelle pictured her ringing the bell at the gate: a woman in her late thirties by her reckoning. The Little Sisters of Gethsemane seemed a strange choice for the times. Most women of Miss MacDonald's age during the war volunteered for the Wrens or to help in the Home Guard or a branch of the Women's Voluntary Service. What had made Bang Bang come here, so far out of the way?

Flipping forward, Mirabelle found Evangelista, the next year, following her aunt into the convent just before Christmas in 1942. She made a very young novice, Mirabelle noted, at only sixteen or thereabouts. She recalled the photograph she'd found in Paul Thompson's briefcase: two children on Hampstead Heath with their gas masks. The young boy had presumably been Paul. Was the older girl Helena, and had Evangelista been cropped out? She wondered about the date: their mother, Mrs Thompson, had been killed in the Blitz. The most intense period of German bombing had preceded both women enrolling at the convent. Yes, she thought, it might be assumed that both Bang Bang MacDonald and Evangelista had arrived at the Little Sisters after Mrs Thompson's death, leaving the two younger children at home in London or wherever they might have been evacuated to. That, she thought, must have been a big decision. Looking back, the spirit had been for families to stick together where they could. For children to be looked after. Retreating into a convent was hardly doing something for the nation or for the family. And, she thought, this meant the aunt and her niece must have spent months, even years, here together, before Bang Bang had voided her vows and moved to Shore Cottage, leaving her family once more, in effect. Perhaps it had been grief, she thought, Cressida losing a sister, Evangelista losing her mother. Maybe that had compelled them.

Letting this settle in, Mirabelle continued to read. Evangelista, the book said, had been admitted to the hospital when she arrived. This surprised Mirabelle. Her sense had been that the hospital at the Little Sisters had been closed for a long time. There was, she considered, the possibility that Dr Alexander's diagnosis of Evangelista's self-harm had not been the first time the nun had cut herself from guilt, shame or desperation. Faith, she thought, was no guarantee of happiness. Clearly. She returned to the text, searching forwards.

Helena had arrived later. After the war. Her clothes had not been sent to charity but had been burned, the book said. Burned? Mirabelle squinted and read the word again. She could hardly think why: 1947 had heralded many difficulties but contagious disease had not been among them. Did it mean Helena's clothes were damaged, perhaps beyond repair?

The entries for the Thompsons being complete, instead of closing the book Mirabelle scanned the pages more closely this time. Women arriving at the Little Sisters often came with troubles, the Thompson and MacDonald clan were hardly unique, but it seemed unusual for novices to be so interrelated. The same surnames were not repeated over and over. She read several of the notes going back as far as the 1890s, covering the entry of most of the seventy women resident in the convent at present. The handwriting varied and so did the details recorded. In the 1920s the nun who had overseen admissions had had a good, clear fist. This woman noted the weather and had also written down the tides at the time novices arrived. *Rainy, neap tide* or *Very warm. Diurnal.* Here and there she had also added the time of day at which the supplicant had presented herself, not the time by the clock but by the convent's prayers. *Arrived just after low tide matins.*

Mirabelle ran back over her time at the convent. The other evening when the sun went down, the nuns hadn't held a service, she remembered. When Vesta found Mother Superior's body, matins was over, but on another morning it did not take place until well after breakfast. She leaned back on the high stool and it came to her. Mother had mentioned the tide that very first day. 'We washed up on the tide,' she said. Something like that. The Little Sisters of Gethsemane prayed with the water not the light. It was the tides that were important. The vestige of a history where pilgrims had arrived and left with the flow of the water.

A dark shadow flitted past the window and on instinct she closed the book and dropped to the floor, huddling behind the desk. The door opened and a priest came in. Beyond the threshold, the bishop was leaving. Sister Mary accompanied him to the gate. The priest pulled the heavy ledger off the desk and into his arms. The smell of soap and leather reached her, cutting through the room's stale, musky scent. A small cloud of dust flew into the air. The man paused a moment. Mirabelle realised she must smell too: of bluebells, if the scent she'd sprayed on this morning had lasted. No nun smelt of Yardley. 'Come on!' a man's voice called from outside, and the priest moved off, taking the book and leaving the door open behind him.

The sound of the bar being lifted on the gate reached her, the back and forth of farewells: nothing friendly in tone. When the men had gone, Sister Mary walked back up the pathway with another nun. 'It doesn't matter at all,' she said. 'What is he going to do? We have our mission, Sister.' As the nuns passed the admissions office they closed the open door. Mirabelle waited, her heart pounding and her fingers quivering. She gave a little smile. It was ridiculous! If she got caught, what were the nuns going to do other than lock her up again? What would the bishop do, for that matter? It was hardly dangerous in any real sense. Still, best let the adrenalin settle.

After a few minutes she stood up and crept out of the door, bypassing the gate and making her way down the slope towards the graveyard, where she could slip over the burn and back into the real world. She hoped she would come across McGregor. She certainly had information she needed to share.

Chapter Twenty-five

I would rather go to Heaven than to Purgatory

Vesta sipped her tea in the kitchen and nibbled the fig roll that Mrs Grieg had placed in front of her on a side plate as she made her list. The nuns, it came to her, talked almost in riddles and she was excited by how much she had found out, without realising it: the formula, for a start, or at least what she could decipher from the windows. The rhythm of a nunnery too. The self-reliance and independence of the women in the face of the bishop. Sister Bernadette's medical competence had also surprised her. At first she'd considered it a duty to look after the old nun but, looking back, her conversations with Bernadette had been most illuminating. The nunnery had been a women's hospital, Vesta surmised. That must have been unusual in an era when most women had given birth at home. Bernadette was worldly and that was why – this part of the nunnery's mission. Prayer and refuge: for women in particular. Women who had been damaged and attacked. As the centuries passed, that hadn't changed.

She considered Bernadette's assumption that she was pregnant because she had been raped. The old woman had definitely been accustomed to dealing with victims and outcasts, which meant that several such women must have presented themselves over the years. Vesta recalled what the old nun had said about Evangelista's nightmares waking her, screaming, even though she had been at the convent for more than a decade. What horrors might stay with someone all that time and still wake them in the small hours? Vesta had experienced the nunnery as a refuge, despite the drama and the deaths. But the same environment hadn't healed Evangelista. And then there was the third pillar of the nuns' mission, which Bernadette had referred to but not spelled out. Vesta wrote a row of question marks on the paper next to the figure three.

Mrs Grieg came downstairs brandishing a duster and removed a pail from the cupboard, going to fill it at the sink. A cool breeze snaked across the kitchen from the open back door. 'Are you all right, Sister?'

Vesta finished her tea and pushed the cup and saucer away. 'Yes,' she said. 'Thank you. I'll be going back to my own order soon.'

'Nice to get back to Africa, I should imagine. Warmer than here. You don't have seasons, do you?'

'The weather has been lovely while I've been in Scotland,' Vesta replied vaguely. She did not add that she was from a place a mere four hundred miles to the south and, besides, Africa was the world's second-largest continent and benefited from several different kinds of weather, which, she was sure, was seasonal in some places and not in others. 'I've enjoyed my stay at the Little Sisters,' she said. 'Most illuminating.'

Mrs Grieg put the bucket onto the floor with a clatter and poured a generous amount of bleach into the water. 'That's a charitable way to put it,' she said.

Vesta continued, 'I didn't know that the Little Sisters were a nursing order for women. The Gethsemane Salve is for everyone, of course, but it seems . . .'

'Oh, the girls used to come from all over. Not nowadays but when I was a bairn. My mother used to call them the Little Mothers of Gethsemane,' Mrs Grieg said with a smirk.

So, Vesta thought, she was right and the nuns had helped women who were pregnant. It occurred to her that the chapel's stained-glass windows didn't hold only the secret of the formula but also of the nuns' whole mission. Every woman depicted had been holding a child, and in the sacristy, where Mirabelle had been trapped, the window showed a baby in a cot – not a manger. Not Jesus – simply an everychild floating on blue water, brought to them on the tide. 'Prayer and respite then.' She named two of the three pillars.

'And making the world right,' Mrs Grieg chimed in, without thinking, as if this was the natural third thing.

'Making the world right?'

'Och, aye. Justice,' she said. She pulled a mop from the cupboard, lifting the pail of water and heading back into the hall.

Vesta wrote the words on her sheet of paper. Making the world right. Justice, she underlined. She wondered what the nuns could possibly do to achieve that. It seemed a tall order from behind the convent's high stone wall. She read through everything she'd written – Cressida MacDonald's chosen name as Sister Grace, Saint Grace being the patron saint of lost children, and a timeline that ran from the lapsed nun's death to Grace Farquarson-Sinclair's pregnancy on to Evangelista's retreat and Sister Monica's body being found. And then Mother's corpse, of course. She sat back. There was a lot to tie together.

Through the open door, the garden looked inviting. Vesta left her writing things on the table and stood framed by the door. It was then she saw the woman through the trees at the bottom of the garden. It was impossible to say who she was but she was heading towards the beach. She had every right, Vesta supposed, to walk along the shore. The Crown owned Britain's beaches. In the bathroom she could hear Mrs Grieg scraping the bucket along the tiles as Vesta stepped onto the grass and, without thinking about it, walked towards the water.

As she reached the foreshore beyond the trees, the woman had disappeared. The cove was sheltered and Vesta wondered if the interloper had continued more quickly than might have been expected, across the burn and onto the convent's land. She was about to head back to the kitchen when she heard someone moving in the boathouse so she lifted the hem of her habit and made her way across the sand onto the jetty. The door was ajar. She pushed it open. 'Hello,' she said, into the gloom.

The woman was pulling a canvas cover off a small sailing boat. 'Go away, Sister Joseph,' she said. 'This is nothing to do with you.'

Vesta tried to make out who it was in the darkness. The woman had used her name. 'Who's that?' she said. 'I can't see.'

A figure stepped out from behind the boat. She was dressed in a loose gingham frock, a pair of bobby socks, sneakers, and her tawny hair was held back with the kind of Alice band a child might wear. She was, Vesta noted, on the old side for such teenage clothes, 'I'm sorry. Do I know you?'

'Oh, for Heaven's sake!'

The tone was familiar. The bad temper, certainly. 'Sister Evangelista?' Vesta said, as she finally recognised her. 'What on earth . . .?'

'I suppose it's good you didn't know me in this thing.' Evangelista picked at the fabric of the skirt.

'What are you doing here?'

The nun looked as if she might cry. She kicked the side of the boat in frustration. 'It seemed the best place to come,' she said. 'I always liked it here. I always felt safe, anyway.'

'Can I help you?' Vesta asked gently.

'How on earth would you be able to help?' Evangelista snapped.

'Why don't you come up to the house? I could make you a cup of tea.'

'Old Grieg is in the house,' Evangelista said flatly. She got up. 'I thought I might take it out.' She nodded at the boat.

'You can sail?'

'Of course I can. I'm not a total ninny. People think nuns can't do anything but pray and run the kitchen garden. Most nuns think that way too, if you're anything to go by.'

'Not at all. The order here is amazing,' Vesta said. 'For its prayer, its respite and making the world right.' Evangelista did not take issue with this. The words seemed to soothe her. Yes, they were definitely familiar. 'Why are you wearing ordinary clothes?' Vesta asked.

'Hideous, isn't it?' Evangelista said. 'I caught sight of myself in a mirror earlier.' She walked to the front of the boathouse and opened the bar that was blocking the boat in.

Vesta tried to remember how Sister Bernadette had put it, not much more than an hour ago, but she could not approach Evangelista in the same way. Saying she should not be embittered by what had happened to her didn't seem appropriate and Evangelista had too much of a temper to dismiss that kind of comment. Instead she decided to take a more factual approach to her assumptions. 'What happened to your baby?' she asked.

Evangelista did not stop what she was doing and did not

meet Vesta's eye. She untied the rope that tethered the boat in place. Then she hopped on board and took up an oar to push away from the mooring. Vesta wasn't going to let her leave. She stepped onto the boat decisively. 'Sister Joseph!' Evangelista objected.

Vesta sat on the little bench, trying not to feel nervous. She disliked anything that swayed. She avoided fairground amusements and donkey rides on the beach. Charlie had once tried to take her on the dodgems when the circus came to town, but she had flatly refused. Come to think of it, she had been pregnant with Noel at the time. Yet here she was. 'I'm staying with you, Evangelista,' she said. 'I want to know why you're here.'

'They took my sister,' Evangelista replied. She waited a moment, clearly realising that she couldn't force Vesta to get out of the boat. 'Suit yourself,' she said, and pushed off into the firth, rowing out a few yards before she set about raising the boat's dusty canvas sail with surprising efficiency. 'We learned to sail in this boat when we were children. There were fewer ships in those days on the water,' she said.

'It must have been nice coming here. To visit your aunt, wasn't it?'

'She was a good person.'

'I can see that. She must have taught you a lot. I can imagine summertime here, swimming in the water, playing on the beach.'

'I never learned to swim,' Evangelista said. 'I don't like being in the water.'

'That still doesn't answer my question,' Vesta pushed, 'about why you're here.'

Evangelista laughed. She tacked the sail and, as the boat moved, she leaned over the water, using her body to help steer the vessel. 'Sister Mary said we ought to leave for a while,' she said. 'We were hiding in the village before we could get away, but the police came and they took Helena. The water's so huge, isn't it?' she said. 'So out of control.'

Vesta's eyes were on the huge rail bridge and the villages along the Fife coastline with their pretty cottages. Specks of water from the swell splashed her habit as the boat picked up speed. 'It's quite invigorating, isn't it?' she said.

'The world,' Evangelista snapped, sounding almost disgusted.

'Does it remind you of your child?' Vesta asked. The nun did not reply but Vesta decided to keep pushing. 'The fact you won't talk about it makes me feel as if something awful happened. What do the sisters do with the children born at the convent?'

'He's fine. Don't be ridiculous.'

'It was a little boy?' Vesta almost added that she had a little boy, but she didn't see how that would help.

Evangelista nodded. 'The sisters make it right. Every time there is a girl who can't keep her baby, there's a married couple somewhere desperate for a child.'

'Like an adoption agency?' Briefly, Vesta felt relieved.

'I thought I'd forgotten. Well, not forgotten exactly,' Evangelista offered up.

'And then your brother came?'

'Everything was brought up at once, really.'

'No wonder you went into the anchorite's cell.'

Vesta began to wonder what direction Evangelista might take when they reached open water. She considered the map of the coastline: north towards Peterhead or south past Newcastle. It wouldn't be possible to reach either port in daylight in a tiny boat like this. 'Do you know where you're going?' she asked.

'He will take me,' the woman said.

Vesta did not find this encouraging. 'Perhaps we ought to make a plan,' she suggested. 'It sounds as if you've had a particularly painful time.'

'Helena won't tell them anything,' Evangelista added.

'About what?'

The nun shrugged.

Vesta leaned forward, her palm curled around the edge of her seat. 'Evangelista, do you know who killed Mother Superior?'

'He did,' Evangelista said insistently. 'He must have.'

Vesta sighed. The nuns' reliance on God's will was becoming tiresome but, still, it was difficult to make an argument against it, particularly dressed as she was.

'I'm not going back,' Evangelista added, much to Vesta's alarm.

'Where were you supposed to go?' Vesta asked. 'Before the police took Helena.'

'Sister Mary was to send word. She was arranging things. There wasn't time to plan it.'

Vesta looked longingly towards the shore. The graveyard was receding now and there was quite a swell on the water.

Evangelista stood up. 'I'm sorry,' she said. 'You'll make it back, Sister. It isn't difficult.' Then she kicked off her shoes and, without hesitation, jumped into the water.

'Evangelista!' Vesta shouted, and reached over the side, scrabbling in the freezing firth to try to grab hold of the woman. Soaked, the sleeves of her habit felt as if they were weighted. Evangelista splashed helplessly for a few moments, and then her head disappeared under the surface. Vesta looked round. The nearest boat was on the other side of the firth and, besides, she didn't know how to signal for help.

She tore at her wimple and pulled the habit over her head. 'Damn,' she said, before she jumped in.

The cold took her breath away. The firth was tidal and the water came from the North Sea so it was icy even in summer. The swell was clear, however, and she could see Evangelista under the surface, the gingham dress blousing in the water. She tried to stay collected and remember the lessons she'd taken as a child. Her mother had insisted Vesta and her brothers learned to swim. One of her uncles had drowned in Jamaica. 'You're going and that's that,' she had said whenever the children took issue with the lessons, which happened particularly in wintertime after Vesta's hair had frozen at the ends on the way home because she had lost her hat. She dived, trying to grab Evangelista's body. 'Keep away from the arms. Come at them from behind. A desperate person will drag you down,' the teacher had said. Vesta had been proud of herself. Practising in the pool, she'd rescued her brother, who was larger than she was. She'd teased him about it.

She couldn't get hold of the nun, though. The skirt of the gingham dress floated upwards, obscuring Evangelista's figure, and the nun kept trying to pull away. As Vesta tried once more, Evangelista pushed her off. The nun surfaced again. It was clear she was reciting a prayer in Latin, holding her hands together in front of her. Vesta took her chance, slipping an arm around Evangelista's torso from behind and grabbing her by the chin.

'Get off me!' Evangelista shouted. She thrashed around but Vesta kept hold. She pulled Evangelista towards the boat but quickly realised it was going to be difficult, if not impossible, to get them both safely on board without the nun's cooperation. She eyed the shoreline, estimating the distance back to the boathouse. It would be a long haul, but she couldn't see another way so she began to kick in that direction, hauling Evangelista through the icy swell. The prayer had stopped now. 'Let me go,' Evangelista squealed. 'Let me go.'

A hundred yards nearer shore, Vesta lost her temper. 'Look, I'm not going to let you go,' she snapped. 'That much is obvious. I'm taking you to land and then we can discuss it.'

'It's not your life,' Evangelista panted, and continued to squirm. 'I must be punished. I have to be punished.'

Vesta needed to focus on swimming. The beach was still a few hundred yards off and the water was cold. She tightened her grip along Evangelista's jawline so the nun would find it more difficult to distract her. Her body was acclimatising to the temperature, though it was a lot more difficult to effect a rescue than she remembered it being when she'd hauled her brother's body to safety at the local swimming pool. She kept her eyes on the sandy beach and thought how lucky she was that it was a sunny day. The tide must be coming in. It was pulling them westwards but that wouldn't make much difference, as long as they made it to shore.

With a little more than a hundred yards to go, her feet reached the silt on the bottom and she began to walk on tip-toe through the water towards the cove. As it got shallower, Evangelista dug her heels into the mud and fought off Vesta's hold. She was furious. 'This is nothing to do with you,' she shouted.

'Did you want me to just sit there and watch you die? It's a sin, Sister.' Vesta surprised herself. She hadn't rescued Evangelista to avert a sin being committed. Not really. Though this quietened the nun. 'I think you owe me a few answers,' Vesta added. 'Why on earth did you want to hurt yourself?'

Evangelista turned. 'I want it to stop,' she said simply. 'I get so angry sometimes.'

'Like when you smashed the stained-glass windows?'

'It is a sin to be angry. But when someone has been hurt . . . I can't help it. I had just found out about my brother. About Mother too. And today those men took my sister away.'

'What men?'

'The police. They took Helena and I didn't do a thing. I just wanted it to stop. To disappear.' Behind them, the little sailing boat was making its way out to sea entirely unmanned. Evangelista shrugged. 'I suppose the coastguard will bring it in. And your habit,' she said.

Vesta took this observation as a good sign. That alongside the fact she was talking about her suicide attempt in the past tense. 'I'm sure they won't mind. It's not my habit, really,' she said.

Evangelista regarded Vesta's lace-edged underwear, which was clearly visible now and certainly not issued by a nunnery. 'I came to find out what happened,' Vesta admitted. 'To your brother and then to Mother. Paul, wasn't he? Sister Monica. I'm not really a nun.'

'We called him Jesus,' Evangelista said.

Vesta recalled his middle initial. 'Really?'

'My mother was half Spanish,' the nun added. 'My aunt as well.'

'I can see that in you.'

'He was musical. He played jazz – not when we were children but later, after I'd taken vows. He told me he had been playing in a club in Soho. A man asked him to go to America to make a record. A talent scout.'

'My husband plays the drums. That's how I met him,' Vesta said.

Evangelista's face betrayed her shock. 'Husband,' she repeated.

The light summer breeze along the surface felt like an icy wind, cold enough to have come from the Russian steppes. Vesta sneezed and her teeth began chattering. 'I'm pregnant,' she said. It was the first time she'd volunteered information about the baby. The first time she'd said it out loud properly.

'Are you all right?' Evangelista asked.

'I'm freezing.' Vesta grinned. 'We should go back to the house.'

The nun acquiesced with only slight reluctance and the women began to wade towards the shore. With her curiosity piqued and both of them safe, Vesta asked simply, 'Was it you, Evangelista? Were you God's instrument to kill Mother? To kill your brother? Did you leave the anchorite's cell to do it?'

'I stayed my term in the cell,' Evangelista said, sounding offended. 'Well, almost. It's not a hotel, you know. I made a vow.'

'There have been enough deaths, don't you think?' Vesta said.

The nun began to cry gently. 'I didn't kill anyone,' she whispered, hanging her head. 'Not a soul. But, God forgive me, I prayed for it.'

Mrs Grieg provided towels and hot sweet tea and searched out dry clothes that fitted neither Sister Evangelista nor Vesta but which they put on nonetheless.

'You're bone cold. I could go to the nunnery and have them bring the car to get you,' she offered, but both women refused. Vesta lit the fire in the sitting room and they sat on the comfortable sofa in silence for a while.

'This house,' Evangelista said at length, with a sigh. 'All my life. It's been the real refuge and I've always loved it and hated it. I don't know why.'

Mrs Grieg brought extra hot water for the teapot. Then she reappeared with a leather shooting bag, an old shotgun and a cardboard box full of books, which she deposited on a side table. 'Since I have you here, miss,' she said, 'I wasn't sure what to do with these.' She propped the gun on the mantel.

Evangelista picked up a couple of the books, read the titles and laid them aside. When she got to the bottom of the box, however, she pulled out a photograph album. Vesta peered over her shoulder as she opened it. The photographs were small square prints of the family, held in place by yellowing glue. 'That's me,' Evangelista said, pointing to a picture of a small girl in a large hat. Vesta sipped her tea.

'Brandy?' Mrs Grieg offered. 'It'd warm you up.'

'Good idea,' Evangelista said. 'We need to look after Sister Joseph. She's with child.'

Mrs Grieg let out a squawk.

'My name is Vesta Lewis,' Vesta said. 'Mrs Lewis, in fact. I'm not a nun. I'm an investigator.'

'With the police?' Mrs Grieg asked.

'Not the police.' Vesta leaned over Evangelista's shoulder. 'Who's that?' she asked.

The photograph was of a blonde toddler playing on the back lawn, the rest of Shore Cottage's garden in the background, the door to the kitchen open just as it was today, with two of the Thompson children sitting on the step behind – Paul and Helena. Bang Bang MacDonald was to one side, wearing a nun's habit. She was watching the child playing in a dress-up box, a long string of beads draped around her neck and a pair of clogs that were too big for her.

'That's Grace Farquarson-Sinclair,' Mrs Grieg said. 'She used to come here to play. Miss MacDonald was terribly fond of her.'

Vesta pulled the photograph out of the album. 'I need to find my friend,' she said. 'Do you know where Miss Bevan might be, Mrs Grieg?'

Chapter Twenty-six

Doubt is the beacon of the wise

There was no sign of McGregor anywhere and Mirabelle did not feel like running into Mrs Grieg so she avoided Shore Cottage. Instead she stopped at the edge of the wood, considering her options. In the end she wandered along the track in the direction of St Clair's Vale. Belinda Farquarson-Sinclair had been extraordinarily unfriendly earlier but that meant there was something she did not want to talk about and, like it or not, Mirabelle reasoned, she was tangled up in this, at least tangentially. It irked her that she still had no idea of the motive for either Sister Monica or Mother Superior's deaths beyond some vague notion of a secret being kept at the nunnery. The Thompson family, however, were clearly involved and the Thompsons had been neighbours to the Farquarson-Sinclairs for more than a century.

As she passed the front gate of the nunnery a truck trundled up the track, overtaking her and coming to a halt. Mirabelle peered as a monk jumped down and knocked enthusiastically at the gate, which took some time to open, revealing two nuns. Neither the events of the last few days at the convent nor the visit of the bishop, it seemed, was going to halt production of Gethsemane Salve. Mirabelle lurked in the trees as the monk opened the rear of the truck and pulled down several baskets of vivid orange flower heads. 'Marigolds,' Mirabelle murmured under her breath. Katja had been right, though the flowers were not grown at the nunnery. The nuns had some operation. She smiled. You just had to keep your eyes open and all the secrets unfolded – all the connections. As one nun brought the monk a glass of water and stood at the gate exchanging small talk, Mirabelle slipped up the track through the trees, approaching St Clair's Vale from the rear.

The Bentley was parked outside a large garage behind the house. Mirabelle hesitated to continue. Faint heart never won fair maiden, she thought, but what excuse could she give? Both Farquarson-Sinclairs had made it clear her intervention was not welcome, not that that usually stopped her, but she'd have to come up with something. She was jolted out of this dilemma when the handsome young butler, who had opened the door on the day of Sister Monica's funeral, appeared with a Louis Vuitton suitcase, which he loaded into the boot of the car. The Farquarson-Sinclairs were going somewhere, or one of them was. This prompted Mirabelle, who stepped out of the bushes into plain sight.

'Miss Bevan,' the butler greeted her, looking quizzically towards the main path.

'I'm sorry,' she apologised. 'I don't know your name.'

'Shields,' the man introduced himself. 'Can I help you, miss?'

Mirabelle allowed her nervousness to show. 'I hope so,' she replied, feeling her way. 'It's about Mrs Grieg, you see.'

Shields rolled his eyes. 'It was my view that Mrs Farquarson-Sinclair ought to have alerted you,' he said. 'Is something missing?'

'Missing?'

'Taken? Stolen?'

Mirabelle decided that to answer in the affirmative would get her further than answering no. 'Yes,' she said. 'That's what I've come about.' She looked at the car behind her. 'Are Mr and Mrs Farquarson-Sinclair going somewhere?'

The butler, who clearly did not subscribe to Mrs Grieg's indiscreet habits, looked extremely uncomfortable.

'I met Mr Farquarson-Sinclair at the church in South Queensferry this morning. He told me the news about Miss Grace in Italy,' she encouraged him.

The man's expression softened. 'Mrs Farquarson-Sinclair will fly to Ciampino tonight,' he said.

Rome, Mirabelle noted. 'At a time like this I hate to bother the mistress,' she continued smoothly. 'Both of the Farquarson-Sinclairs have enough on their plates. I wonder, might I speak to you about Mrs Grieg?'

'As I understand it, it is only ever petty theft,' Shields volunteered. 'Pocket change and such. Since the war it's been difficult to get staff and Mrs Grieg is only part time here. She's restricted to the kitchen and the laundry – nowhere else.'

'Miss MacDonald must have been extremely loyal to her. Given her . . . proclivities.'

'She was a forgiving kind of lady. Though perhaps she owned fewer items of interest to Mrs Grieg.'

Mirabelle nodded. It did not entirely surprise her that Mrs Grieg was light-fingered. This chimed with what she already knew about the woman who, after all, had continued to stay at Shore Cottage when it suited her despite her employer's demise. It also might explain why Paul Thompson had chosen not to leave anything of value at Shore Cottage, stowing his getaway funds in the locker at Waverley. Mrs Grieg's dishonesty was clearly common knowledge. 'It's very kind of you,' Mirabelle said. 'I wonder, might I have a written reference?'

Shields acquiesced and led Mirabelle through a chipped wooden outer door into the Vale's large kitchen, which smelt of Scotch broth and baking bread.

He continued along a corridor into a private office with two worn but comfortable chairs on either side of the fireplace. He checked his desk.

'I need to fetch more ink,' he said, and disappeared. Mirabelle's eyes strayed round the office, which could not have changed much since the Victorian era, with its wrought-iron fireplace and highly varnished, dark wooden dresser. It had the air of a shrine. Quickly she took in the items on the shelves and the mantel: a few books on the subject of household management and on the top shelf, right at the back, a black-and-white photograph in a long frame, which at first she thought must have been taken at a school. As she brought it down, though, she saw it featured the family and staff of St Clair's Vale seated in front of the house. It looked older than it was, she thought, picking out a young Belinda Farquarson-Sinclair next to her husband, a nun in white robes and a woman who, as she held the photograph as far away as she could manage, to bring it into focus, was, yes, pregnant.

Shields returned with a fresh bottle of Indian ink. 'I hope you don't mind,' Mirabelle said. 'I was drawn to this. It's lovely.'

'It was taken during the war,' he said. 'My father was the butler in those days. It seems a long while ago now. There were some officers convalescing at Hopetoun House and one of them had a camera.'

'I recognise this person, I think.' Mirabelle pointed at the pregnant woman.

'That's Mrs Farquarson-Sinclair's cousin. She stayed here for a few weeks that summer.'

'Ah,' Mirabelle said lightly.

'Mr Farquarson-Sinclair's cousin too, of course. The master and the mistress are related. They married young, as you can see.'

'Sounds rather complicated.' Mirabelle smiled.

Shields opened a drawer and withdrew a sheet of paper. He paused, then took out a cardboard-backed notebook. 'It was my father's hobby,' he explained, opening the book at the centre pages. 'Genealogy. This is the master's family tree. It goes back three hundred years. On his days off my father used to visit the archive at the National Library to research it.'

'How interesting.'

Shields picked up a magnifying glass from the brass pen tray and handed it to Mirabelle. 'Perhaps you'd find this helpful,' he said.

Mirabelle felt torn. He was right, but still. 'And the nun?' she said, passing the glass over the photograph. 'She's wearing a different habit from the one the sisters use.'

'She was Mrs Farquarson-Sinclair's tutor. She joined the Little Sisters not long after. She became the Mother Superior.'

'Gosh.' Now she could magnify the faces, Mirabelle could see it. Younger, but, yes, it was Mother Superior in white robes. She looked like an angel. 'She died, didn't she?' she added. It seemed odd not to say it.

'Yes,' Shields said. 'Quite recently.' He began to scribble the reference.

Mirabelle turned her attention to the family tree. Old Mr Shields had done a thorough job and it was complex. Like many people, the Farquarson-Sinclairs had had large families over several generations. 'So Mr and Mrs Farquarson-Sinclair's cousin . . .' Mirabelle put her finger on the family's main branch.

'The MacDonald line,' Shields said helpfully, without looking up.

'MacDonald?' It was a common name, of course. Mirabelle scanned the tree, left and right, and there she was: Cressida MacDonald and her sister, Julia, who had married James Thompson, side by side on the page.

'Ah, yes, that's the branch of the family who lived in your house,' Shields said. 'Shore Cottage. They are second cousins to the main line. The children of a younger son two generations back. The MacDonalds are not directly in line to inherit but, really, they are quite close to Mrs Farquarson-Sinclair's line, in particular.'

Mirabelle let this fall into place. 'So Mrs Farquarson-Sinclair, that is Belinda, was tutored by the nun who became Mother Superior. And she is a distant relation of Bang Bang MacDonald, Cressida, who also went into the nunnery and who is with child in this photograph?'

Shields became suddenly uncomfortable. He closed the notebook with a snap. 'Here is what you asked for, Miss Bevan.' He handed her the reference, blotted and folded neatly in two.

'Mr Shields,' Mirabelle said firmly. 'What happened to Miss MacDonald's child?'

'Child?'

'Miss MacDonald is pregnant in this photograph but the child is not shown on this family tree. Did your father not record illegitimate births?'

'I wasn't here then. The lady only came to stay for a few weeks as I understand it . . .' the butler said dismissively, not wanting to admit that Miss MacDonald's baby had been born on the wrong side of the blanket. 'I have said that Mrs Grieg is certainly light-fingered but we find if we keep her out of temptation's way she does not . . . transgress. My advice would be to keep hard liquor locked up and make sure no petty cash or small valuables are within her grasp. Her needlework is excellent. I am sure Mrs Farquarson-Sinclair would want me to be frank.'

Mirabelle tried not to laugh. Mrs Farquarson-Sinclair clearly could not have been less frank all along. Every family had connections, of course, but what was suggested by the photograph felt positively incestuous. There were so many points of contact to explore that Mirabelle had consciously to slow down her thoughts. Grace Farquarson-Sinclair was sixteen, Dr Alexander had said, or, rather, she had been when the doctor had examined her. That meant the girl was born in 1943.

'Grace was Miss MacDonald's baby,' she said out loud. 'Wasn't she? The Farquarson-Sinclairs adopted her.'

It made absolute sense. Cressida MacDonald had stayed close to her daughter – at first in the convent but, devout or not, that hadn't really suited her and she'd moved to Shore Cottage. 'Belinda couldn't conceive at first, could she?' Mirabelle guessed.

'Miss Bevan!' Shields objected, but Mirabelle ignored him and kept on reasoning.

Cressida had had this unwanted pregnancy, and now Grace had fallen pregnant with an illegitimate child of her own. Like mother like daughter. Or was it?

'There are worse crimes than murder,' Mirabelle said out loud, as it fell into place. Which man had taken advantage of a pious young woman during wartime? Who had taken advantage of Grace? Mirabelle's eye fell to the face of Ruari Farquarson-Sinclair beside his wife in the photograph. Had they taken in Cressida's baby girl because she was his?

'You can't . . .' Shields began, but Mirabelle was already on her way out of the butler's office, striding down the corridor into the main house.

Shields followed her. 'Stop!' he shouted.

'How could you work for these people?' Mirabelle snapped, and kept going. Ahead of him, she scaled the service staircase, bursting into the main hallway through a baize-backed door that gave a muffled bang as it closed. Taking her bearings, she continued towards the morning room. Inside, Belinda Farquarson-Sinclair was standing by the long windows that looked out over the garden, and Ruari Farquarson-Sinclair was sitting on the sofa to one side. They both turned as Mirabelle came through the door.

'What the hell?'

'It was you, wasn't it? You're the common factor,' Mirabelle said, confronting him. 'You adopted Grace because she was yours. You got Cressida MacDonald pregnant.'

'What nonsense are you spouting now?' Belinda spat, as Shields appeared in Mirabelle's wake.

'I'm sorry, madam,' the butler said. 'Miss Bevan came to enquire after a reference for Mrs Grieg. I didn't mean to say anything out of turn.'

Ruari Farquarson-Sinclair waved him off. 'It's all right,' he said. 'You can get on, Shields.'

The butler looked nervous but he turned to go, closing the door behind him.

Mirabelle glared at Belinda Farquarson-Sinclair. 'This place!' she gasped. 'Everything was connected all along! Everyone is in each other's pockets. The Queensferry way?

Isn't that what you called it? Well, I've worked it out.' She turned towards Ruari Farquarson-Sinclair, who had got out of his seat. 'It wasn't only Cressida you violated, was it? It was Grace! Your own daughter. You're a monster.'

Belinda's eyes flashed. She lashed out, slapping Mirabelle hard. 'How dare you? Ruari is an honourable man. He'd never—'

But Mirabelle hadn't finished. 'And the nunnery helped you cover everything up. How a man like you can stand for Parliament! It's a travesty. And you, Belinda! How could you cover for him? That's not what marriage is about.'

'How would you know?' Belinda snapped back cattily.

'Taking advantage. With your child. Or your cousin's child, rather. That's the truth about Grace, isn't it? She was born his victim and now she's suffering from his actions. It's depraved!'

Belinda stamped her foot. 'Stop it!' she shouted.

Ruari Farquarson-Sinclair put both his hands in front of him as if he was trying to quieten a child having a temper tantrum. 'Belinda, sit down,' he said. This calmed his wife and she sank quietly onto the end of the sofa. 'I must say, Miss Bevan,' he continued, 'you have got all this rather profoundly wrong.' He looked charming, suddenly. Almost charismatic. 'Not that I am entirely without blame. But a rapist who takes advantage of vulnerable women? No. And to answer one of your concerns, this morning I withdrew my candidacy for election.'

'The Tory will win now,' Belinda said regretfully. 'There's no other Liberal who could fight the seat like you, Ru.'

'Nevertheless,' Mr Farquarson-Sinclair said, 'I shan't be standing. We need to look after Grace.'

'You should be kept as far away as possible from Grace,' Mirabelle said steadily.

Ruari Farquarson-Sinclair walked to the drinks trolley and poured himself a whisky. He gestured but neither Belinda nor Mirabelle took him up on his offer. Then he downed the drink in one. 'It's not even lunchtime yet,' he said. 'You know, when I think of the Vale, it has never really felt like home.'

'What are you talking about?' Belinda snapped. 'You've always lived here. I always wanted to live here too. Since the first time I came for the summer.'

Ruari shrugged. 'There's just so much . . . history. I've never been able to be myself. It's always felt as if I was playing a part. Though I have loved you, my darling.'

Belinda looked out of the window. A tear slid down her cheek. She brushed it away, her eyes hardening. 'See what you've done,' she snarled at Mirabelle.

Mirabelle felt a wave of anger. 'Me?' she said. 'All I've done is try to work out this whole mess.'

'It is a mess,' Ruari said. 'You're right about that.'

'I think it's time to call the police,' Mirabelle replied. 'It would be best to come clean, don't you think?'

He looked as if he was about to agree, but before he could, Belinda jumped to her feet. 'No!' she shouted.

'It's all right, darling. I'll take responsibility for everything.'

'No,' Belinda repeated. 'It's our business. It's nobody else's.' She picked up the bronze figurine of a hunting dog that stood on one of the side tables and threw it, aiming for Mirabelle's head.

Mirabelle dodged but the ornament hit her shoulder and a jagged pain bloomed like a flower along her arm. 'What are you doing?' she shouted, but Belinda wasn't listening. Having missed her target, she now jumped to her feet.

'Belinda!' Ruari said, as if he were calling a disobedient

dog to heel. 'Belinda!' He was pleading now, but Belinda was advancing towards Mirabelle, her eyes on fire.

Mirabelle scrambled towards the door. Her left arm felt stiff and shaky, which made running more difficult, but she made it down the hallway with Belinda in pursuit and through the front door. Behind her, Belinda picked up a sturdy stick from the stand as she passed and brandished it. 'You've spoiled everything!' she shouted.

Ruari Farquarson-Sinclair appeared behind his wife. 'Stop!' he begged again. 'Please, let me deal with this. Belinda!' But his wife was not listening. 'Think of Grace!' he added, which Mirabelle, still running, considered rich. It made her turn. She realised her mistake immediately but it was too late. Belinda Farquarson-Sinclair was close now. She brought the walking stick down with a crack on Mirabelle's skull. A wave of nausea swept over her but no pain. No more pain, anyway. She had a sudden vision of a group of heavily pregnant women – Cressida MacDonald, as she had appeared in the old photograph, Grace, a slip of a girl at sixteen, and Belinda herself. And then a nun, or a woman in a nun's habit, black like those of the Little Sisters of Gethsemane. Was it Sister Evangelista? Or Sister Helena? Or both of them? The habit was worn loose, without the plain black belt roped round the waist. They are all one family, it came to her – Farquarson-Sinclairs, MacDonalds and Thompsons. All victims of one man. Creating such havoc. A sting of rage preceded the all-encompassing pain when it finally hit. Then everything went black.

Chapter Twenty-seven

Fear follows crime

McGregor was finding that he quite enjoyed being in a police station again. It was strange how easily old habits came back – the bonhomie of feeling part of a large team. It quickly became apparent at Torphichen Street that the baby's skeleton from the shoreline was more a matter for the National Museum than for the city's police force. The pathologist proclaimed the bones 'at least Victorian. I can't say the child wasn't killed,' the man added thoughtfully. 'That was common enough if an unmarried woman got caught out. But we'll never know. The mother must be long dead anyway.'

After this pronouncement, the file was forwarded to the fiscal's office and Rennie diverted his attention away from the tiny skeleton towards Sister Helena, who had been detained in one of the interview rooms. 'Any trouble?' he asked the desk sergeant.

The man smirked. 'She's a nun, sir.'

'We have two nuns dead,' Rennie pointed out. 'It might well be a nun who killed them. Have you found out why she isn't wearing a habit?' The man looked sheepish. 'Has she asked for anything?'

'No, sir. We offered her a cuppa but she refused. She's just sitting at the table. She's been like that for more than an hour. I think she might be praying.'

Rennie paused. 'Penny for them?' McGregor asked.

'We got nothing from the nuns in the convent,' Rennie said. 'They all refused to comment. It was as if they had taken a vow of silence.'

'You interviewed them after Mother's body was found but you didn't know then about Paul Thompson – who he was.'

'True,' Rennie said. 'We've that.'

'And Helena's not in the nunnery any more. You could let me sit in,' McGregor offered cheerfully.

Rennie shrugged. 'All right,' he said. 'Let's try that.'

They peered at Sister Helena through the hatch in the interview-room door. She didn't look up. McGregor nodded at Rennie and the inspector turned the handle.

'I'm Detective Inspector Rennie and you know Mr McGregor, don't you?' he checked, as they entered.

Helena nodded. The men sat down.

'We were wondering what you were doing wearing . . . mufti,' Rennie asked.

'The habit is not what makes the nun,' Helena replied serenely.

Rennie pulled a packet of cigarettes from his pocket, clearly happy that Helena was at least talking today, if only to refute his questioning. 'Do you mind?'

Helena shook her head and he lit up. 'What were you doing outside the convent, Sister?'

'Our vows do not limit us to nunnery ground.'

'When was the last time you left?' Rennie asked.

'It is not a criminal offence, is it?'

'No.'

'I don't understand why you're keeping me. I have nothing to do with the bones that were found by the shore. I give you my word.'

'We know that, Sister,' Rennie said reassuringly.

McGregor leaned over the interview table. 'It's the matter of your brother,' he said. 'That's why you're here. We wanted to talk to you about his death. Paul Thompson was your brother, wasn't he?'

Helena nodded. 'I said everything I had to say the other day.'

'You didn't say anything, from what I hear. And now we have even more questions,' McGregor replied. 'The other day, Inspector Rennie was not aware of the family connection. Were you, Inspector?'

'No,' Rennie confirmed, 'I was not because Sister Helena did not inform us.'

Helena continued to look impassive.

'Do you know why Paul Thompson came to the nunnery?' McGregor asked.

'No.'

'It was to see you, wasn't it?'

'He shouldn't have come,' Helena said.

'It must have been terrible for you. A dilemma. Did you feel ashamed?' McGregor had hardly let her get the words out. If he could make the questions and answers spitfire, the nun would have less time to think. Less time to cover anything up.

Helena gave a sharp little nod.

'But you didn't tell Mother? You didn't tell anyone that he wasn't really a novice?'

She shook her head.

'It's quite the decision for a young man to do what he did. And quite the decision for you not to reveal him.'

'God forgive me,' Sister Helena said.

'Had you been clearer, earlier, he wouldn't have died, would he?'

'I don't know. It was an accident.'

'Was it?' McGregor asked sharply. Still no real reaction. 'You must have been thinking about what you did and didn't do, a nun like you, with a conscience. We only want to get to the bottom of what happened.'

Still nothing.

Rennie stubbed out his cigarette. The policemen waited, allowing silence to settle uncomfortably in the room. Sister Helena collected herself and showed no sign that the silence troubled her. After a minute or so, McGregor resumed. 'Poor Paul. It must have been difficult for him to enter the Little Sisters under false pretences. To live like a nun. But then a great deal had happened in your family. Your father had just died. Christmas time, wasn't it?'

Helena nodded once more.

'And then your aunt . . .'

The nun remained impassive at the mention of Miss MacDonald.

'That must have been difficult,' McGregor pressed on. 'Were you fond of her?'

Helena paused, then nodded again, this time with more feeling. She looked quite suddenly as if she was going to cry. McGregor took his handkerchief out of his pocket. 'Here,' he said.

Helena took it.

'We're only trying to understand, Miss Thompson,' he said.

She began to cry softly.

'Your aunt interests me,' McGregor continued, realising this was a rich seam. 'I find myself coming back to the way she kept her gun with her all the time. We keep hearing that. She took the gun to the chapel. She had the gun by the door. It sounds as if it's a joke. People made light of it with that nickname of hers, Bang Bang. But it wasn't a joke, was it?'

Helena sobbed loudly. 'No,' she said. 'She was marvellous. Please. Stop.'

'What did she feel so threatened by that she had to carry a weapon? Do you know?'

Nothing.

'And your brother? My guess is he wanted to help. But it wasn't a help, was it?'

'He didn't even believe in Our Saviour! He used to go to clubs and play cards for money and . . . he wasn't a good person, Mr McGregor.'

'Why wasn't he?'

'Look what he did! Coming to the nunnery like that. Intruding on us. Evangelista told him we didn't want to see him. It wasn't his business. She told him!'

'Told him? At your father's funeral, you mean?'

'She wrote to him too. I knew it was a bad idea, but she thought it would hold him off. I said she was wrong. I told her!'

'So why did he come?'

'He was a selfish person.'

'Selfish?'

'All about himself. Before anyone else.'

'Before you, you mean?'

Helena blew her nose loudly. 'Excuse me,' she said, visibly pulling herself together, drawing herself up in the chair. Retreating.

'It must be strange, wearing normal clothes. Where did you get the dress?' McGregor asked.

'Someone gave it to me.'

'Someone?'

'In the village.'

'So you would blend in? Was it dangerous for you to stay in the nunnery, Sister Helena? Is there a reason you had to leave?'

'He is always with us.'

'Jesus?'

Another nod.

'What was Paul so intent on talking to you about that he was prepared to give up the life you've described? The life he enjoyed. The cards. The drinking. We know you're right. He enjoyed a drink. The doctor who performed his post-mortem examination was clear about that. You say he was selfish, yet he was prepared to give up all his worldly pleasures, Miss Thompson.'

'Sister Helena,' she corrected him.

'Sister,' McGregor conceded. 'It doesn't sound to me as if your brother was selfish. It sounds as if you were the selfish one, refusing to talk to him. Evangelista at least had the kindness to try to reason with him.'

'Sister Evangelista,' Helena insisted.

'Yes. Sister Evangelista, Sister Helena. But you weren't very good *sisters* to Paul, were you? Especially you.'

A flash of defiance flared in Helena's eyes. It burned for only a moment before she brought herself under control again.

'I feel sorry for Paul,' McGregor said.

'I'm sorry he died.'

'And sorry he came to South Queensferry?'

'Yes.'

'That's not very welcoming. Tell me, if Mother Superior had found out who Paul really was before he died, what would have happened?'

'She'd have sent him away.'

'Don't you think she would have asked you to speak with him first? It seems such a modest request. So humble, really.'

'Humble!' Helena sounded outraged at this suggestion.

'What did he want to talk about, Sister? What was worth the world to him? What did he want that only you and Evangelista could give him?'

'It wasn't his business.'

'What wasn't his business?'

Helena pushed the handkerchief back across the table. 'Thank you,' she said. 'I don't need this any more. You have no right to talk to me like this. I haven't done anything wrong.'

'Haven't you? Because it seems to me that in refusing to speak to Paul Thompson you as good as killed him, Sister. That's how it seems to me.'

'That's preposterous!'

'Are you prepared to answer to that? I don't mean in a civil court. You believe in a higher authority. So this man, this selfish man, as you'd have me believe, gave up everything just to try to speak to you. And your refusal of his modest request resulted in his death. What will your higher authority make of that?'

'My faith is certain,' the nun said.

'That seems conceited to me.'

The policemen let silence fall once more. Rennie put his cigarettes back into his pocket. 'Sisters,' he said. 'Like a double cherry – two lovely berries moulded on one stem – you and your sister, miss. That's Shakespeare. *A Midsummer Night's Dream*,' he explained. 'If you won't tell us, then I'm sure Evangelista will. She's the one who was prepared to talk to her brother, after all.'

'Leave her alone. She's finding things difficult enough as it is.'

Rennie leaned across the table. 'What is she finding difficult exactly? You know, I'm minded to go out to the Little Sisters and pick her up.'

Helena smirked.

She's not there, McGregor thought.

'I need to use the bathroom,' Sister Helena said.

'We should take a break.' McGregor got to his feet.

A female officer accompanied the nun to the single women's lavatory, which was situated downstairs, at the back of the station. Rennie leaned against the wall of the interview room. 'That was you just sitting in, was it?' he said, and then conceded. 'You're a good interrogator. We learned a lot. More than we got from interviewing dozens of them at the convent.'

McGregor couldn't help but feel proud. He hadn't lost it, then. All those years on the force. 'It's something the boy found out,' he said. 'You realise that, don't you? After the father died. Something pressing. The father dies and Paul comes to see his aunt, who is also dying, and his sisters. It's as if the boy's life had unravelled with the estate and only the women could help him make sense of it.'

Rennie nodded slowly. 'Something about the mother's death, perhaps?'

'That was a long time ago. Whatever it was, it propelled the girls behind the convent's walls. The aunt too. The Little Sisters provided sanctuary. There's something angry or desperate about him following them.'

Rennie considered this. 'We can't hold her much longer. She hasn't done anything.'

McGregor checked his watch. It was almost three in the afternoon.

'Let's leave her for a little longer, then give her something to eat. She must be hungry.'

'All right,' Rennie said. 'I'll get a sausage roll from the canteen.'

'And another thing,' McGregor added, 'I think I should call my solicitor.'

Rennie's expression asked the question.

'He's also their solicitor. He might know something, but he might not know he knows it.'

In Rennie's office, McGregor sat behind the desk and raised Mr Wallace on the telephone.

'Hello,' he said, when the secretary put him through. 'I'm calling from Torphichen Street police station.'

Wallace sounded perturbed. 'Good Lord, Mr McGregor. What on earth has happened?'

McGregor laughed. 'I'm on a busman's holiday. I'm helping one of the detectives. I wanted to ask you about the woman who owned Shore Cottage, Miss MacDonald. Did you ever meet her?'

'Oh, yes,' Wallace said. 'She was a bit of a man-hater,' he confided.

'And on her death the house passed to her nephews and nieces, did it?'

'Her nephew. Not her nieces. They're nuns. It was quite complicated, actually. And unusual. According to the deed, the house passes down the female line where it can. But the girls being nuns there was only the boy to inherit. The deed allows for that but only where the female line is ended. I saw to the whole thing myself.'

'And the nephew decided to put the house on the market?'

'He called the place gloomy, as I recall. Which is most unfair – the light from the firth is lovely. Can I ask . . . are you having second thoughts about the purchase?'

'You might not know yet, but Paul Thompson, Miss MacDonald's nephew, has been found dead,' McGregor explained.

Mr Wallace paused. 'Dead?' he said. 'But he was a young man.'

McGregor did not want to go into the fact that Paul Thompson had died inside the nunnery. 'The police are making enquiries but it seems it was an accident. I wondered if this affects our purchase. Who inherits the place now?'

'I'll look into it,' Wallace said. 'With his sisters excluded and with no issue, it may fall to a generation of cousins, if there is one. As far as I'm aware he hadn't made a will. I advised him to do so but young men seldom take advice of that nature before they marry.'

'Will you keep me abreast of what you find?'

'I will,' Wallace said, and hung up.

When Rennie and McGregor returned to the interview room, Sister Helena was on her knees, praying next to the table. She got to her feet and eyed the sausage roll Rennie placed in front of her, slipping onto the seat and sipping the cup of tea that accompanied it. Rennie cut the pastry into three pieces. 'You need to eat something,' he said gently.

Sister Helena paused and took a piece from the plate. She nibbled tentatively, then more quickly. It seemed she was hungry and reached for a second slice. 'What do you think happened to your brother, Sister?' Rennie asked.

'I think he slipped and fell.'

'Really? He was seen arguing with Sister Evangelista the afternoon before he died.'

'None of my sisters in the convent would hurt anybody.'

'So if it wasn't an accident and it wasn't a nun, you

310

think it was somebody from outside the convent?' Rennie asked.

Sister Helena licked her fingers. She pushed away the plate, the third slice of sausage roll uneaten. 'It was an accident,' she said. 'It was God's will. I'm not going to say anything else. You can't make me. And you can't hold me here.'

There was a tap on the door and the female police officer put her head round. 'Might I have a word, sir?' she asked.

The men trooped into the corridor where she pulled out a piece of paper. 'The suspect dropped this,' she said. 'I went to the loo and it was on the floor.'

Rennie took the paper from her hand.

'Are you sure it's hers?' McGregor asked.

The constable nodded. 'I'm the only female PC in the station today,' she said. 'It wasn't there when I took Sister Helena to the lavatory. She must have dropped it.'

'Oh, it's hers all right,' Rennie said with a grin. 'I think we'd better get ourselves back to South Queensferry. He offered the letter to McGregor, who read the signature first. *Aunt Cressida.*

My Dear Girls
  He is gone and I am going. You have been so brave and now you must be brave again . . .

Chapter Twenty-eight

Courage is the greatest of all virtues

Mirabelle opened her eyes. It was dark. Not dark outside, she realised, as she took in the bright outline of daylight around the door. She was simply in a room with no windows and the light was off. She felt confused and her head and shoulder ached. Slowly, she got to her feet and fumbled for the door knob. To her surprise, it wasn't locked. She opened it and stepped into a well-proportioned bedroom decorated in pink toile-de-Jouy. She looked behind her. She had been bundled into a large closet. Looking out of the window, she ascertained she was still at St Clair's Vale. Across the canopy of trees she could just make out the steep, slated roof of the convent and beyond it a long line of blue – the firth. Judging by the light it was afternoon.

On the bedside table there was a flask of water and a glass with cornflowers painted along the rim. She poured a splash and gulped it down. That helped. Then she made her way to the bedroom door, which was locked. She did not have her picking kit but the lock was standard. She pulled a pin out of her hair and went to work. It took less than a minute. Outside, the hallway was quiet and she crept along the plush red-patterned carpet and slipped downstairs, her eyes on the main door ahead. Through the sidelights she could see the Bentley had been brought round to the front of the house. Belinda Farquarson-Sinclair hadn't yet left for Italy, she thought.

Turning in the other direction, she caught sight of herself in a mirror on the opposite side of the hall. She looked paler than usual and a bruise was forming on her left temple. She was about to move, to get away, when someone spoke. 'Oh, God,' the voice said. 'You're up. I told you the bedroom door wouldn't hold her, darling.'

Mirabelle turned. Belinda was standing in the doorway to the morning room.

'Don't run,' she said. 'I'm sorry I hurt you. I lost my temper. Are you all right?'

'My head hurts,' Mirabelle said. 'And my neck.'

'I was furious, and you will go poking about in matters that don't concern you.'

'I want to leave,' Mirabelle said stoutly.

'I'm trying to apologise.' Belinda sounded affronted.

Mirabelle decided not to take issue with this. She bit back the fact that the woman had knocked her out, put her into a cupboard and locked the door of the room. Or, more likely, Ruari had.

'I need medical help,' Mirabelle said. 'I'm going to the convent to ask them to call Dr Alexander.'

'Oh, that busybody!' Belinda snapped impatiently. 'I can fix you up. Shields will bring ice and some Gethsemane Salve. That's what you need.'

'I'm not going to stay here,' Mirabelle said, eyeing the stand with walking sticks and umbrellas next to her in which Belinda had found her weapon earlier. 'Don't be ridiculous.'

Ruari Farquarson-Sinclair appeared from the drawing room. 'Good Lord,' he said. 'This is a real mess, isn't it?'

'I want to leave,' Mirabelle repeated, thinking if she had to run this time, she'd pull a stick from the cluster by the door with which to defend herself before she took off. She'd give as good as she got this time.

Ruari pushed past his wife. 'Absolutely,' he said. 'Just not quite yet. If you don't mind.'

'Do you usually bash women over the head and stick them in cupboards when they try to leave your house?' Mirabelle spat. 'Or do you only kill the people who find out what you've done?' She couldn't bear the sight of him – this man who had abused the women around him. This killer.

'Oh, God,' Belinda said again, as if this were even more tiresome than Mirabelle's last utterance.

Ruari took control. 'Miss Bevan. Please sit down in the day room. I promise Belinda won't hurt you again. I'll have Shields bring the first-aid box.' Mirabelle glanced fleetingly at the walking sticks. 'If you'd feel safer, please bring one of those with you.'

He was personable, she'd give him that. But, then, he was a politician, or had intended to become one. 'If you don't mind,' Mirabelle said, and picked out a mahogany stick with a bulbous silver handle, which she saw, as she took it in her palm, was shaped like a skull.

Ruari Farquarson-Sinclair was as good as his word and Shields arrived with a large first-aid kit, a bowl of ice and some hand towels. Belinda stubbed out her cigarette and got to work, sitting next to Mirabelle on the sofa to attend to her. 'We have boys,' she explained, as she efficiently put Mirabelle's damaged arm in a sling and applied an ice compress to her collar bone. 'They're always falling off things,' she added. 'You're a bit bruised, is all.'

Ruari stood opposite. He was too still to be described as

hovering, Mirabelle thought, but that was what it felt like. Perhaps Belinda was his victim too – unable to get away. It was difficult for women, almost impossible sometimes. 'You have the advantage of us, Miss Bevan,' he said. 'I am going to be absolutely honest with you. Belinda and I are leaving this evening.'

'Rome?' Mirabelle asked.

'Belinda had intended to see Grace. You're right. To be with her now her son is born. Our grandchild.'

Mirabelle bit her lip. She did not say what she wanted to, that the boy was not only Ruari's grandchild but his child as well. She decided it was just best to keep him talking. If Ruari Farquarson-Sinclair got away, she wanted to know where he was headed so the police could pick him up. 'She had a boy, did she? And the child will be adopted, I imagine.'

'That's what we've arranged. Mother Superior helped us find a suitable family in Spain in need of an heir.'

'Mother Superior?'

Ruari smiled. 'The nuns have been brokering adoptions among the best families for centuries. The Little Sisters of Gethsemane are well connected across Europe. Queensferry seems like a backwater now, I know, but . . .'

'. . . it was once the centre of the world,' Mirabelle finished his sentence.

'It seems that way,' Ruari said. 'Hard to believe but, yes. Grace is finding the situation difficult. It's only natural. The baby came early and that hasn't helped. She isn't ready to let him go.' Mirabelle bit her lip. His concern sounded genuine. 'However,' he continued, 'given what you have discovered and what will now inevitably come out, my wife and I are leaving for good. I've organised power-of-attorney papers so the children will be looked after. We're

315

abdicating our positions, in effect. It's not ideal, not what we wanted. But Henry will get the house when he comes of age and there's plenty of money. I hope the children do better than we did.'

Mirabelle cocked her head. It felt as if her arm was swelling as the bruises bloomed on her skin. Ruari Farquarson-Sinclair seemed too controlled, she thought. Too civilised. And she couldn't tell if Belinda was really willing to leave everything and stick with her husband, no matter what. Was he making her leave with him? Belinda offered her a glass of water and two Anadin tablets. 'Here,' she said. Mirabelle looked dubious. 'God,' Belinda snapped, as if Mirabelle's suspicions were unreasonable. She scrabbled in the first-aid box and produced the packet. 'Go on. Take the pills out yourself.'

Mirabelle did so. 'So where are you going?' she asked casually, swallowing.

'Somewhere without an extradition treaty,' Ruari said bluntly. 'We have rather made a hash of things. Best disappear. For the children's sake.'

'You ought to go to prison, Mr Farquarson-Sinclair. They ought to throw away the key.'

'I'm sure it will feel like a prison, Miss Bevan, if that makes you feel better,' he said smoothly.

'You're a rapist and a killer, sir,' Mirabelle said stoutly, her fingers closing around the stick. 'I don't know where you're going but I doubt it'll be as much of a prison as, say, Barlinnie.'

Ruari sank onto the chair opposite. 'I feel the need to clear that up. It's not that I care what you think, really.'

'Of course.'

'But you have me wrong. I'm a killer. Yes. A murderer. There, I've said it.'

Belinda got up. 'Don't, Ru,' she said.

'I want to,' he replied simply. 'I admit it freely. I murdered him. Someone had to.'

'Why? Was he about to expose you?' Mirabelle sat forward. 'Who?'

'Paul Thompson. Sister Monica.'

'Oh, Miss Bevan, you have everything wrong. You don't understand at all. I killed Paul's father. Don't you see? And I don't regret it.'

'James? Why did you kill James?'

'Because of what he did. Because he was the scum. It's a different offence, isn't it, when you premeditate a murder? Well, I premeditated killing James Thompson. He hurt my little girl. He took everything from her. He did what you're accusing me of and I killed him for it. I hope that means I'm not quite as bad as you think and it explains my actions. I had to.'

'James Thompson died of cancer. That's what's on his death certificate.'

'He had cancer.' Ruari nodded. 'That's true. Quite advanced cancer. But I killed him. I held a pillow over his face in the spare bedroom at Shore Cottage until he stopped breathing. It was Christmas time. I'd do it again.'

Belinda let out a long sigh. 'You see, he's a hero,' she said. 'People always think the worst but Ruari is a hero. Grace knows it. She knows what he did for her. It's important for a girl to feel protected. No matter what.'

'So you didn't—' Mirabelle started.

'No,' Ruari cut in. 'I did not. Grace understands.'

'You told your sixteen-year-old daughter that her father was a killer?'

'I avenged her,' Ruari said. 'Those poor bitches at the nunnery didn't have anyone to stand up for them and look at

317

how they turned out. I wish I'd stepped in before. Perhaps it would have saved Grace. But I didn't. I wanted my little girl to know that I'd do anything for her. She's the most important thing. More important than this house or the estate. More important than all of it.'

'We discussed it,' Belinda added. 'We decided together.'

Mirabelle let this information fall into place. 'So, you're saying James Thompson was a predator. He raped Grace. He was the father of her child.'

Belinda's cheeks were flush. 'He came for the horse racing. We had a weekend at the end of the autumn. The track at Musselburgh. He was visiting Bang Bang, you see. To say goodbye. He knew how ill he was. She was ill by then too. They had reconciled after a fashion. She thought he couldn't do any more harm. I expect the bastard looked on that weekend as his last chance for a bit of fun. Why Julia married him, I don't know. He made her life a misery, and when she died he turned his attentions to the women who were left.'

'Bang Bang,' Mirabelle said, thinking of the figure of the pregnant woman in the old photograph. The year after her sister had died. It fell into place.

'At first. Yes. He forced himself on Cressida. She had moved in to help look after the children. When she came to the sisters for help, he turned his attention to his own girls. One after the other. She'd had no idea he'd do that. They were only children – Evangelista is only a couple of years younger than I am, and we'd just got married. Poor Bang Bang never forgave herself for leaving them. After Evangelista, they tried to get Helena away. She was sent to boarding school. They thought that would save her, but it didn't.'

'And Paul?'

'Paul had no idea about any of it until James's funeral. He came across letters Evangelista had written to her father. She's never got over what happened to her. I can't say I blame her. The others seemed to recover. But not Evangelista. She wrote to him for years. I think she hoped he would apologise. Or repent. She wanted salvation or something. I don't know. It tortured her, anyway.'

Mirabelle remembered Dr Alexander having to attend to Evangelista – the self-imposed cuts that had become infected.

'Paul was shocked,' Belinda continued. 'He wanted to open it all up again. He wanted to understand, he said. Get some justice. As if that were his right. Bang Bang and the girls were quite happy James had died. Bang Bang called it an act of God, didn't she, darling?'

'A gift from God,' Ruari corrected his wife. 'She was glad it had happened before she went. We encouraged her to invite him, you see, Miss Bevan. When we found out what he'd done to Grace. She became quite shy suddenly, in November of last year. Quite removed from everything.'

'Dr Alexander didn't examine her until later,' Mirabelle said.

'That's right. We hoped she wasn't pregnant. We didn't know then. But when we found out what he'd done, that was enough. We told Bang Bang it had been such fun and she should invite him for Christmas. Then I broke into Shore Cottage. I'd like to have strung him up, of course, but it seemed unlikely I'd get away with that. And the plan was to get away with it. Scot-free. Though now that isn't possible.'

'I'm sorry, darling,' Belinda said. 'Me and my stupid temper.'

'I think we've told Miss Bevan enough, don't you?'

'I misjudged you,' Mirabelle said. 'You're not a rapist. Only a murderer.'

Ruari ignored this. 'I'm sure you can understand why we'll keep you here until after we've left, Miss Bevan. There has been enough death, don't you think? So I want to be clear – we're not going to hurt you. Only detain you.'

'Did you kill the others?' Mirabelle asked. 'I mean, confessing to killing your second cousin's husband is all very well but there are two other deaths that remain unexplained, one of them a nun's.'

Ruari Farquarson-Sinclair froze for a second. 'Paul's death was accidental,' he said. 'He had been in touch with Grace. He wanted to apologise to her, he said. Make amends on his father's behalf. He felt the need to beat his chest a lot. It was clear he intended to talk about it all in public. A bloody bull in a china shop. I went to warn him off. We argued. I pushed him. It was an accident.'

'And Mother Superior?'

Ruari nodded curtly. 'I lost my temper. She asked me to come. She got suspicious after Paul's death, after she had engaged you. It seems Helena said something to her. Let something slip. The family connection would have been enough for someone who knew our secrets. When I went to meet her, she said something about atonement. As if it were my fault. Justice, she said, was important, but I had done the wrong thing. I hadn't realised the pressure it had put me under and I snapped. I will atone for that for the rest of my life.'

Mirabelle eyed him. He did not seem like somebody who easily lost control. 'Mother Superior was slashed to death. There were eleven stab wounds,' she said.

Ruari moved forward. If he had hoped she would trust him or simply acquiesce to his departure, he had another think coming. This time, before he could grab her to lock her away, Mirabelle was ready. She sprang off the sofa, brandishing the walking stick. Belinda interposed herself between the seating and the door of the room but Mirabelle backed in the other direction, towards the French windows, and opened them, stepping onto the paved area outside. Ruari lunged at her and she hit him so hard that the silver skull folded in on itself. He reeled backwards into the glass door, which cracked as he fell against it; a long, jagged shard shattering across the floor of the day room, like water spilling from an overturned glass.

Mirabelle didn't wait to check if he was all right. She took off across the lawn, past the comfortable garden chairs and the pond, on towards the garage and into the woods. Behind her the Farquarson-Sinclairs had rallied. She could hear them but this time she didn't look back. The ground was uneven beneath her feet as she dodged between the trees, and the house disappeared from view. Her shoulder ached but she tried to ignore it. For a minute or two she thought they wouldn't be able to catch up but she didn't slow. The main thing was to get to a telephone. She had to tell McGregor, the police, anyone, what she had found out. Whatever the Farquarson-Sinclairs said, once someone else knew, she'd be safe. Or safer.

Through the trees to her right, she could make out the dark outline of the Bentley crawling along the track. It was difficult to tell who was at the wheel – Belinda, she guessed. Yes, he'd follow her into the woodland and Belinda would try to cut her off in the car. They had the advantage. They knew the ground like the backs of their hands. She tried to visualise the woods and the winding track on the map: the convent, then Shore Cottage, the works, the naval yard and the village. She wasn't sure she could keep up this pace as far as the village, if she was honest. And there was only one direction to run in – St Clair's Vale behind her and everything else bounded by the water. As she approached the point where she would have to turn for the convent, she made a decision not to go to the nuns. At the door she'd either have to ring the bell and wait, exposed until they answered, or cut down the side and over the garden wall again. For this, however, she would need full use of both arms and her left arm was too battered and weak. Her best bet, she decided was to get to Shore Cottage – through the back door, straight to the telephone and the sanctuary of a 999 call. With luck Mrs Grieg wouldn't be there today to hinder her with questions or offers of help. To put herself in danger.

She decided to keep dodging through the trees until she reached a little way beyond Shore Cottage. Then she'd cross the track, turning back on herself on the other side and towards the safety of the house. There was a double bend in the road there that would shield her from view in both directions. If she could cross without encountering the car, the Farquarson-Sinclairs wouldn't know which side of the track she was on. She was out of breath now, but her arm had stopped aching as adrenalin flooded her system and the pills she'd swallowed took effect. As she reached the edge of the wood, she saw she had run too far and the double curve was behind her. She was about to turn back under the cover of the trees when she heard a crack and a man's voice swearing. 'Damn.' It was Ruari Farquarson-Sinclair and he was closer than she would have either liked or guessed. He must have fallen.

With split-second timing, she jumped down onto the track. It was wider here and the trees on the other side more sparsely planted, but there was a huge fir that had been felled. She made for that and dived behind the trunk for cover. A few seconds later, Ruari limped out of the wood. He'd hurt his ankle. His injury would slow him down, she thought. The

Bentley glided around the kink in the road. Belinda jumped out. 'What happened?' she asked her husband.

'I tripped,' he said, leaning his hand on the bonnet of the car.

'You drive,' she offered. 'I'll go into the woods. If you find her, honk the horn.'

Ruari hauled himself into the driver's seat and closed the door. He put the car into gear and was about to pull off when he wound down the window and peered towards the fallen tree trunk. Mirabelle sank down as far as she could but he'd spotted something out of place. He pulled on the handbrake and she heard the click of the car door opening. Belinda turned back.

'Check over there!' he shouted. 'The undergrowth is disturbed. The moss.'

Mirabelle didn't wait for them to get closer. She jumped up and started to run again with both Belinda and Ruari in pursuit. Underfoot here, near the firth, the mud was softer. This slowed Ruari with his newly injured ankle, but Belinda was fresh and sprinting fast through the trees. She launched herself at Mirabelle, who lashed out behind with the cane, catching Belinda's forearm and causing her to yelp in pain. Far from slowing her, the attack seemed to speed her up and she hit out at Mirabelle's injured arm and grabbed hold of her hair, pulling hard. Mirabelle let out an undignified squeal. She struck Belinda's arm again and managed to pull away, losing a clump of hair in the process. 'Meddler!' Belinda shouted. 'What the hell has it got to do with you?'

From behind, Ruari shouted, 'Stay calm, Belinda. Stay calm.'

Mirabelle pulled away and kept running. That was an odd thing for him to say, she thought. Then it came to her. Ruari might have killed James Thompson but it was Belinda who had the temper. His modus operandi was to plan, but it was Belinda who lost control. He had avenged his daughter, but it was Belinda who had committed the crimes at the nunnery. It had been Belinda who was able to slip in and out unnoticed. There was a strange kind of decency in Ruari Farquarson-Sinclair, as if justice and fate were the same thing. He intended to take the blame for his wife's actions. He'd be hanged for one murder if he were caught so he might as well save her and admit to the others. It was a strategic move. Intelligent. Now, running, almost out of breath, Mirabelle understood that it was Belinda who was more likely to kill her. She had killed in temper before. Paul Thompson and Mother too: just as Ruari Farquarson-Sinclair had described, but Belinda had done it, not him. Mirabelle speeded up.

She burst onto the lawn at Shore Cottage with Belinda Farquarson-Sinclair only a few feet behind. She was glad now that the back door was open. 'Mrs Grieg,' she shouted, as she wheeled towards it. 'Mrs Grieg.'

It wasn't Mrs Grieg who appeared in the doorway, but a younger woman. Mirabelle scrunched her eyes. 'Evangelista,' she breathed.

Evangelista stood back to let her pass and, seeing the emergency, slammed the door before Belinda could get through. Unable to stop in time, Belinda barrelled into it and began to bang hard, shouting, 'Let me in! Let me in!'

There was the sound of shattering glass as Mirabelle raced into the hallway. 'I need the telephone!' she shouted.

The shadowy outline of Ruari Farquarson-Sinclair appeared behind the frosted glass sidelight of the front door. He rang the bell insistently. Mrs Grieg appeared at the top of the stairs as Mirabelle scrambled to lift the handset and dialled 999.

'Hello,' she gasped, before the operator could get a word out. 'My name is Mirabelle Bevan.'

'Miss Bevan!' Mrs Grieg exclaimed.

The sidelight shattered and Ruari Farquarson-Sinclair's hand grappled for the door knob inside. When it didn't turn, he reached in further, feeling for the lock. 'I'm at Shore Cottage,' Mirabelle shouted down the line, reaching out singlehanded to bash him off with the cane. The hand withdrew. 'I want to report three murders in South Queensferry,' Mirabelle shouted, her tone garbled. 'Superintendent Scott at Torphichen Street is the officer in charge. I know who did it!'

Before she could get the names out, there was a loud scream of terror from the kitchen and Evangelista flung herself into the hall, banging the kitchen door closed behind her and pulling the handle with all her might to stop Belinda opening it. Then Vesta appeared in the doorway to the sitting room. She was wearing an extraordinarily ill-fitting summer dress. 'Mirabelle!' she said.

'It was the Farquarson-Sinclairs,' Mirabelle babbled, half into the phone and half towards Vesta. 'Mr Farquarson-Sinclair killed James Thompson. Mrs Farquarson-Sinclair killed Paul and Mother Superior.'

Mrs Grieg let out a sound like a balloon deflating. She sank onto the top stair. Evangelista stared blankly at what Mirabelle had said, and then lost her grip on the handle. The kitchen door opened but Vesta pushed past her in time to pull it shut before Belinda could get through. 'Did you understand that?' Mirabelle shouted at the operator.

But she could not hear the reply. Ruari Farquarson-Sinclair was now battering down the front door, which was flimsier than she might have hoped. The hinges buckled quickly and the surround splintered. 'You have to send the police! Now!' Mirabelle shouted down the wire.

She was about to turn and address the Farquarson-Sinclairs – hold them off, somehow. There was no point in them hurting her or anyone else now she had shared what she knew. If she could keep them talking, keep them here, the police would be able to detain them when they arrived. But as Mirabelle turned away from the telephone she realised Evangelista had other plans. She had fetched Cressida MacDonald's gun and was holding it to her shoulder, aiming at the front door. 'No!' Mirabelle shouted, but as Ruari Farquarson-Sinclair finally made a gap in the doorway big enough to get through, Evangelista fired. The report was deafening in the enclosed space and the smell of cordite filled the hallway as he fell with a dull thud onto the carpet and let out a long, low moan, like that of a wounded animal.

Mirabelle rushed to him. Whether Evangelista had aimed to kill or not, she couldn't be sure, but she had hit Ruari Farquarson-Sinclair in the leg at close range. There was a good deal of blood but he wouldn't die. Mirabelle pulled the linen runner off the hall table and staunched the wound efficiently. 'Oh, God,' she murmured. 'This is my fault. He was following me. I'm an idiot.'

Shocked, Vesta let go of the kitchen-door handle and Belinda burst into the hall. She grabbed Mirabelle, pulling her viciously off her husband's prone figure and flinging herself on top of him. 'Ru! What have you done? What have you done?' she shouted, and began to wail.

Ruari Farquarson-Sinclair seemed too calm for someone who had been injured. 'Shush, darling. Shush,' he said.

As Mirabelle reached a hand to comfort Belinda, she kicked out. 'Keep off him! Stay away! This is all your fault.' Mirabelle didn't deny it. 'What did you shoot him for, you stupid, stupid woman?' Belinda turned her ire towards Evangelista. 'He helped you. He avenged you. That bastard!'

Behind the Farquarson-Sinclairs, Vesta was bent over as if she was about to be sick. Evangelista stood in the doorway to the sitting room. Her lips were moving. It took Mirabelle a moment to realise she was reciting the Lord's Prayer.

Chapter Twenty-nine

Being good is easy, what is difficult is being just

Helena and Evangelista sat on the sofa in the sitting room at Shore Cottage with their arms around each other, crying for a long time. An ambulance had arrived to take Ruari away for treatment at the Royal Infirmary. Outside, the nuns said goodbye to him quietly. Both of them kissed his uninjured hand as he lay on a stretcher. 'He did free us, you see,' said Evangelista.

'What do you mean?' Rennie asked, and Mirabelle took him into the kitchen with McGregor and told the men everything.

'I'm not sure the nuns will be able to talk about it,' she said. 'They've spent their entire adult lives atoning for what happened to them – as if it was their fault. They never discussed it. It's so personal for all of them, you see: Ruari avenging his daughter and Belinda losing her temper with Paul and later with Mother. I'm sure she didn't mean to kill either of them. She just felt threatened. That is, she felt her daughter's reputation was threatened. It sounds like Mother Superior discovered what had happened on the morning she died and invited Belinda to talk about it. They had known each other since Belinda was a child. Mother was such a fair woman, the type to ask Belinda to give herself up. But Mrs Farquarson-Sinclair believes herself to be . . . I'm not sure how to put it. Righteous, perhaps. That her ends, whatever they are, justify her means.'

'This mess is partly at your door, Miss Bevan,' Rennie replied, with a stony expression. 'I don't understand what you were doing here in the first place.'

'Mother Superior asked Mirabelle to look into Sister Monica's death,' McGregor told him.

Rennie exhaled in exasperation. 'I should never have encouraged you two. You need to control your fiancée, McGregor.' He sounded angry.

'It was hardly Mirabelle's fault,' McGregor defended her.

'No. He's right,' Mirabelle said. 'You're right. I got too caught up.'

'You could have been killed. All of you,' Rennie said. 'I specifically said you should stay away from South Queensferry today and you walked right into this off your own bat.'

'You think we'd have got to the bottom of it without her?' McGregor's blood was up.

'I think Ruari Farquarson-Sinclair wouldn't have been shot,' Rennie said flatly.

'We're just lucky nobody died.'

Mirabelle nodded. 'I know,' she said. 'I'm sorry.'

'You have to leave this to me now. Do you think you can manage that?'

Once the ambulance had gone, Belinda was detained in the pantry away from the others until she was removed by two burly policemen for questioning at Torphichen Street. As she was taken through the hallway she caught sight of Mirabelle and broke free, rushing towards her, hitting her injured arm and screaming, 'This is your fault! I'm glad I killed Paul – that little pervert!' Still-eyed, Rennie noted the admission but Belinda didn't let up. 'He wasn't fit to talk to my little girl. He wanted to tell everyone what had happened. How hard it'd been for him to find out about his bloody father! She'd never have recovered from it. He was the last man in that line and they were all rotten.'

Once Belinda had gone, Rennie did not rush the nuns. 'Just keep out of the way of the officers doing their work,' he said.

Mirabelle hovered in the sitting room near the sisters. 'I'm sorry,' she apologised again. 'The Farquarson-Sinclairs told me what happened to you. You don't have to tell me anything more. I just wanted you to know.'

Evangelista turned her face away. Helena stared blankly. 'All of this is because of Paul,' she said. 'He acted as if he was the one who had been hurt. He kept going on about how his childhood was a lie. But what happened, happened to Evangelista and me. To Auntie Cress. And to Grace.'

'But how could Belinda do that to Mother?' Evangelista sobbed.

'You know what she's like,' Helena said. 'Her whole life she's had everything her own way.'

'Your brother stayed at the Little Sisters for a long time,' Mirabelle said.

Evangelista's eyes were bright and furious. 'He wouldn't leave. He wouldn't listen. He just kept pushing. It started when our father died and he found out about us. When he knew what had happened to Grace he sneaked out to talk to her. Once she'd gone he wrote to her in Italy. She wrote to her mother begging her to get him to stop. He wouldn't leave us alone. It's all going to come out now, isn't it? Everyone is going to know.'

Helena squeezed her sister's hand and Evangelista stopped speaking as if a button had been pressed. 'Will my sister be charged, Miss Bevan?' Helena asked. 'The gun . . .'

Mirabelle shrugged. 'I don't know,' she said. 'It's my fault. I led the Farquarson-Sinclairs here. They followed me. I'll do anything I can.'

After photographs had been taken of the shattered glass and the blood, Mrs Grieg set about cleaning. Mirabelle and Vesta remained at the kitchen table with untouched cups of tea in front of them. Tears welled in Mirabelle's eyes and Vesta slipped her arm round her friend. 'I put you in the most awful danger,' Mirabelle said regretfully. 'I'm sorry.'

'Don't be silly,' Vesta replied. 'No one could have anticipated what happened. We thought it was all about the nuns.'

At that moment the doorbell sounded and they both looked up.

'There isn't even a door any more,' Vesta said, peering into the hallway, curious about who might have bypassed the police officer now stationed at the gate. In the hall, the robed figure of Sister Mary stepped inside and Inspector Rennie went to greet her.

'I heard what happened,' she said. 'Is there anything we at the convent can do to help?'

'Not at this stage,' Rennie said. 'We may wish to talk to you later.'

'Then I shall simply fetch my sisters back into the fold.'

Evangelista and Helena appeared from the sitting room. 'That isn't possible, I'm afraid, Sister,' Rennie said.

'I'm Mother now,' Sister Mary replied firmly. 'We held a ballot today and I am here as Mother Superior of the Little Sisters of Gethsemane. The prioress of the order.'

'Praise be,' said Helena. 'Out of darkness He brings light.'

'That's as may be, but I need to hold Sister Evangelista,' Rennie said. 'She shot Mr Farquarson-Sinclair. Charges will have to be considered.'

'Shot him?' Sister Mary sounded horrified.

'He was coming for us,' Evangelista said. 'He wanted to hurt us.'

'He did, Mother,' Helena added, backing up her sister. 'She told me everything. He battered down the door.'

Evangelista laid a hand on her sister's arm. 'I will face the charges,' she said serenely. 'I'm not going to run away. I will take my punishment.'

Mother Mary nodded slowly. 'If she is to be charged, Sister Evangelista must be allowed to wear her robes. She is a nun in orders. She must be seen to be so. The Little Sisters of Gethsemane will commission legal counsel on her behalf. Very good legal counsel, Sister. To make your case.'

'I will also need to ask more questions of you, Mother,' Rennie added. 'And Sister Helena. The inquiry has progressed quite a bit today.'

'Do you know who killed our previous incumbent?'

Rennie nodded. 'Mrs Belinda Farquarson-Sinclair has been charged with two murders – that of Mother Superior and of Paul Thompson.'

'Belinda!' Mother Mary exclaimed. 'You must be mistaken. She came to the chapel the day of the murder. Afterwards. She prayed.'

Rennie paused a moment to take this in. 'Returned to the scene of the crime,' he said thoughtfully.

'She made a donation,' Vesta added. 'To the African mission. She seemed . . . elated almost.'

'You'll all have to give statements,' Rennie instructed. 'We need to find out how Mrs Farquarson-Sinclair got into the convent on the occasion of both murders without being detected. Though that seems easier than might be expected. Especially if one looks like a nun.' He cast a glance at Vesta through the kitchen door.

'Mrs Farquarson-Sinclair has Miss MacDonald's old habit,' Mrs Grieg said. 'She asked me to fetch it after Miss MacDonald's death. Nobody would mind, she said, and she had been invited to a fancy-dress party at the officers' mess in Edinburgh Castle.'

'Thank you, Mrs Grieg,' Rennie said. 'That's helpful. We will require a statement to that effect. Everyone will have to come to Torphichen Street.'

'There'll be blood on that habit,' McGregor added sagely. 'If that's what Mrs Farquarson-Sinclair wore when she committed the crime.'

'It'll be in her dressing room,' Mrs Grieg added, 'not that I'm allowed in there.'

The party paused, as if in Mother's memory, the stab wounds and the puddle of her blood on the chapel floor. Sister Mary nodded a silent amen. 'But Sister Helena is free to go? After these statements are given?' she checked.

'I don't see why not,' Rennie said.

Helena stood, her weight shifting from foot to foot. 'I can't hide in the convent while Evangelista is in the world,' she said. 'I don't know if I want to go back at all. I'll stay here, I think, Mother. Please. As my aunt did.'

Mother Mary considered this. 'I can have a habit sent for your use.'

Helena shrugged. 'I don't want one. Evangelista should have one, of course, but I'm not sure . . . about anything. I need time to think.'

'You can stay here, miss. I'll look after you,' Mrs Grieg said stoutly.

'It all seems so senseless,' Helena added.

'Murder usually is,' Rennie said. 'To be frank, this seems to make more sense than most. There's more real offence been caused.' He studied the two younger nuns' faces but concluded Mirabelle might be right – they were unlikely to be able to talk about what had happened to them. 'I'll take you into custody now, Sister,' he said to Evangelista. And she stepped forward bravely.

As they took Evangelista away, Vesta turned to Mother Mary. 'Does your new position mean that the bishop . . .?'

Mother let amusement play at the corners of her mouth. 'Foiled entirely,' she said. 'Men! They try to take everything. They removed our ordained women in 1276. Our female bishops and deaconesses. I have never forgiven them for that.'

Vesta did not point out that eight hundred years was a long time to hold a grudge. 'So the formula is safe.'

Mother patted the side of her nose. 'We must decide what to do with it, of course, for we are falling in numbers. Perhaps another order might help us. Perhaps,' she hazarded, 'the Poor Clares.'

Vesta looked bashful. 'I'm sorry about that,' she said. 'Lying to you.'

Mother Mary's eyes fell to Vesta's stomach. She pulled her to one side. 'I hear there is to be a happy event,' she whispered.

Vesta nodded.

'All is forgiven then,' Mother said. 'Of course.'

★ ★ ★

334

It was late by the time Mirabelle, McGregor and Vesta left Torphichen Street after giving their statements. Mirabelle had cried, been comforted and cried again.

'I will have to live with this on my conscience,' she said.

'Yes. You have to live.' McGregor stroked her face. 'We all do.'

Mr Wallace had attended and McGregor asked him back to Heriot Row for a drink afterwards. In the drawing room, Mirabelle and Vesta flopped onto the sofa and McGregor poured four double whiskies. 'Please,' he said, gesturing Wallace towards one of the chairs.

'I'm starving,' Vesta proclaimed. 'I want a steak. No, a stew.'

McGregor checked his watch. It was long after midnight and the flat was poorly provisioned. He doubted there was as much as a tin of game soup in the kitchen cupboards. Outside the long windows Edinburgh's streets were deserted. Up on Queen Street the windows lay dark. 'I can go out if you like,' he said doubtfully, 'but I expect everywhere is closed.'

'There's a bakery at Stenhouse that starts work about this time,' Wallace offered. 'They sell from the back door. The local bobbies use it.'

'You're a very useful solicitor.' McGregor grinned.

'A bakery?' Vesta said wistfully. 'I wonder if they might have a steak pie? And an iced bun? Something with cream? And jam, perhaps? Is that terrible after everything that's happened?'

Mirabelle sipped her whisky. She couldn't face a thing. 'Do you remember when you were pregnant with Noel and we used to have pasties in the office in the afternoon and those apple cakes from the bakery on St George's Road? Once you'd got over the morning sickness . . .'

Vesta blushed.

'Oh,' said Mirabelle. She got to her feet. 'Vesta! Why didn't you tell me?'

'I only realised once I was inside the convent and there was so much else going on,' Vesta said. 'I haven't even told Charlie. Though the nuns copped on. Can you believe it?'

McGregor laughed. 'Congratulations, Mrs Lewis. Well, Wallace, we have a very important mission. Shall we to Stenhouse? Steak pie it will be. And a box of cream cakes.'

Wallace downed his whisky in one. 'Indeed,' he said. 'Good news.'

'I feel shallow,' Vesta added. 'But I'm starving! What will happen to Evangelista, Mr Wallace?' She did not add that she had saved the nun's life by fishing her out of the water earlier in the day.

Wallace turned. 'She shot in self-defence and the man survived. Given the circumstances, I can't see anything more than a short custodial sentence being handed down and the fiscal may well decide it's not in the public interest to try her at all. I will do my best on her behalf. I promise.'

'And the Farquarson-Sinclairs?' Mirabelle added.

Wallace shook his head. 'They'll be lucky not to face the hangman's noose, Miss Bevan. I'm not their solicitor or their advocate but if I were I might certainly question the woman's mental state. She killed a nun. Mr Farquarson-Sinclair clearly knew what he was doing.'

'But he killed for justice,' Vesta said. 'With Belinda it was fury – a kind of madness. Most people would believe James Thompson deserved to die. After what he'd done.'

'Indeed,' Wallace said. 'But one life cannot be judged more valuable than another.'

'And you're solicitor for the Thompson line?'

'The MacDonalds, yes.'

'What will happen to our house?' Mirabelle asked. 'If we're asking shallow questions.'

McGregor put down his glass on the side table. 'Yes,' he said. 'You have a child of the MacDonald line, it seems. Grace's son. A new heir, though illegitimate. And Paul Thompson's estate to process.'

'Well, as *your* solicitor, Mr McGregor, my question is do you still want to live at Shore Cottage? If not, I'm sure I can terminate the purchase. The missives are not completed and, as you say, a good deal of new information has come to light.'

McGregor looked in Mirabelle's direction. They both wondered whether they would ever forget Ruari Farquarson-Sinclair's body lying on the hall carpet or that James Thompson had been murdered in the bedroom upstairs.

'I might look for somewhere in Fife,' McGregor said. 'Why don't we discuss it in the car?'

As the front door closed behind the men, Vesta pulled up her legs, curling up comfortably next to the open fireplace. 'Your wedding, Mirabelle,' she said. 'What are we going to do? There's hardly any time.'

Mirabelle flicked her hair to one side. 'I have a dress coming,' she admitted bashfully. 'So it's flowers, I suppose. And something to eat. And a haircut.'

Vesta squinted at her friend. 'Your hair seems . . . lopsided.'

'Belinda pulled some out.'

Vesta made a face. 'And what about your arm?'

Mirabelle stretched it ahead of her. The bruises were up now – yellow and a deep red – and she was slightly swollen. 'I'll heal,' she said. 'I've had worse. Look, tomorrow is Sunday. Nothing will be open. Frankly we deserve a rest. You especially. When do you think you're due?'

337

'She isn't going to be a Christmas baby,' Vesta said. 'Thank goodness – after Noel. My guess is February.'

'She?'

'One of the nuns said it was a girl.'

'How could she tell?'

Vesta gestured above her head mysteriously. Mirabelle laughed. 'Well, it's wonderful news. I'm going to feed you up. They have a carvery at the George Hotel on a Sunday. It's jolly good.'

Vesta grinned. 'Thank goodness,' she said. 'I was worried you were going to suggest going to church.'

Epilogue

Dancing is the poetry of the foot

The bride looked particularly lovely. She had chosen a bouquet of pale pink roses, thistles and rosemary, and in the end she had accessorised the taupe dress in pink, not black, because, she decided, there had been enough darkness. The swelling in her arm had gone down and the bruises were covered with a cashmere wrap. She squinted as she signed the register but the groom did not say a word about it, and afterwards they ran through the squall of a summer shower with the rest of the wedding party to the North British Hotel where a private room had been taken for the reception.

Charlie, freshly arrived off the train from Brighton, played the piano next to the bar with Inspector Rennie keeping time on the lid. Noel danced with Katja to general amusement as everybody sipped champagne around them. Mr Wallace danced with his secretary.

'So you're really not a nun at all?' Mrs Grieg tackled Vesta. The housekeeper had surreptitiously swept a few sandwiches into her handbag from the buffet table, but now seemed to have settled down to enjoy herself.

'I'm a debt collector,' Vesta admitted. 'I liked my time at the convent, though. I know that sounds odd. But it's so peaceful. It's made me see that perhaps I've been focusing too much on worldly concerns.'

'Worldly concerns, Sister Joseph?' Mother Mary cut in.

'Money, Mother. It might be time for a change.'

'Well, you have this little boy to look after and another child on the way . . . quite right.'

'Yes. Noel is my only Black baby. So far. I've never been to Africa.'

Mother Mary regarded the champagne saucer in her hand. 'His ways are wondrous,' she said mysteriously.

'Aren't they, though?' Wendy Lamont said, as she passed on her way to the bar. She had been sitting beside the fire, deep in conversation with Dr Alexander. The women had quit champagne after two glasses and instead ordered Percy Specials. 'What is that?' Vesta asked, pointing at the glass with its maraschino cherry and glistening ice.

'Cherry brandy and whisky,' Wendy offered delightedly. 'It's all the rage.'

Later, as Inspector Rennie helped pour the women into a taxi, Vesta overheard Wendy saying, 'Let's go to the Hawes Inn. All this talk of South Queensferry is making me feel positively romantic about Robert Louis Stevenson. I think I might write a column about historical dress. Have you read *Kidnapped*?' As the car pulled away, Vesta couldn't help thinking all the girls loved a doctor. She hoped the women had fun.

'Do you need a cab too?' she asked Rennie.

'I'll walk,' he said with determination and pulled up his collar.

After that, the guests left one by one until it was only the Lewises and the McGregors at the bar. They ordered a last bottle of Dom Pérignon and Charlie turned his attention to the blues. 'Mother Mary took it well,' Vesta said. 'I thought she would be upset about the wedding being in a registrar's office. Oh, Alan,' she added, suddenly remembering, 'you didn't give a speech!'

McGregor got to his feet solemnly. 'When I first saw this woman . . .' He indicated his wife.

'In a graveyard in Brighton,' Mirabelle added.

'Yes. Then. I knew immediately—'

'That isn't true,' Mirabelle interrupted. 'You were flirting with somebody else. A widow. Quite shamelessly. She offered to cook you dinner.'

'When I second saw this woman,' McGregor continued smoothly, 'I knew. Not only that she would never cook me dinner but that she was the brightest star, the most precious gem, the best of all of us.'

Mirabelle blushed. She removed McGregor's glass from his hand. 'Thank you, darling,' she said, kissing him. 'I think it might be time to go home.'

'Oh, no,' McGregor said. 'Not on our wedding night. Here.' He withdrew the key to the flat on Heriot Row from his pocket and gave it to Vesta, who hugged Mirabelle tightly.

'Mrs McGregor,' she said. 'I'm very glad to meet you.'

McGregor took his wife's hand and pulled her out of the bar, into the grand hallway and up in the lift to a floor where there was, she noted, a view of the castle out of the rain-spattered window. The sign on the door said 'Honeymoon Suite'. He took another key from his pocket and opened it, turning to sweep Mirabelle into his arms and carry her over the threshold. 'We'll be here until at least Sunday,' he said.

Mirabelle laughed.

He laid her on the bed. 'You look beautiful.' She pulled him close and kissed him. 'Do you mind me not telling you about taking a room?' he said. 'I had to have you to myself, just for tonight.'

She shook her head. 'There are a few things I haven't told you, as a matter of fact.'

'Really?'

'I bought myself a car. It's ridiculous that we have to share the one we have.'

'You bought a car without me?'

'Sister Triduana gave me advice. It's a rather smart Jaguar that's being driven up from London. I thought it was a better wedding present than . . .'

'Shore Cottage?'

'It is a lovely house. But I never want to go back. What do you think will happen to it now?'

McGregor stood up. Another bottle of champagne was icing on the side table alongside two plates, one with smoked salmon canapés and another with strawberries glazed with dark chocolate. 'They think of everything,' he said, and popped the cork, pouring two glasses. 'Wallace says Grace Farquarson-Sinclair's child will inherit the place. If there's any justice. Perhaps Grace will want to live there with the baby.'

'Like Bang Bang MacDonald did? Sort of.'

'She's very young, of course.'

'But the nuns could help. Sister Helena, perhaps?'

'Who knows? Wallace is seeing to it. There are two trust funds, I understand. One for the Farquarson-Sinclair children and one that's MacDonald money.'

'Money, money, money,' Mirabelle said with a sigh.

'Not very romantic,' McGregor agreed.

'I'm not sure I'll ever get over it, really,' she said. 'I could have died. I led those people right to Vesta. Right to all of us.'

'You did your best, Mirabelle. You always do your best,' he said. 'Will you make some wishes? For us. A bride's toast?'

Mirabelle regarded the view over Princes Street Gardens. 'I want to feel free,' she said. 'And modern . . .'

McGregor followed her sightline. 'You don't mean . . . one of these dreadful new towns they're going to build, do you?'

Mirabelle laughed. 'No. But I took risks, didn't I? I stirred things up – like an idiot. I'm not sure I'm fitted for this any more, digging things up all the time. The thing is, I get pulled in, like some kind of addiction, and I can't see what's in front of me. I couldn't even see you in front of me, darling. I hardly organised our wedding. There's a darkness in me, I think.'

'The wedding was perfect. The wedding is done. And you are who I have chosen – darkness and light,' McGregor said.

'It's going to be a whole new decade soon, 1960,' Mirabelle added.

McGregor raised his glass and she clinked hers against it. 'To the sixties,' he toasted. 'Whatever they may bring.' They drank. 'Mrs McGregor,' he said, trying out the name as he joined her on the satin quilt. 'Mrs McGregor,' he repeated, and there was no more talk about houses or cars or darkness or guilt or what the new decade might bring. There was only love.

Author's note

This book was written during the Covid crisis of 2020 and early 2021. I was living in Edinburgh and could go to South Queensferry with my (very naughty) dog, Dotty, to walk along the shoreline and imagine where Shore Cottage, the Little Sisters of Gethsemane Convent and St Clair's Vale are situated and also the (in 1959) not yet half-built bridge that now is one of three that span the Firth of Forth. It's a beautiful spot and it saved me on some dark days. Writers are blessed in the worlds that exist in their heads!

I owe, as always, a debt of thanks to my agent Jenny Brown, who I know loves Mirabelle as much as I do and supports many of the japes that I go through when writing these stories. Many thanks are also due to the team at Constable, headed by Krystyna Green and editors Amanda Keats and Hazel Orme, who are so enthusiastic about Mirabelle venturing north and keep me right – always. It's been soothing for me to write Scottish stories for a character I know so well, and to dip into the 1950s world in which my own parents met and married.

The Little Sisters of Gethsemane were greatly inspired by the nuns who lived next door to our house when I was growing up. Theirs was a silent order and it disbanded in the 1980s because the nuns became too old to run it themselves. The buildings were Victorian, and there was a kitchen garden and a chapel, all of which I visited as a child. We were woken in the morning by the nuns' cockerel crowing. They were lovely women. After they left, the convent was sold and developed into the flats that now stand on the corner of Ettrick Road and Spylaw Road on the south side of the city – not far from the Bishop's Palace at Churchill. Once the nuns had left and before the works got under way, my brother and I broke in through a window and sneaked round the areas we had never visited. During this foray we were spooked by a large ivory Jesus on the cross halfway up the stairs – just like Mirabelle . . .

Thanks are also due to my parents for their memories of the best places for romantic dinners and shopping in Edinburgh in 1959. I'm happy to say that Mirabelle's wedding dress is markedly like my mother's and *so* chic! My upstairs neighbour and friend Jeanette Alexander kindly lent me her name to use for the convent's doctor – thanks, Jeanette, for that, for seeing me through lockdown and helping me stay sane or sane-ish. Thanks, too, to my friend Eleanor Leech, daughter of Mr Leech, who was the optician at Trotter's in real life as well as in the books. Eleanor is now my optician in the present-day Trotter's, which is situated on George Street these days. Also a big shout-out to the many readers who contact me by email and on Twitter in support of these stories and often make suggestions, Andrew Morton especially – thank you for your tales of nuns you have known! I'm more a reader than a writer, in truth, so readers' responses matter to me.

Lastly, these books could not be written without the patience of my husband, Al, and my daughter, Molly, both of whom take me seriously when I can't decide how to kill somebody. A new addition to our family, my son-in-law Jon, is a fresh Mirabelle inductee and is proving as patient as the rest of the tribe. Thanks to all of you. I couldn't write without your love and support. You are always and ever amazing.

The quotations and misquotations used to open each chapter are taken from the following sources:

Truth lies beyond: Proust. Come, pensive nun, devout and pure: Milton. Opinions are made to be changed: Byron. Where there is mystery there must also be evil: Byron. Our deeds disguise us: John Locke. Where there is no novelty, there can be no curiosity: Aphra Behn. Truth will rise above falsehood as oil above water: Miguel de Cervantes. He was a fiddler, and consequently a rogue: Jonathan Swift. Tears are the silent language of grief: Voltaire. Friends are the siblings God never gave us: Mencius. It is the lot of man but once to die: Francis Quarles. Suspicion is the companion of mean souls: Thomas Paine. Quiet as a nun breathless with anticipation: Wordsworth. That which appears white is really black if the Church so decides: St Ignatius. The envious die not once, but oft: Baltasar Gracian. Deceit: guile, chicanery, duplicity: dictionary definition. Nothing is so aggravating as calmness: Oscar Wilde. When anger rises, think of the consequences: Confucius. Some virtues are only seen in affliction: Joseph Addison. Simplify, simplify: Henry David Thoreau. The cautious seldom err: Confucius. Discovery is not in seeking new landscapes but in having new eyes: Marcel Proust. Some rise by sin, some by virtue fall: Shakespeare. Woman rules us still: Thomas Moore. I would rather go to Heaven than to Purgatory: Charles Spurgeon. Most doubt is the beacon of the wise: Shakespeare. Fear follows crime: Voltaire. Courage is the greatest of all virtues: Samuel Johnson. Dancing is the poetry of the foot: John Dryden. Being good is easy, what is difficult is being just: Victor Hugo.